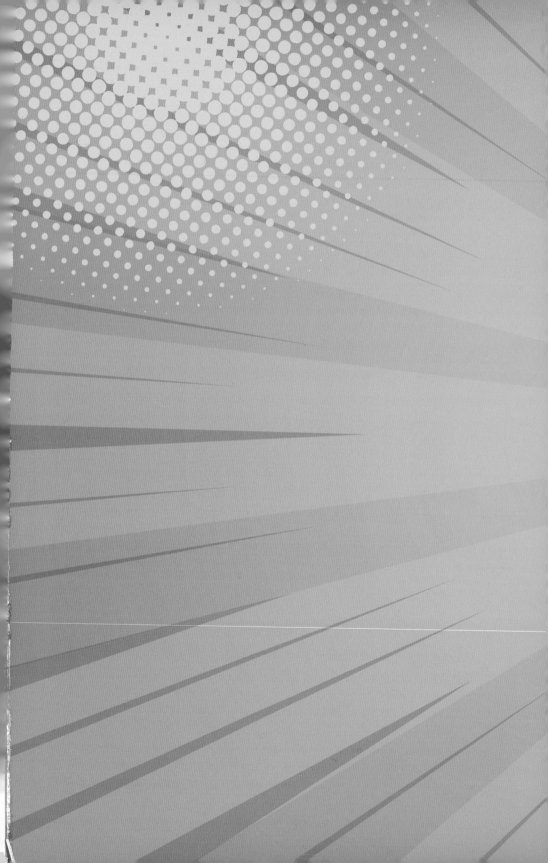

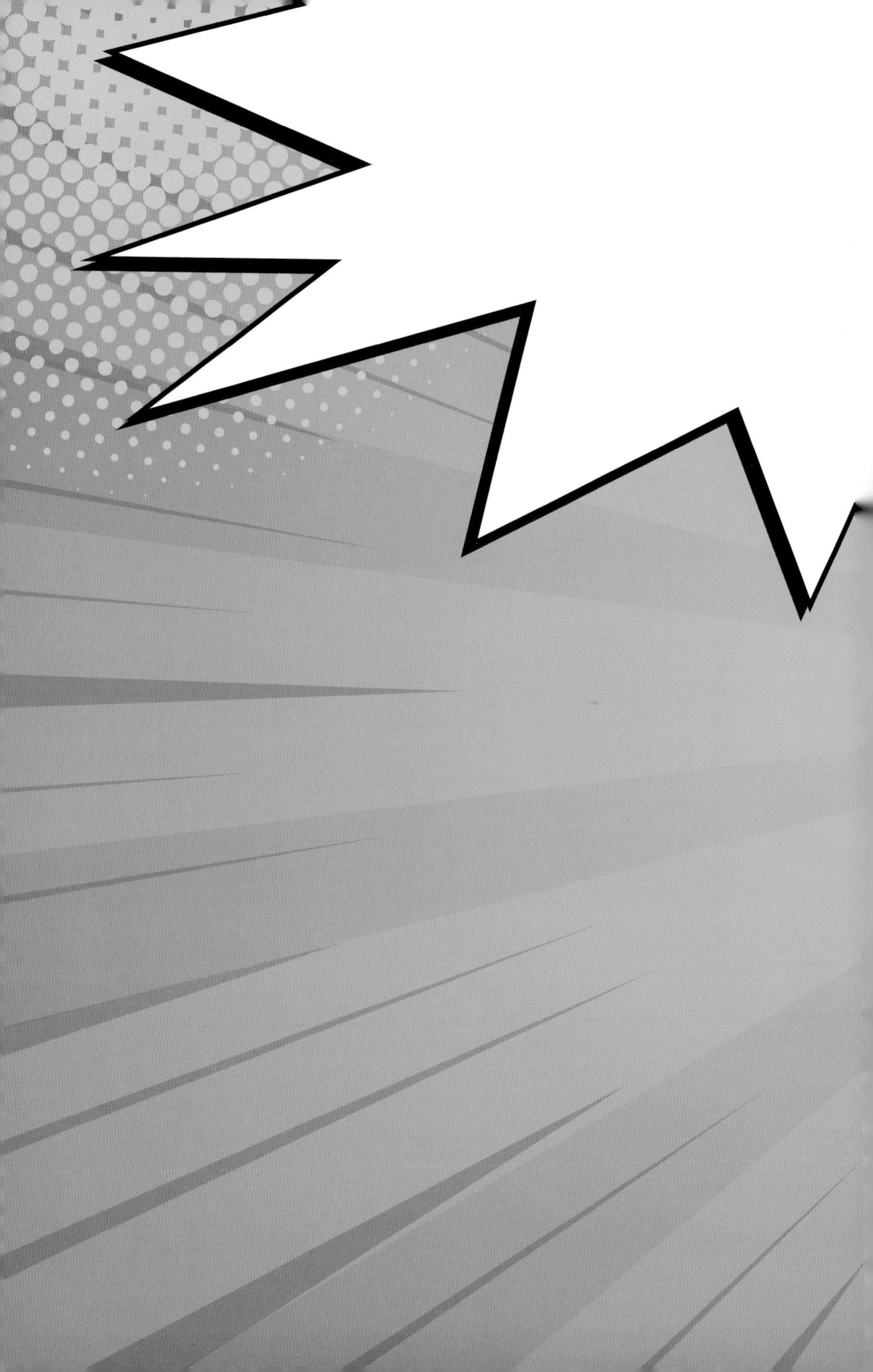

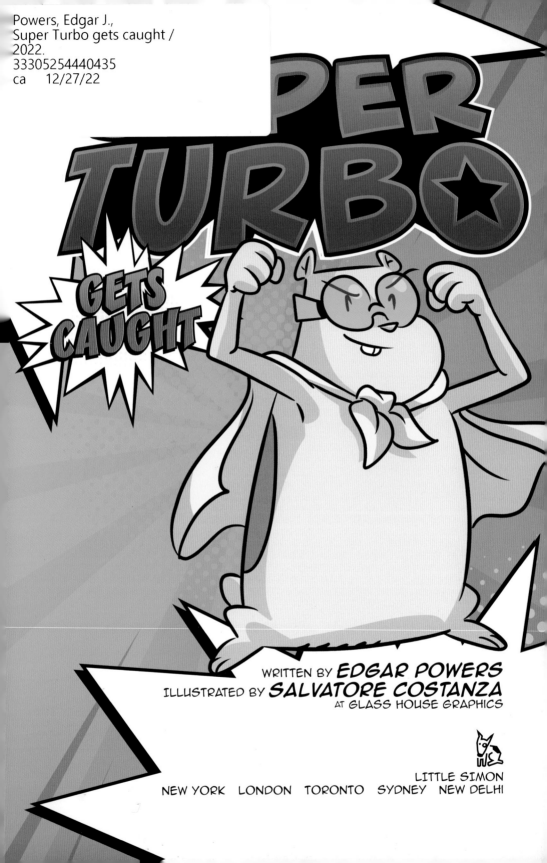

PER TURBO★

GETS CAUGHT

WRITTEN BY **EDGAR POWERS**
ILLUSTRATED BY **SALVATORE COSTANZA**
AT GLASS HOUSE GRAPHICS

LITTLE SIMON
NEW YORK   LONDON   TORONTO   SYDNEY   NEW DELHI

LITTLE SIMON
AN IMPRINT OF SIMON & SCHUSTER CHILDREN'S PUBLISHING DIVISION
1230 AVENUE OF THE AMERICAS, NEW YORK, NEW YORK 10020
FIRST LITTLE SIMON EDITION NOVEMBER 2022 * COPYRIGHT © 2022 BY SIMON & SCHUSTER, INC. ALL RIGHTS RESERVED, INCLUDING THE RIGHT OF REPRODUCTION IN WHOLE OR IN PART IN ANY FORM. LITTLE SIMON IS A REGISTERED TRADEMARK OF SIMON & SCHUSTER, INC., AND ASSOCIATED COLOPHON IS A TRADEMARK OF SIMON & SCHUSTER, INC. FOR INFORMATION ABOUT SPECIAL DISCOUNTS FOR BULK PURCHASES, PLEASE CONTACT SIMON & SCHUSTER SPECIAL SALES AT 1-866-506-1949 OR BUSINESS@SIMONANDSCHUSTER.COM. THE SIMON & SCHUSTER SPEAKERS BUREAU CAN BRING AUTHORS TO YOUR LIVE EVENT. FOR MORE INFORMATION OR TO BOOK AN EVENT CONTACT THE SIMON & SCHUSTER SPEAKERS BUREAU AT 1-866-248-3049 OR VISIT OUR WEBSITE AT WWW.SIMONSPEAKERS.COM. DESIGNED BY NICHOLAS SCIACCA * ART SERVICES BY GLASS HOUSE GRAPHICS * ART AND COLOR BY SALVATORE COSTANZA LETTERING BY GIOVANNI SPATARO/GRAFIMATED CARTOON * SUPERVISION BY SALVATORE DI MARCO/GRAFIMATED CARTOON * MANUFACTURED IN CHINA 0822 SCP * 2 4 6 8 10 9 7 5 3 1 * LIBRARY OF CONGRESS CATALOGING-IN-PUBLICATION DATA NAMES: POWERS, EDGAR J., AUTHOR. | COSTANZA, SALVATORE, 1989- ILLUSTRATOR. | GLASS HOUSE GRAPHICS, ILLUSTRATOR. TITLE: SUPER TURBO GETS CAUGHT / WRITTEN BY EDGAR POWERS ; ILLUSTRATED BY SALVATORE COSTANZA AT GLASS HOUSE GRAPHICS. DESCRIPTION: FIRST LITTLE SIMON EDITION. | NEW YORK : LITTLE SIMON, 2022. | SERIES: SUPER TURBO, THE GRAPHIC NOVEL ; 8 | AUDIENCE: AGES 5-9. | AUDIENCE: GRADES K-1. | SUMMARY: WHILE ON A MISSION TO ACQUIRE SNACKS FOR A PARTY, SUPER TURBO AND BOSS BUNNY ARE CAUGHT IN ONE OF THE JANITOR'S RAT TRAPS AND THEIR ONLY HOPE FOR ESCAPE LIES IN THE PAWS OF THEIR ENEMY WHISKERFACE. IDENTIFIERS: LCCN 2021061351 (PRINT) | LCCN 2021061352 (EBOOK) | ISBN 9781665915779 (PBK) | ISBN 9781665915786 (HC) | ISBN 9781665915793 (EBOOK) SUBJECTS: CYAC: GRAPHIC NOVELS. | HAMSTERS—FICTION. | RATS—FICTION. | SUPERHEROES— FICTION. | PETS—FICTION. | SCHOOLS—FICTION. CLASSIFICATION: LCC PZ7.7.P7 SI 2022 (PRINT) | LCC PZ7.7.P7 (EBOOK) | DDC 741.5/973—DC23/ ENG/20220419 LC RECORD AVAILABLE AT HTTPS://LCCN.LOC.GOV/] LC EBOOK RECORD AVAILABLE AT HTTPS://LCCN.LOC.GOV/2021061352

CONTENTS

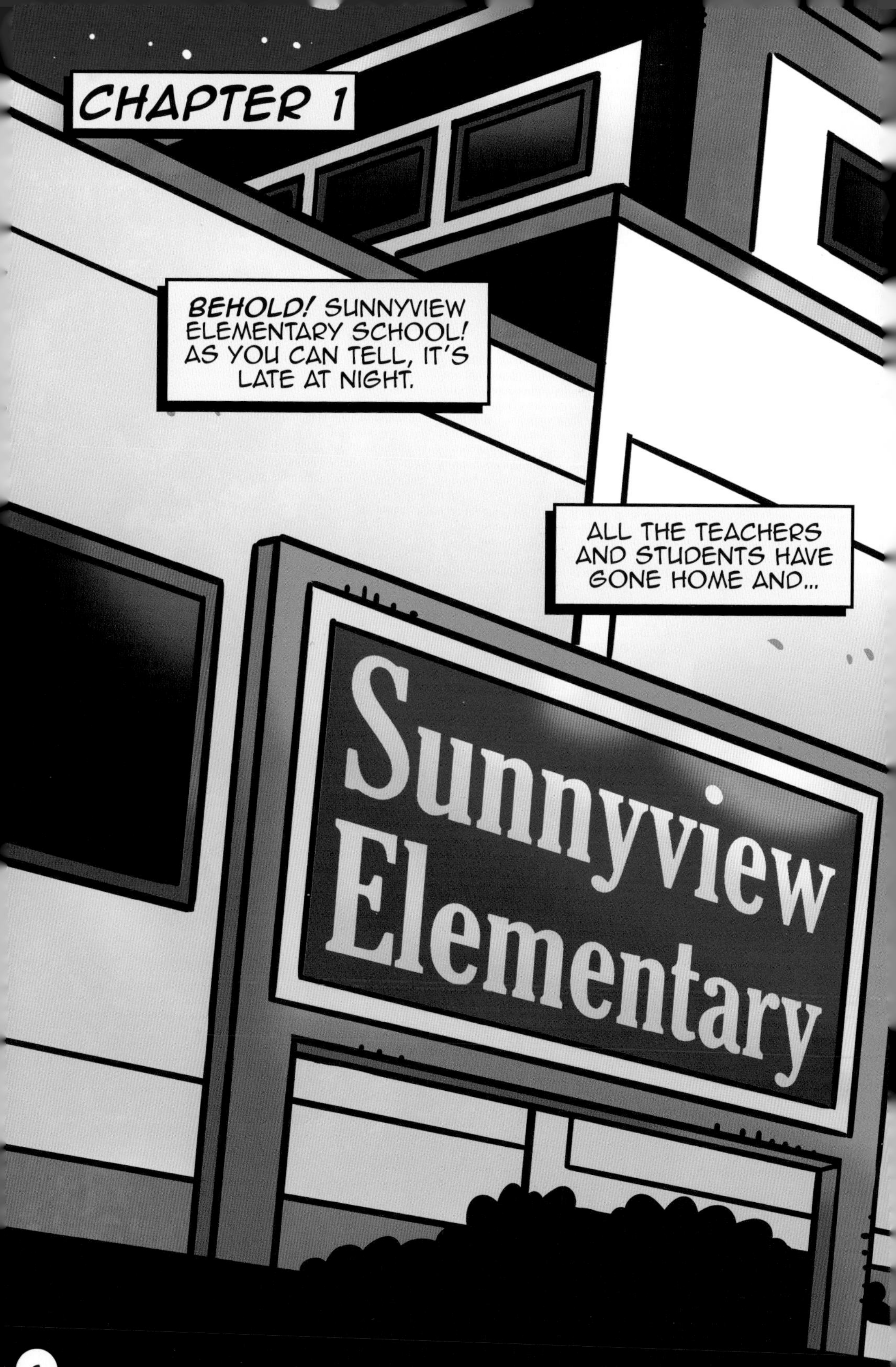
CHAPTER 1
BEHOLD! SUNNYVIEW ELEMENTARY SCHOOL! AS YOU CAN TELL, IT'S LATE AT NIGHT.
ALL THE TEACHERS AND STUDENTS HAVE GONE HOME AND...
Sunnyview Elementary

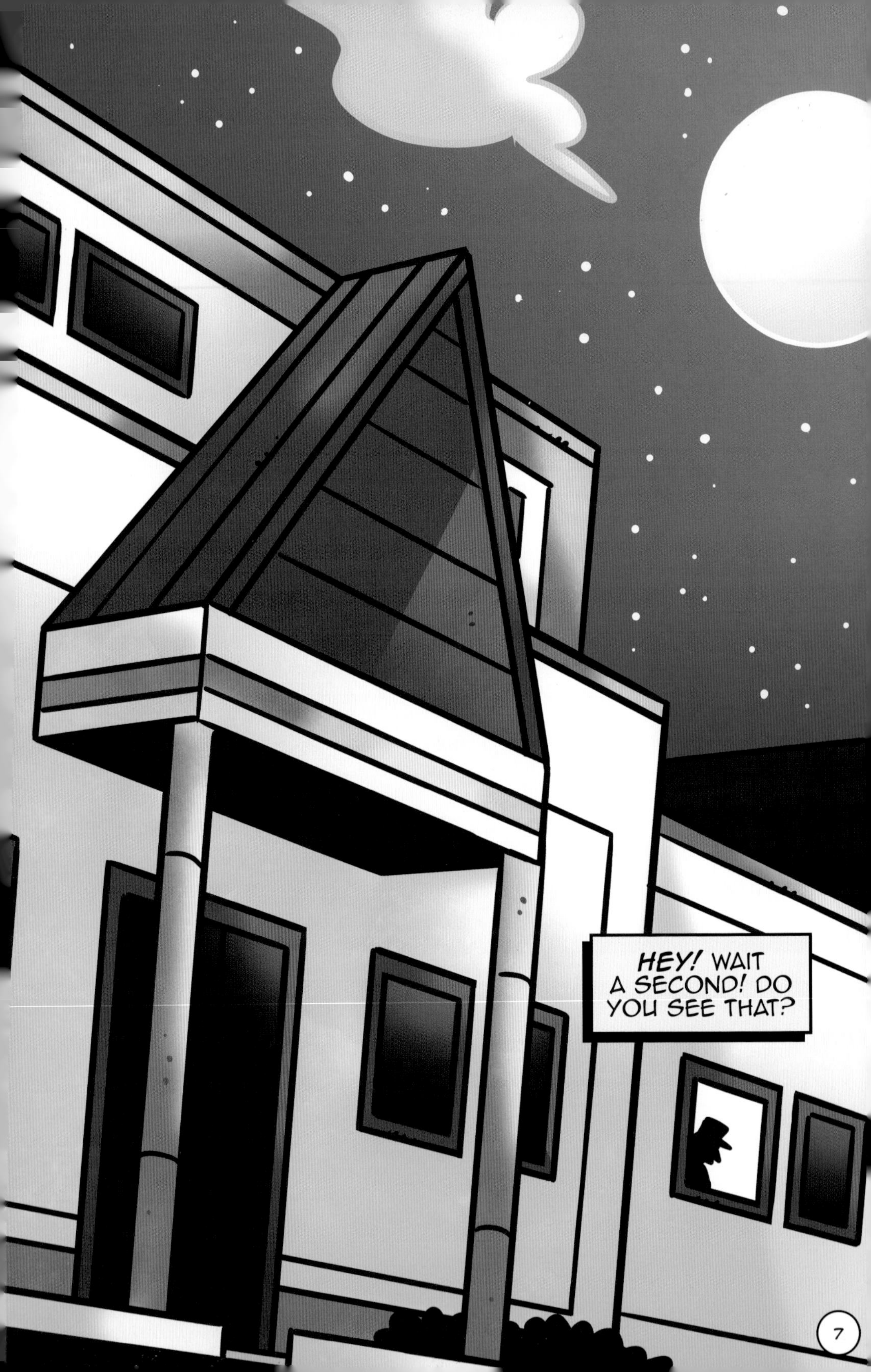
HEY! WAIT A SECOND! DO YOU SEE THAT?

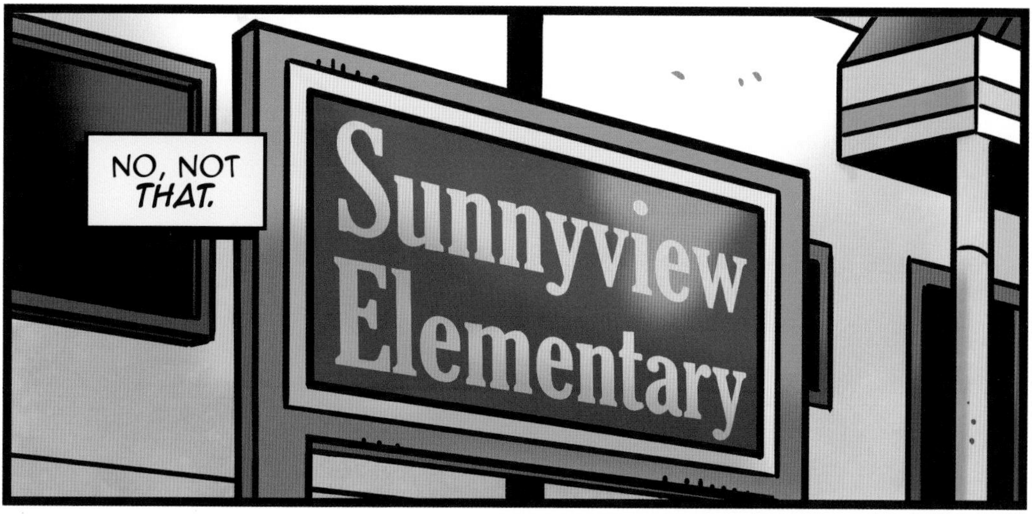
Sunnyview Elementary
NO, NOT *THAT.*

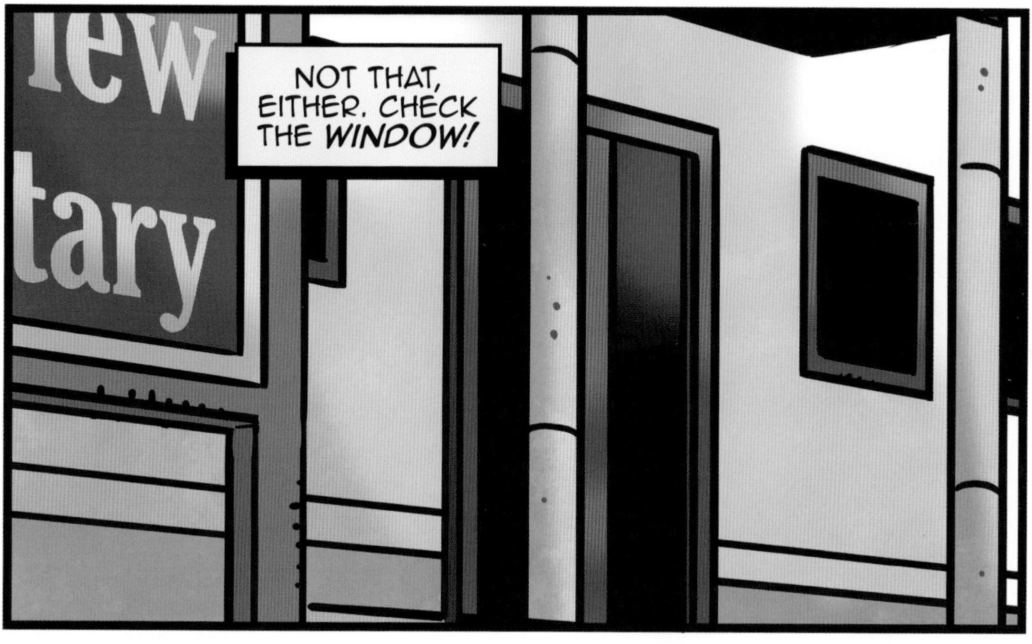
NOT THAT, EITHER. CHECK THE ***WINDOW!***

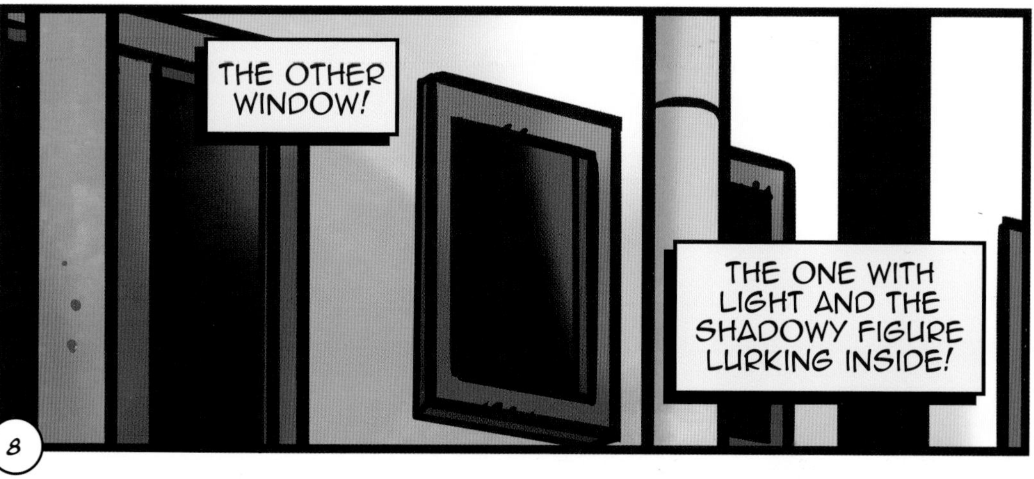
THE OTHER WINDOW!
THE ONE WITH LIGHT AND THE SHADOWY FIGURE LURKING INSIDE!

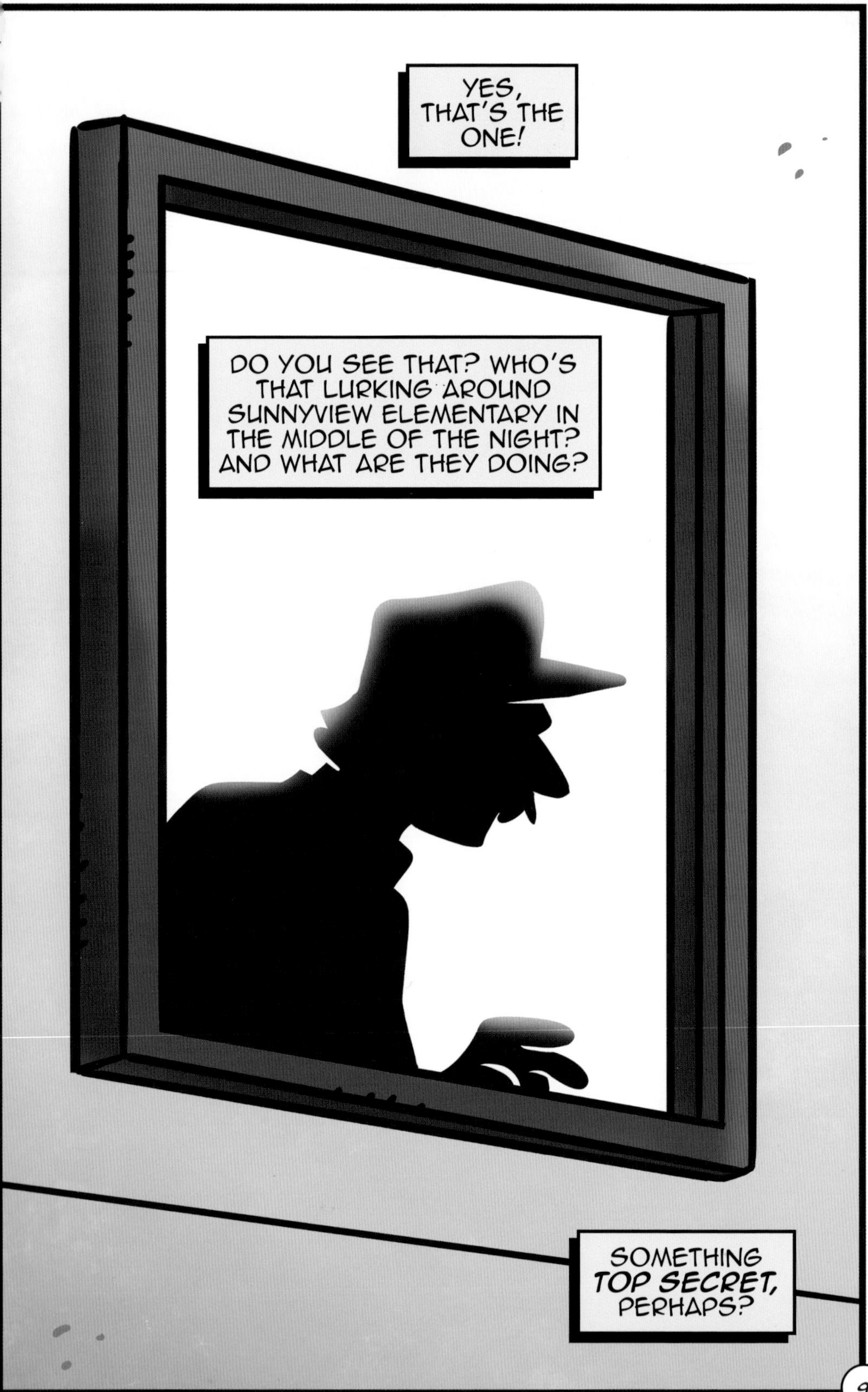
YES, THAT'S THE ONE!
DO YOU SEE THAT? WHO'S THAT LURKING AROUND SUNNYVIEW ELEMENTARY IN THE MIDDLE OF THE NIGHT? AND WHAT ARE THEY DOING?
SOMETHING *TOP SECRET,* PERHAPS?

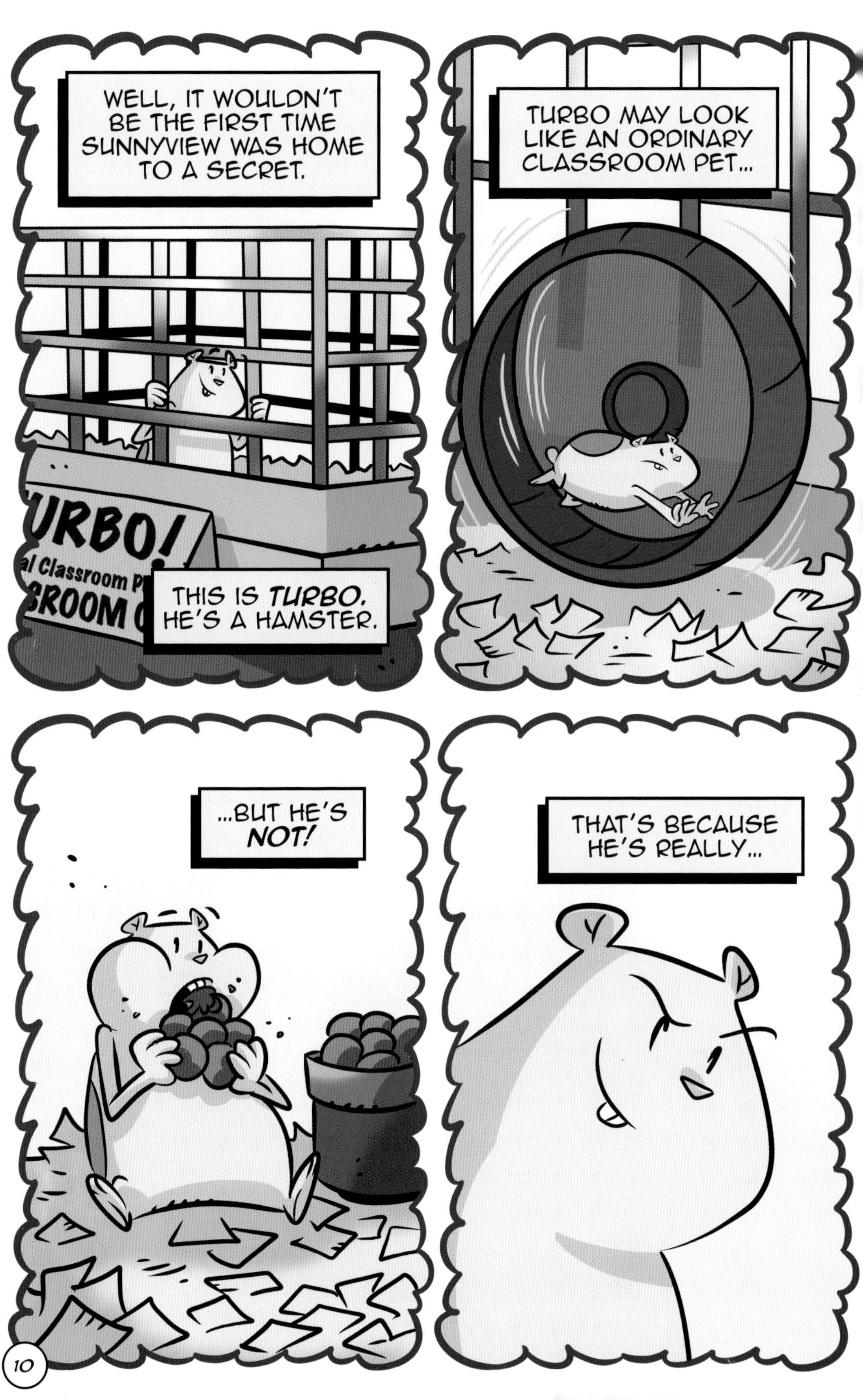
WELL, IT WOULDN'T BE THE FIRST TIME SUNNYVIEW WAS HOME TO A SECRET.
THIS IS *TURBO*. HE'S A HAMSTER.
TURBO MAY LOOK LIKE AN ORDINARY CLASSROOM PET...
...BUT HE'S *NOT!*
THAT'S BECAUSE HE'S REALLY...

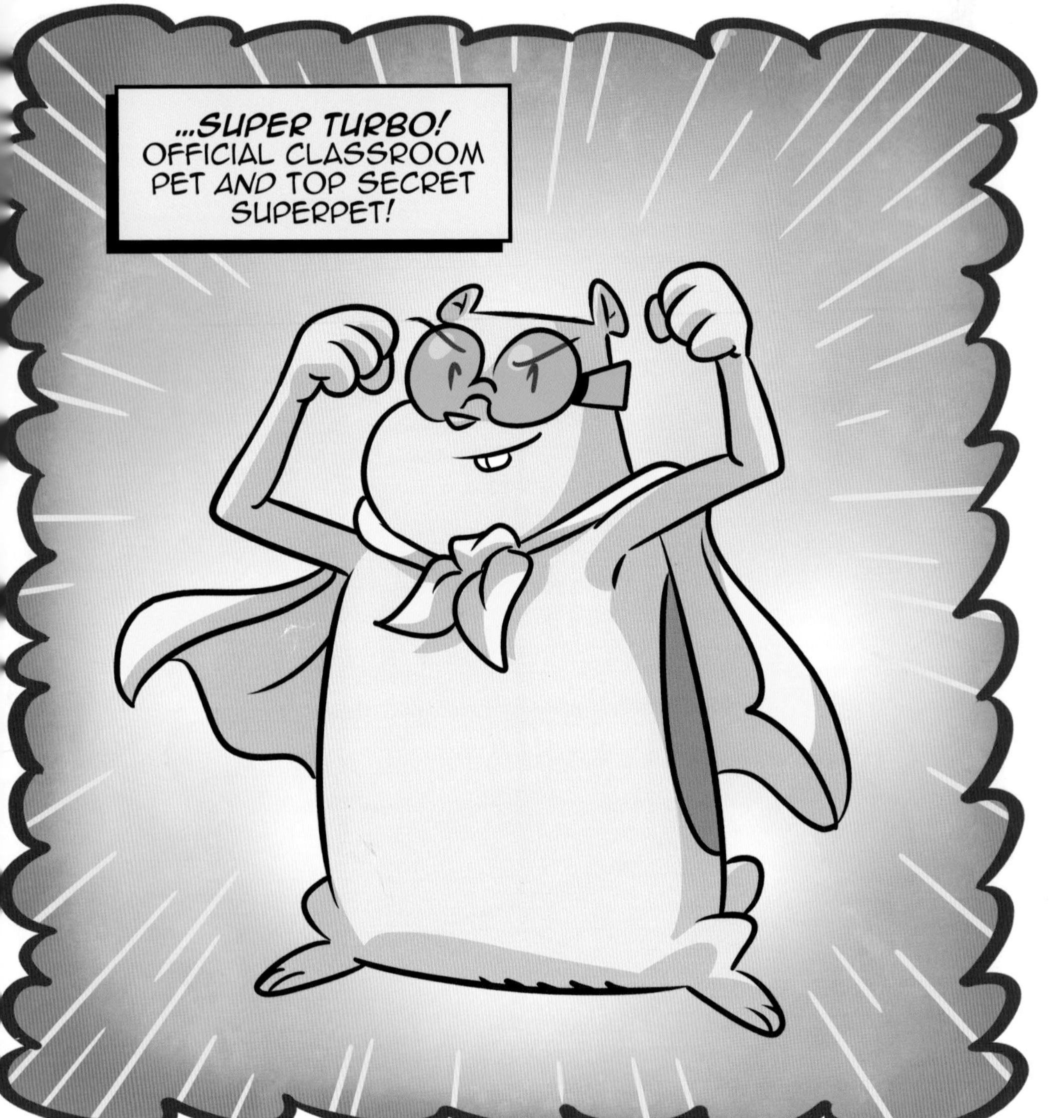
...SUPER TURBO! OFFICIAL CLASSROOM PET AND TOP SECRET SUPERPET!

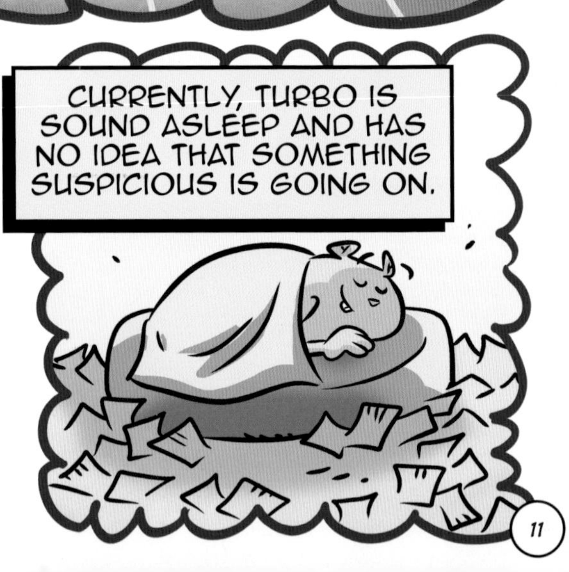
CURRENTLY, TURBO IS SOUND ASLEEP AND HAS NO IDEA THAT SOMETHING SUSPICIOUS IS GOING ON.

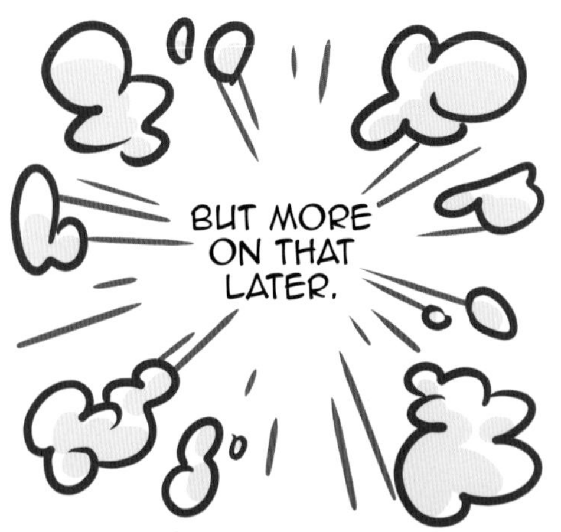
BUT MORE ON THAT LATER.

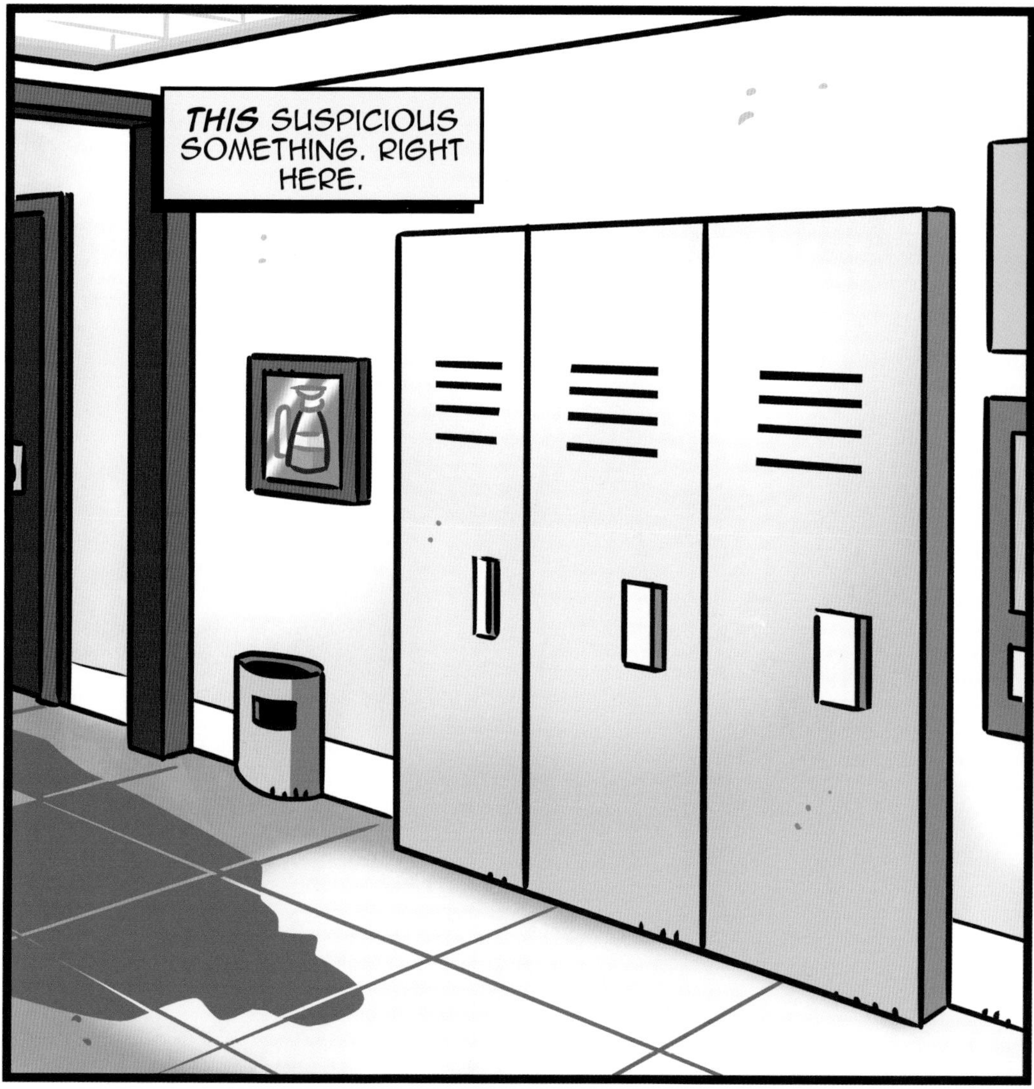
THIS SUSPICIOUS SOMETHING. RIGHT HERE.

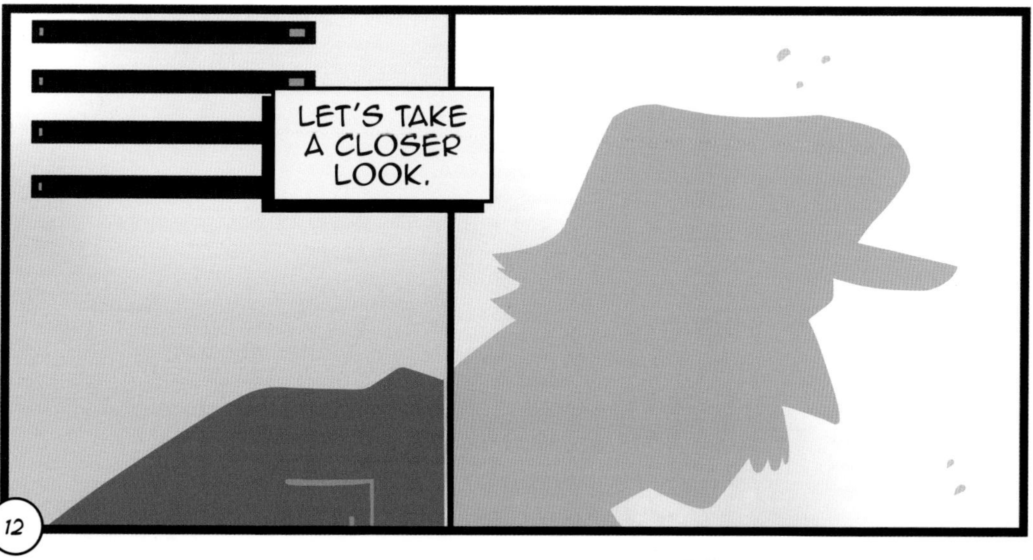
LET'S TAKE A CLOSER LOOK.

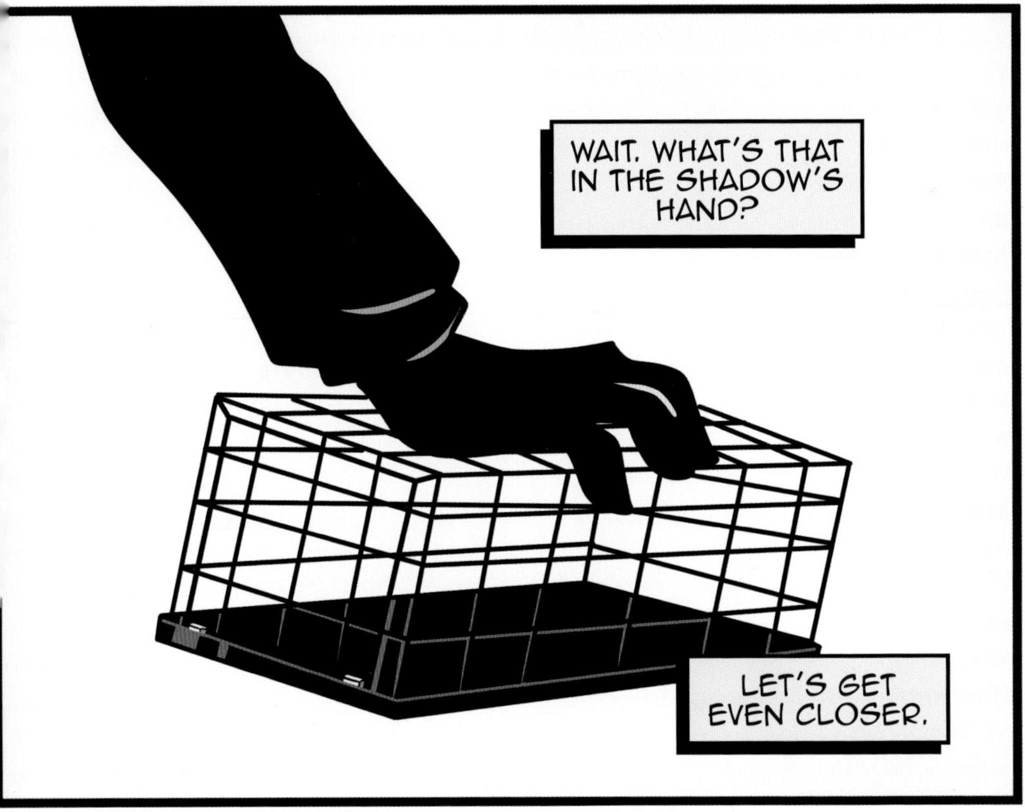
WAIT. WHAT'S THAT IN THE SHADOW'S HAND?
LET'S GET EVEN CLOSER.

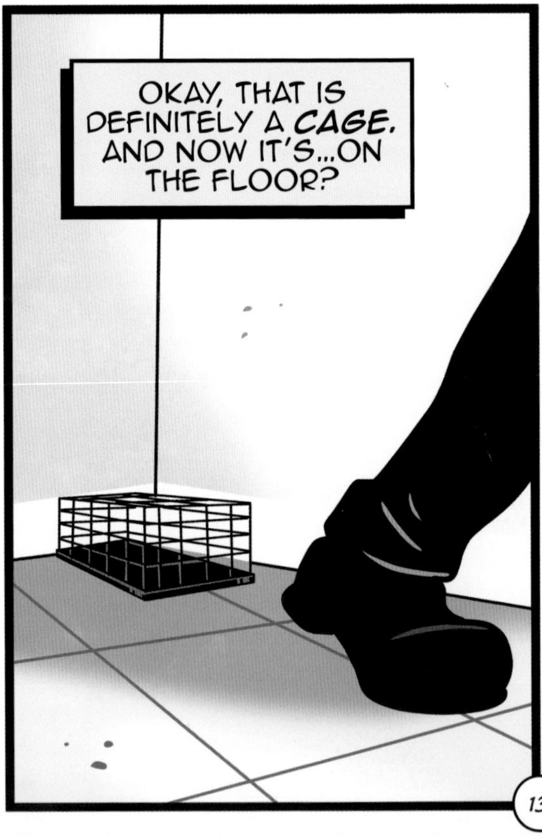
OKAY, THAT IS DEFINITELY A *CAGE.* AND NOW IT'S...ON THE FLOOR?

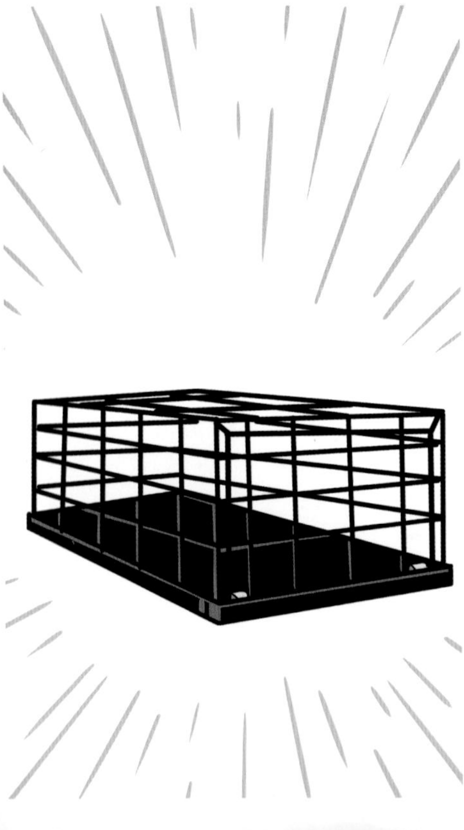

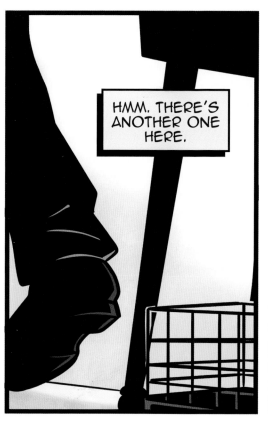

HMM. THERE'S ANOTHER ONE HERE.

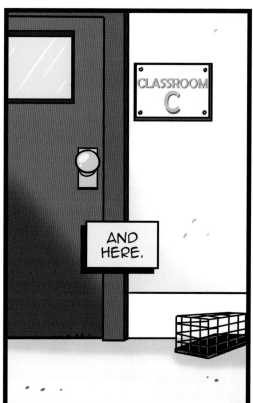

CLASSROOM C

AND HERE.

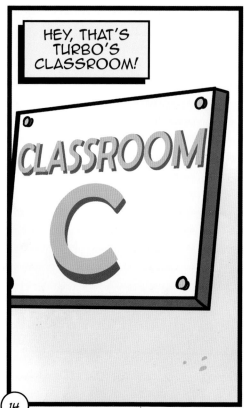

HEY, THAT'S TURBO'S CLASSROOM!

CLASSROOM C

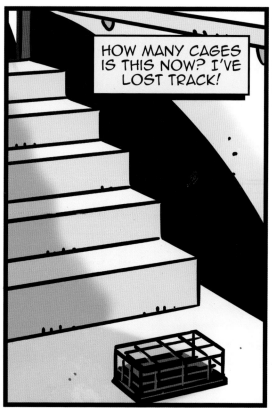

HOW MANY CAGES IS THIS NOW? I'VE LOST TRACK!

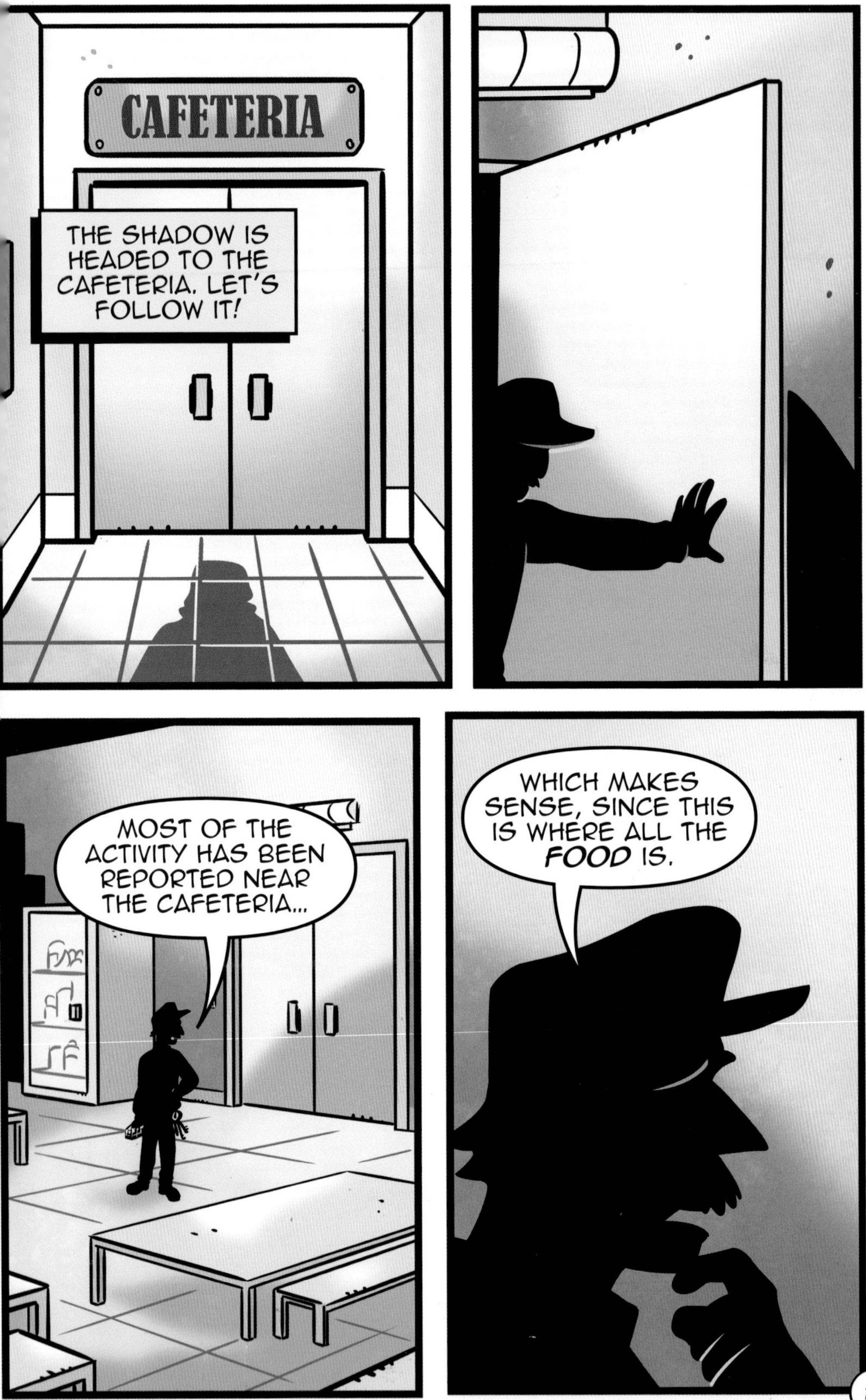
CAFETERIA
THE SHADOW IS HEADED TO THE CAFETERIA. LET'S FOLLOW IT!
MOST OF THE ACTIVITY HAS BEEN REPORTED NEAR THE CAFETERIA...
WHICH MAKES SENSE, SINCE THIS IS WHERE ALL THE *FOOD* IS.

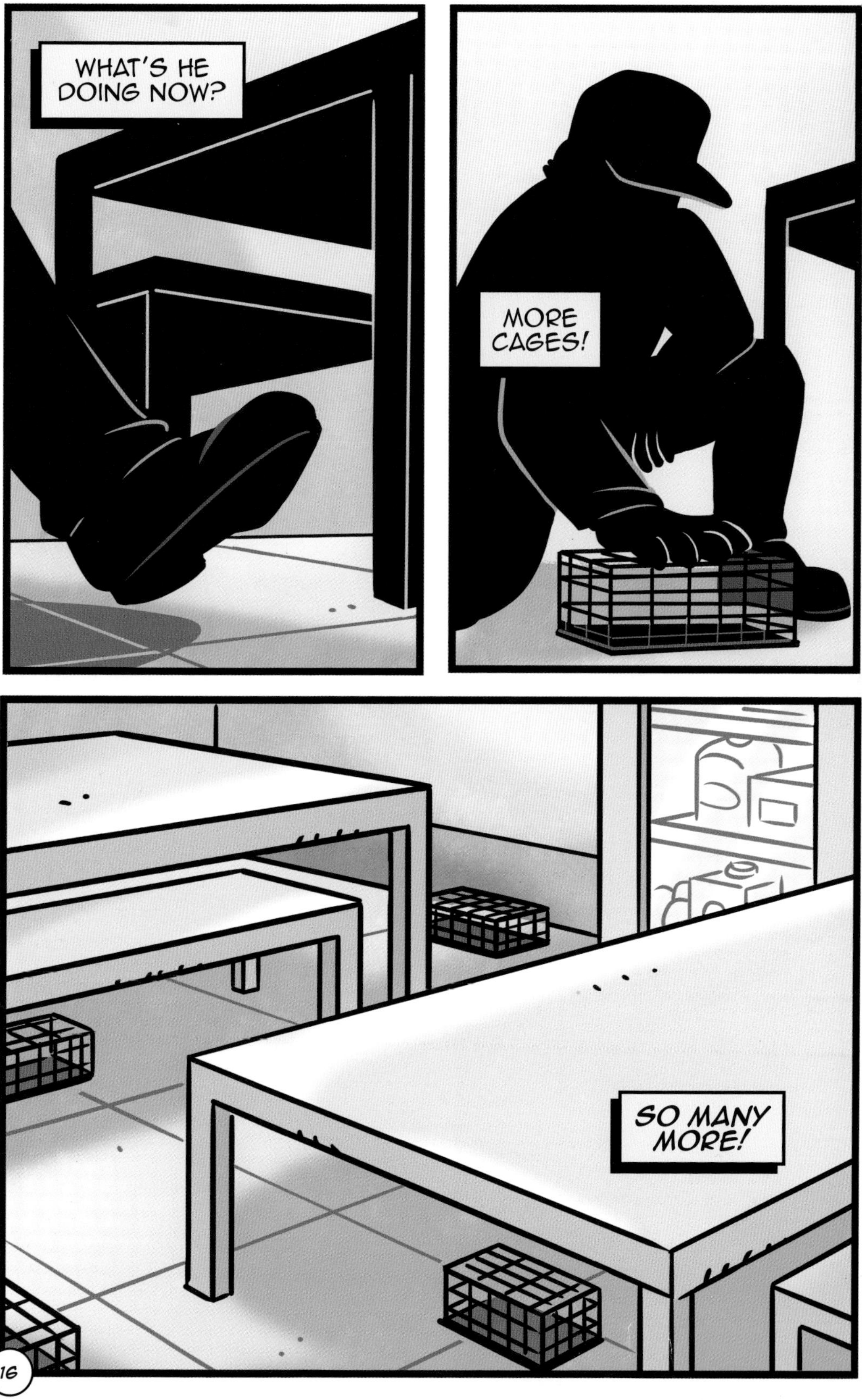
WHAT'S HE DOING NOW?
MORE CAGES!
SO MANY MORE!

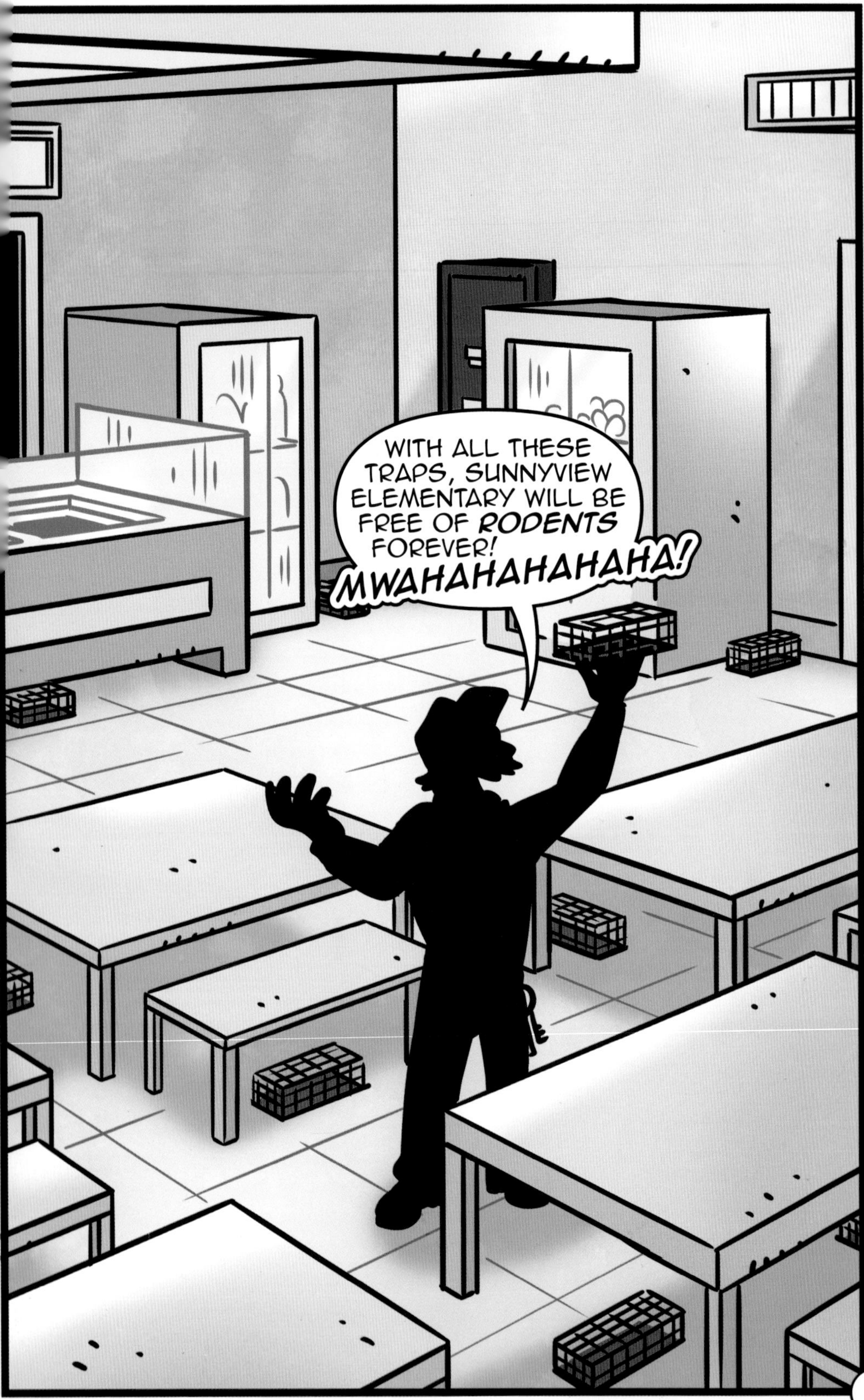
WITH ALL THESE TRAPS, SUNNYVIEW ELEMENTARY WILL BE FREE OF *RODENTS* FOREVER!
MWAHAHAHAHAHA!

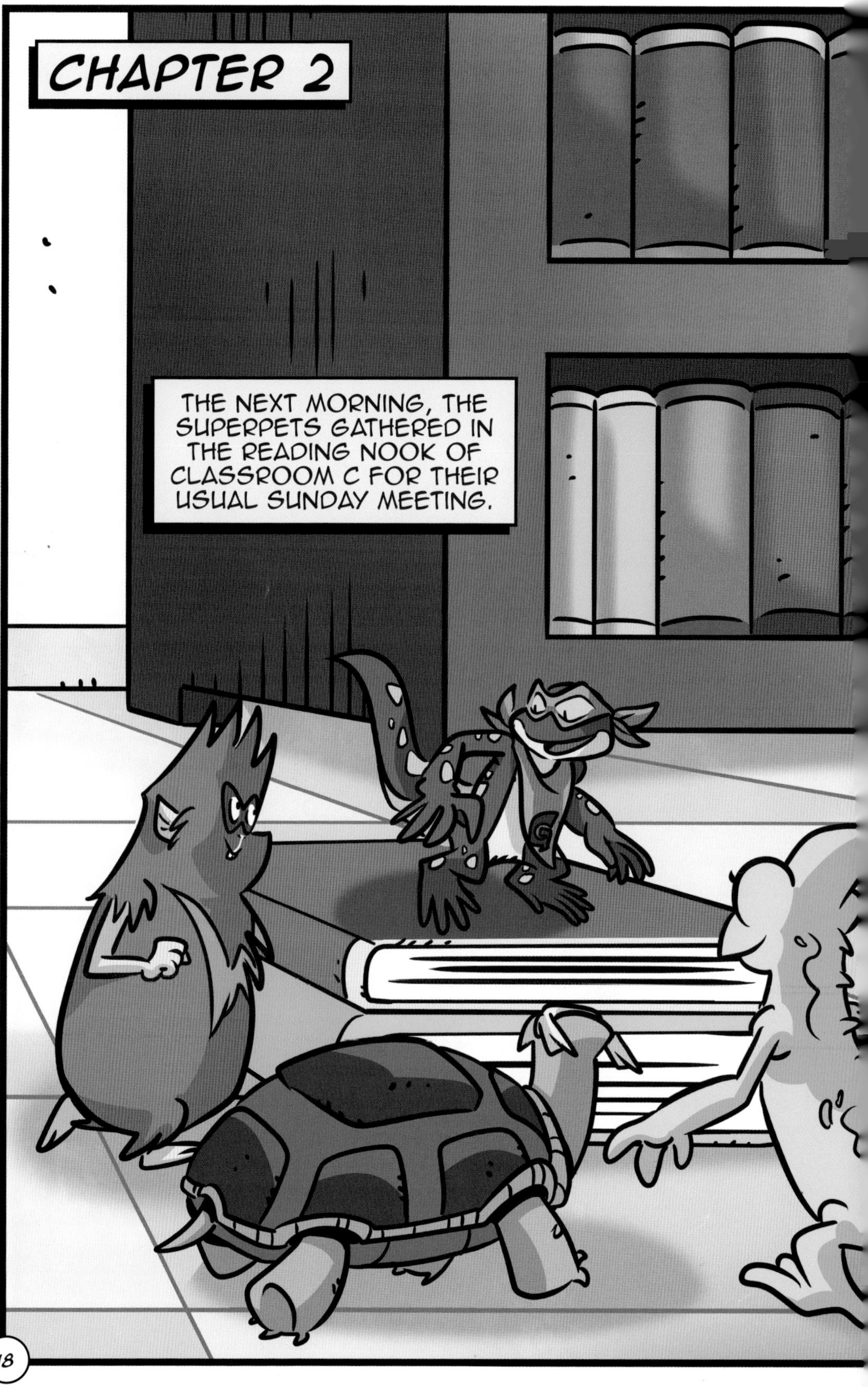
CHAPTER 2
THE NEXT MORNING, THE SUPERPETS GATHERED IN THE READING NOOK OF CLASSROOM C FOR THEIR USUAL SUNDAY MEETING.

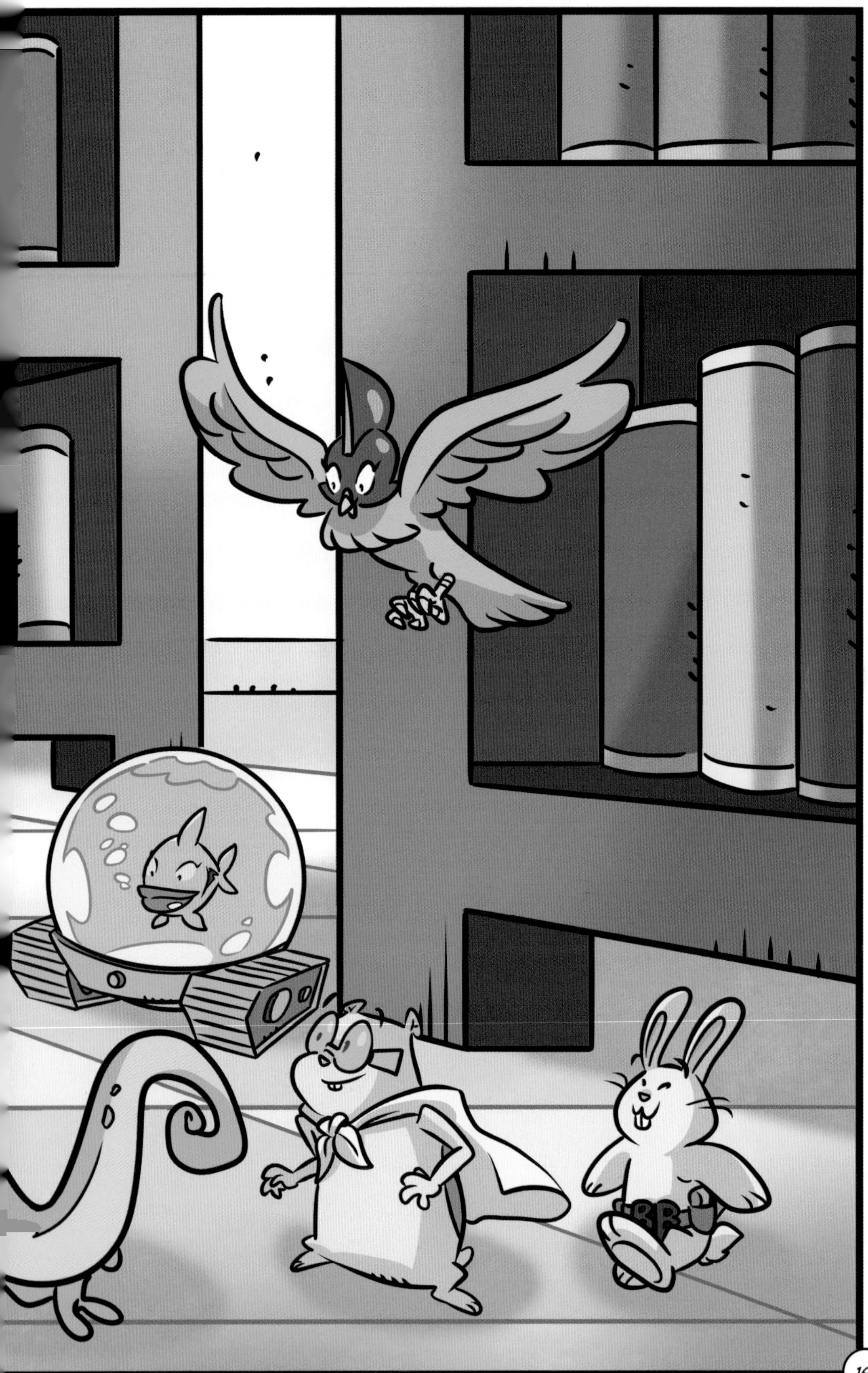

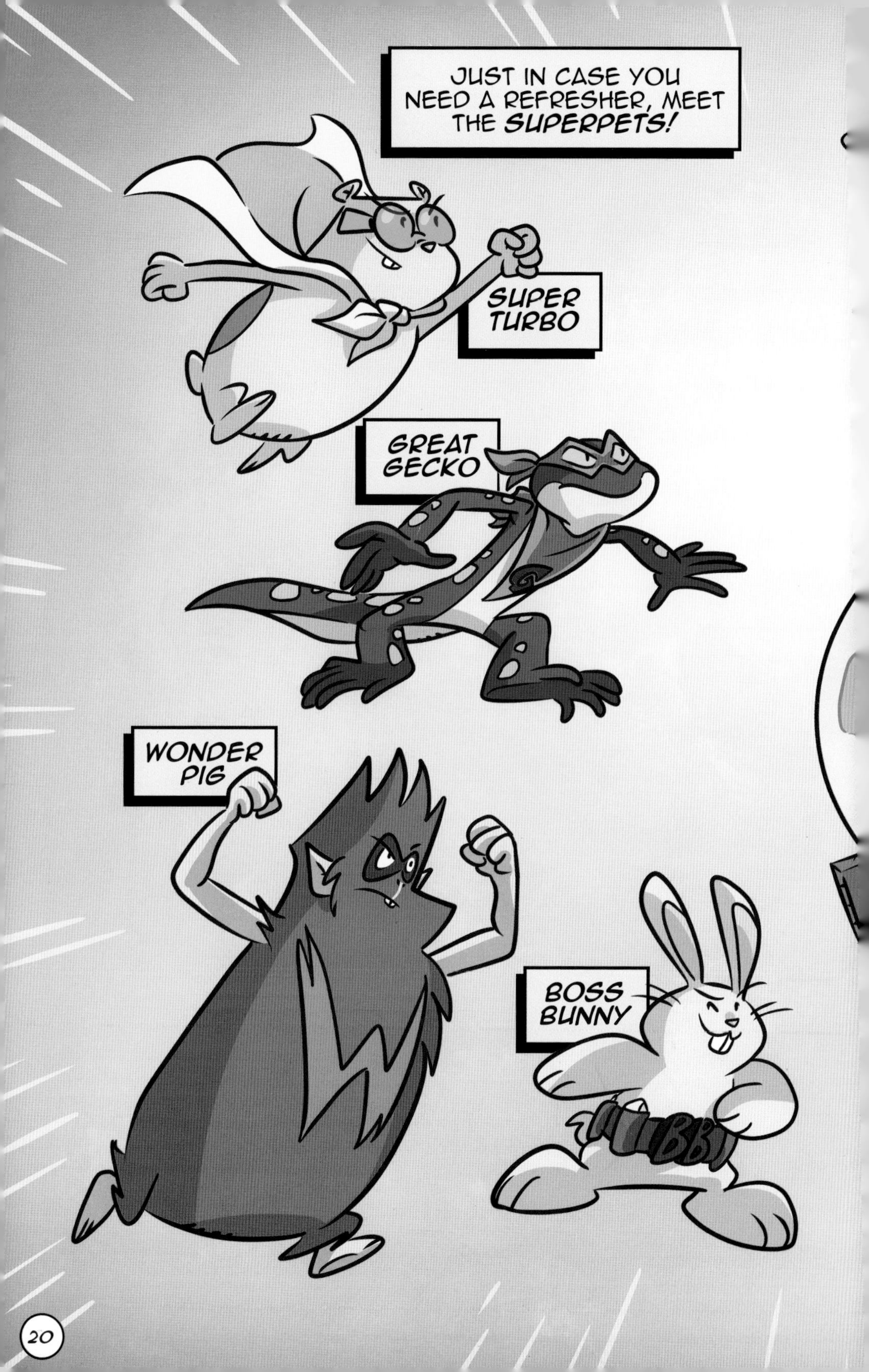
JUST IN CASE YOU NEED A REFRESHER, MEET THE SUPERPETS!
SUPER TURBO
GREAT GECKO
WONDER PIG
BOSS BUNNY
BB

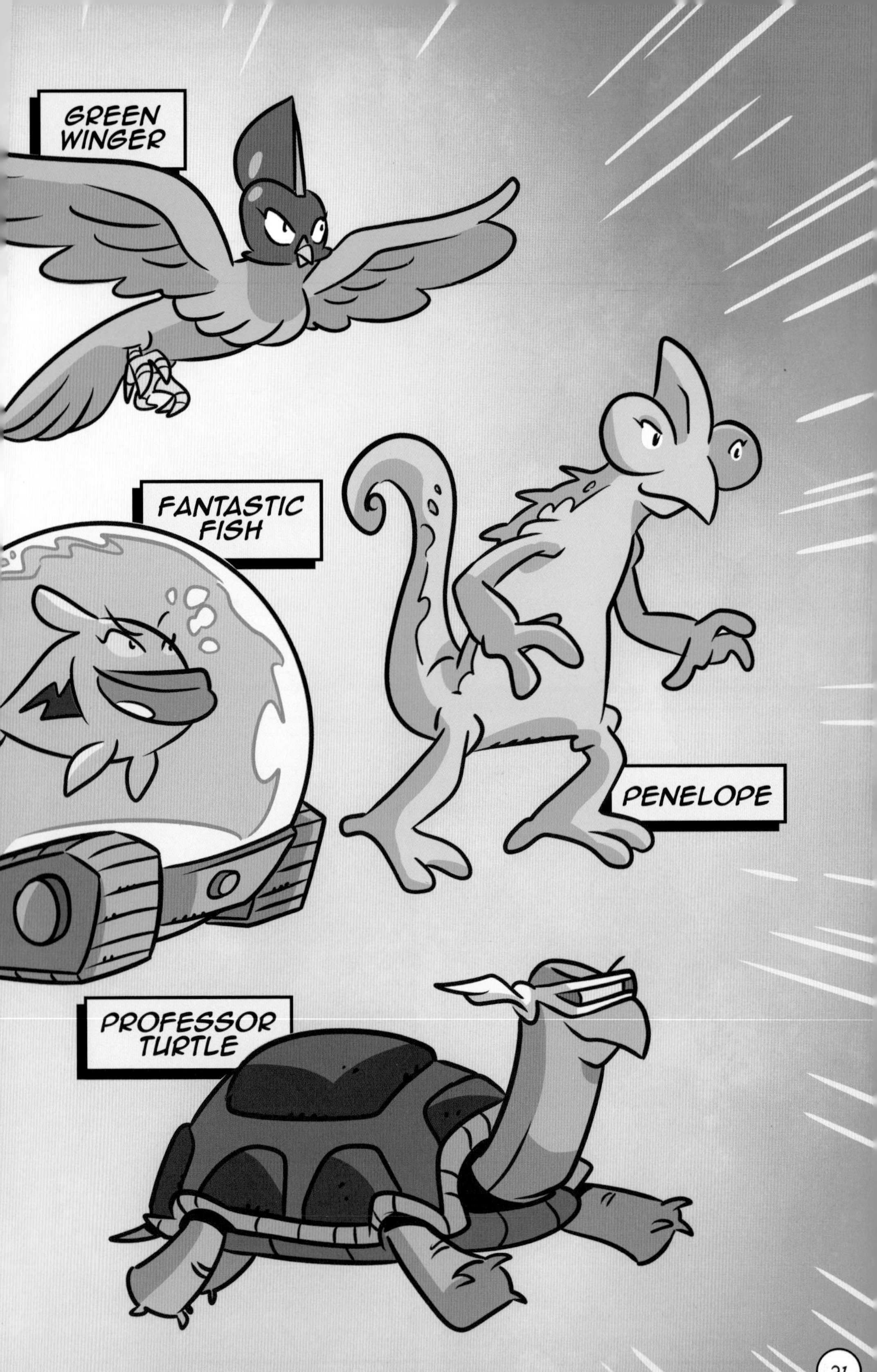
GREEN WINGER
PENELOPE
FANTASTIC FISH
PROFESSOR TURTLE

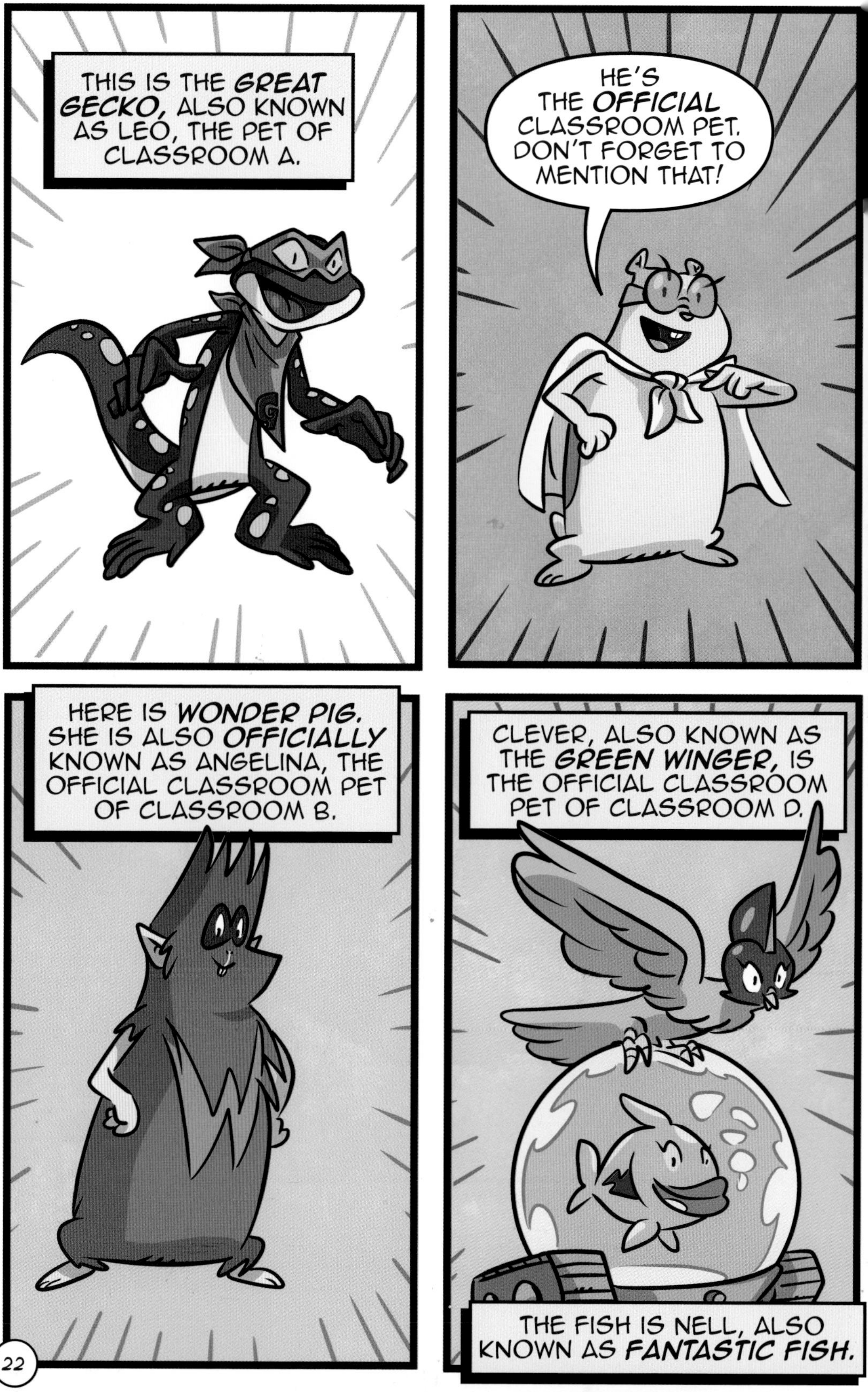
THIS IS THE GREAT GECKO, ALSO KNOWN AS LEO, THE PET OF CLASSROOM A.
HE'S THE OFFICIAL CLASSROOM PET. DON'T FORGET TO MENTION THAT!
HERE IS WONDER PIG. SHE IS ALSO OFFICIALLY KNOWN AS ANGELINA, THE OFFICIAL CLASSROOM PET OF CLASSROOM B.
CLEVER, ALSO KNOWN AS THE GREEN WINGER, IS THE OFFICIAL CLASSROOM PET OF CLASSROOM D.
THE FISH IS NELL, ALSO KNOWN AS FANTASTIC FISH.

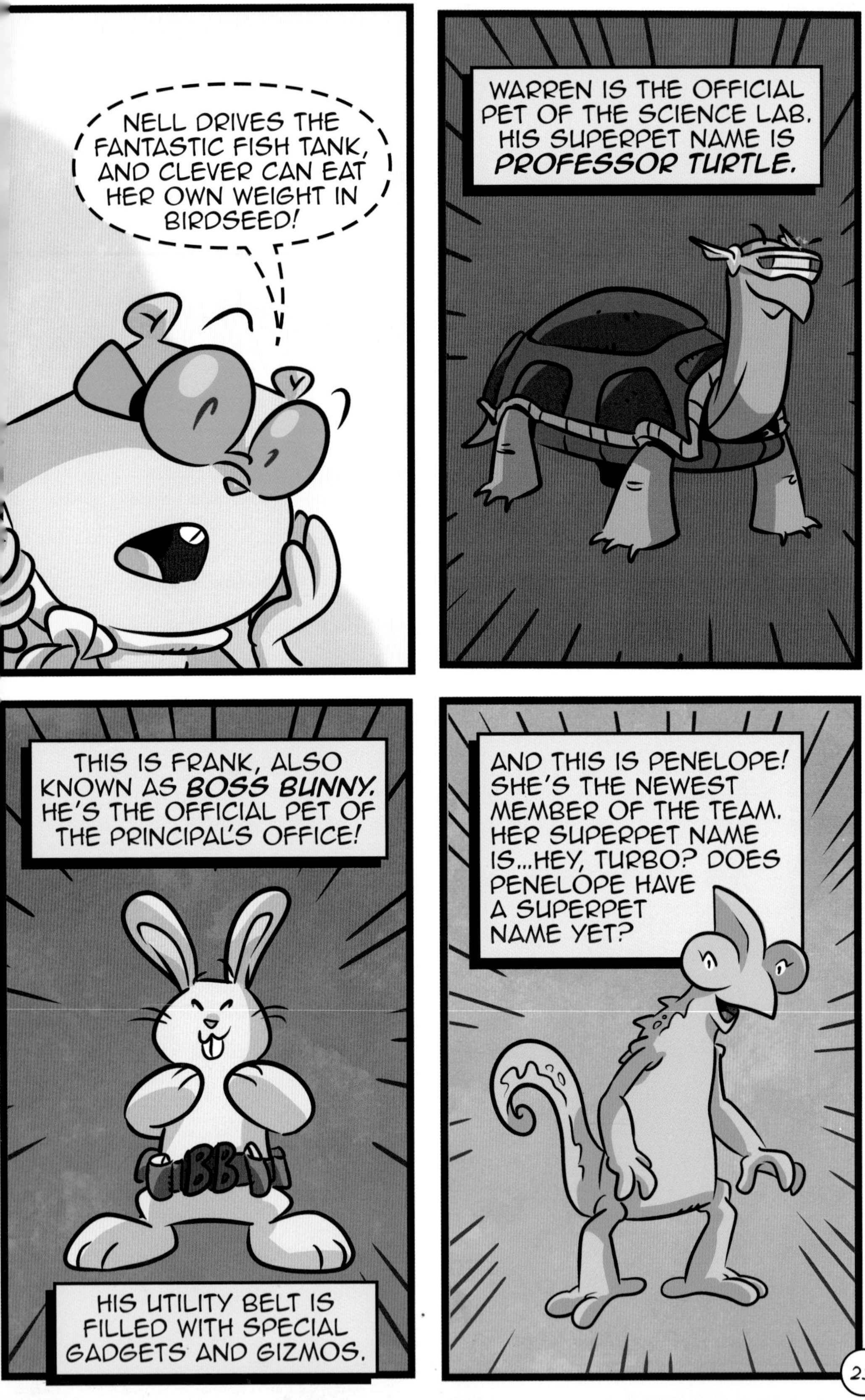
WARREN IS THE OFFICIAL PET OF THE SCIENCE LAB. HIS SUPERPET NAME IS *PROFESSOR TURTLE.*
NELL DRIVES THE FANTASTIC FISH TANK, AND CLEVER CAN EAT HER OWN WEIGHT IN BIRDSEED!
AND THIS IS PENELOPE! SHE'S THE NEWEST MEMBER OF THE TEAM. HER SUPERPET NAME IS...HEY, TURBO? DOES PENELOPE HAVE A SUPERPET NAME YET?
THIS IS FRANK, ALSO KNOWN AS *BOSS BUNNY.* HE'S THE OFFICIAL PET OF THE PRINCIPAL'S OFFICE!
BB
HIS UTILITY BELT IS FILLED WITH SPECIAL GADGETS AND GIZMOS.

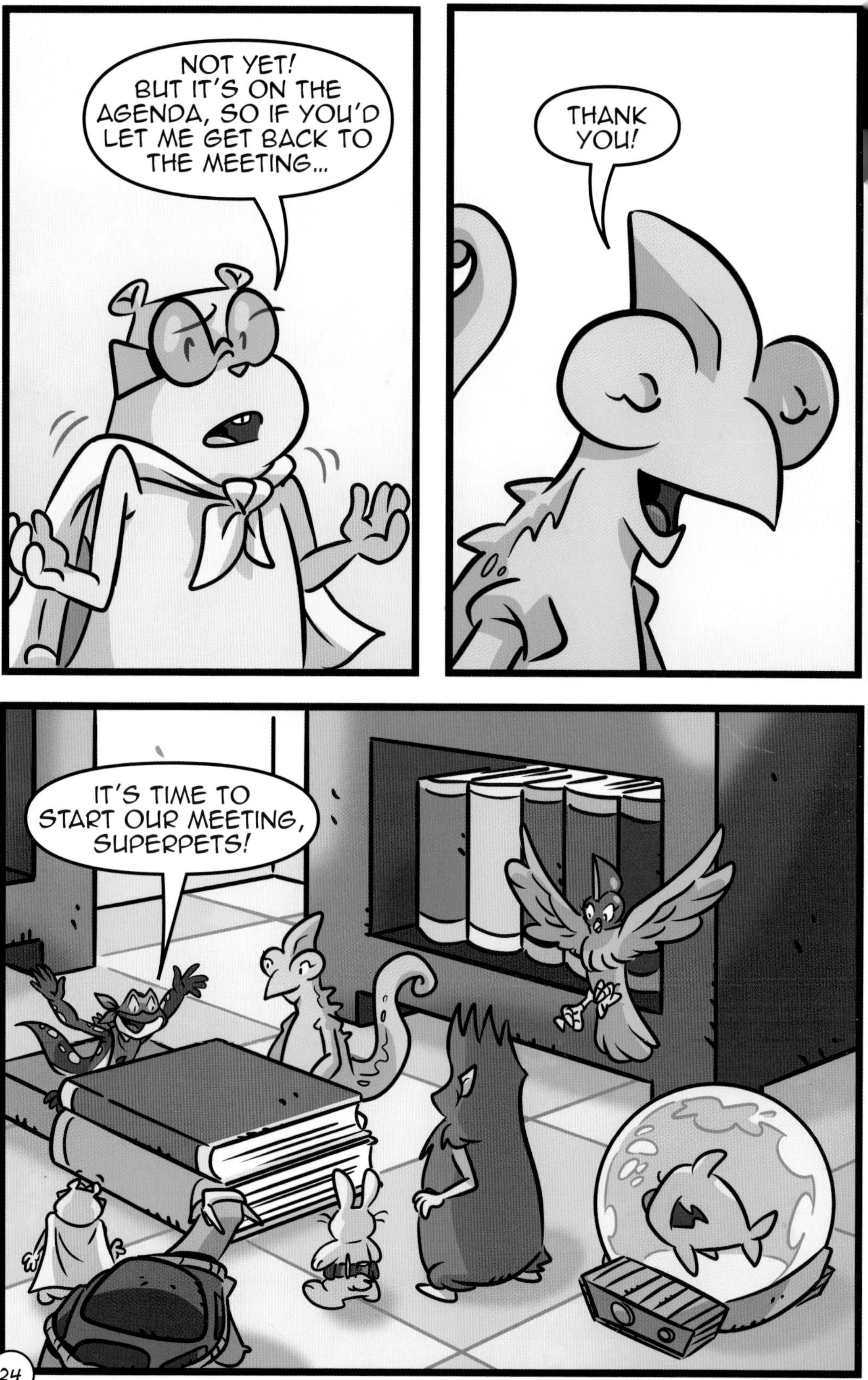
THANK YOU!
NOT YET! BUT IT'S ON THE AGENDA, SO IF YOU'D LET ME GET BACK TO THE MEETING...
IT'S TIME TO START OUR MEETING, SUPERPETS!

THE SUPERPETS ARE PRETTY OBSESSED WITH MAKING THINGS *OFFICIAL*, HUH?

BUT BACK TO THE MEETING...

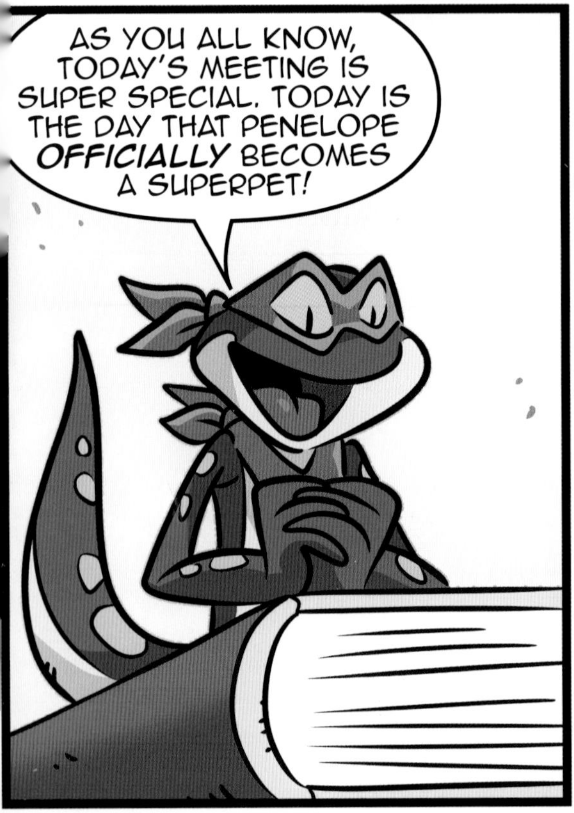
AS YOU ALL KNOW, TODAY'S MEETING IS SUPER SPECIAL. TODAY IS THE DAY THAT PENELOPE *OFFICIALLY* BECOMES A SUPERPET!

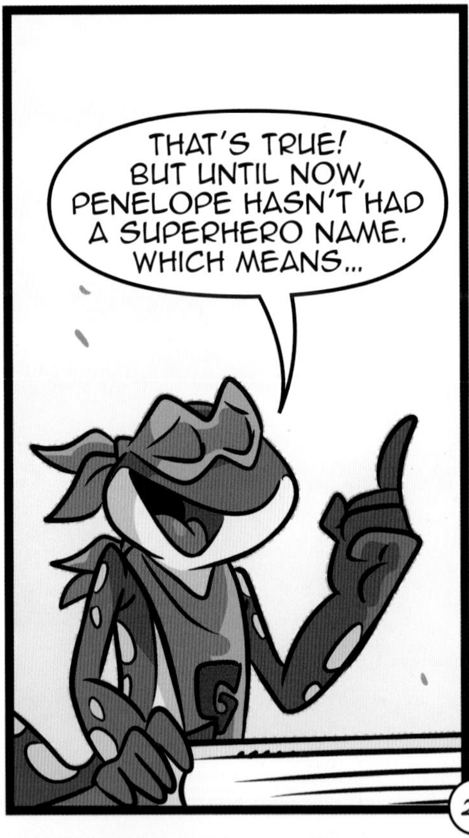
THAT'S TRUE! BUT UNTIL NOW, PENELOPE HASN'T HAD A SUPERHERO NAME. WHICH MEANS...

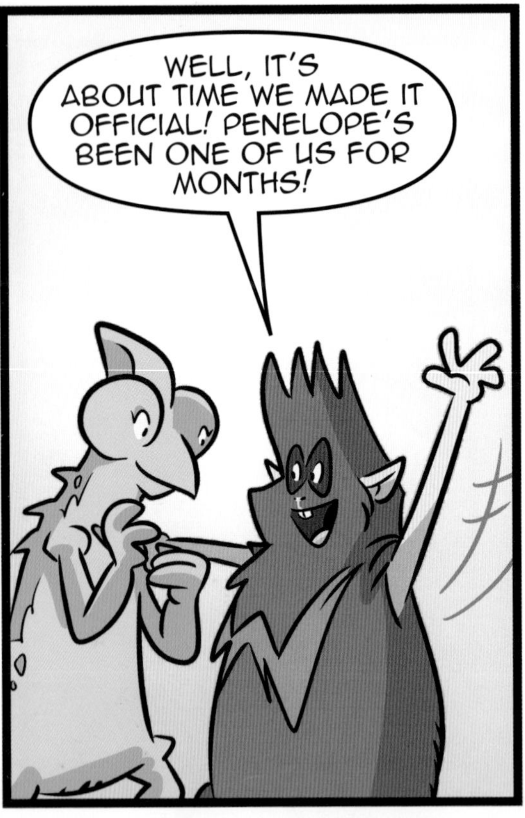
WELL, IT'S ABOUT TIME WE MADE IT OFFICIAL! PENELOPE'S BEEN ONE OF US FOR MONTHS!

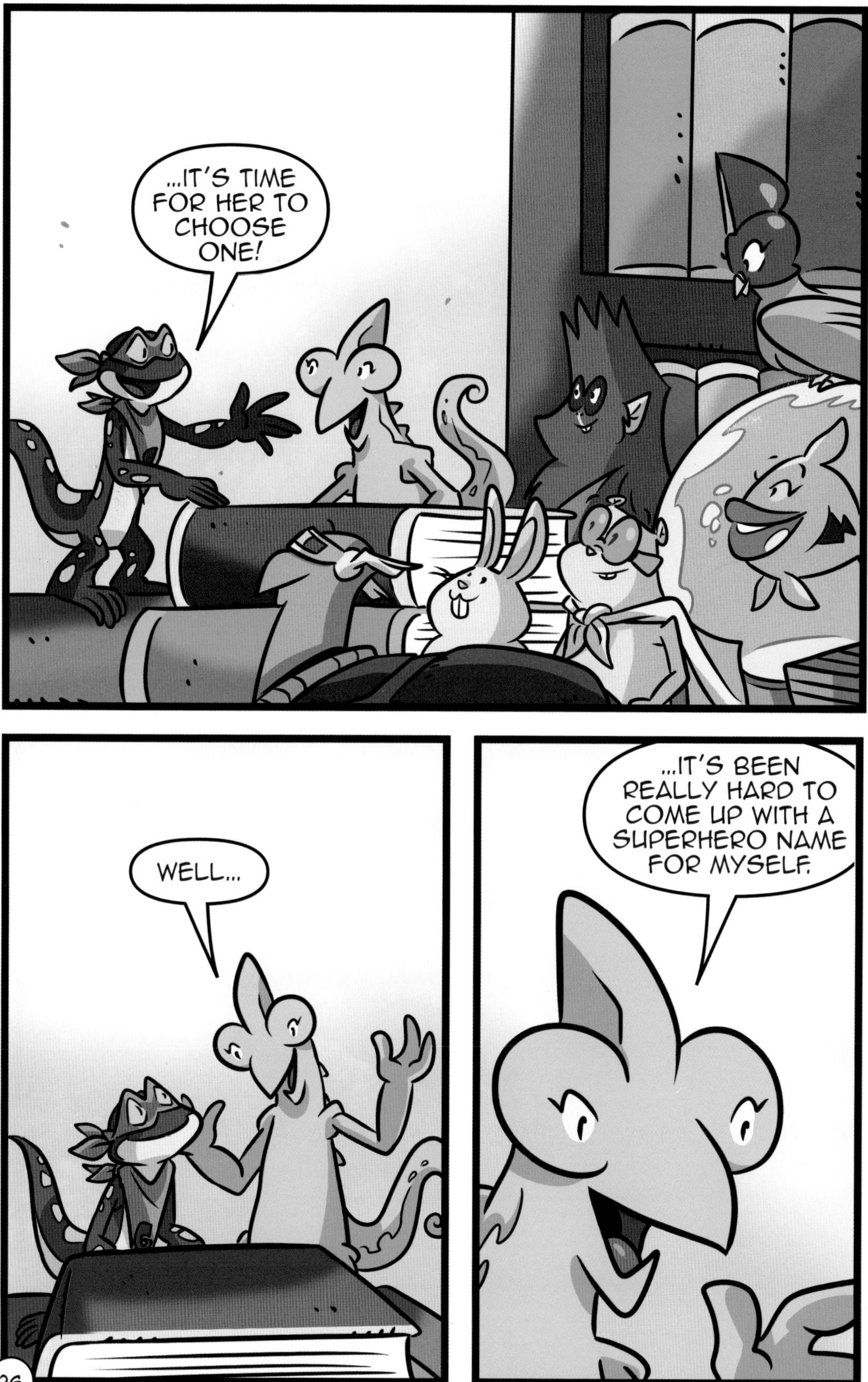
...IT'S TIME FOR HER TO CHOOSE ONE!
WELL...
...IT'S BEEN REALLY HARD TO COME UP WITH A SUPERHERO NAME FOR MYSELF.

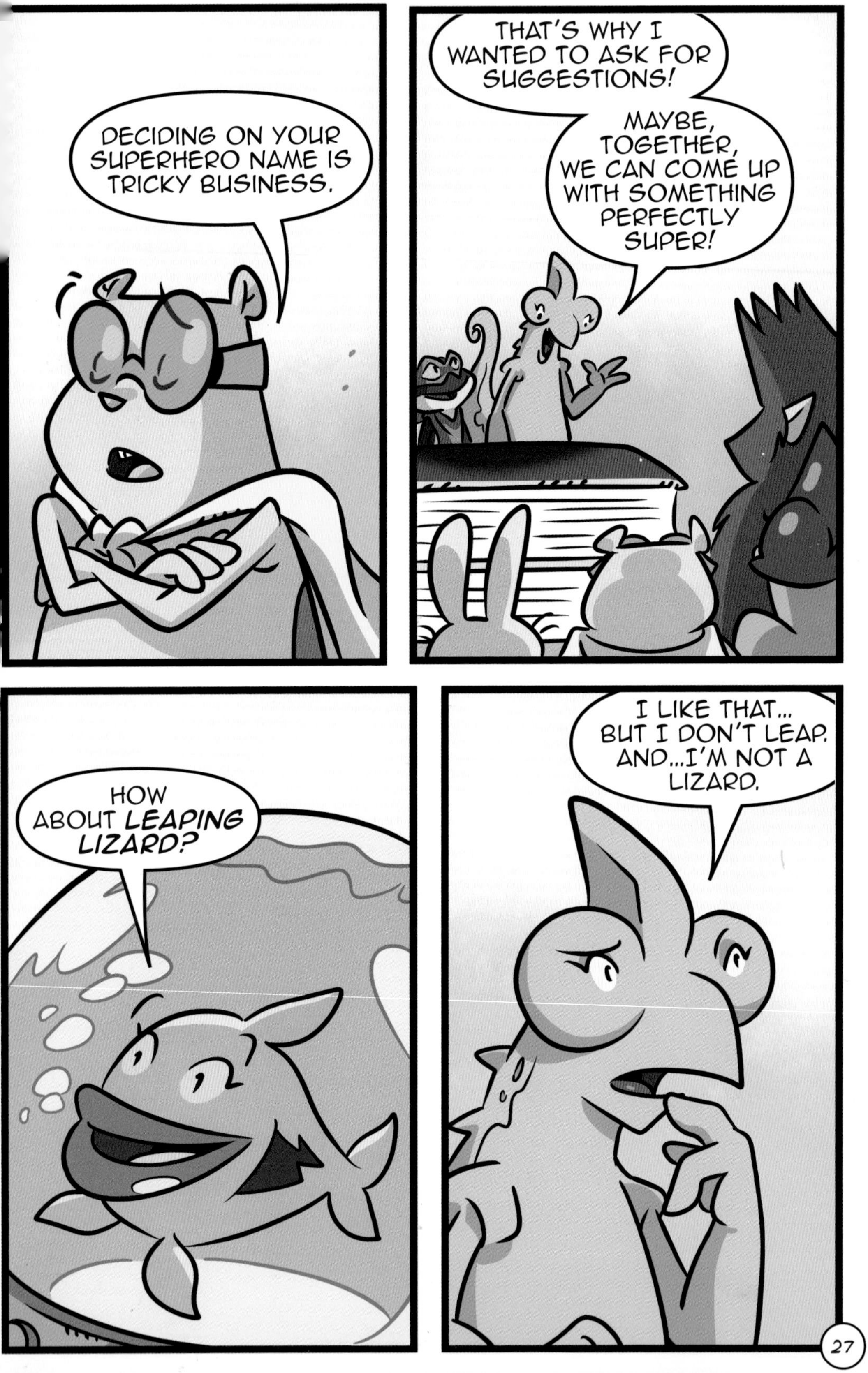
DECIDING ON YOUR SUPERHERO NAME IS TRICKY BUSINESS.
THAT'S WHY I WANTED TO ASK FOR SUGGESTIONS!
MAYBE, TOGETHER, WE CAN COME UP WITH SOMETHING PERFECTLY SUPER!
HOW ABOUT *LEAPING LIZARD?*
I LIKE THAT... BUT I DON'T LEAP. AND...I'M NOT A LIZARD.

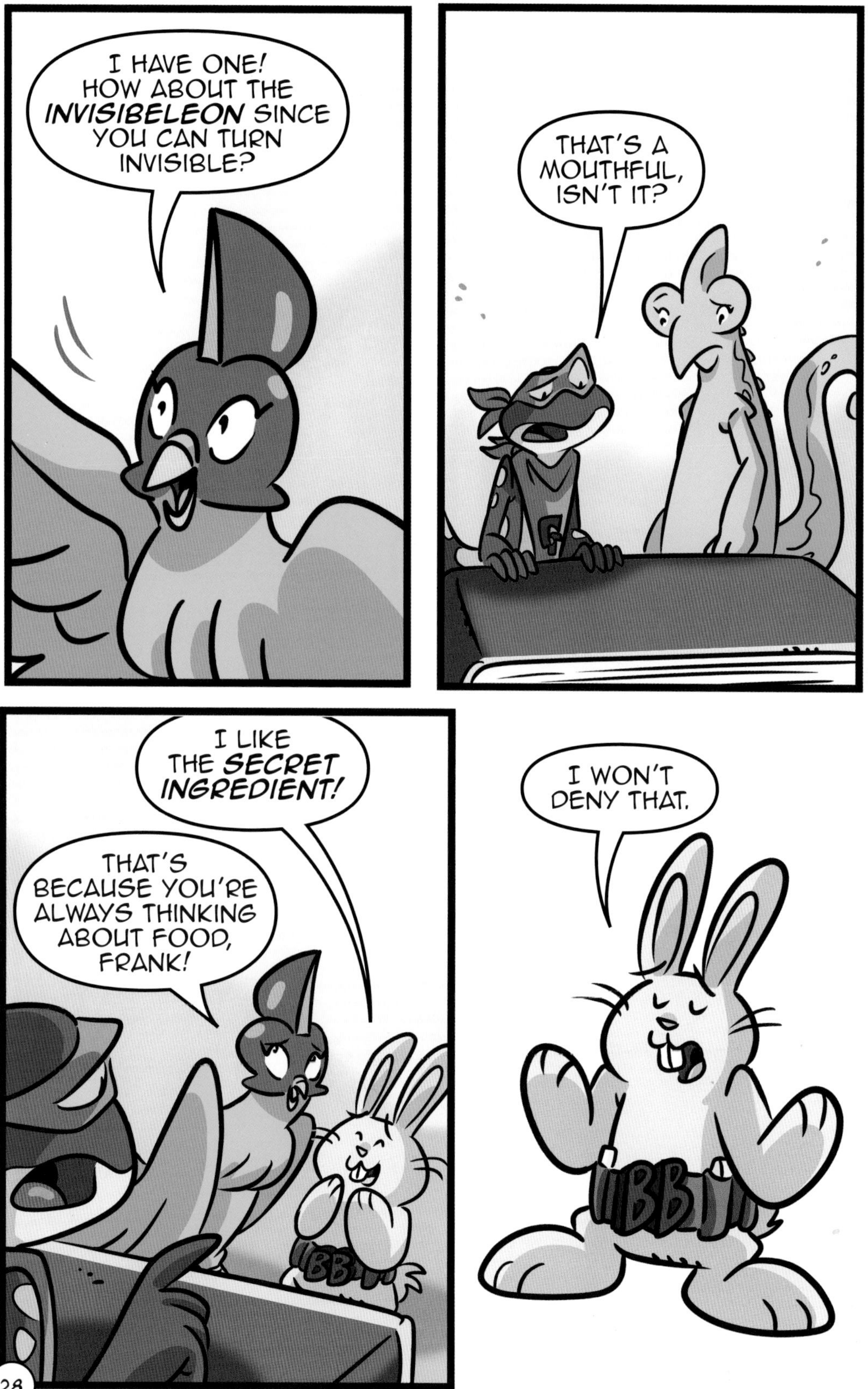
I HAVE ONE! HOW ABOUT THE *INVISIBELEON* SINCE YOU CAN TURN INVISIBLE?
THAT'S A MOUTHFUL, ISN'T IT?
I LIKE THE *SECRET INGREDIENT!*
THAT'S BECAUSE YOU'RE ALWAYS THINKING ABOUT FOOD, FRANK!
I WON'T DENY THAT.

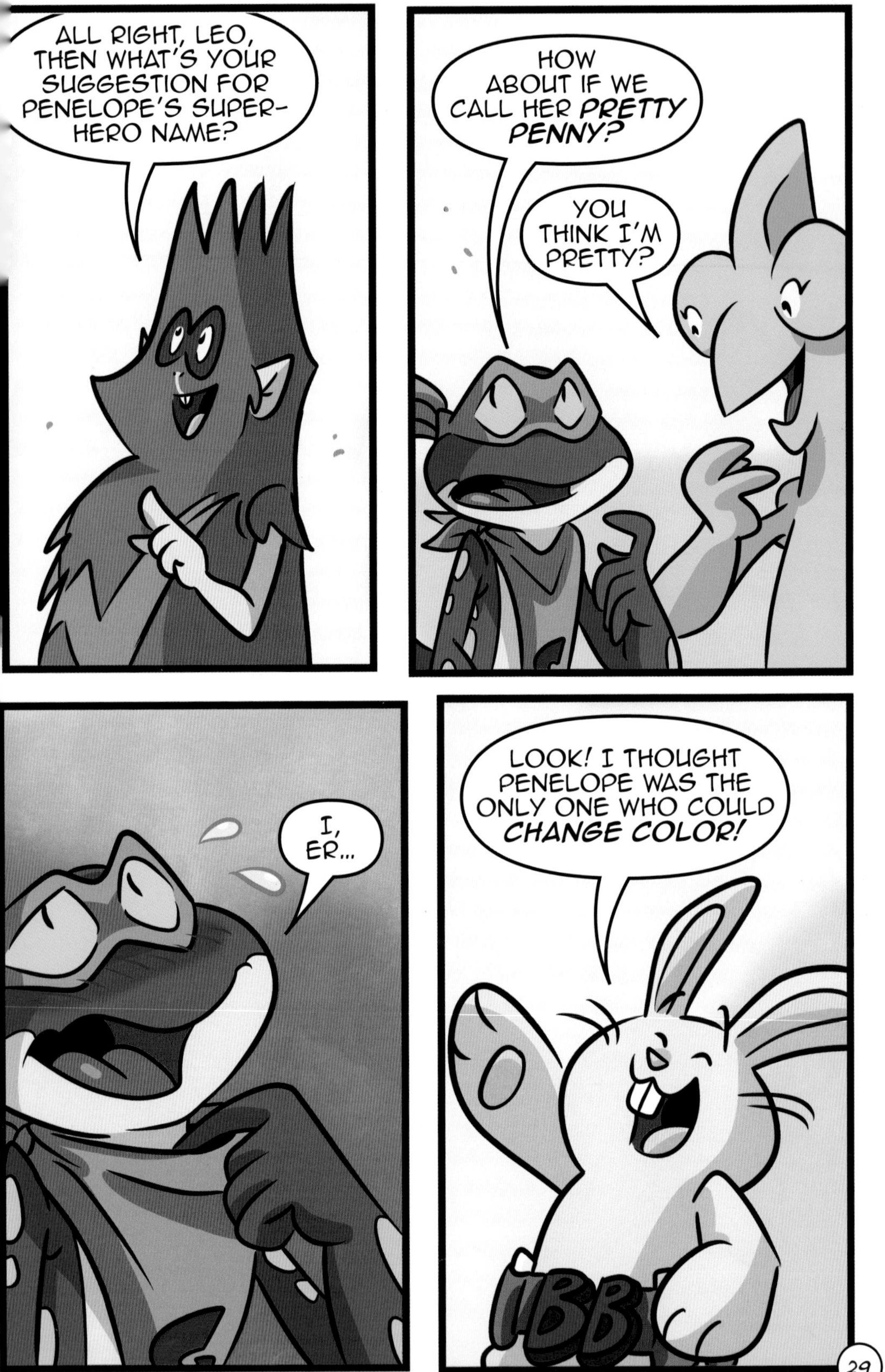
ALL RIGHT, LEO, THEN WHAT'S YOUR SUGGESTION FOR PENELOPE'S SUPER-HERO NAME?
HOW ABOUT IF WE CALL HER *PRETTY PENNY?*
YOU THINK I'M PRETTY?
I, ER...
LOOK! I THOUGHT PENELOPE WAS THE ONLY ONE WHO COULD *CHANGE COLOR!*
BB

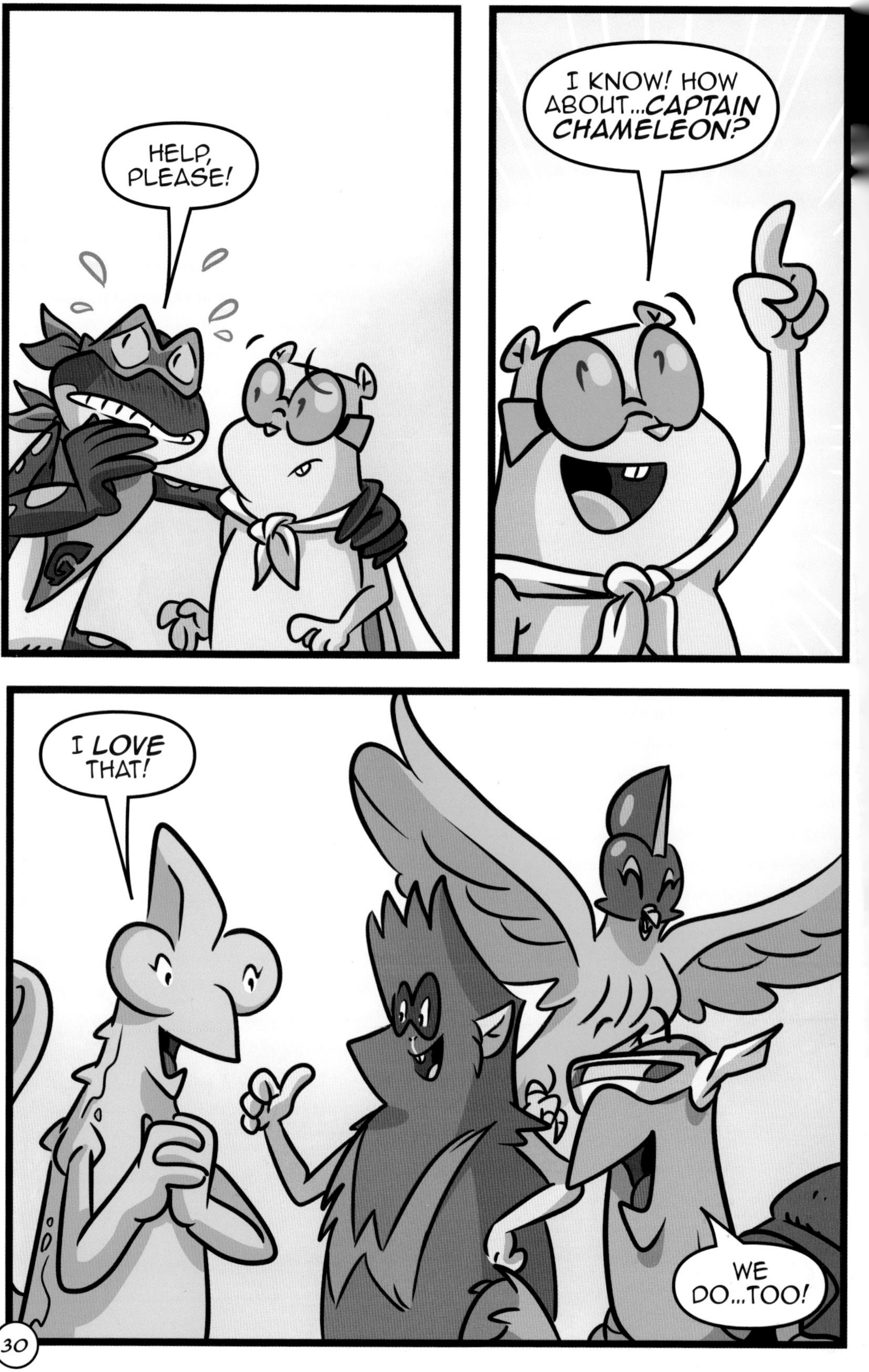
I KNOW! HOW ABOUT...CAPTAIN CHAMELEON?
HELP, PLEASE!
I LOVE THAT!
WE DO...TOO!

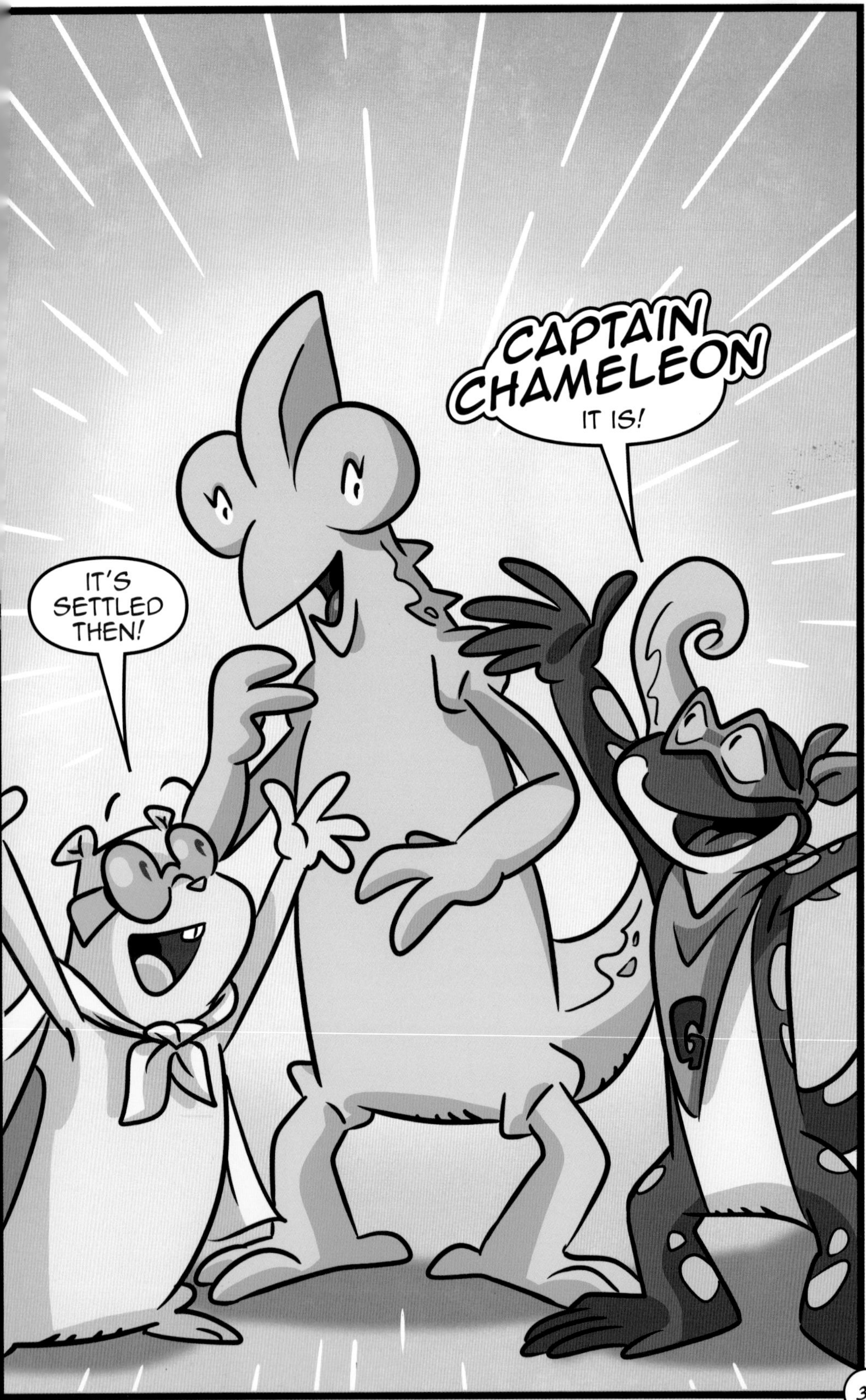
CAPTAIN CHAMELEON IT IS!
IT'S SETTLED THEN!

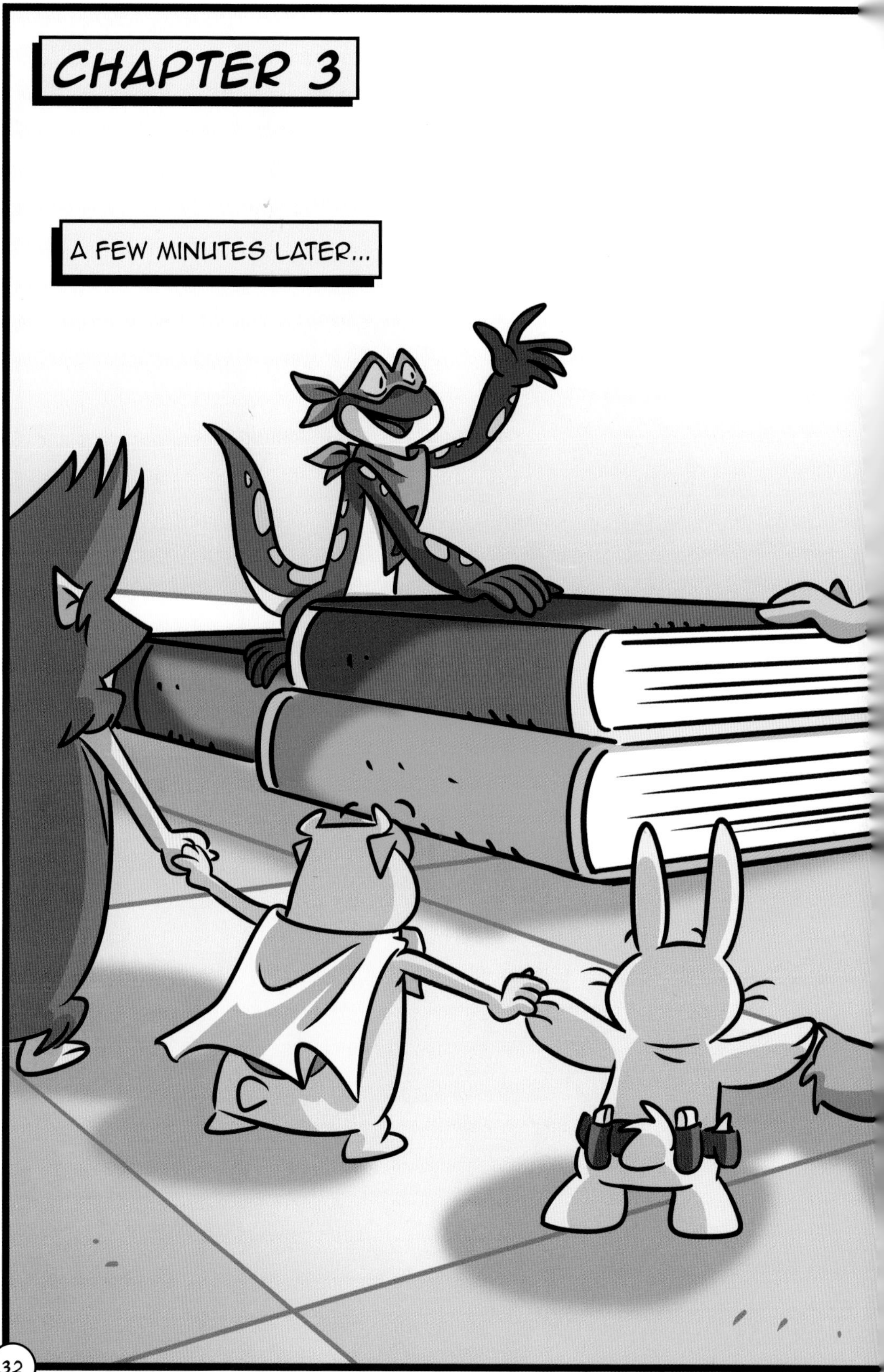
CHAPTER 3
A FEW MINUTES LATER...

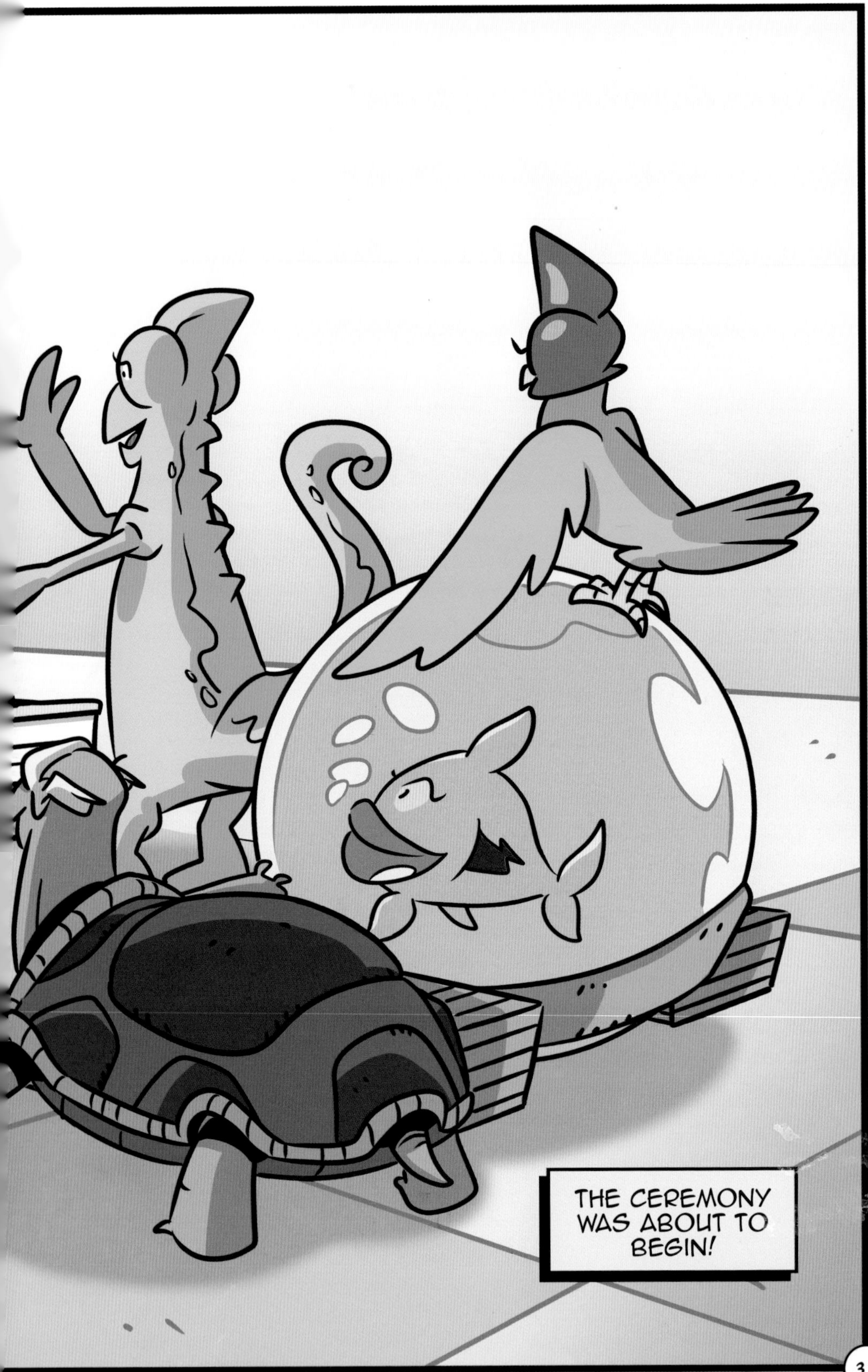
THE CEREMONY WAS ABOUT TO BEGIN!

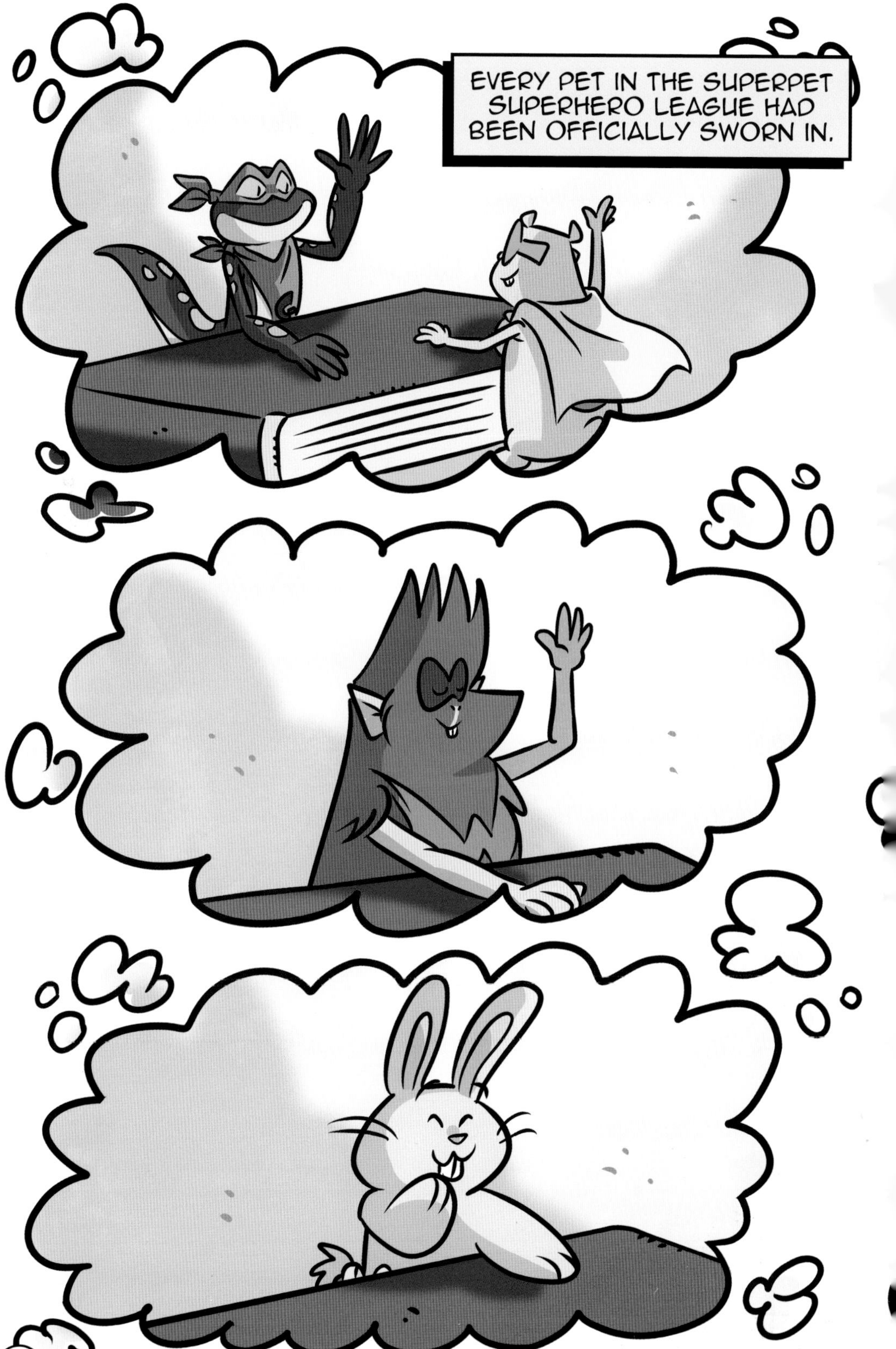
EVERY PET IN THE SUPERPET SUPERHERO LEAGUE HAD BEEN OFFICIALLY SWORN IN.

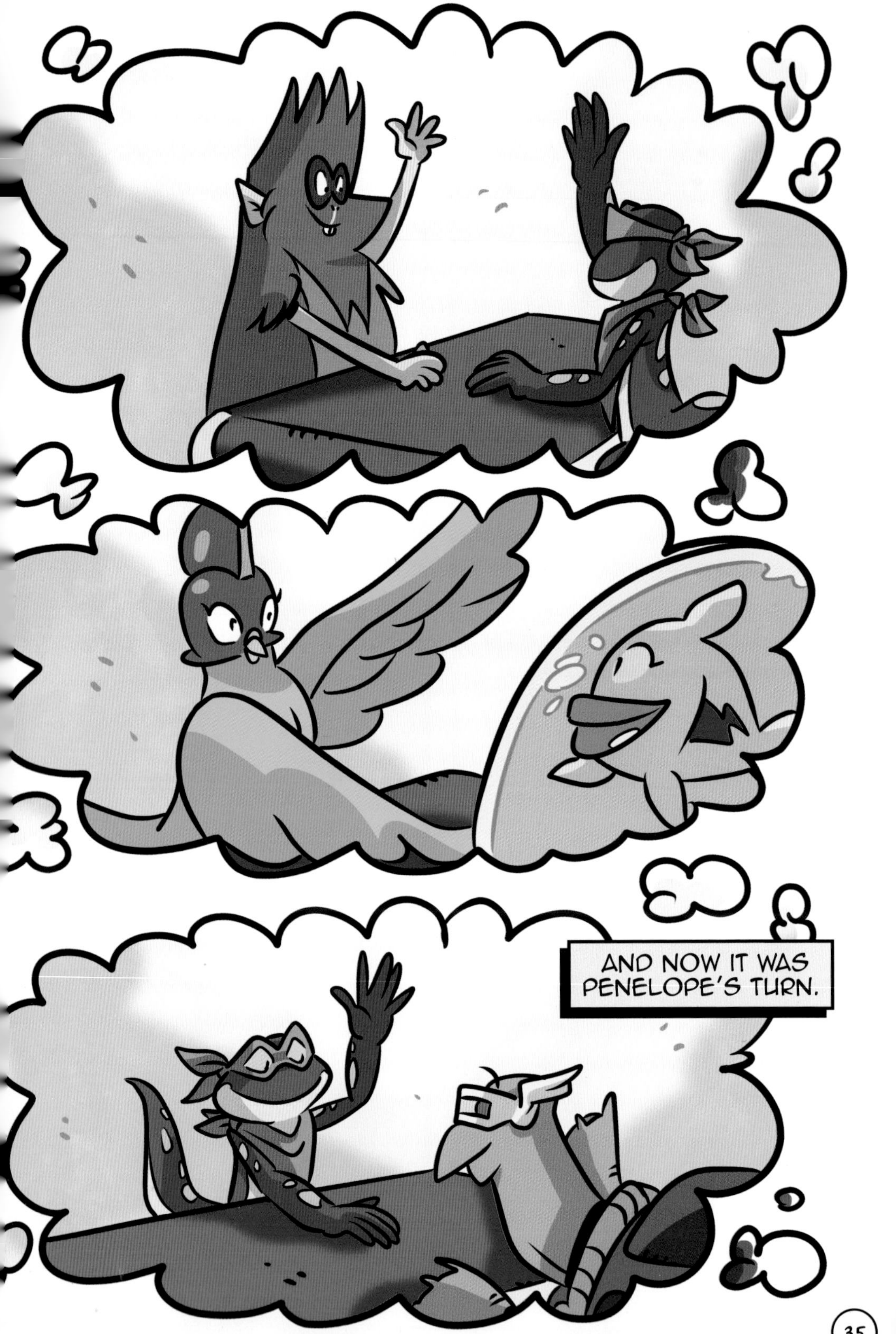
AND NOW IT WAS PENELOPE'S TURN.

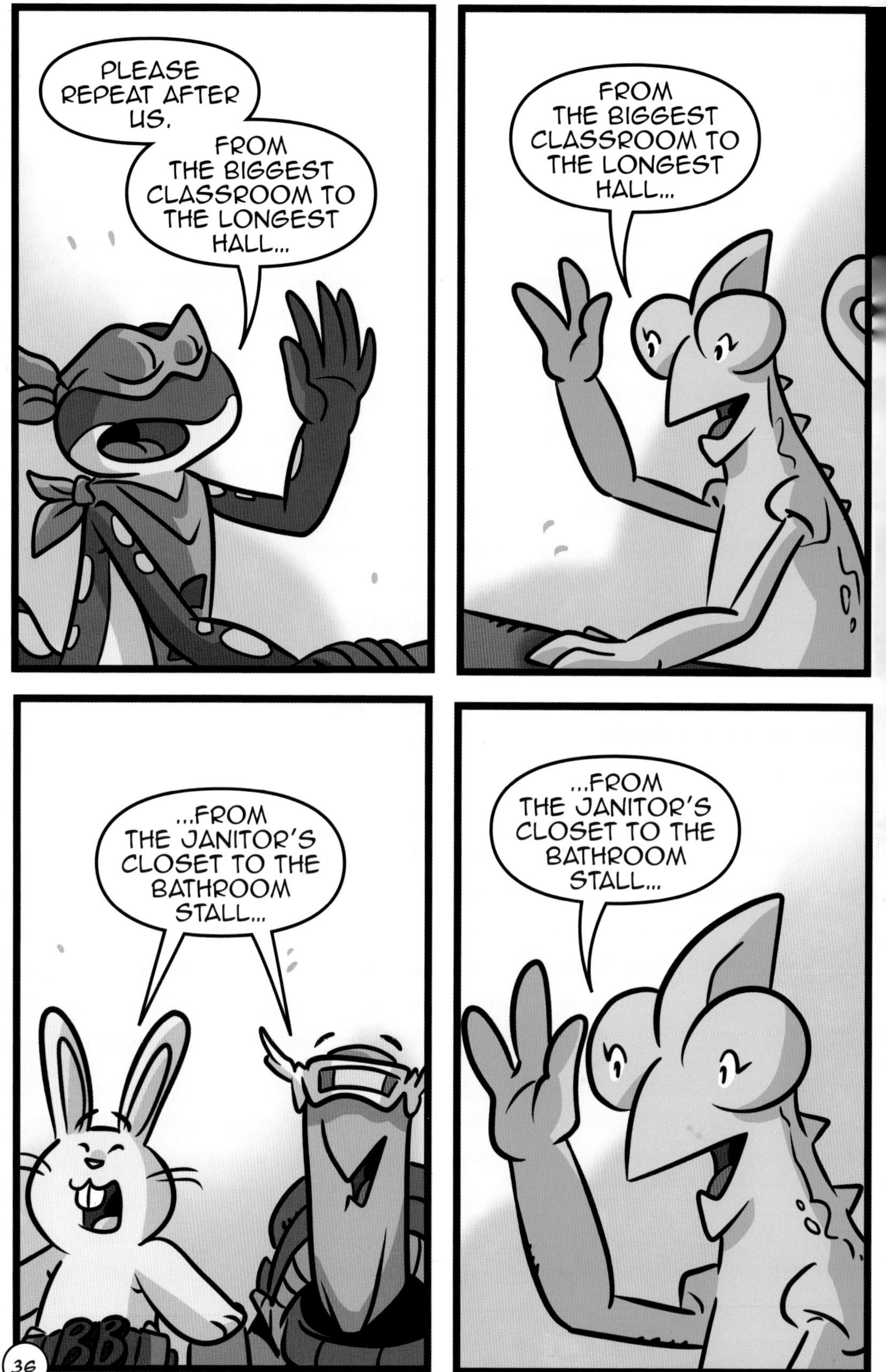
PLEASE REPEAT AFTER US.
FROM THE BIGGEST CLASSROOM TO THE LONGEST HALL...
FROM THE BIGGEST CLASSROOM TO THE LONGEST HALL...
...FROM THE JANITOR'S CLOSET TO THE BATHROOM STALL...
...FROM THE JANITOR'S CLOSET TO THE BATHROOM STALL...

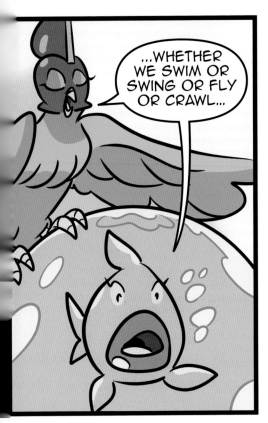

...WHETHER WE SWIM OR SWING OR FLY OR CRAWL...

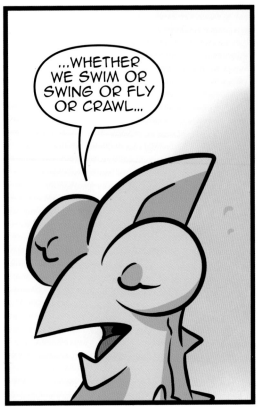

...WHETHER WE SWIM OR SWING OR FLY OR CRAWL...

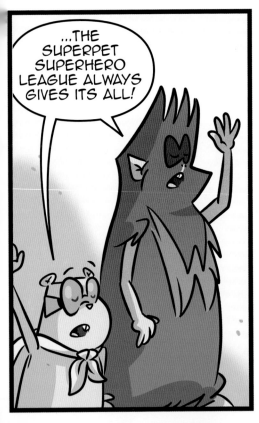

...THE SUPERPET SUPERHERO LEAGUE ALWAYS GIVES ITS ALL!

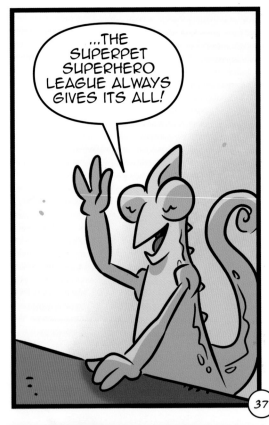

...THE SUPERPET SUPERHERO LEAGUE ALWAYS GIVES ITS ALL!

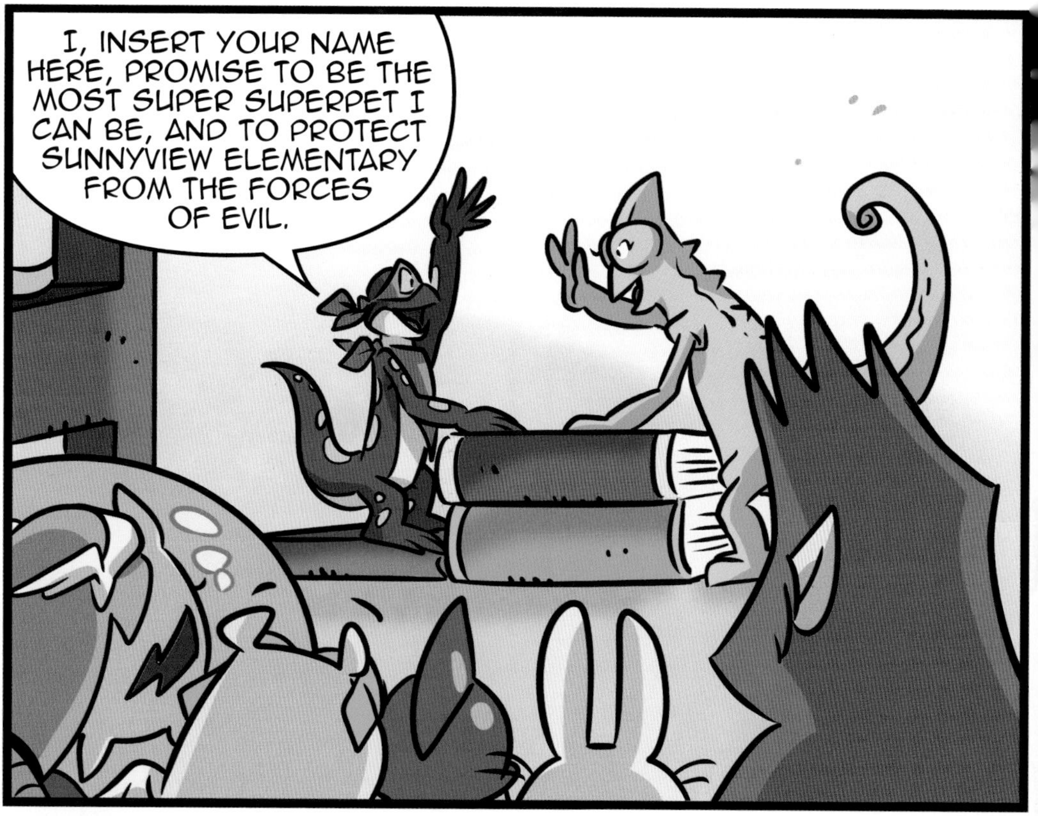
I, INSERT YOUR NAME HERE, PROMISE TO BE THE MOST SUPER SUPERPET I CAN BE, AND TO PROTECT SUNNYVIEW ELEMENTARY FROM THE FORCES OF EVIL.

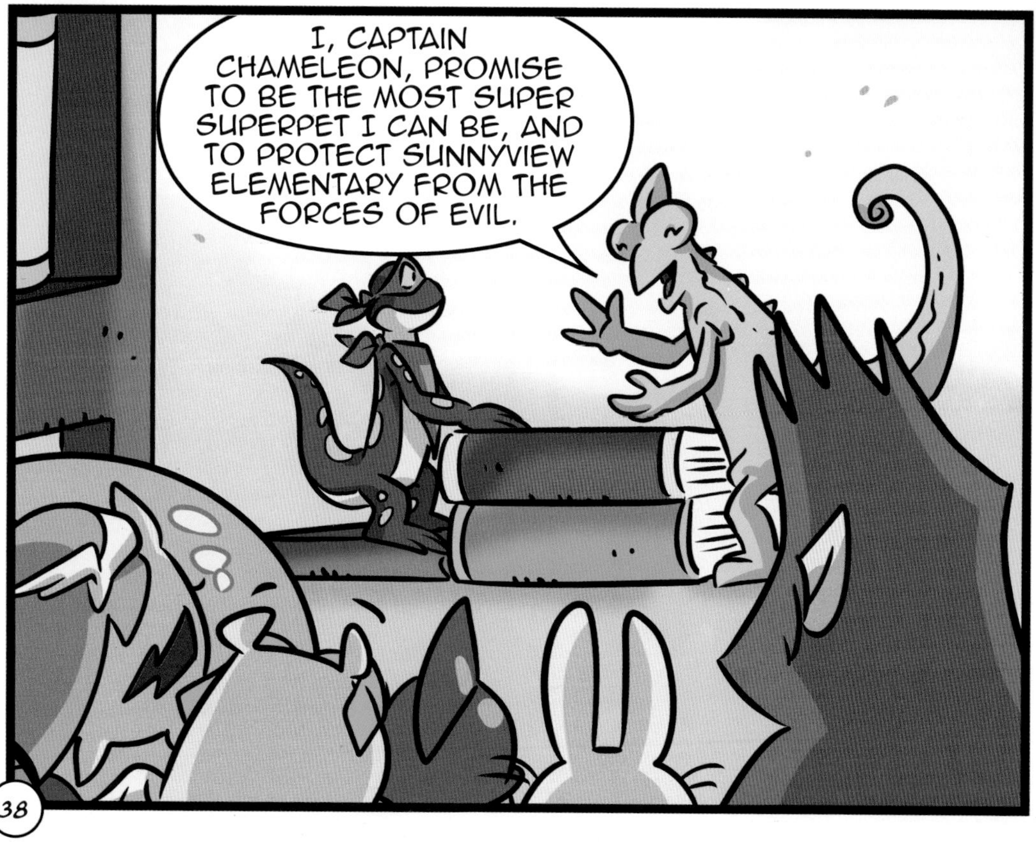
I, CAPTAIN CHAMELEON, PROMISE TO BE THE MOST SUPER SUPERPET I CAN BE, AND TO PROTECT SUNNYVIEW ELEMENTARY FROM THE FORCES OF EVIL.

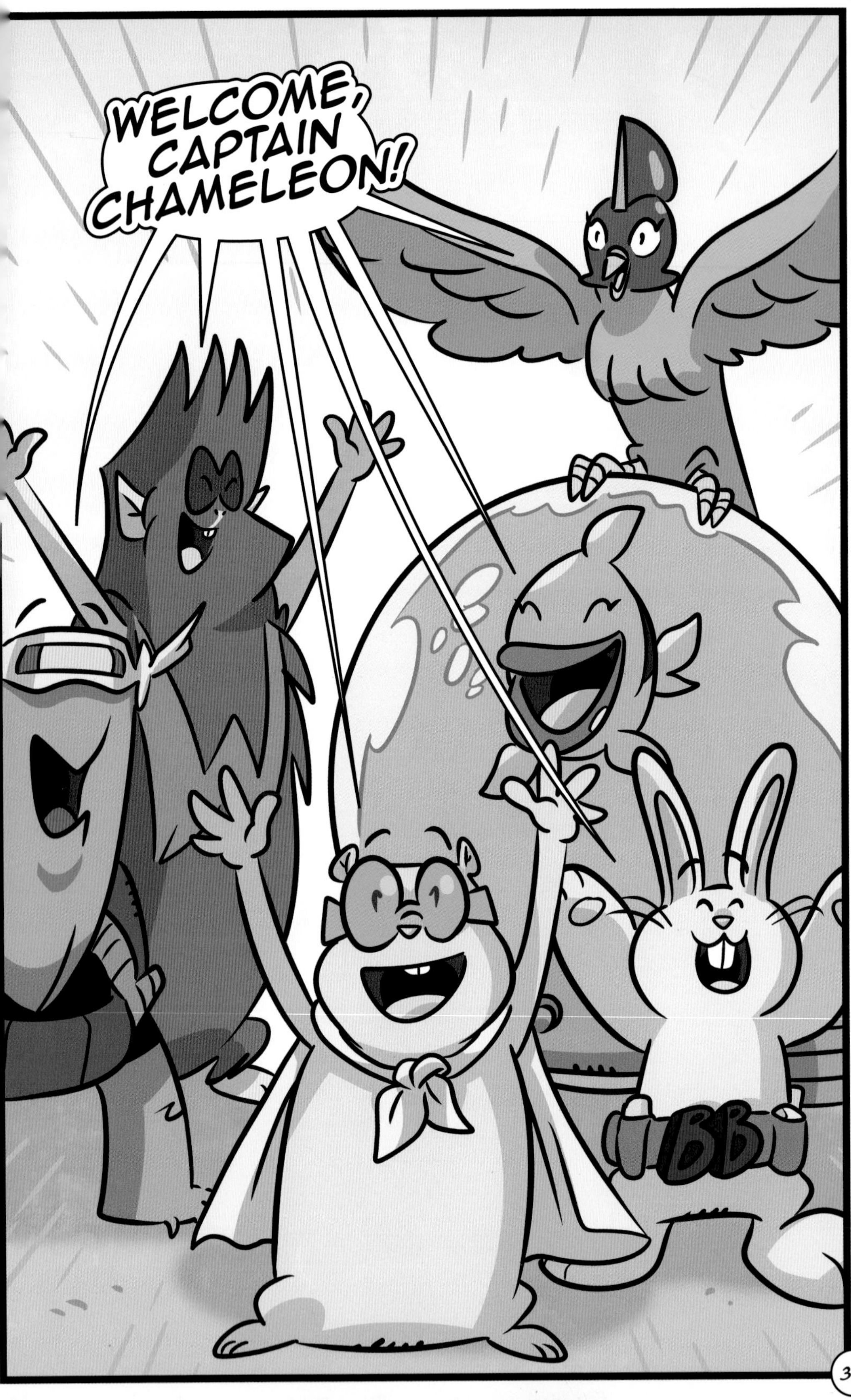
WELCOME, CAPTAIN CHAMELEON!
BB

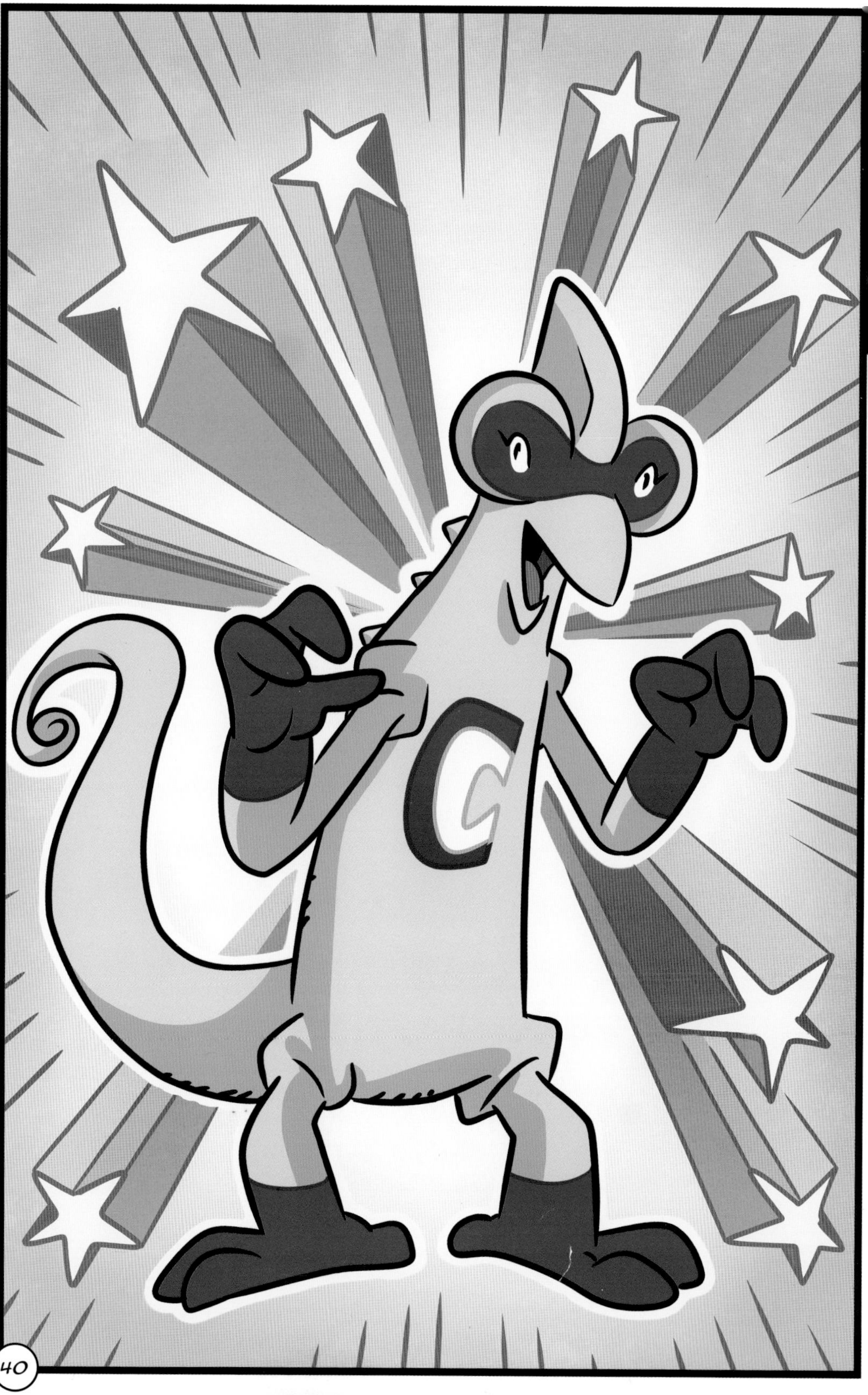

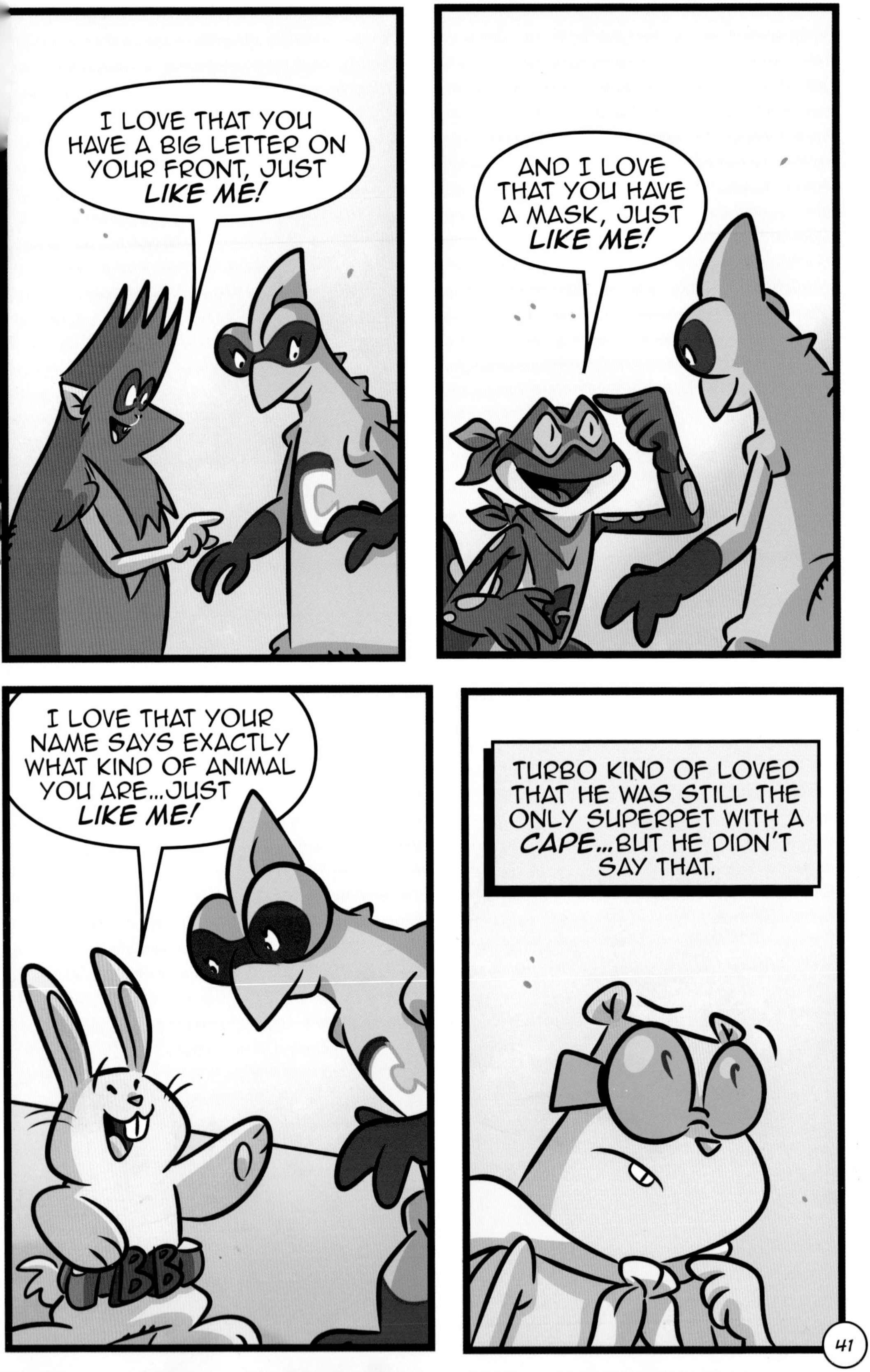
I LOVE THAT YOU HAVE A BIG LETTER ON YOUR FRONT, JUST *LIKE ME!*
AND I LOVE THAT YOU HAVE A MASK, JUST *LIKE ME!*
I LOVE THAT YOUR NAME SAYS EXACTLY WHAT KIND OF ANIMAL YOU ARE...JUST *LIKE ME!*
TURBO KIND OF LOVED THAT HE WAS STILL THE ONLY SUPERPET WITH A *CAPE...*BUT HE DIDN'T SAY THAT.

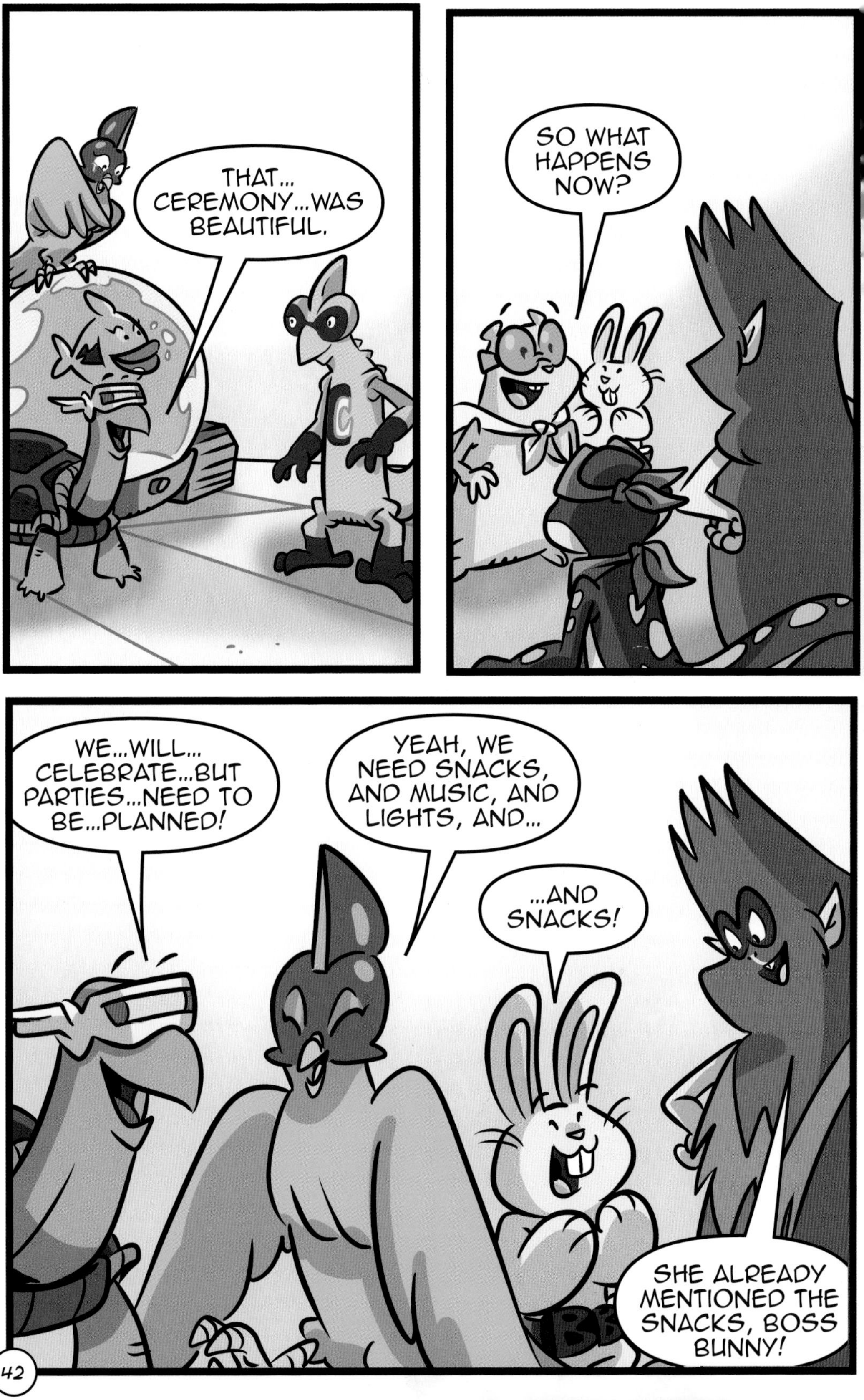
SO WHAT HAPPENS NOW?
THAT... CEREMONY...WAS BEAUTIFUL.
YEAH, WE NEED SNACKS, AND MUSIC, AND LIGHTS, AND...
WE...WILL... CELEBRATE...BUT PARTIES...NEED TO BE...PLANNED!
...AND SNACKS!
SHE ALREADY MENTIONED THE SNACKS, BOSS BUNNY!

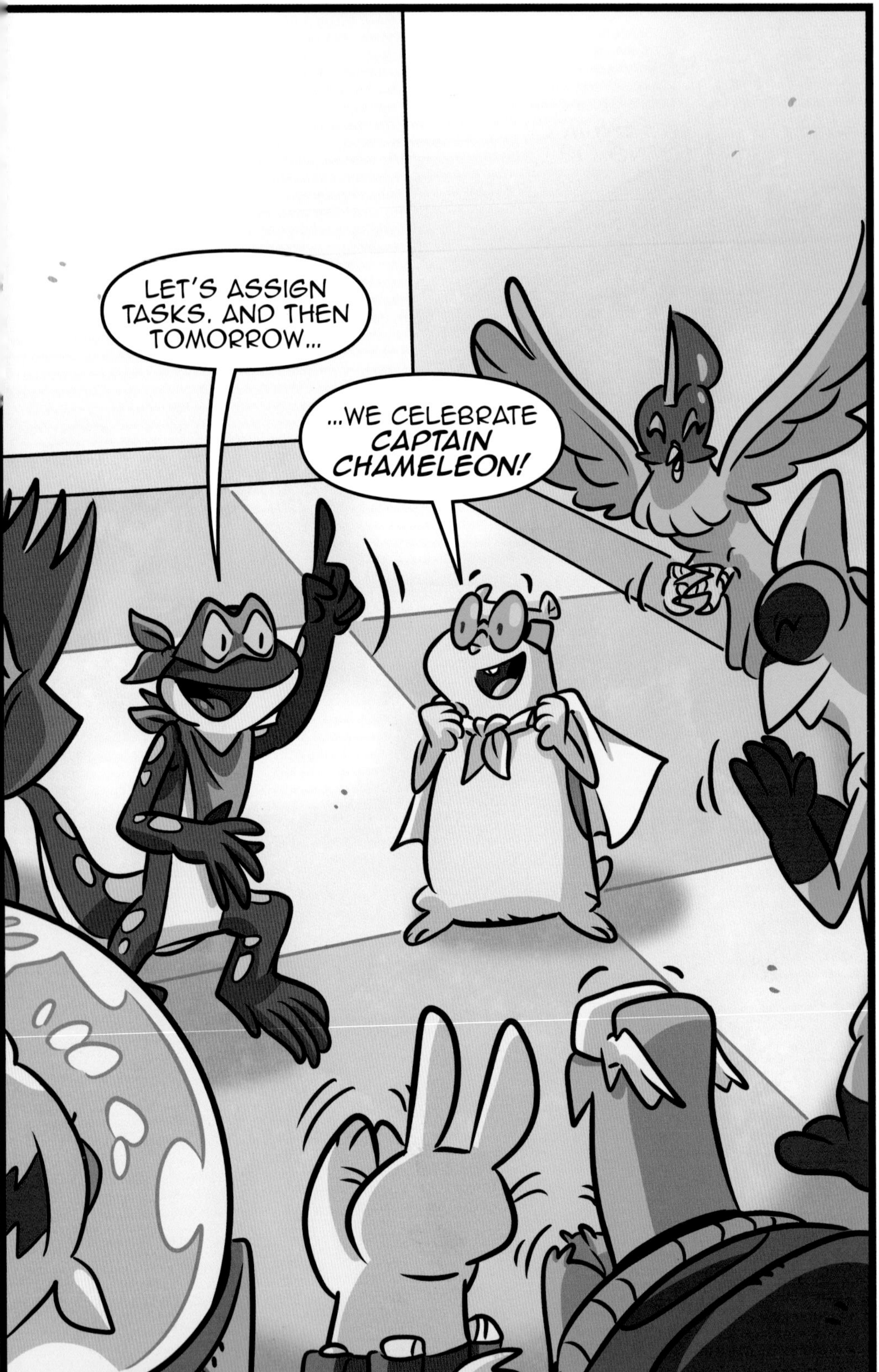
LET'S ASSIGN TASKS, AND THEN TOMORROW...
...WE CELEBRATE *CAPTAIN CHAMELEON!*

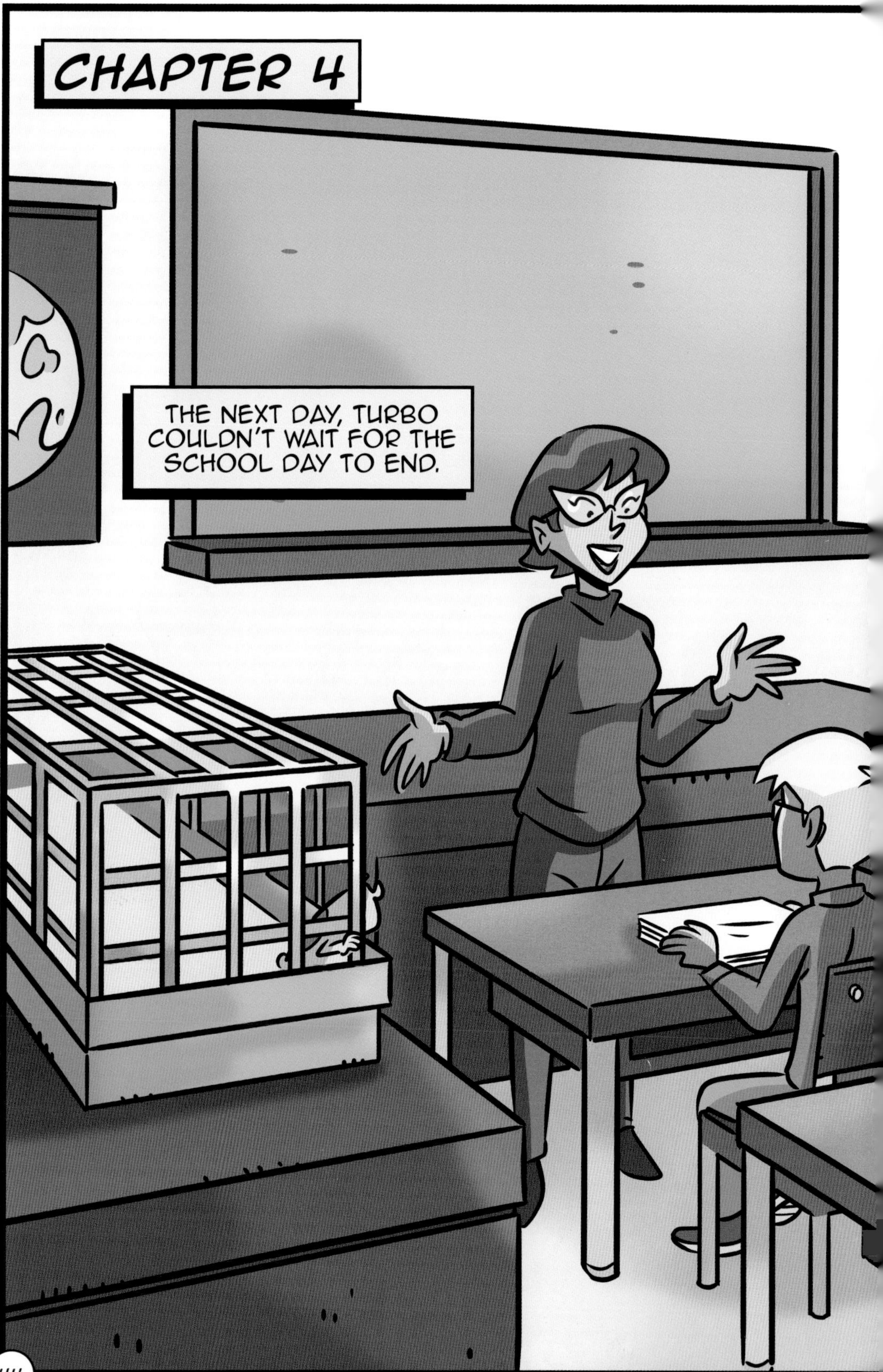
CHAPTER 4
THE NEXT DAY, TURBO COULDN'T WAIT FOR THE SCHOOL DAY TO END.

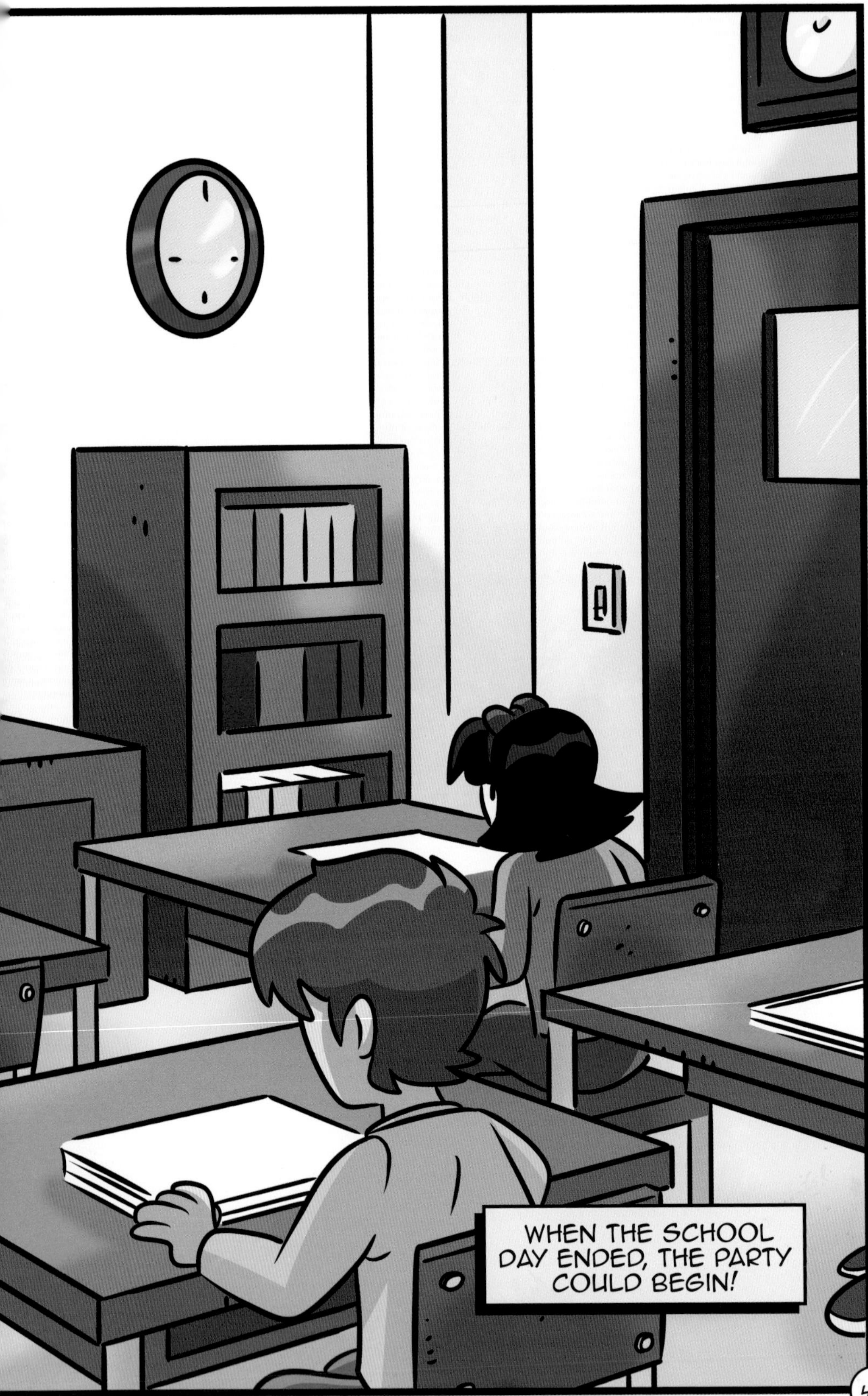
WHEN THE SCHOOL DAY ENDED, THE PARTY COULD BEGIN!

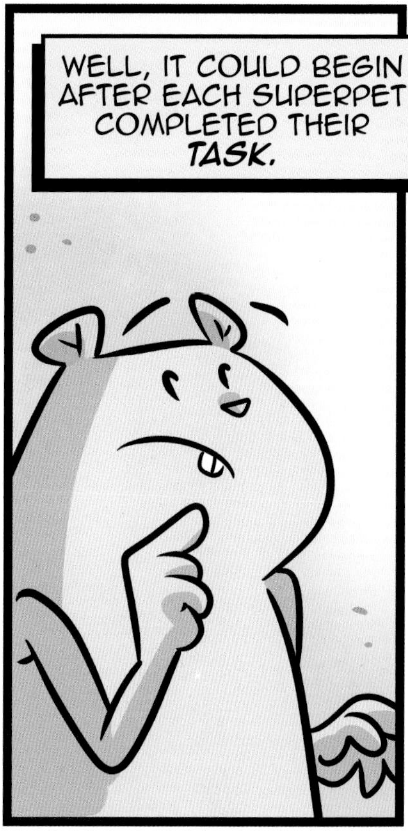
WELL, IT COULD BEGIN AFTER EACH SUPERPET COMPLETED THEIR *TASK.*

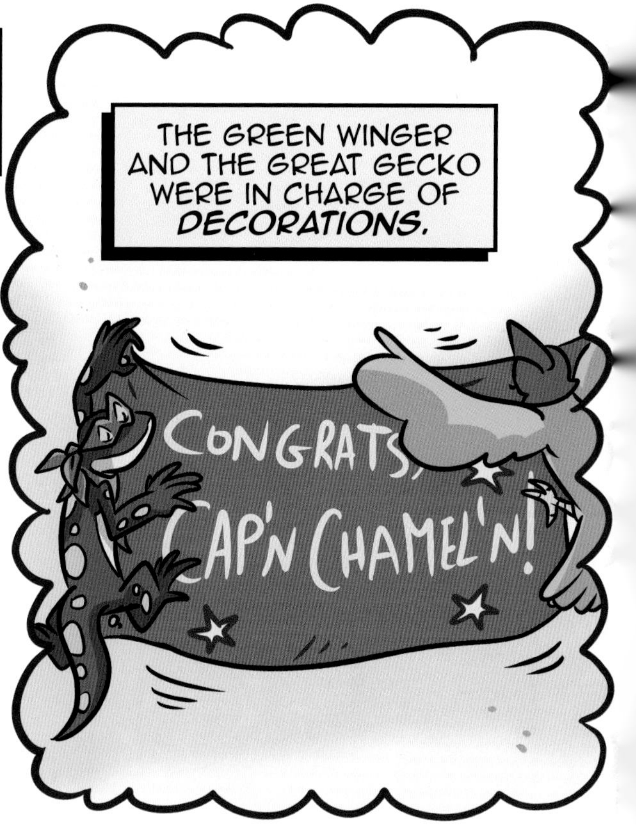
THE GREEN WINGER AND THE GREAT GECKO WERE IN CHARGE OF *DECORATIONS.*
CONGRATS, CAP'N CHAMEL'N!

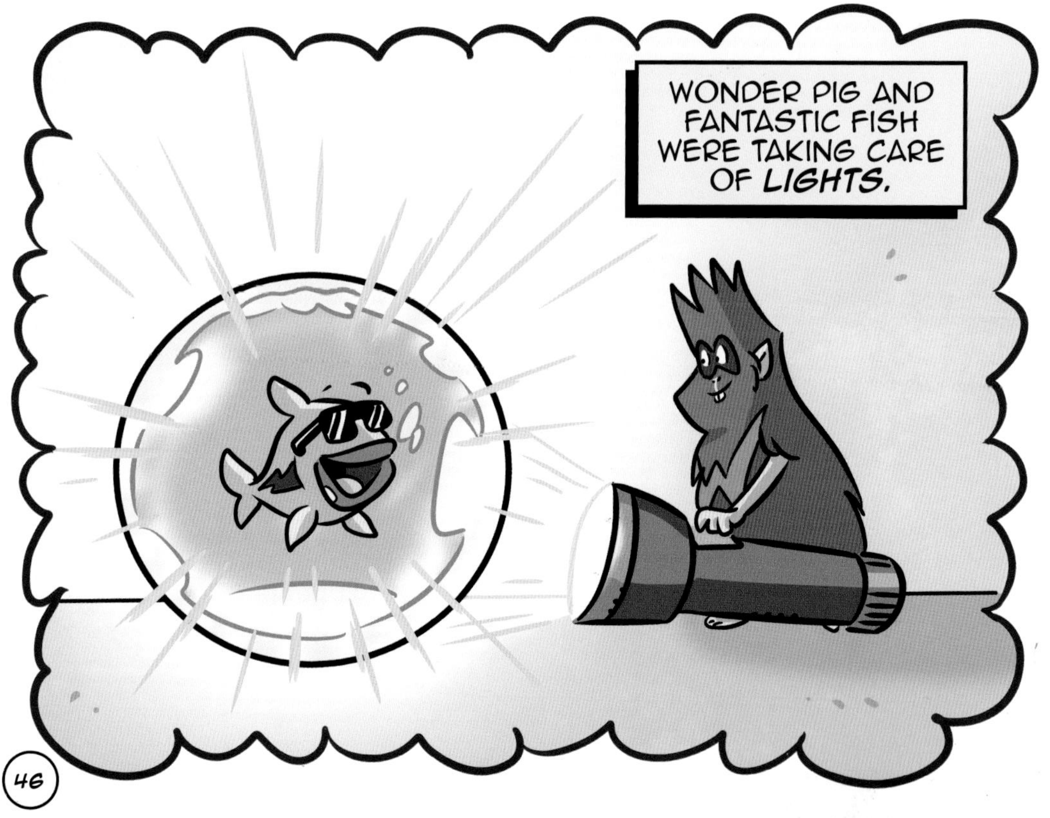
WONDER PIG AND FANTASTIC FISH WERE TAKING CARE OF *LIGHTS.*

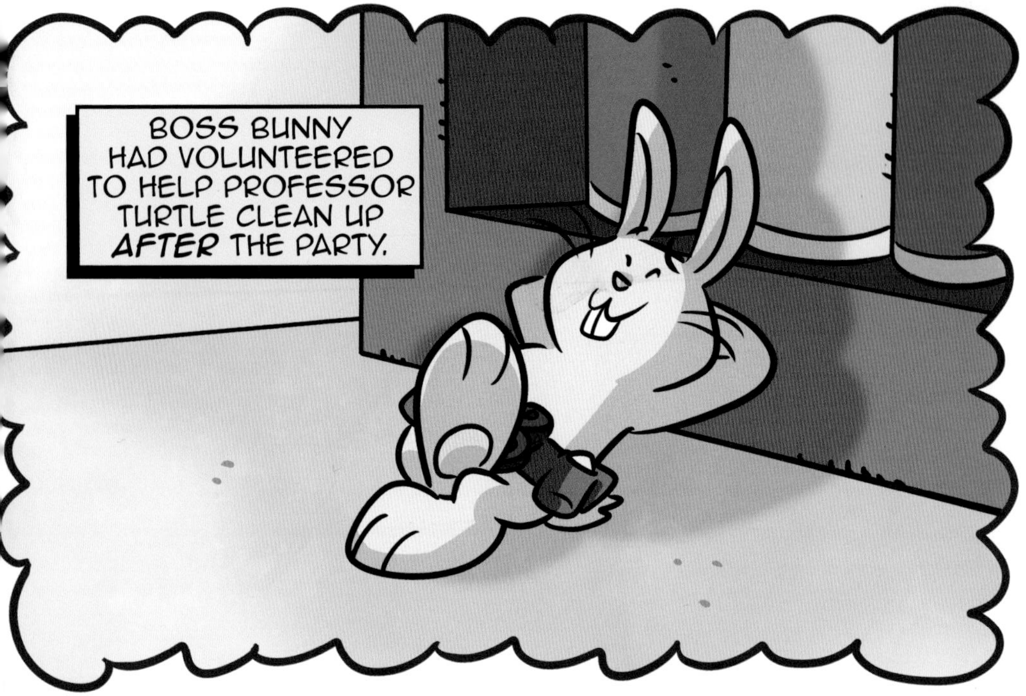
BOSS BUNNY HAD VOLUNTEERED TO HELP PROFESSOR TURTLE CLEAN UP ***AFTER*** THE PARTY.

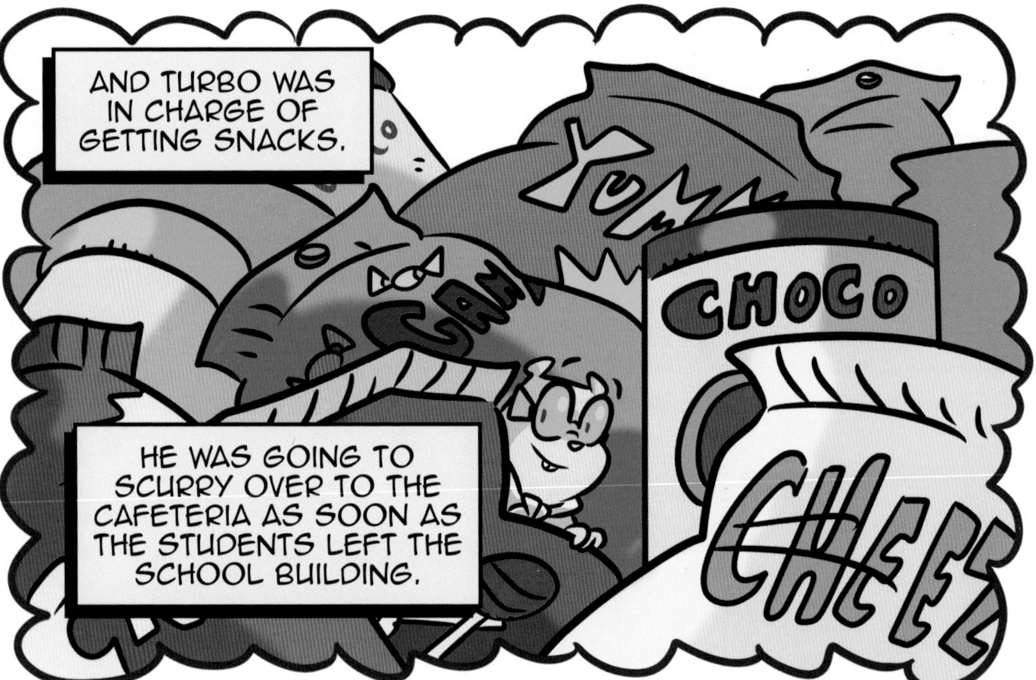
AND TURBO WAS IN CHARGE OF GETTING SNACKS.
CHOCO
HE WAS GOING TO SCURRY OVER TO THE CAFETERIA AS SOON AS THE STUDENTS LEFT THE SCHOOL BUILDING.

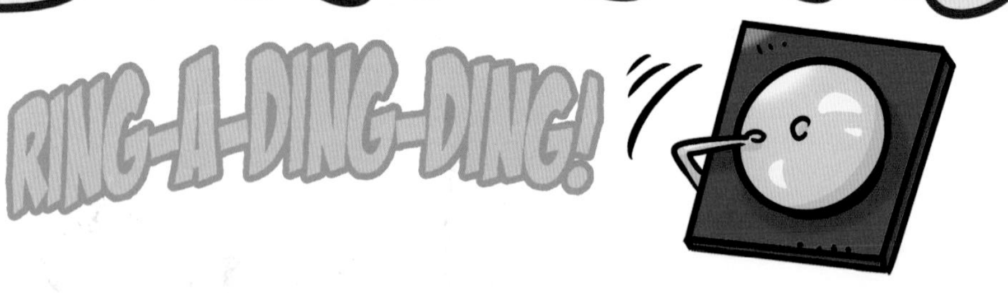
RING-A-DING-DING!

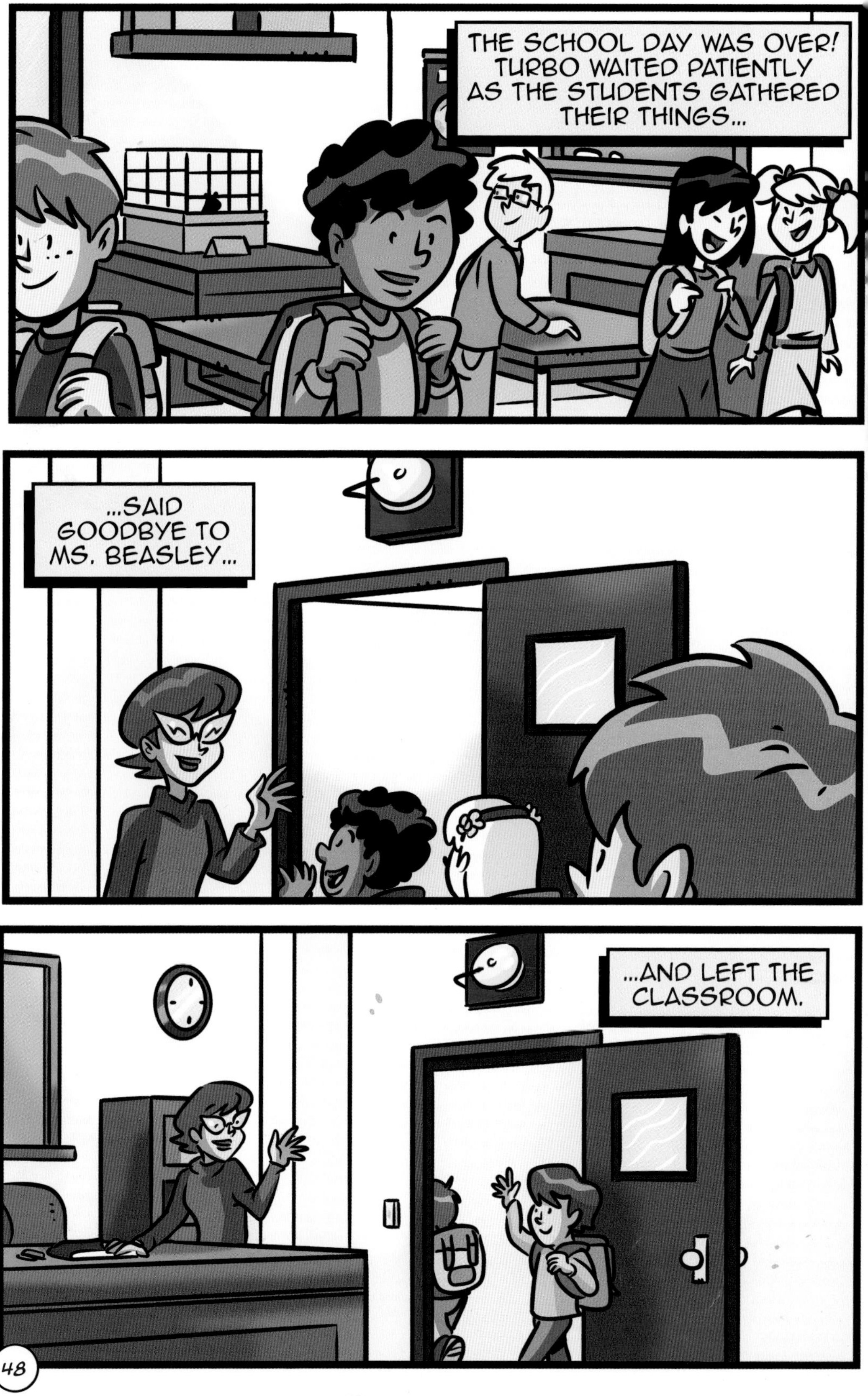
THE SCHOOL DAY WAS OVER! TURBO WAITED PATIENTLY AS THE STUDENTS GATHERED THEIR THINGS...
...SAID GOODBYE TO MS. BEASLEY...
...AND LEFT THE CLASSROOM.

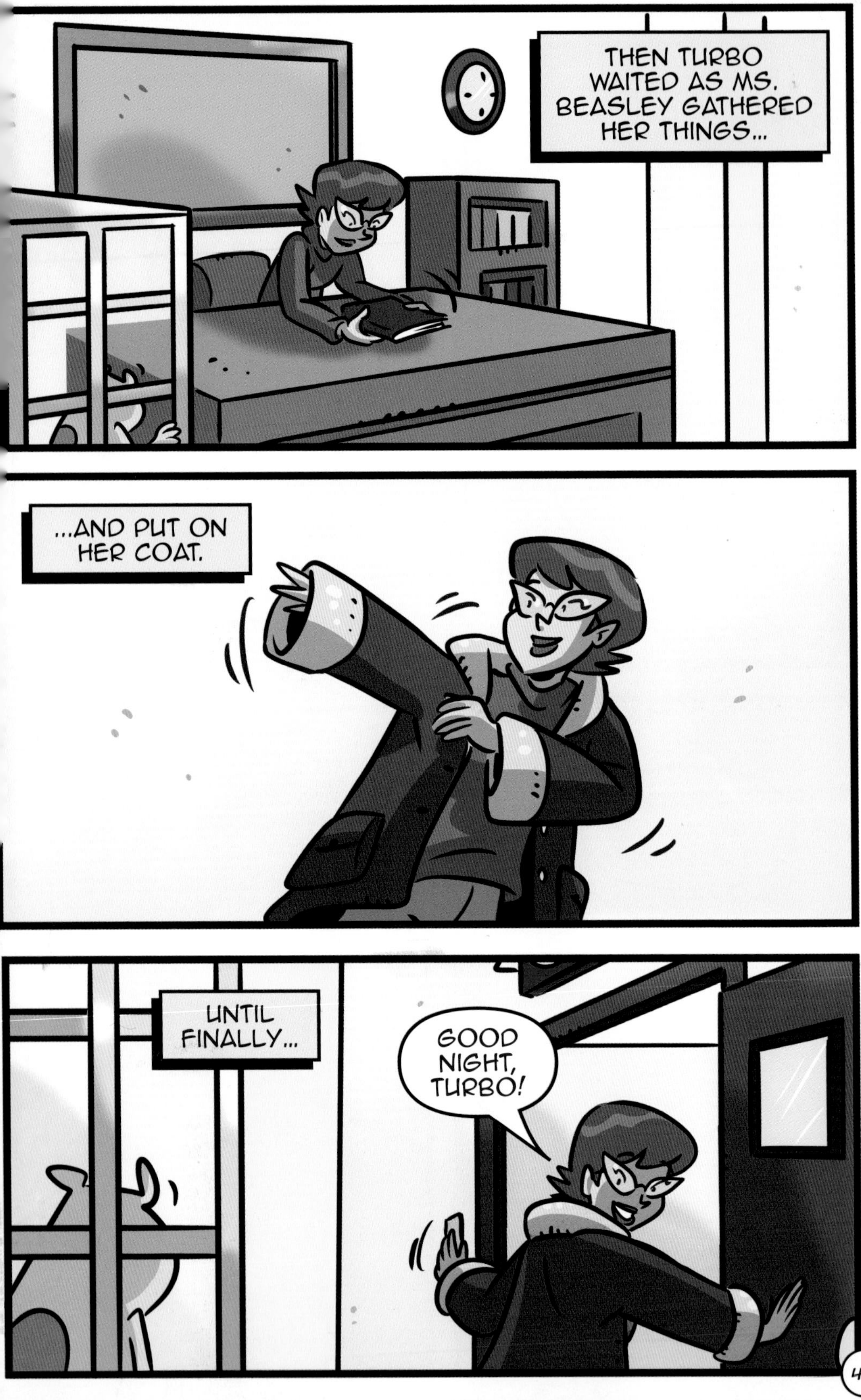
THEN TURBO WAITED AS MS. BEASLEY GATHERED HER THINGS...
...AND PUT ON HER COAT.
GOOD NIGHT, TURBO!
UNTIL FINALLY...

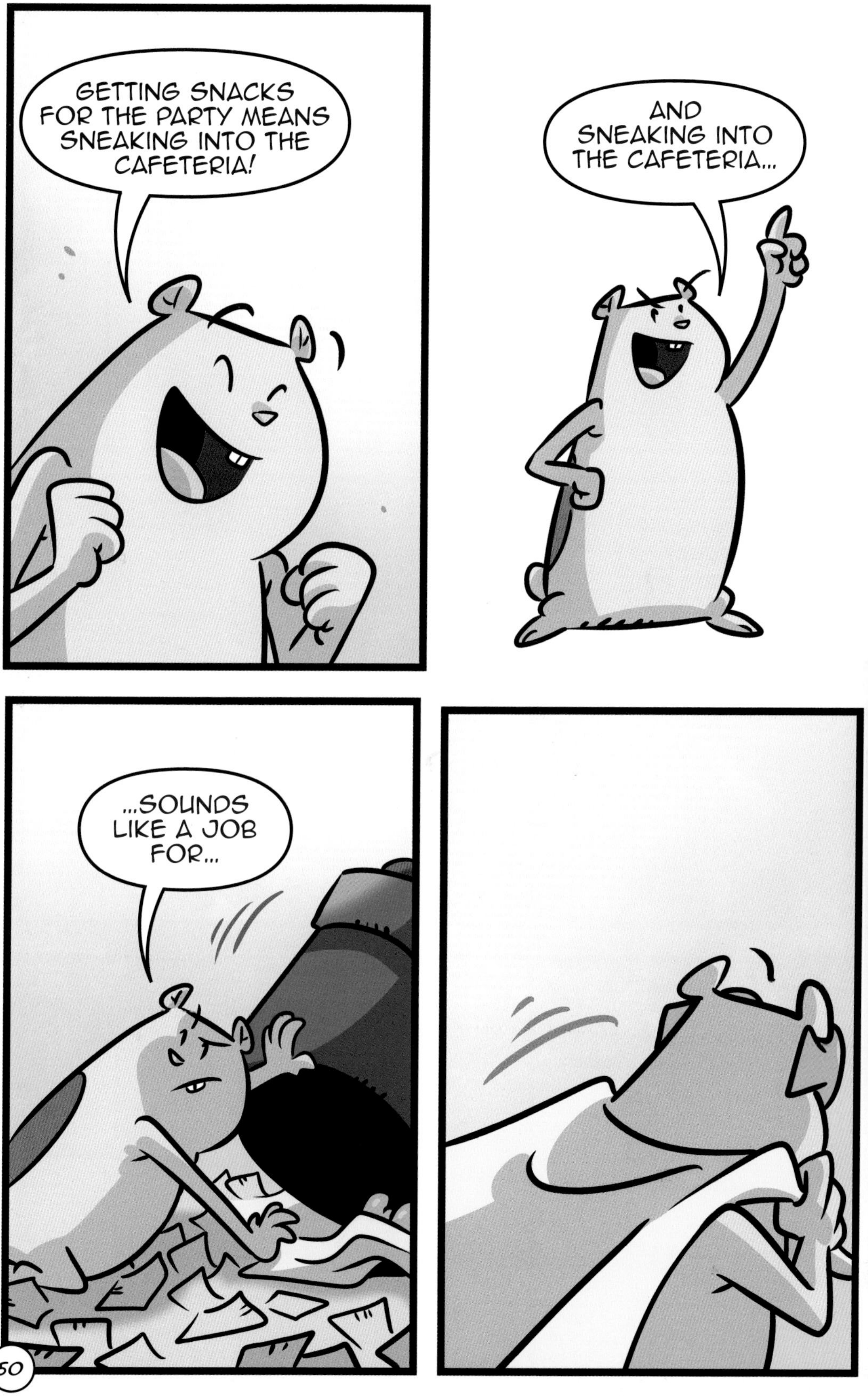
GETTING SNACKS FOR THE PARTY MEANS SNEAKING INTO THE CAFETERIA!
AND SNEAKING INTO THE CAFETERIA...
...SOUNDS LIKE A JOB FOR...

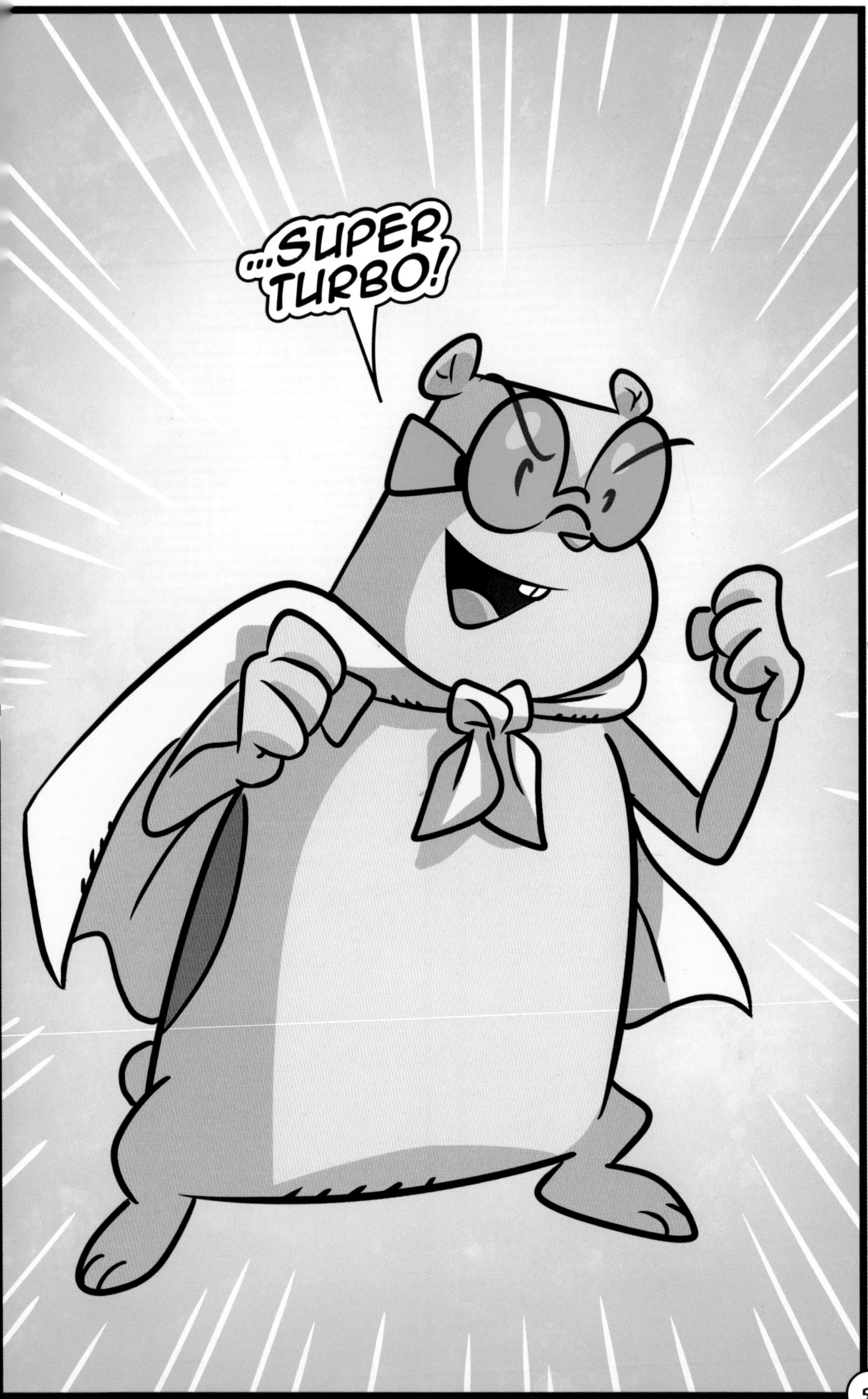
...SUPER TURBO!

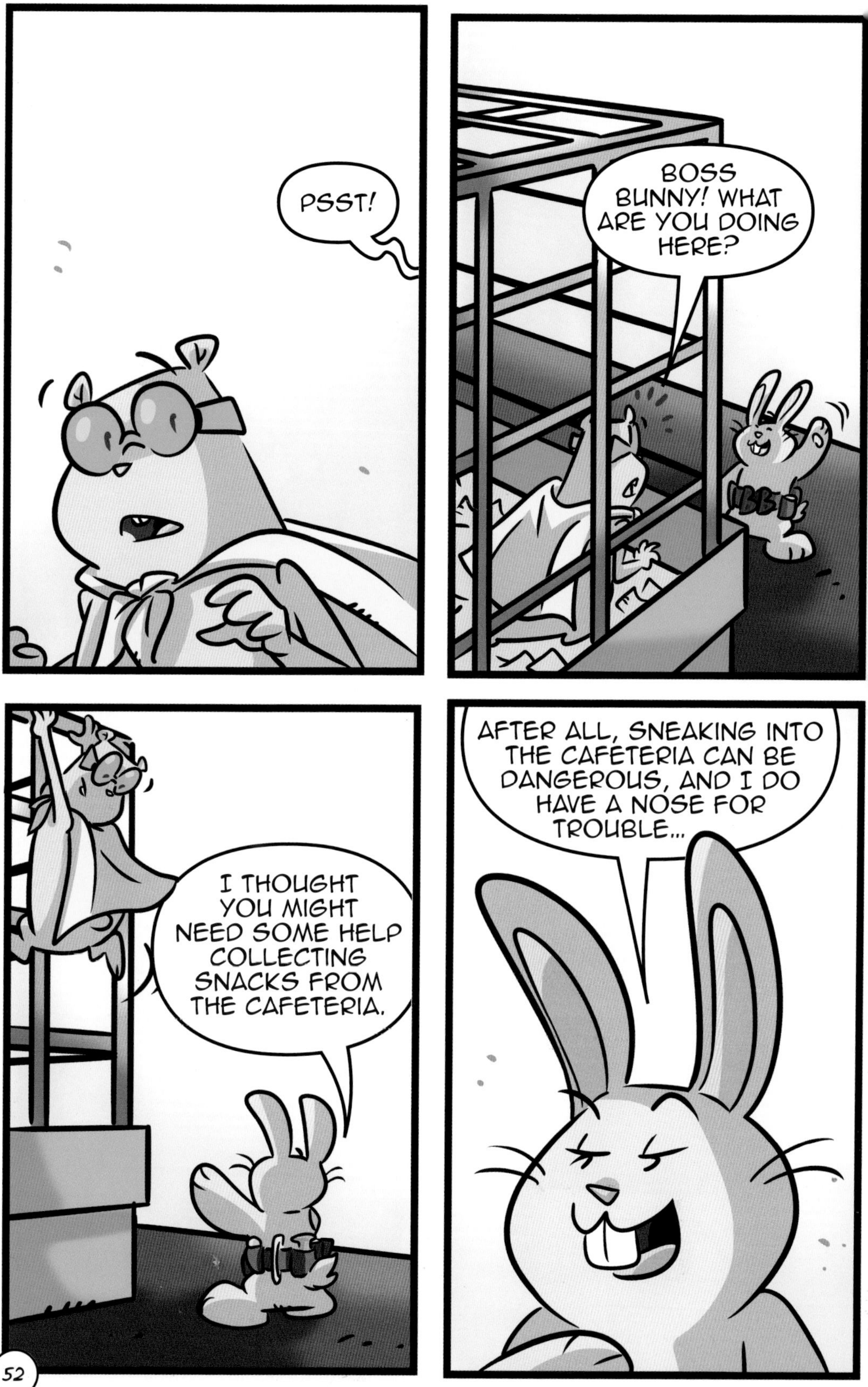
PSST!
BOSS BUNNY! WHAT ARE YOU DOING HERE?
I THOUGHT YOU MIGHT NEED SOME HELP COLLECTING SNACKS FROM THE CAFETERIA.
AFTER ALL, SNEAKING INTO THE CAFETERIA CAN BE DANGEROUS, AND I DO HAVE A NOSE FOR TROUBLE...

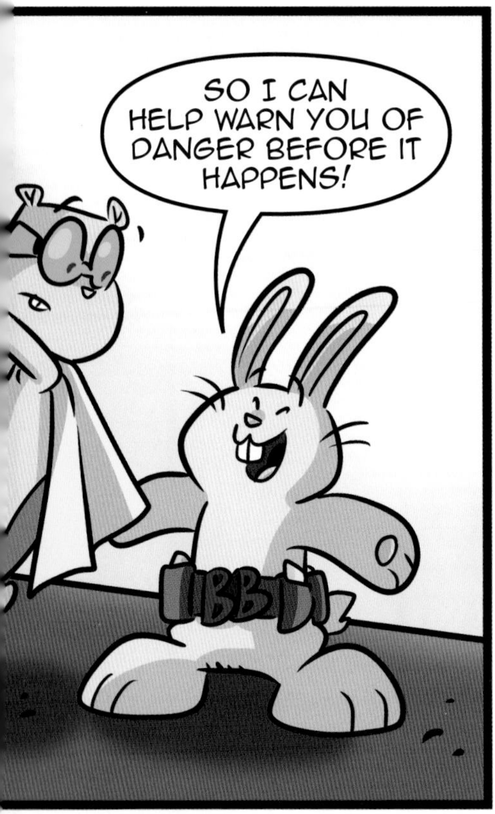
SO I CAN HELP WARN YOU OF DANGER BEFORE IT HAPPENS!

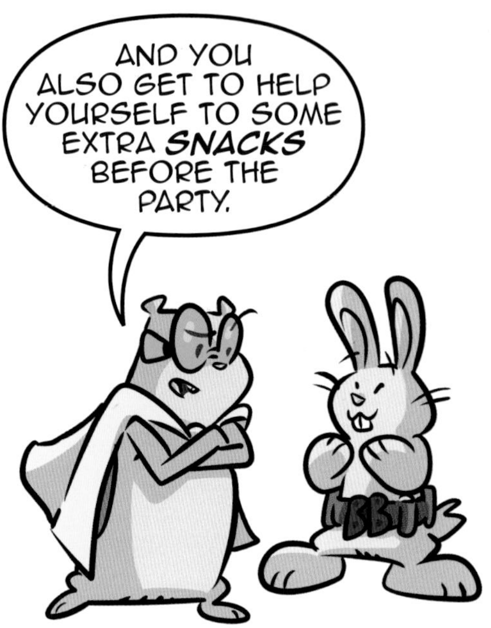
AND YOU ALSO GET TO HELP YOURSELF TO SOME EXTRA ***SNACKS*** BEFORE THE PARTY.

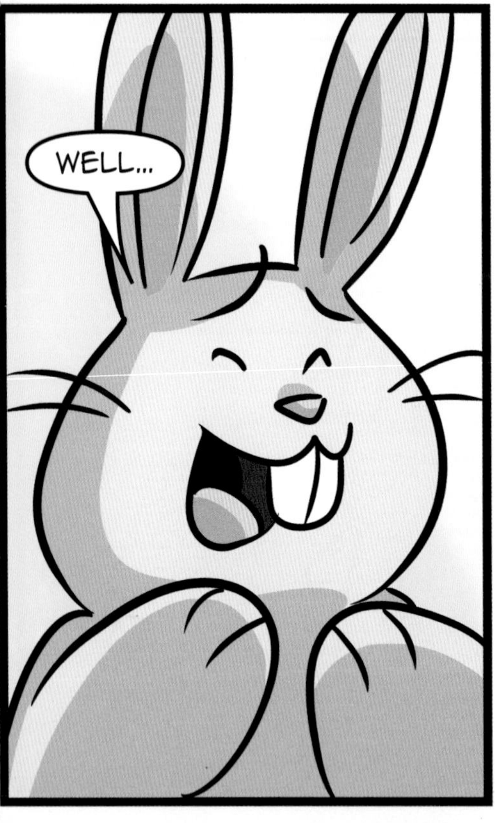
WELL...

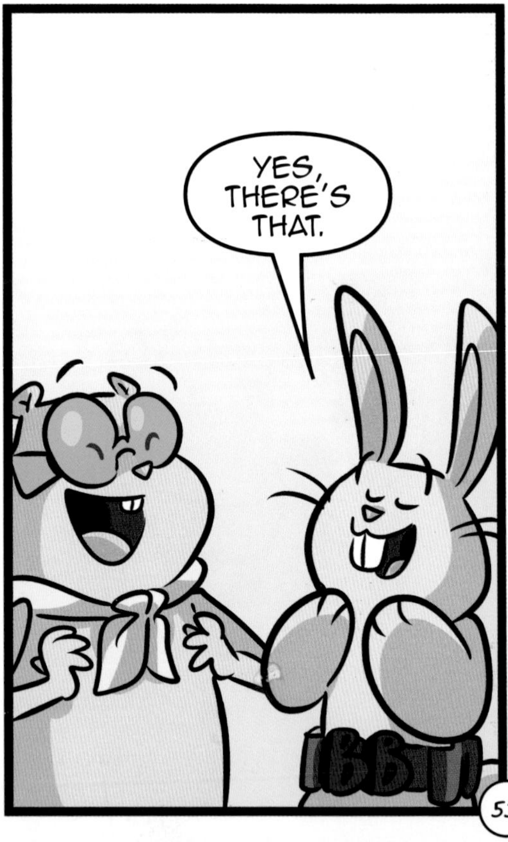
YES, THERE'S THAT.

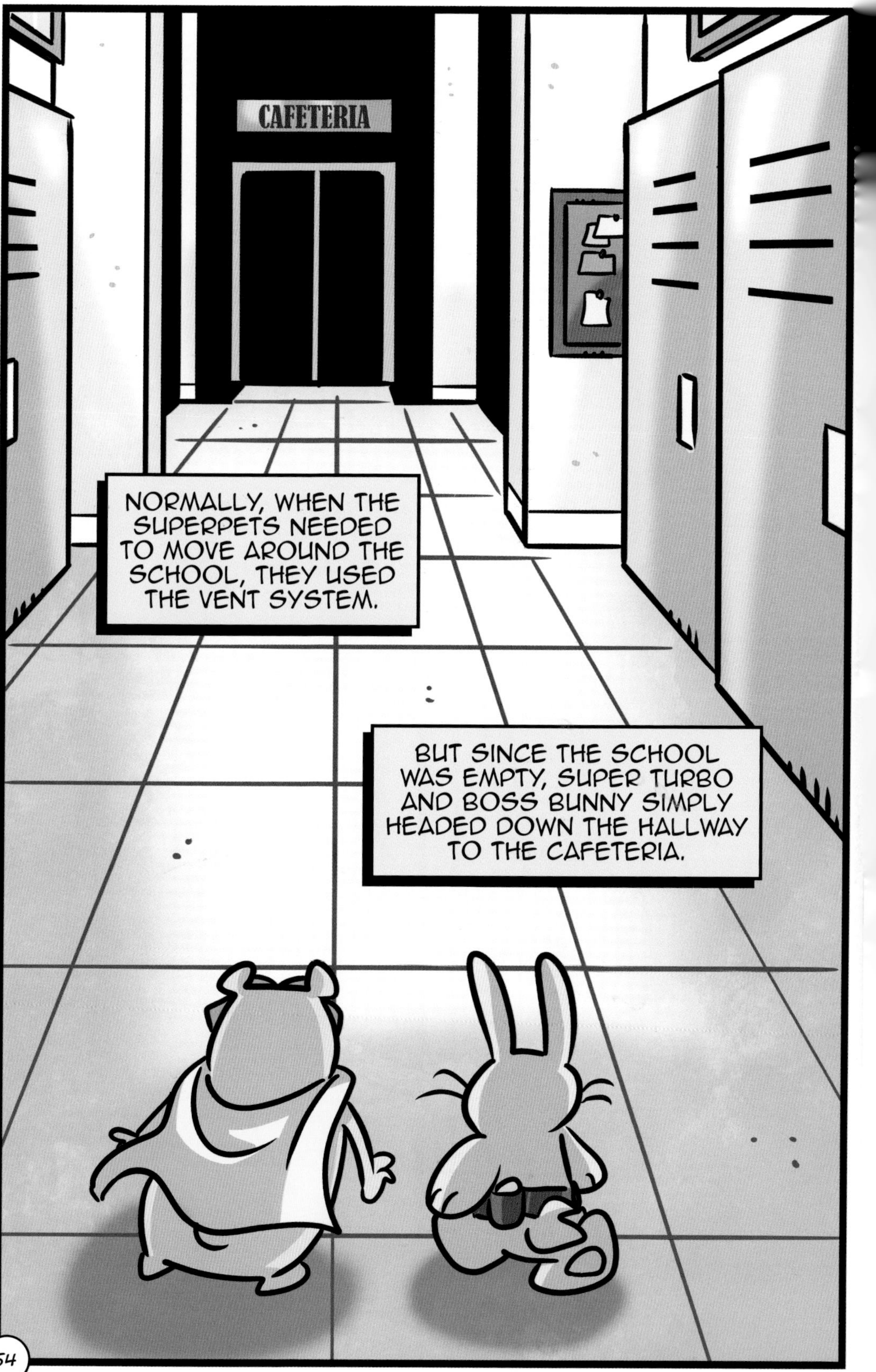
CAFETERIA
NORMALLY, WHEN THE SUPERPETS NEEDED TO MOVE AROUND THE SCHOOL, THEY USED THE VENT SYSTEM.
BUT SINCE THE SCHOOL WAS EMPTY, SUPER TURBO AND BOSS BUNNY SIMPLY HEADED DOWN THE HALLWAY TO THE CAFETERIA.

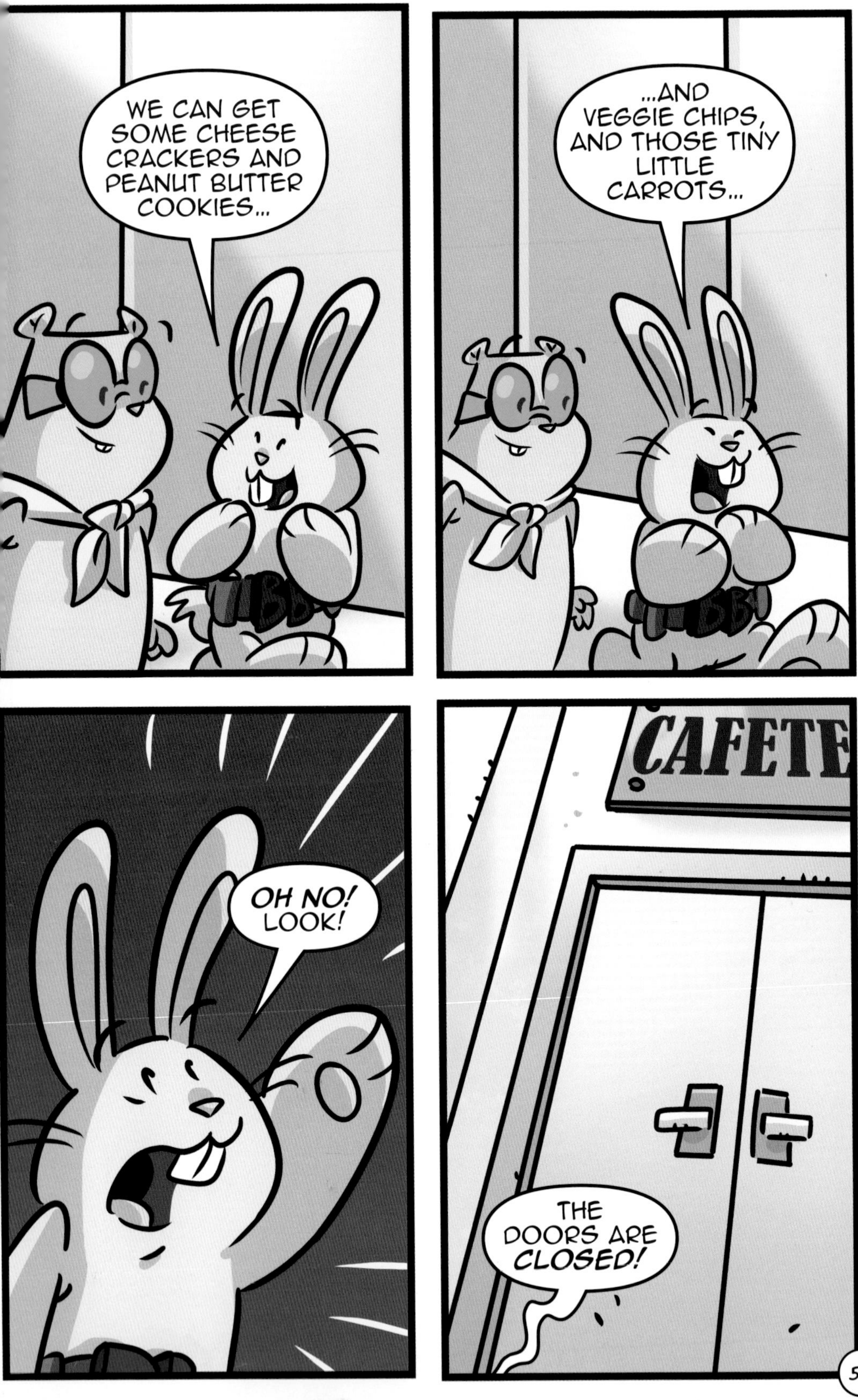
WE CAN GET SOME CHEESE CRACKERS AND PEANUT BUTTER COOKIES...
...AND VEGGIE CHIPS, AND THOSE TINY LITTLE CARROTS...
OH NO! LOOK!
CAFETE
THE DOORS ARE CLOSED!

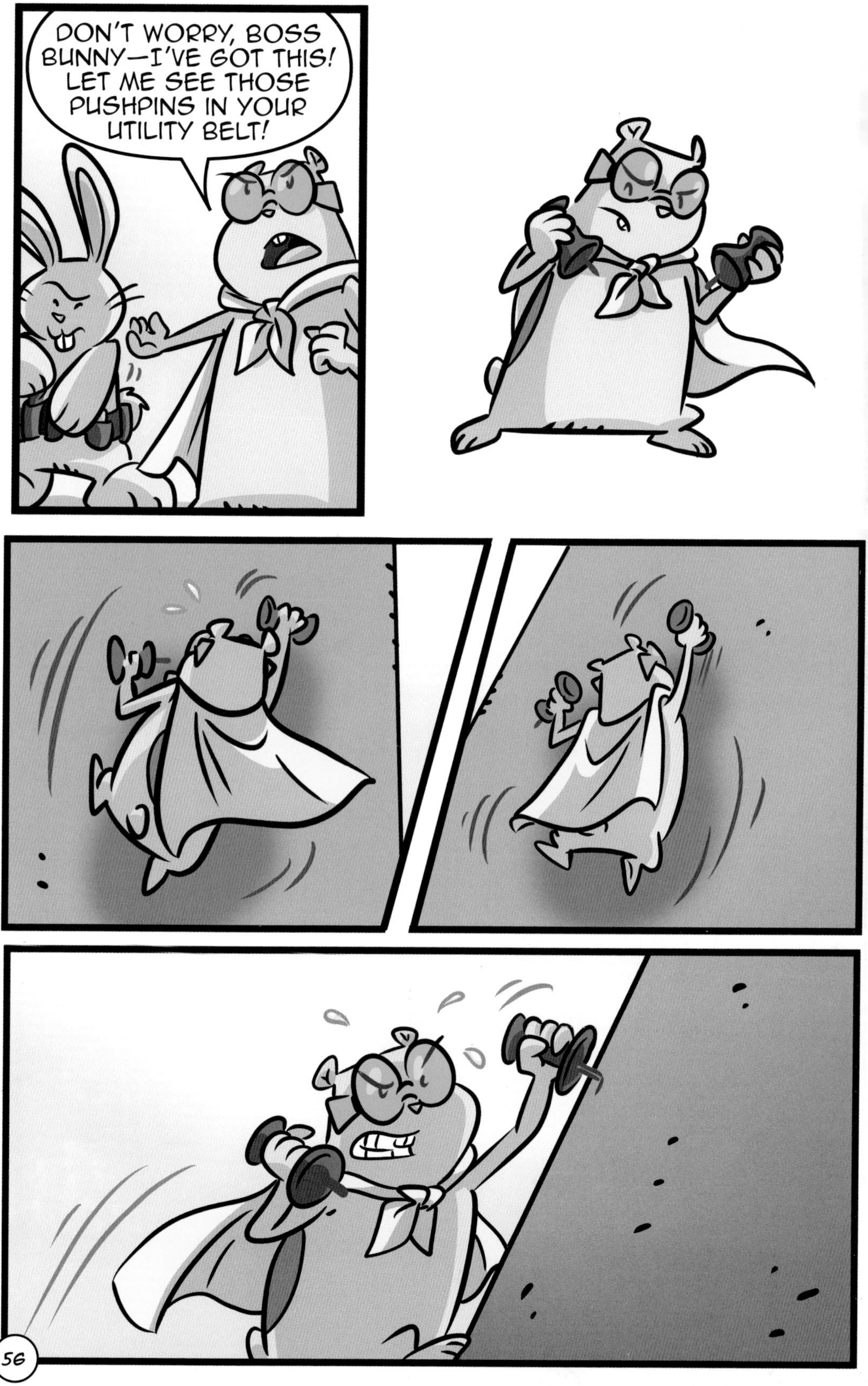
DON'T WORRY, BOSS BUNNY—I'VE GOT THIS! LET ME SEE THOSE PUSHPINS IN YOUR UTILITY BELT!

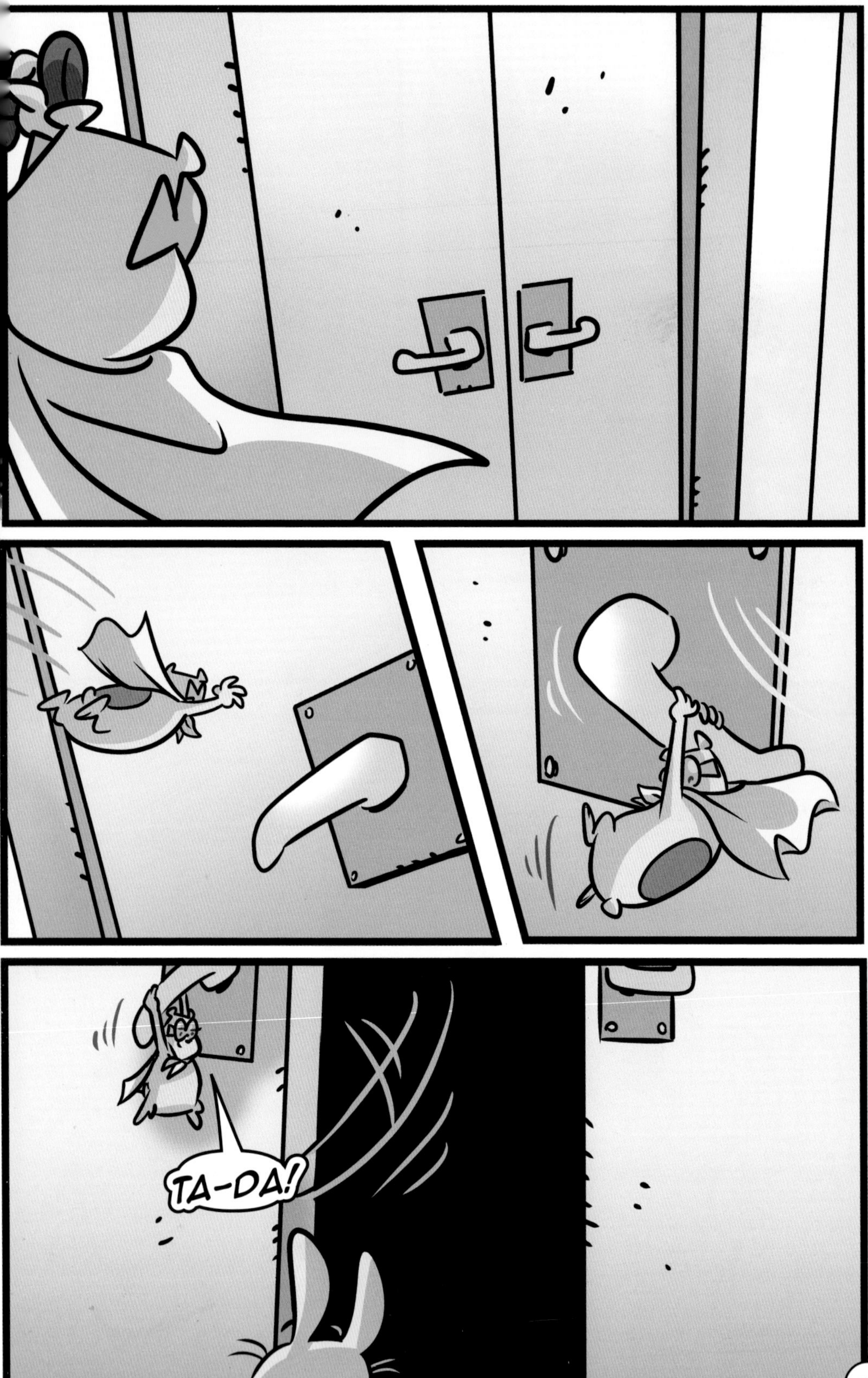
TA-DA!

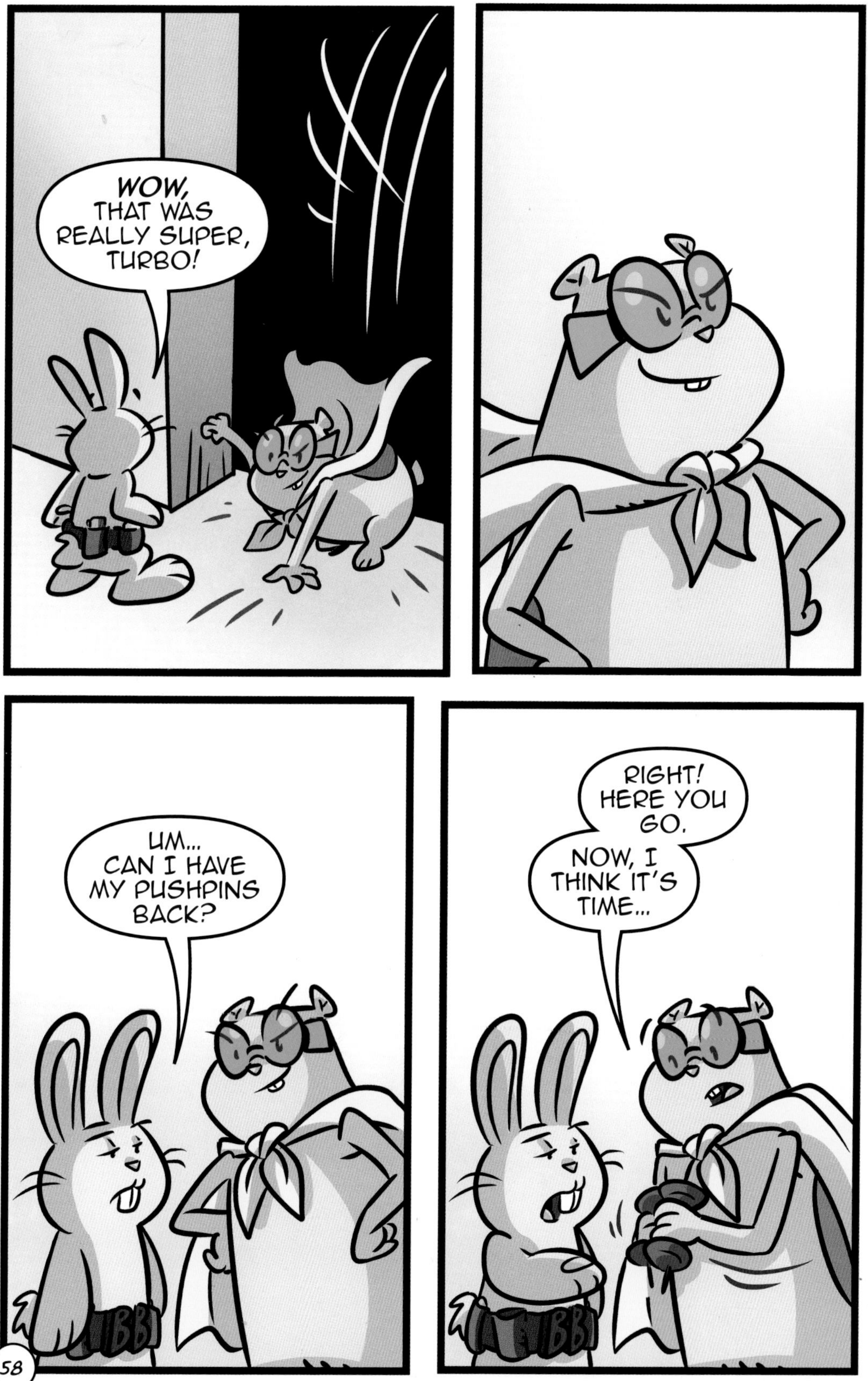
WOW, THAT WAS REALLY SUPER, TURBO!
UM... CAN I HAVE MY PUSHPINS BACK?
RIGHT! HERE YOU GO.
NOW, I THINK IT'S TIME...

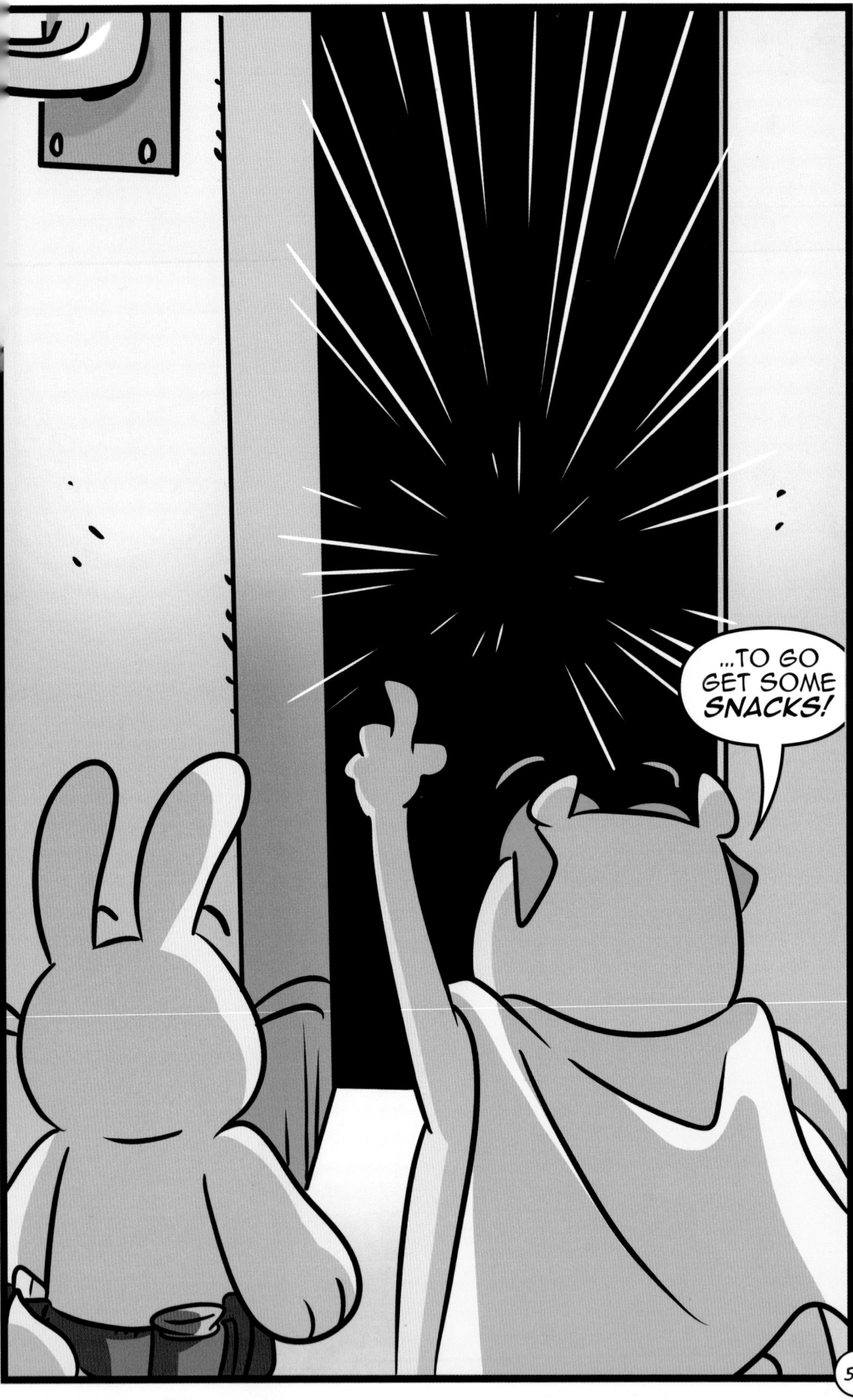
...TO GO GET SOME SNACKS!

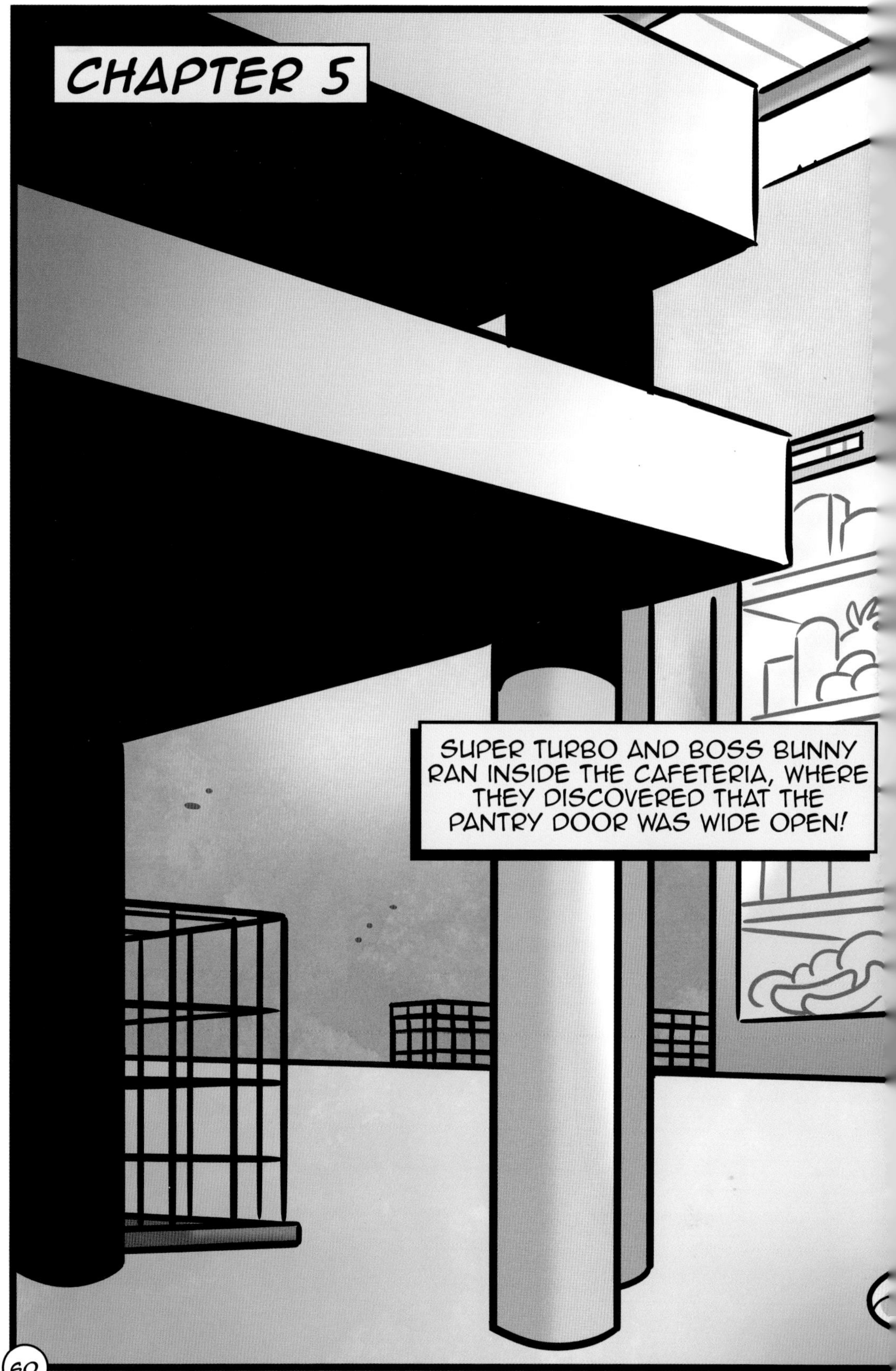
CHAPTER 5
SUPER TURBO AND BOSS BUNNY RAN INSIDE THE CAFETERIA, WHERE THEY DISCOVERED THAT THE PANTRY DOOR WAS WIDE OPEN!

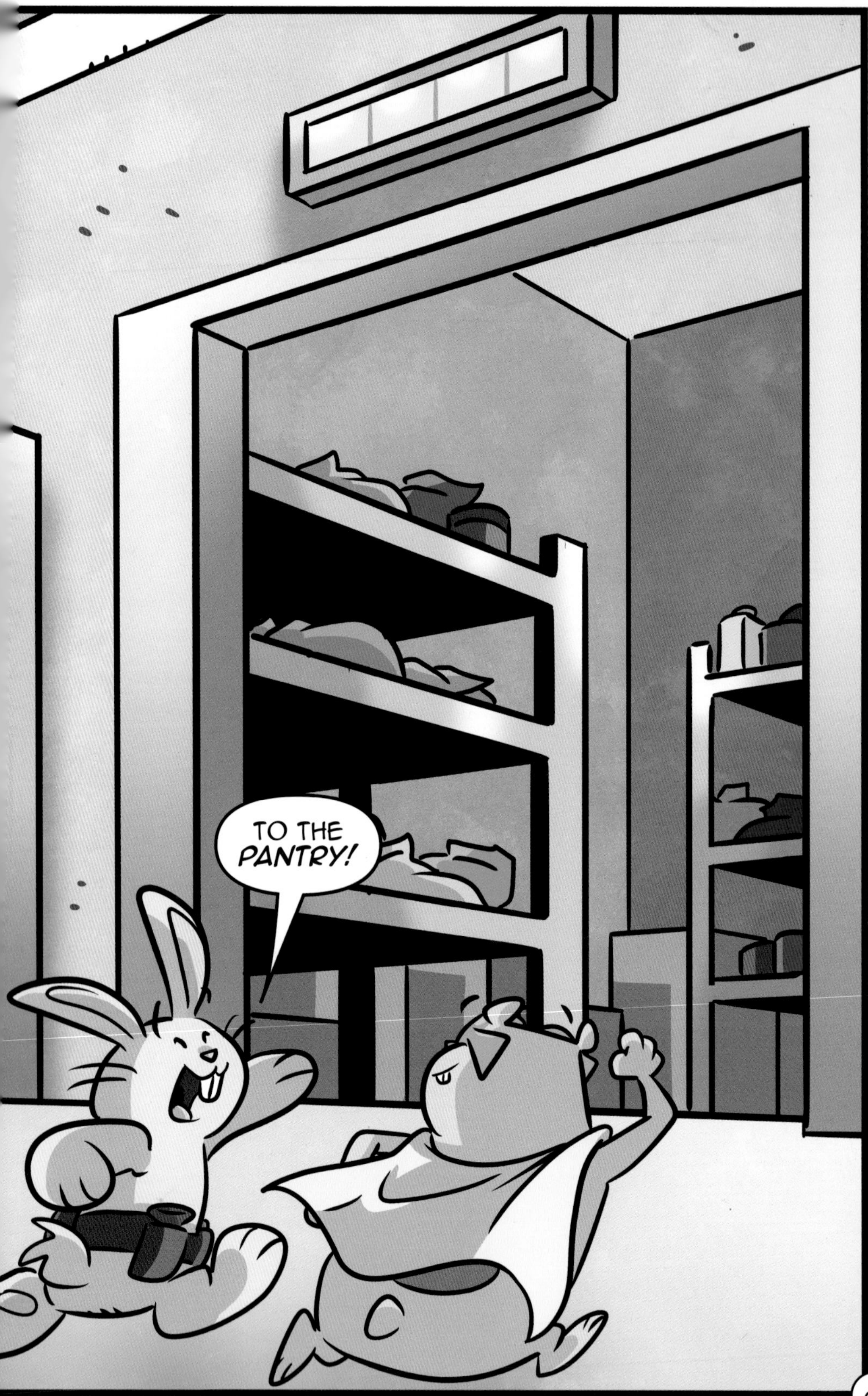
TO THE PANTRY!

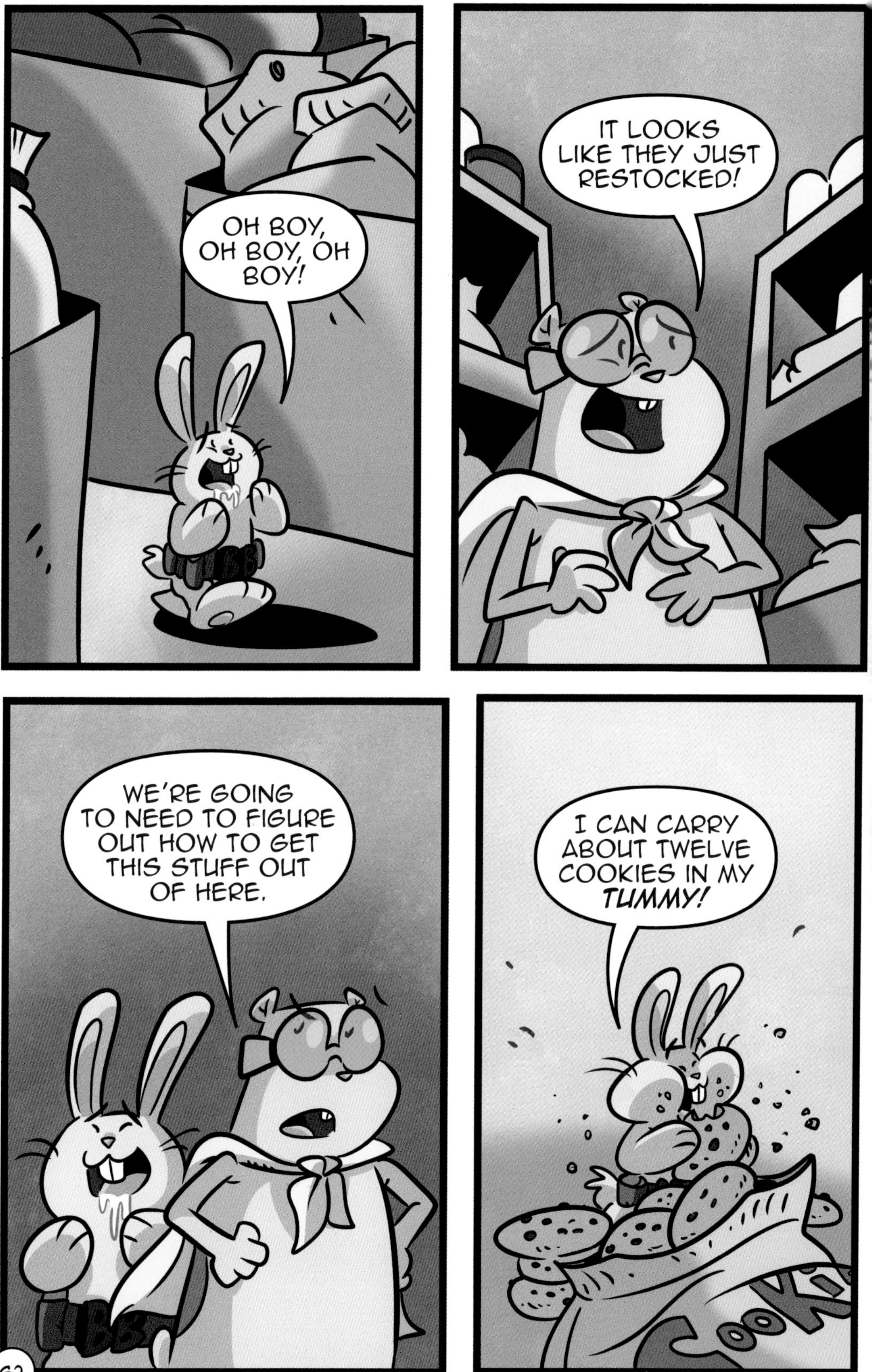
IT LOOKS LIKE THEY JUST RESTOCKED!
OH BOY, OH BOY, OH BOY!
I CAN CARRY ABOUT TWELVE COOKIES IN MY *TUMMY!*
WE'RE GOING TO NEED TO FIGURE OUT HOW TO GET THIS STUFF OUT OF HERE.

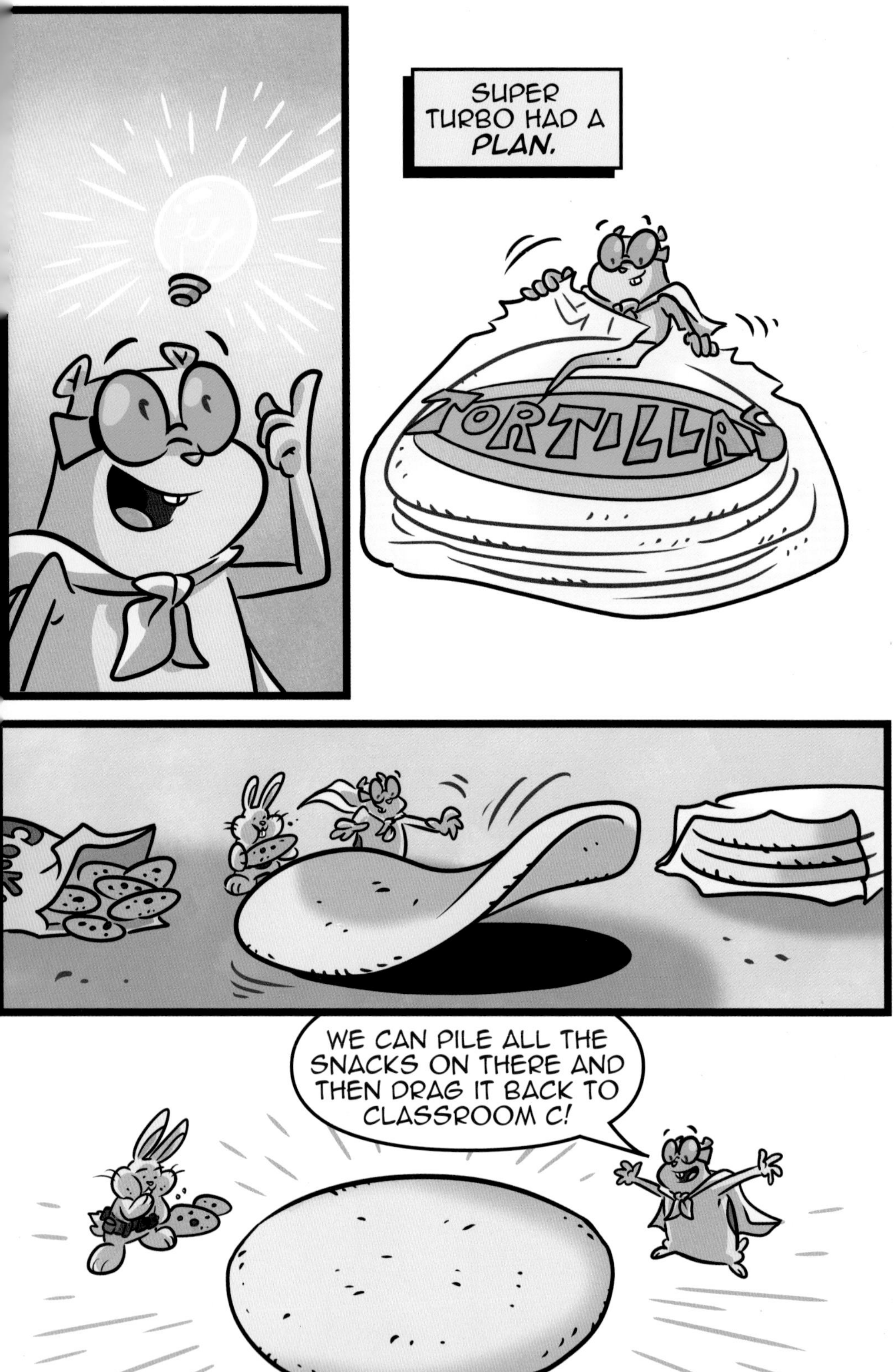
SUPER TURBO HAD A *PLAN.*
TORTILLAS
WE CAN PILE ALL THE SNACKS ON THERE AND THEN DRAG IT BACK TO CLASSROOM C!

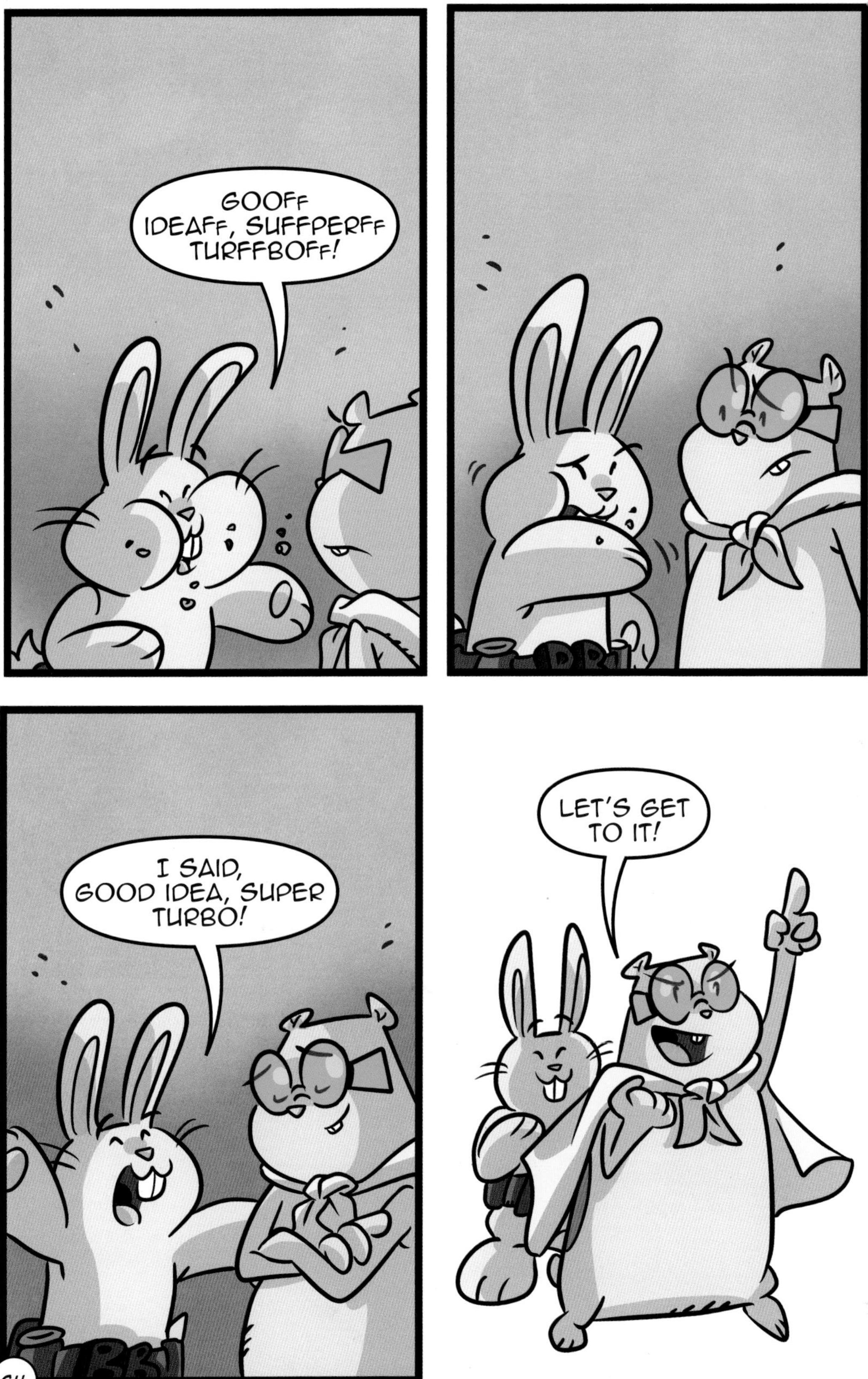
GOOFF IDEAFF, SUFFPERFF TURFFBOFF!
I SAID, GOOD IDEA, SUPER TURBO!
LET'S GET TO IT!

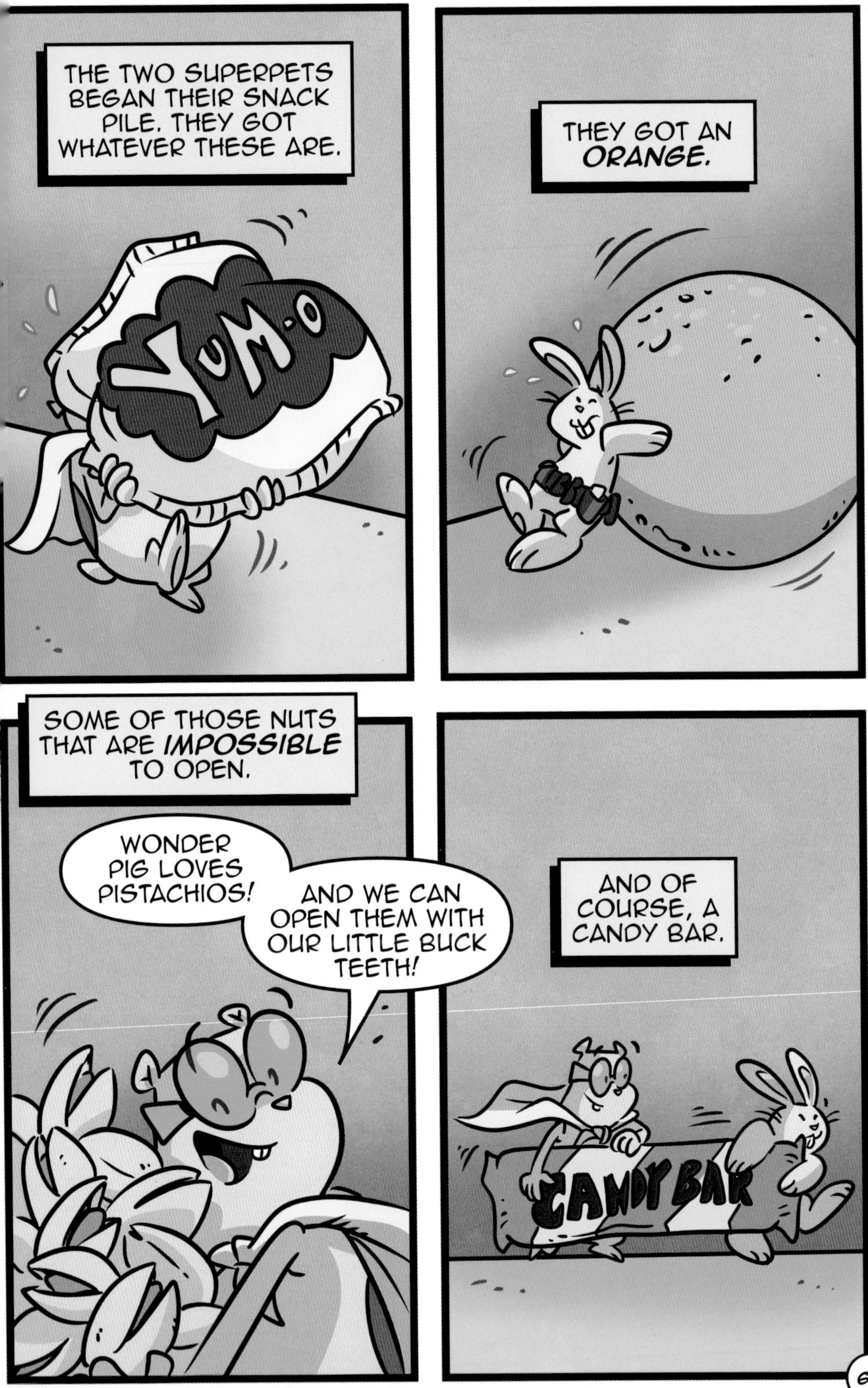
THEY GOT AN *ORANGE.*
THE TWO SUPERPETS BEGAN THEIR SNACK PILE. THEY GOT WHATEVER THESE ARE.
YUM-O
AND OF COURSE, A CANDY BAR.
CANDY BAR
SOME OF THOSE NUTS THAT ARE *IMPOSSIBLE* TO OPEN.
WONDER PIG LOVES PISTACHIOS!
AND WE CAN OPEN THEM WITH OUR LITTLE BUCK TEETH!

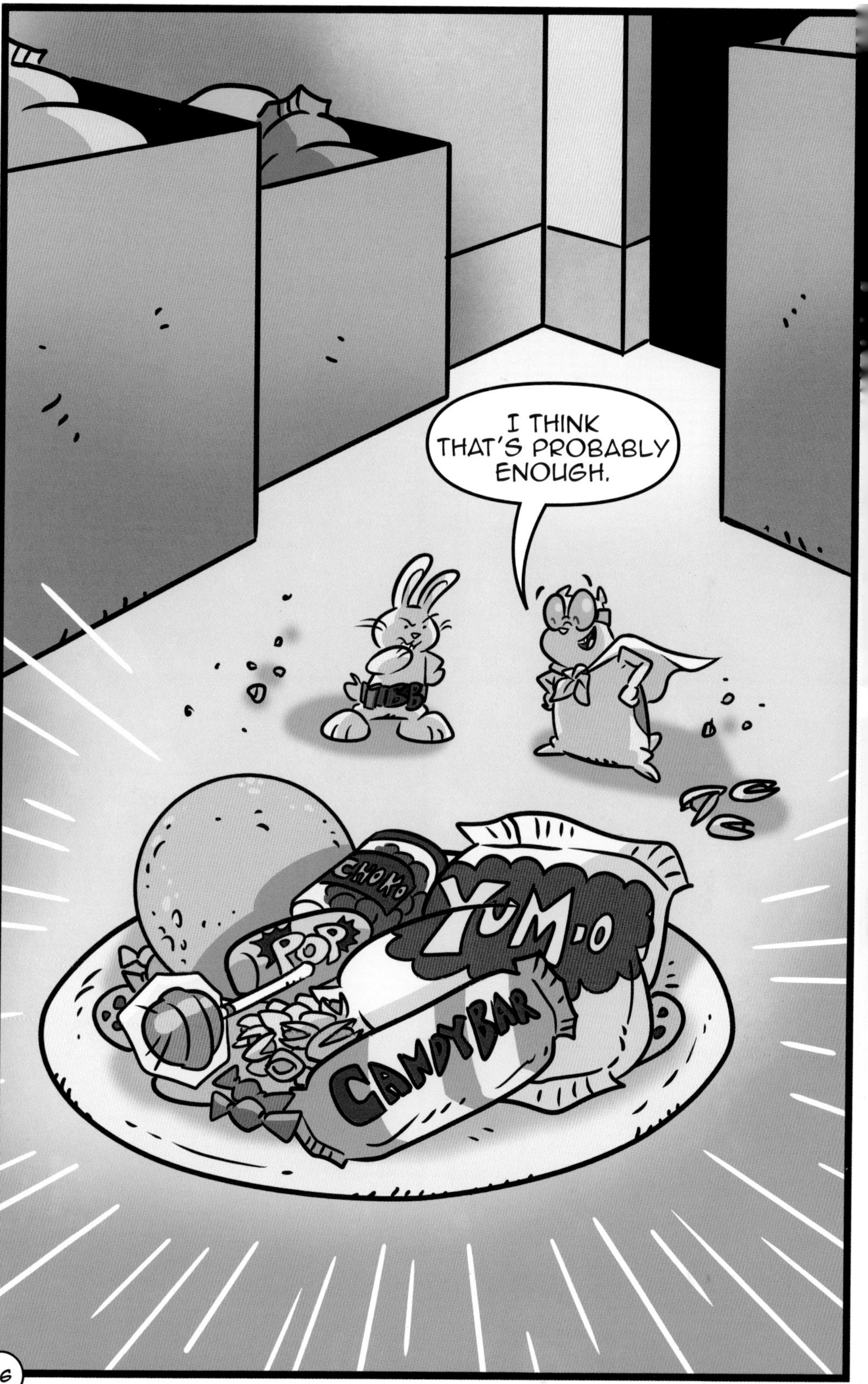
I THINK THAT'S PROBABLY ENOUGH.
CHOKO
POP
YUM-O
CANDYBAR
TBB

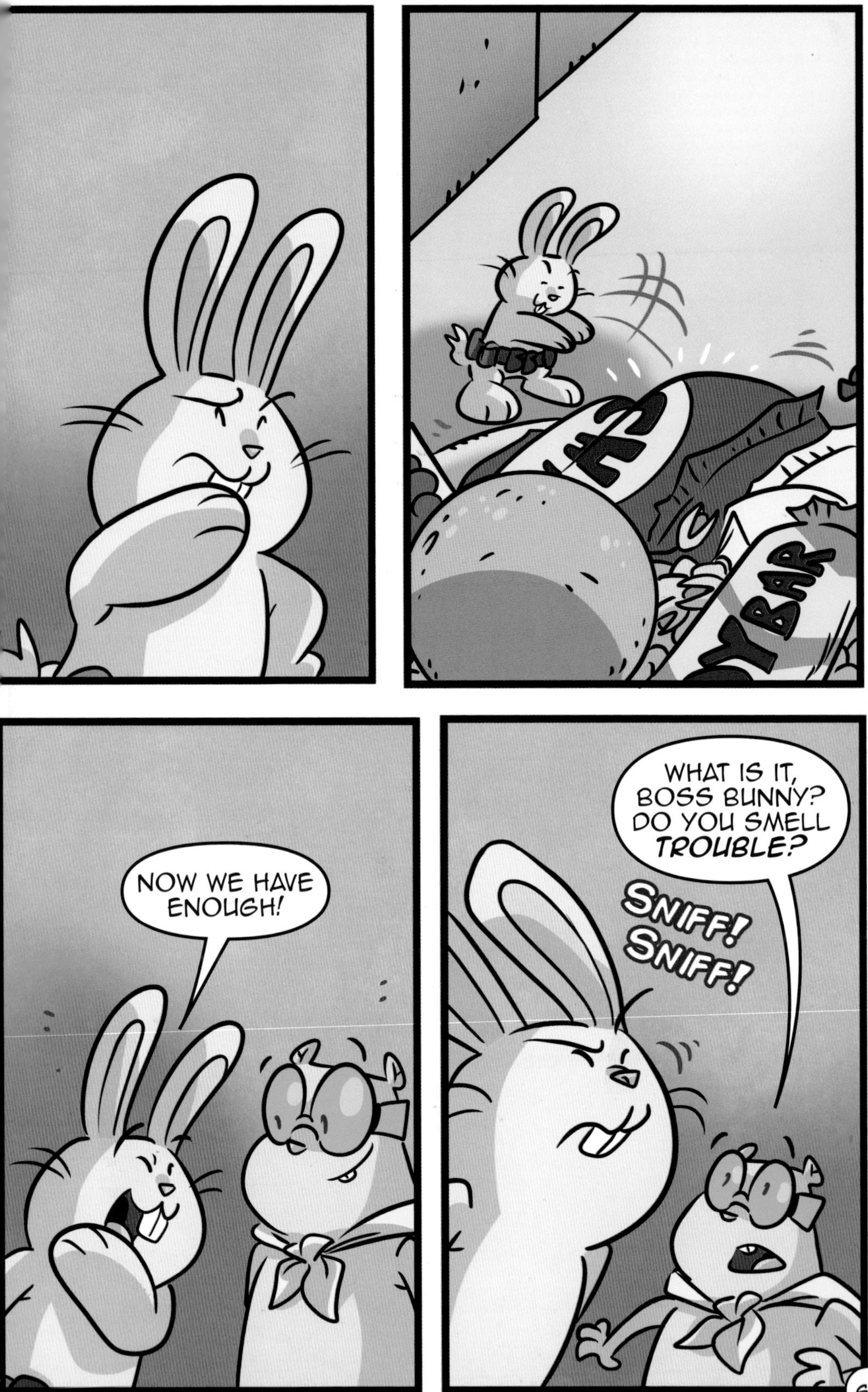
WHAT IS IT, BOSS BUNNY? DO YOU SMELL *TROUBLE?*
SNIFF! SNIFF!
NOW WE HAVE ENOUGH!

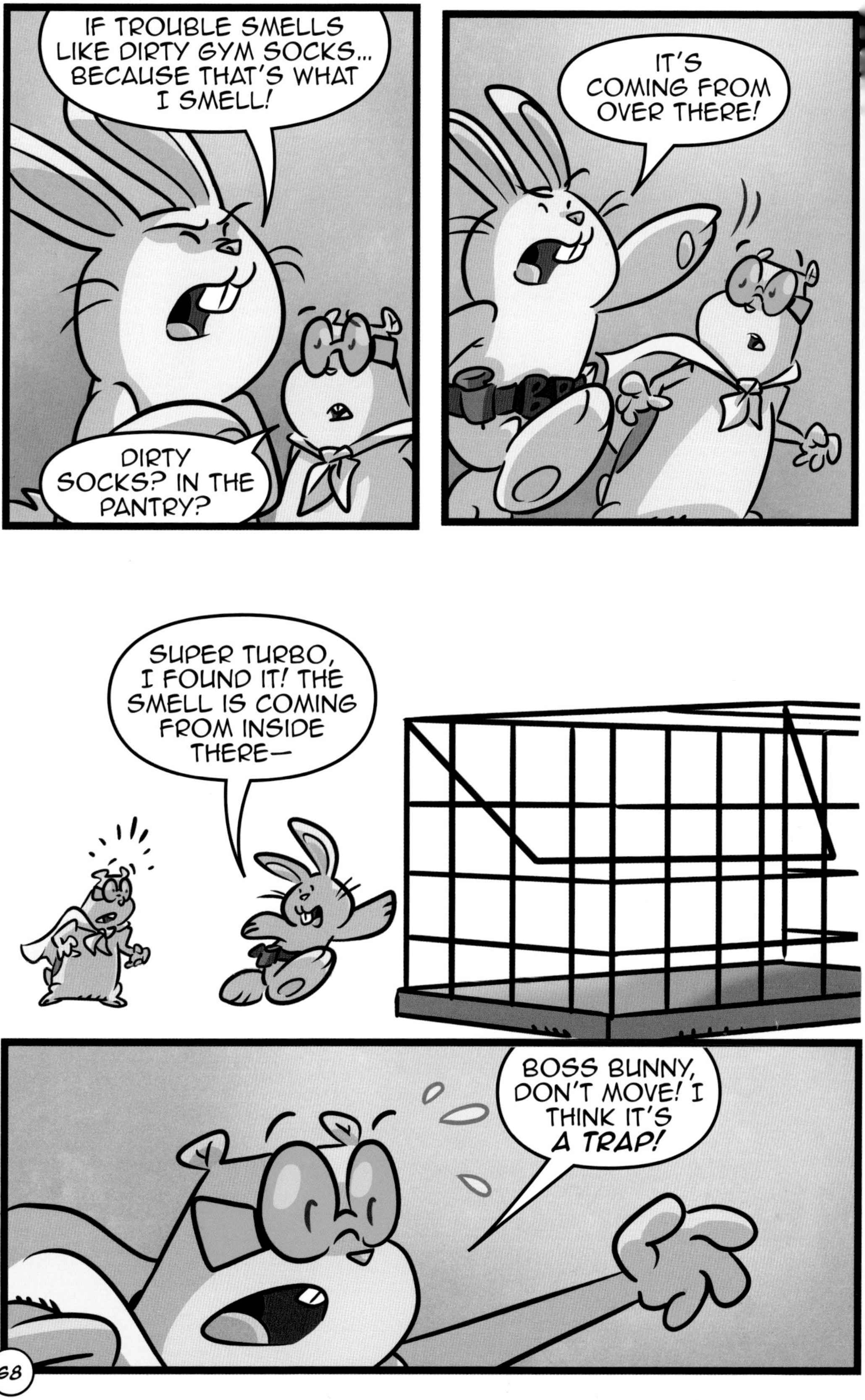
IT'S COMING FROM OVER THERE!
IF TROUBLE SMELLS LIKE DIRTY GYM SOCKS... BECAUSE THAT'S WHAT I SMELL!
DIRTY SOCKS? IN THE PANTRY?
SUPER TURBO, I FOUND IT! THE SMELL IS COMING FROM INSIDE THERE—
BOSS BUNNY, DON'T MOVE! I THINK IT'S *A TRAP!*

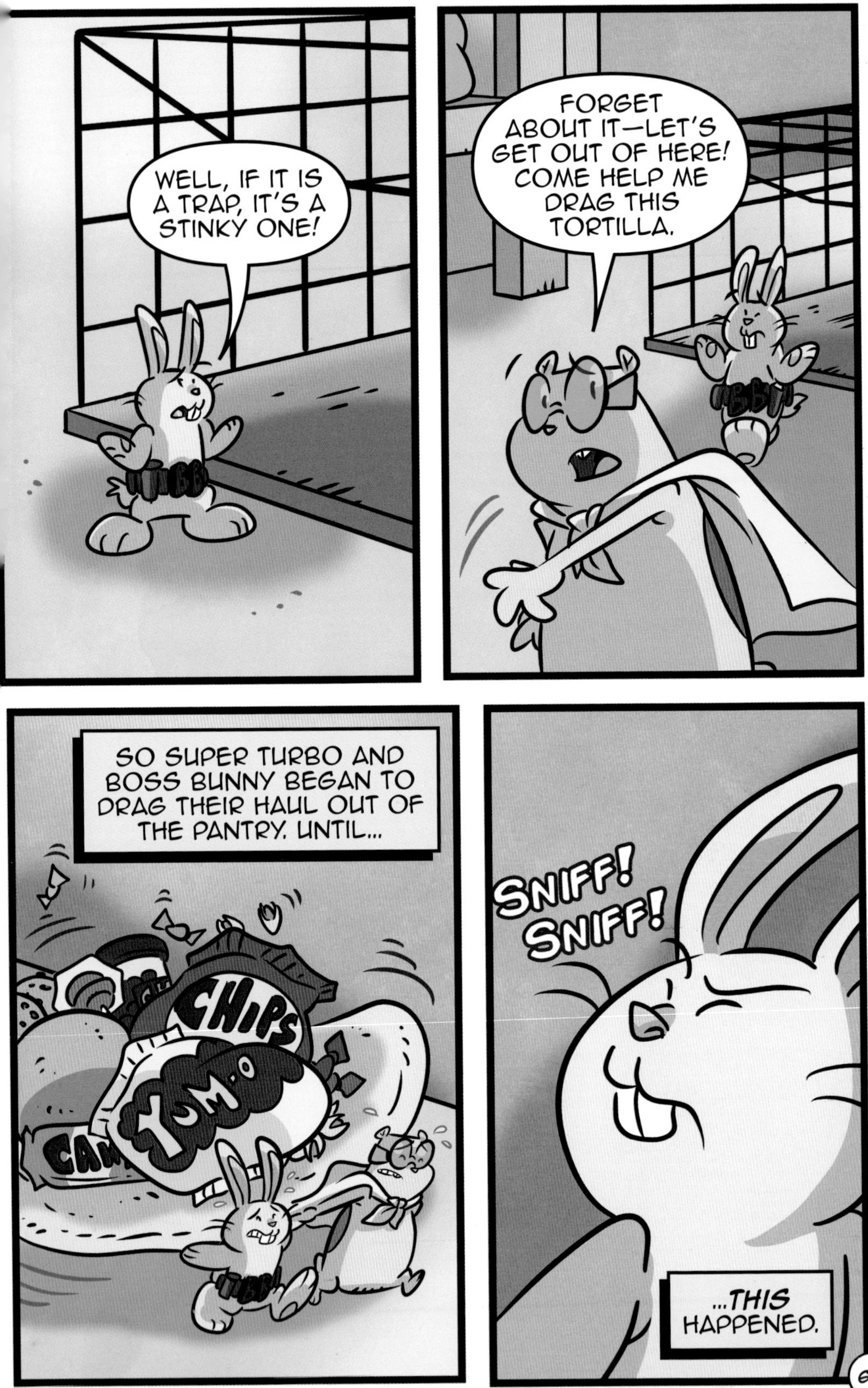
WELL, IF IT IS A TRAP, IT'S A STINKY ONE!
FORGET ABOUT IT—LET'S GET OUT OF HERE! COME HELP ME DRAG THIS TORTILLA.
SO SUPER TURBO AND BOSS BUNNY BEGAN TO DRAG THEIR HAUL OUT OF THE PANTRY. UNTIL...
CHIPS
YUM-O
SNIFF! SNIFF!
...THIS HAPPENED.

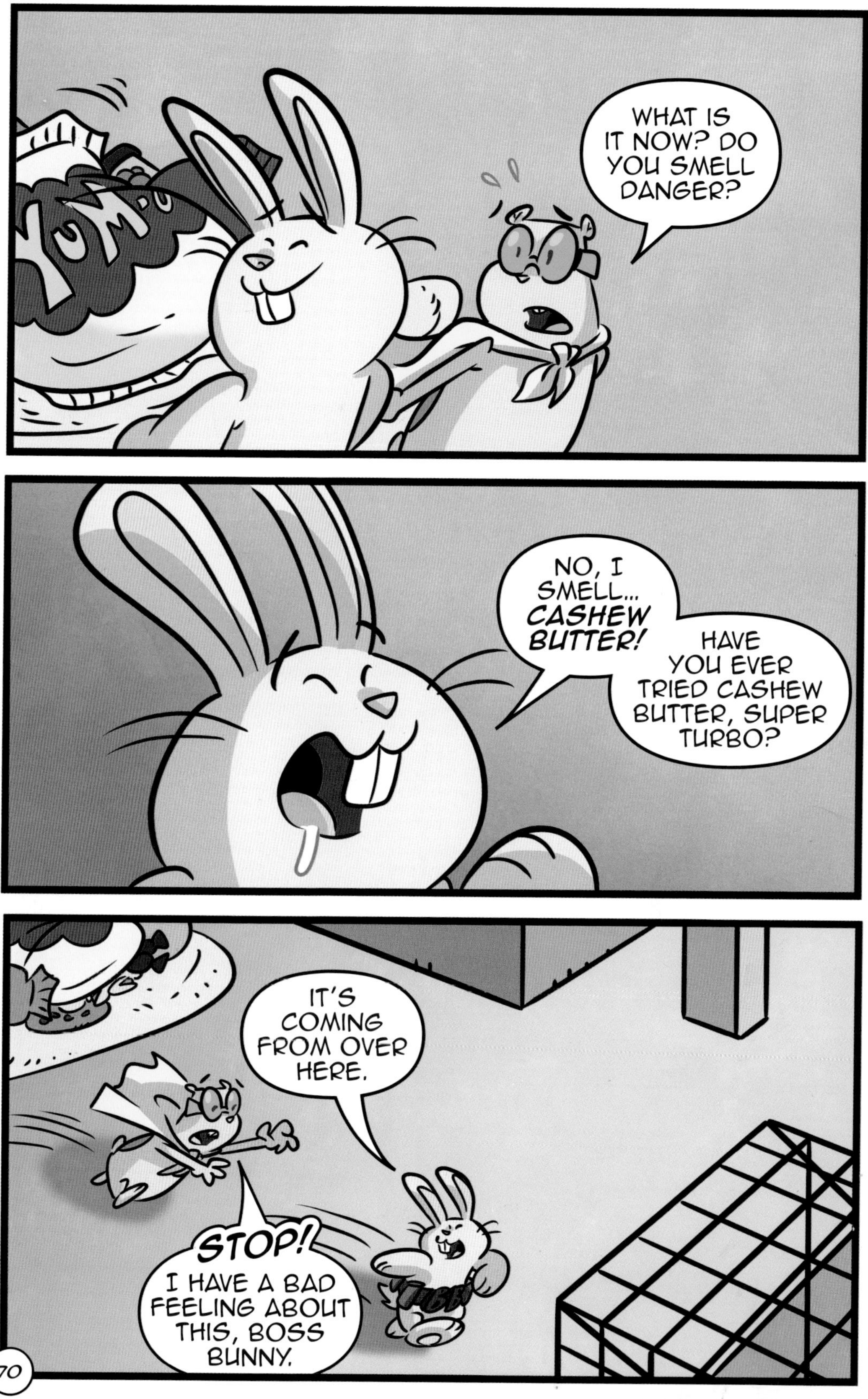
YUM!
WHAT IS IT NOW? DO YOU SMELL DANGER?
NO, I SMELL... *CASHEW BUTTER!*
HAVE YOU EVER TRIED CASHEW BUTTER, SUPER TURBO?
IT'S COMING FROM OVER HERE.
STOP! I HAVE A BAD FEELING ABOUT THIS, BOSS BUNNY.

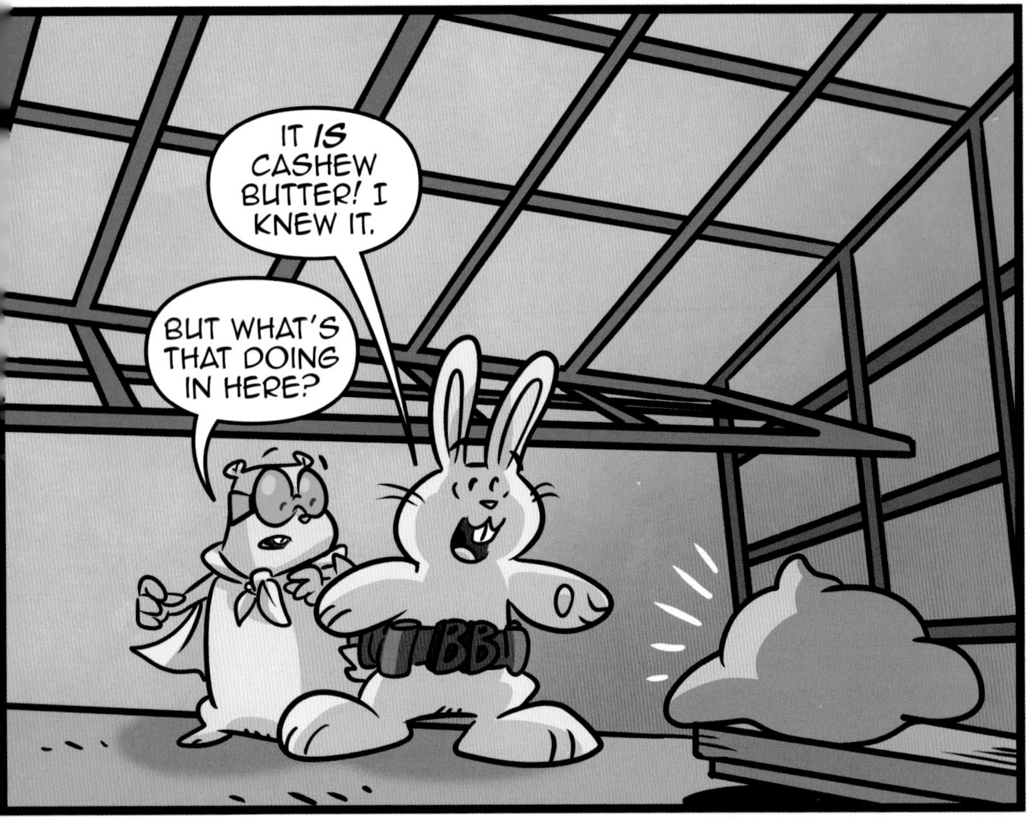
IT *IS* CASHEW BUTTER! I KNEW IT.
BUT WHAT'S THAT DOING IN HERE?

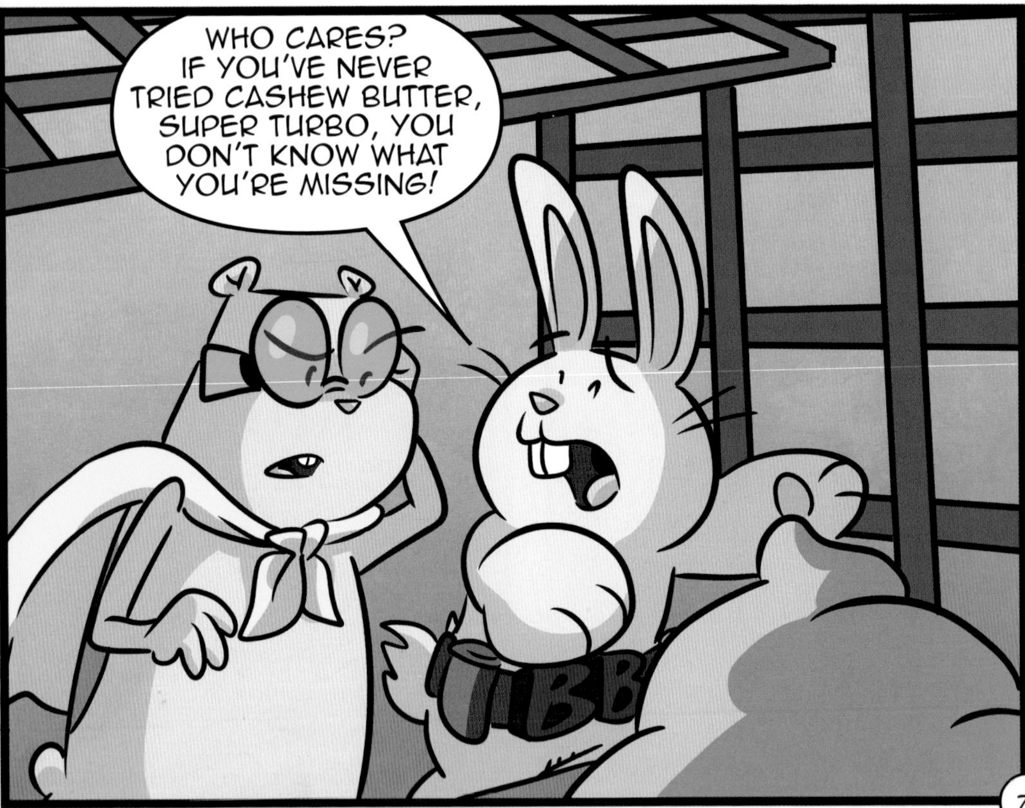
WHO CARES? IF YOU'VE NEVER TRIED CASHEW BUTTER, SUPER TURBO, YOU DON'T KNOW WHAT YOU'RE MISSING!

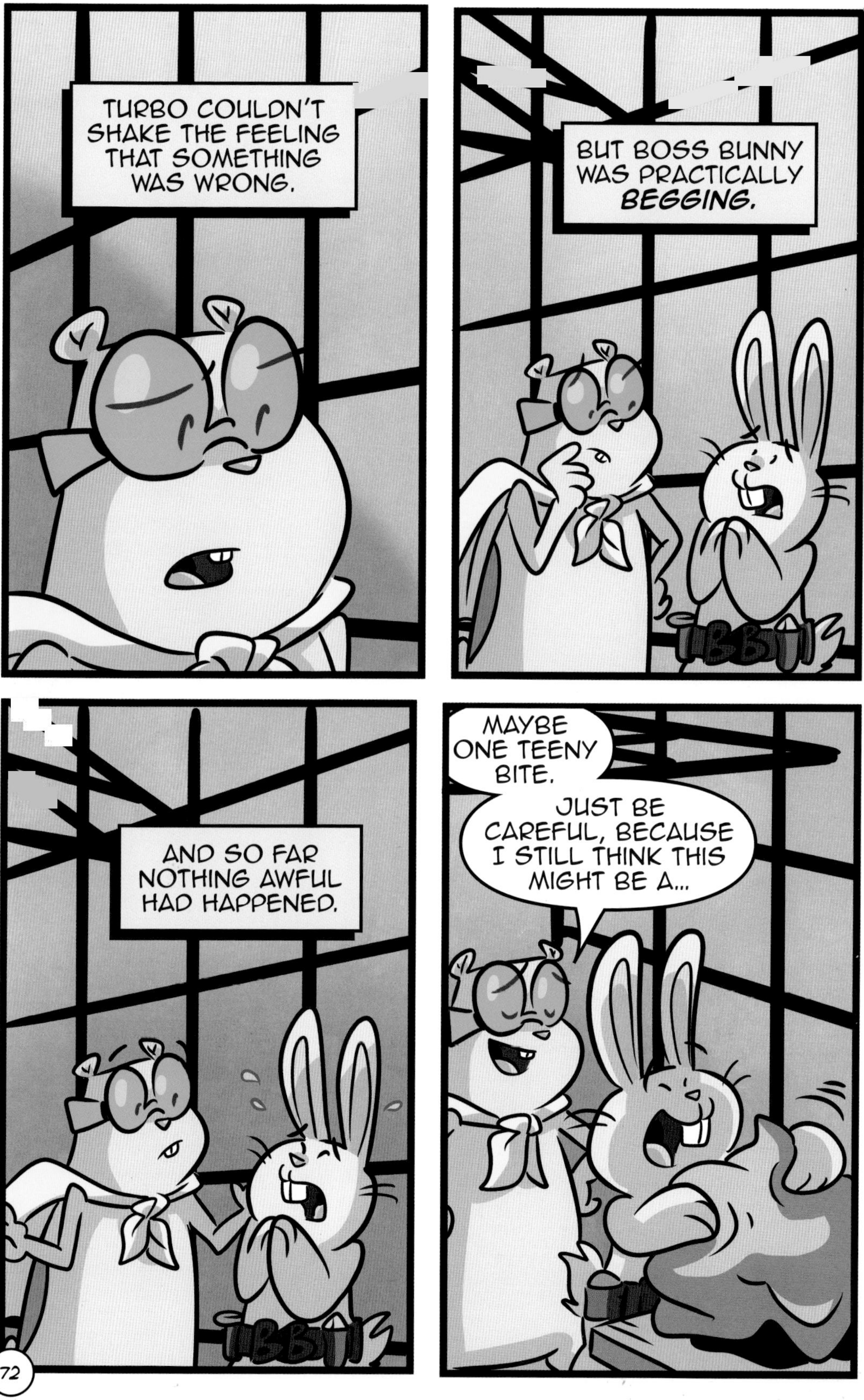
TURBO COULDN'T SHAKE THE FEELING THAT SOMETHING WAS WRONG.
BUT BOSS BUNNY WAS PRACTICALLY *BEGGING.*
BB
AND SO FAR NOTHING AWFUL HAD HAPPENED.
BB
MAYBE ONE TEENY BITE.
JUST BE CAREFUL, BECAUSE I STILL THINK THIS MIGHT BE A...

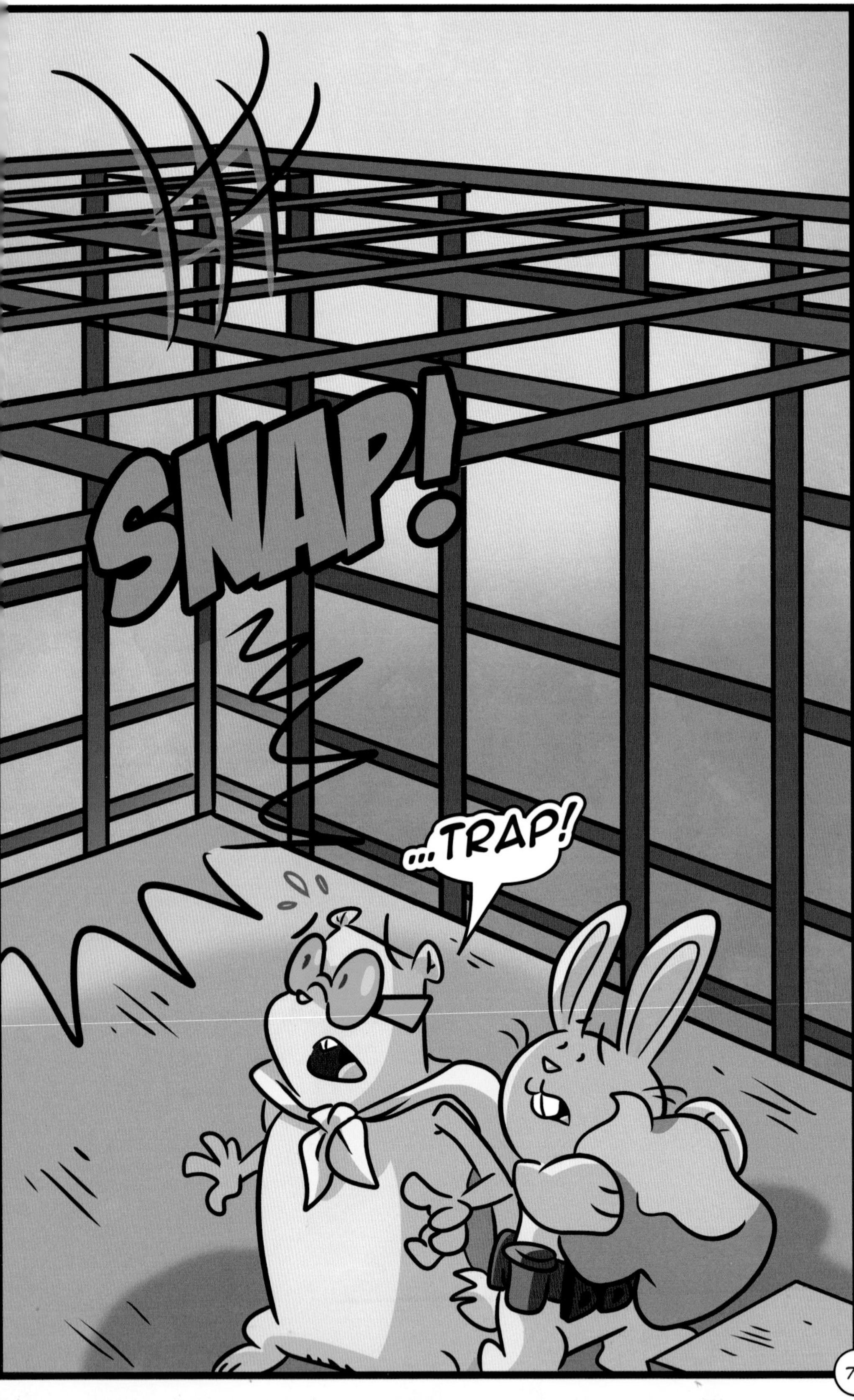
SNAP!
...TRAP!

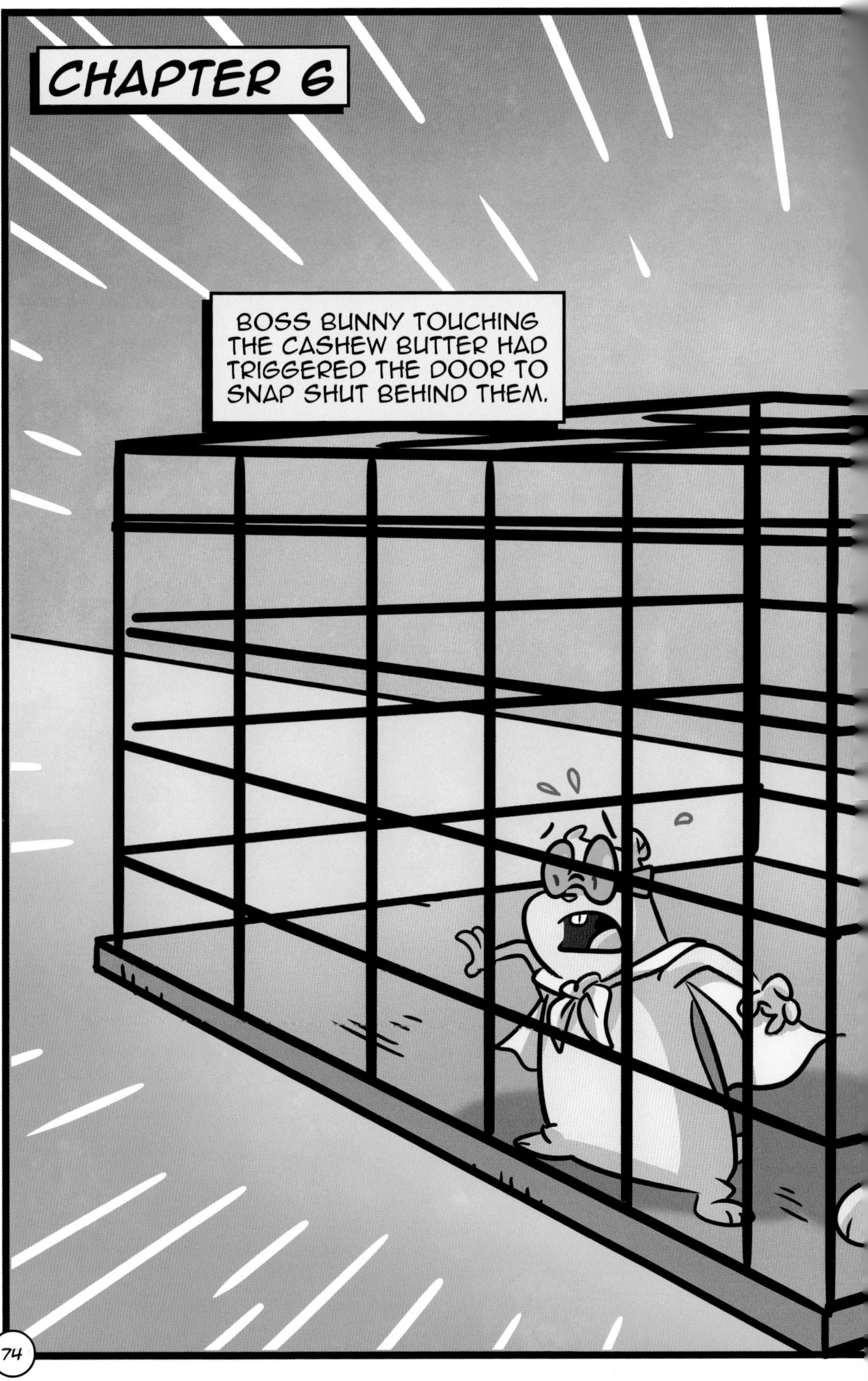
CHAPTER 6
BOSS BUNNY TOUCHING THE CASHEW BUTTER HAD TRIGGERED THE DOOR TO SNAP SHUT BEHIND THEM.

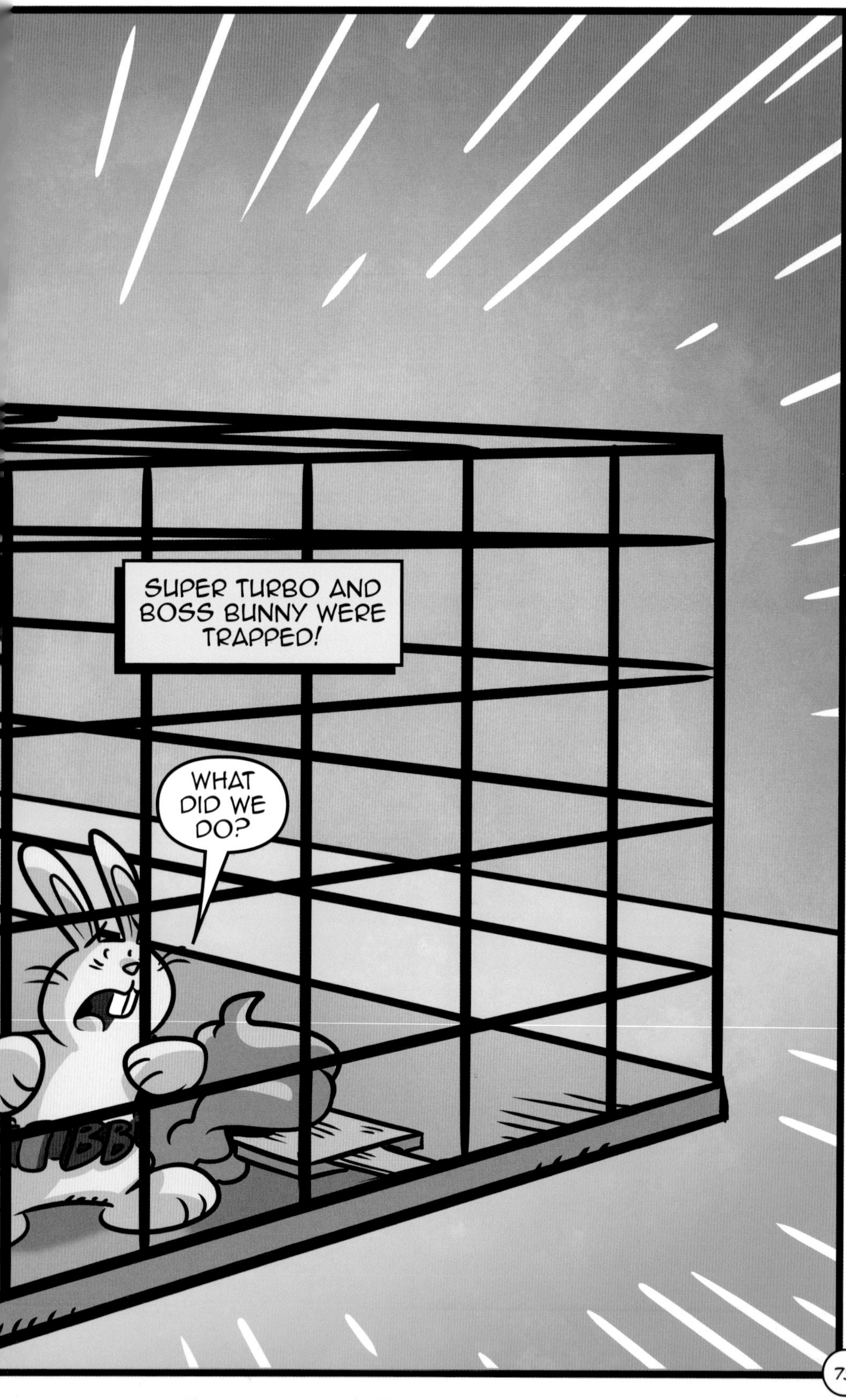
SUPER TURBO AND BOSS BUNNY WERE TRAPPED!
WHAT DID WE DO?

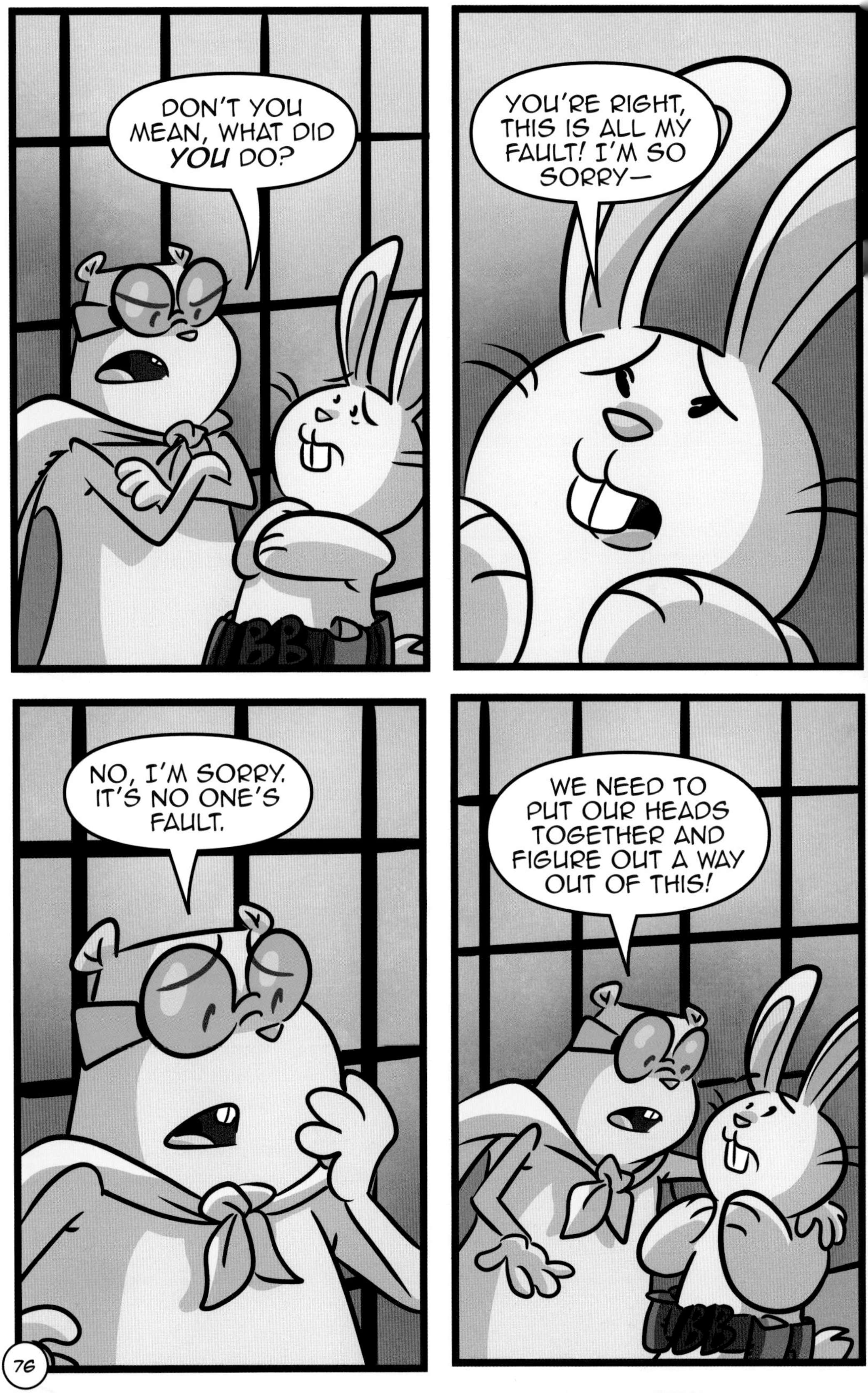
DON'T YOU MEAN, WHAT DID *YOU* DO?
YOU'RE RIGHT, THIS IS ALL MY FAULT! I'M SO SORRY—
NO, I'M SORRY. IT'S NO ONE'S FAULT.
WE NEED TO PUT OUR HEADS TOGETHER AND FIGURE OUT A WAY OUT OF THIS!

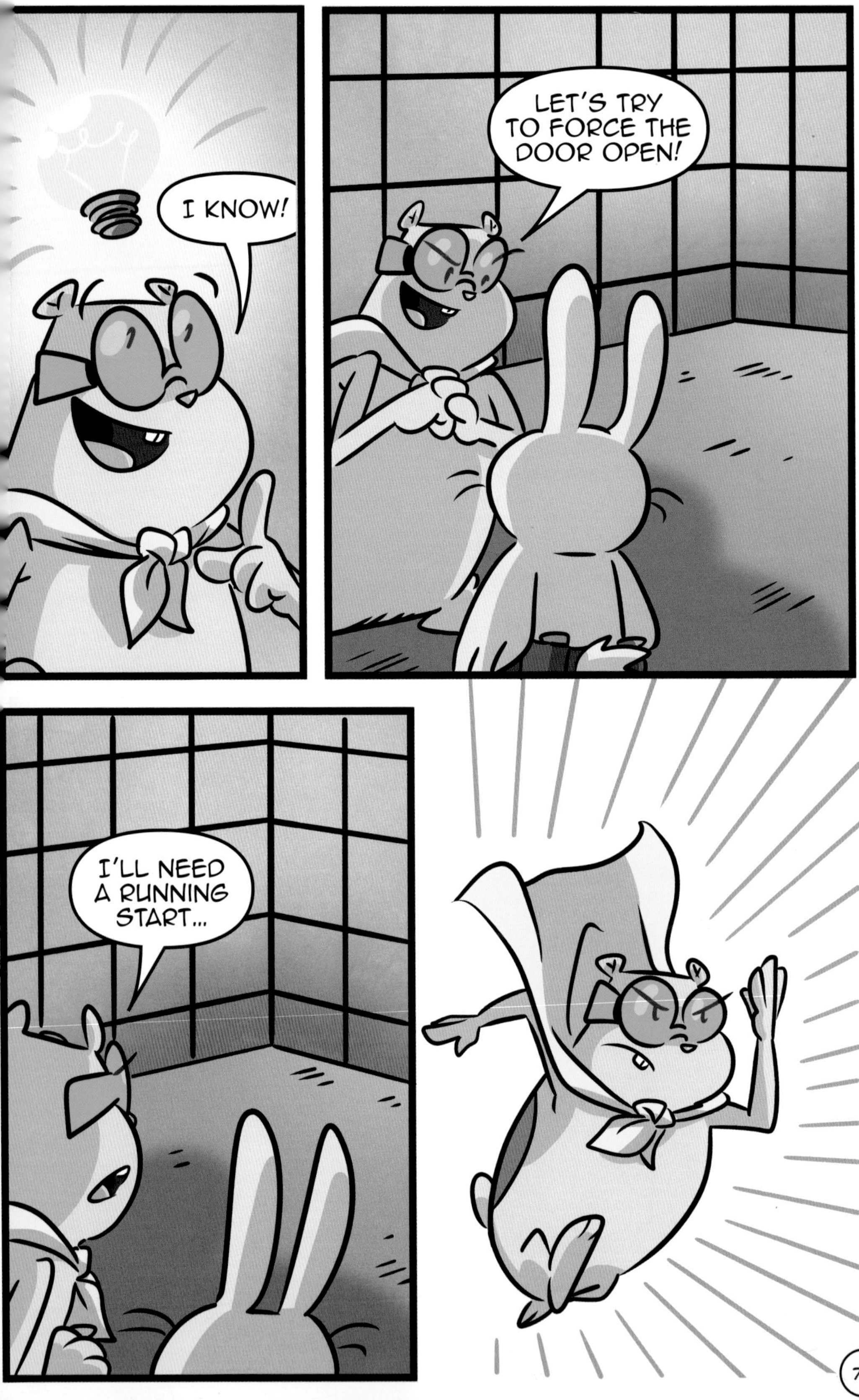
LET'S TRY TO FORCE THE DOOR OPEN!
I KNOW!
I'LL NEED A RUNNING START...

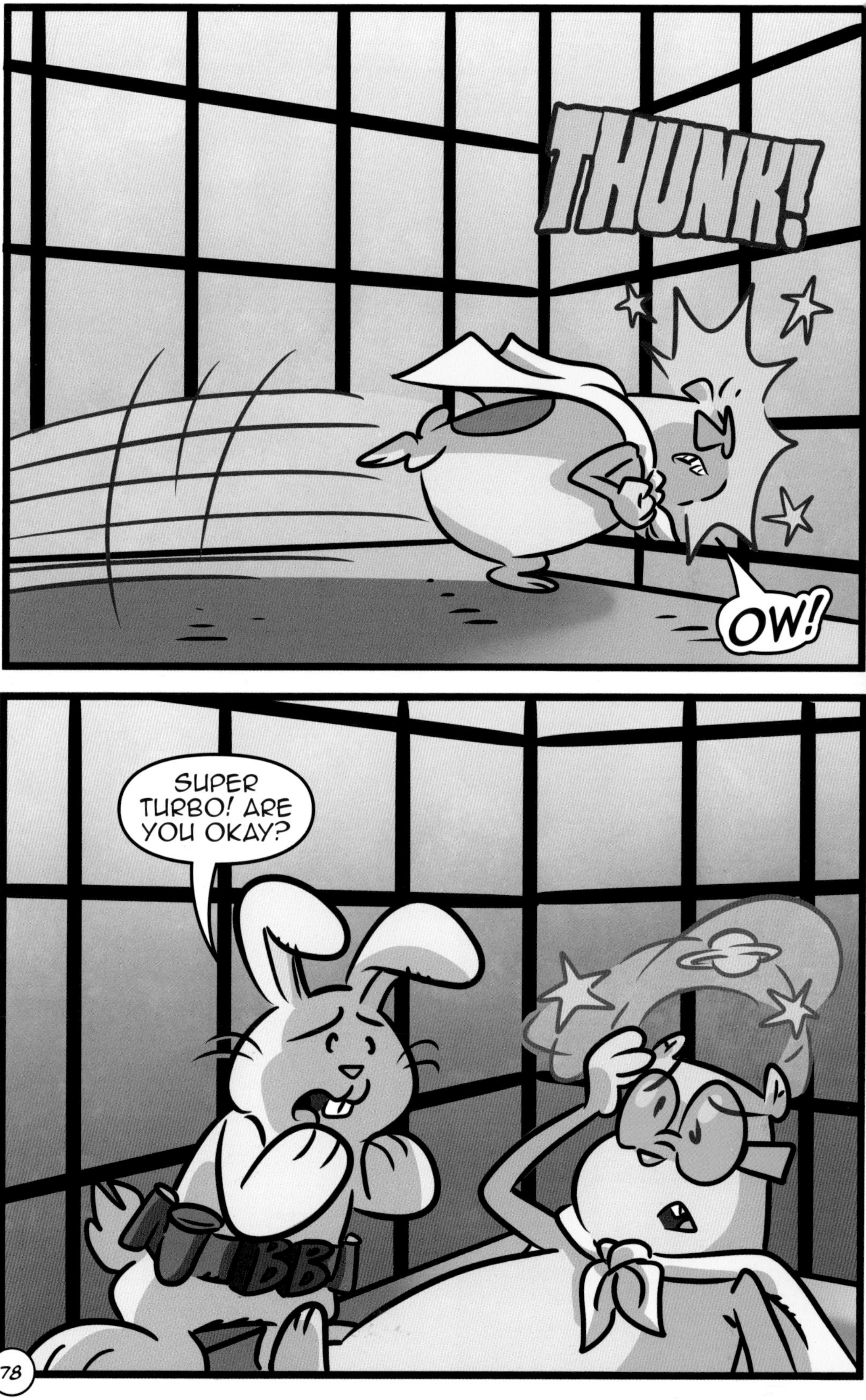
THUNK!
OW!
SUPER TURBO! ARE YOU OKAY?

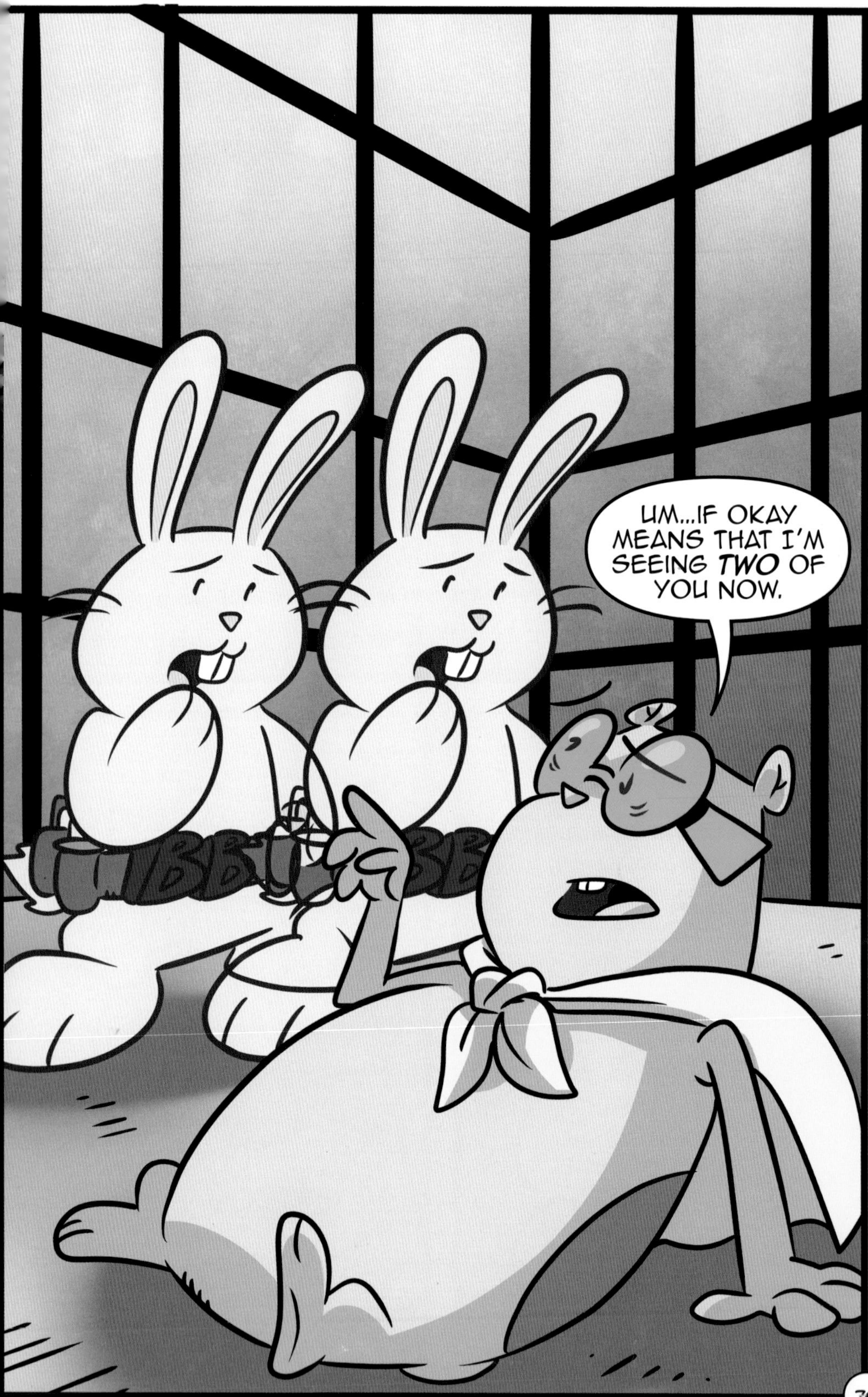
UM...IF OKAY MEANS THAT I'M SEEING *TWO* OF YOU NOW.

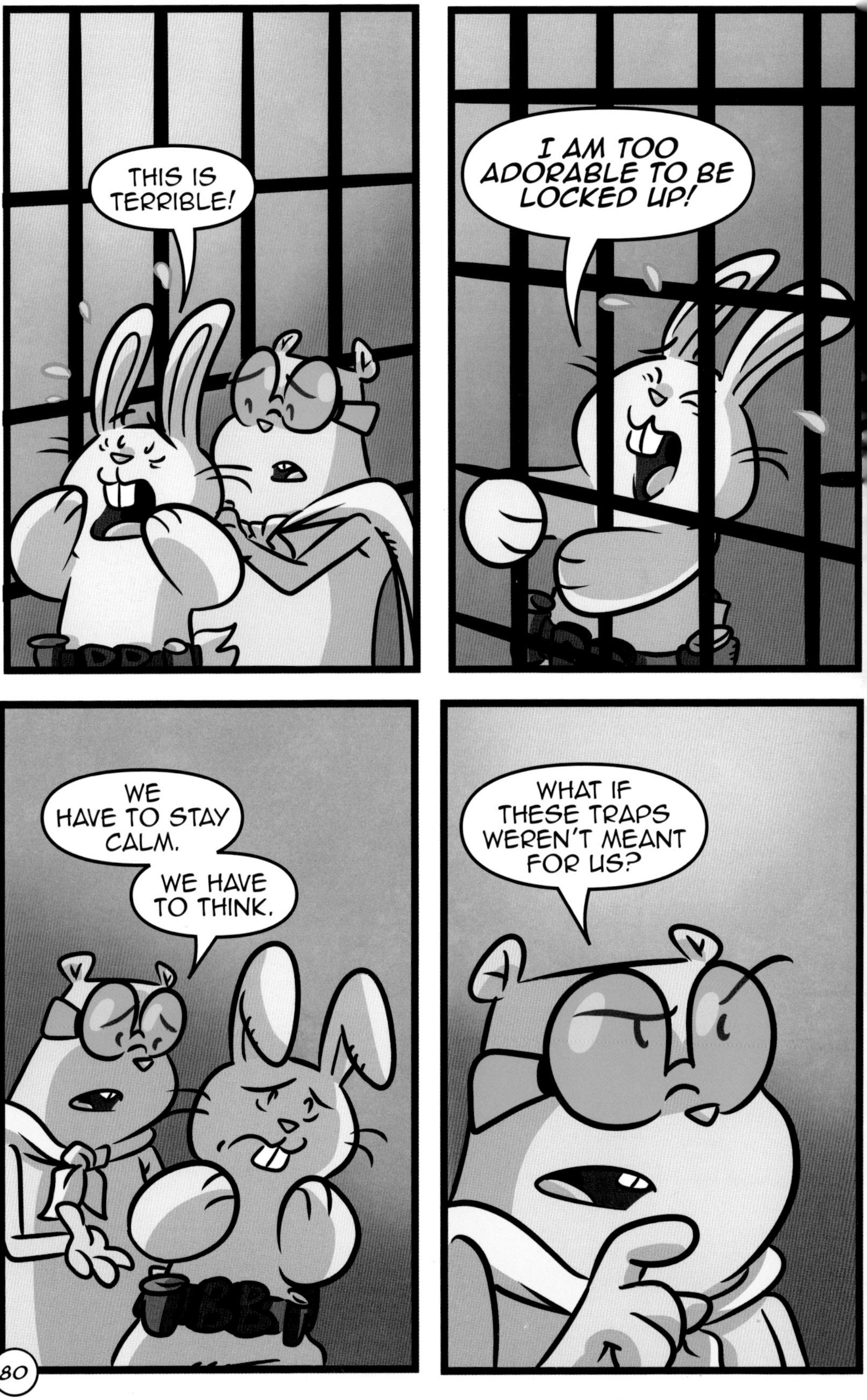
I AM TOO ADORABLE TO BE LOCKED UP!
THIS IS TERRIBLE!
WHAT IF THESE TRAPS WEREN'T MEANT FOR US?
WE HAVE TO STAY CALM.
WE HAVE TO THINK.

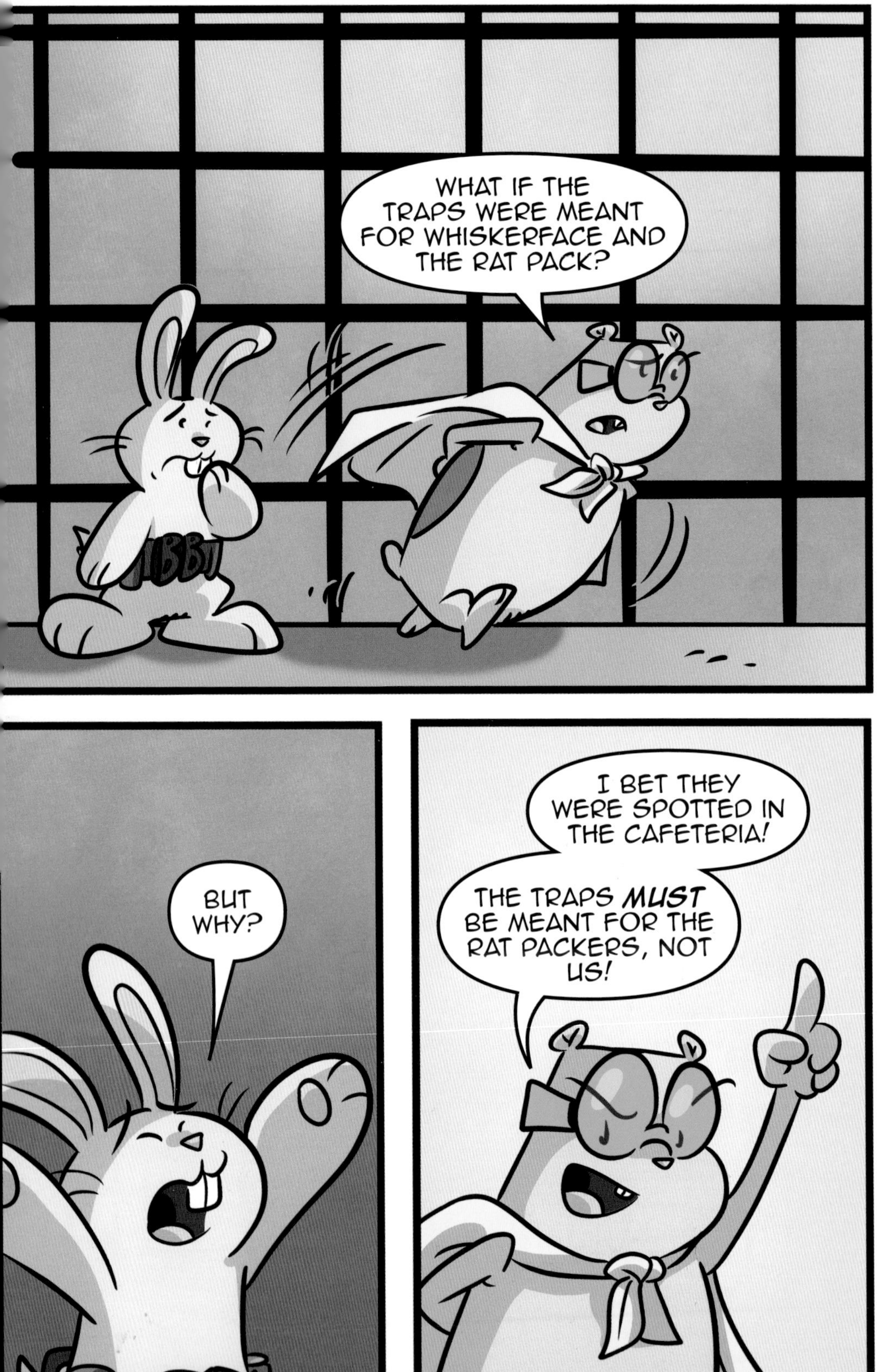
WHAT IF THE TRAPS WERE MEANT FOR WHISKERFACE AND THE RAT PACK?
I BET THEY WERE SPOTTED IN THE CAFETERIA!
THE TRAPS *MUST* BE MEANT FOR THE RAT PACKERS, NOT US!
BUT WHY?

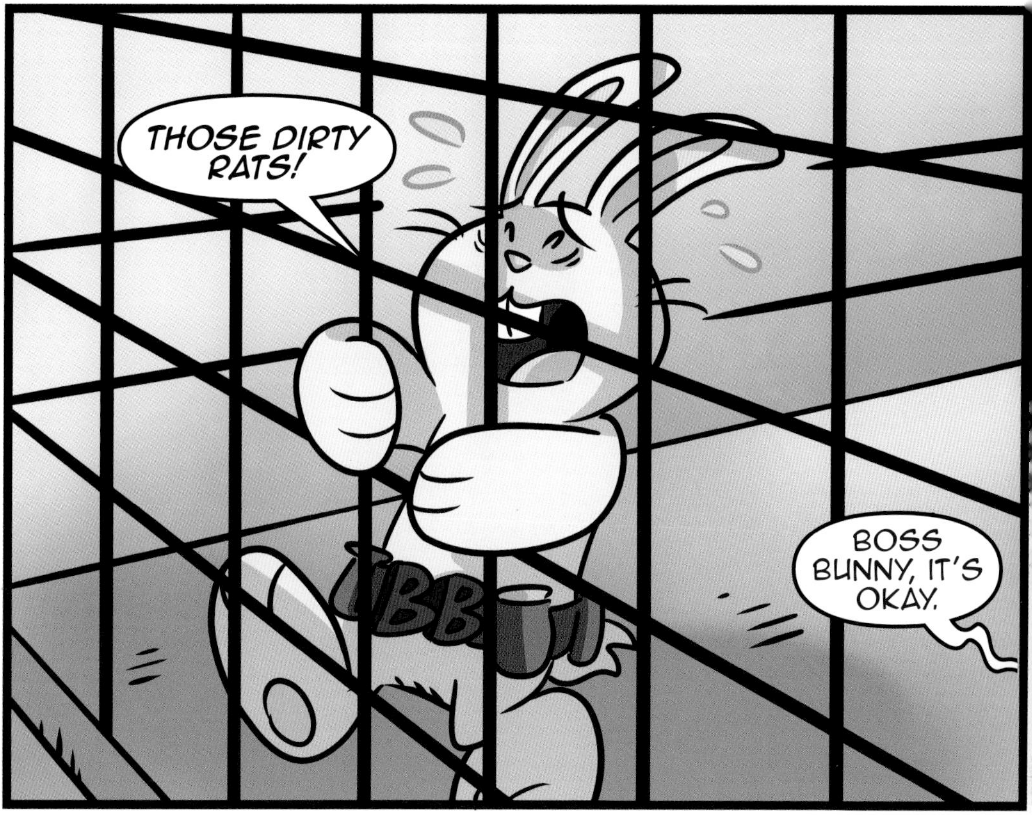
THOSE DIRTY RATS!
BOSS BUNNY, IT'S OKAY.

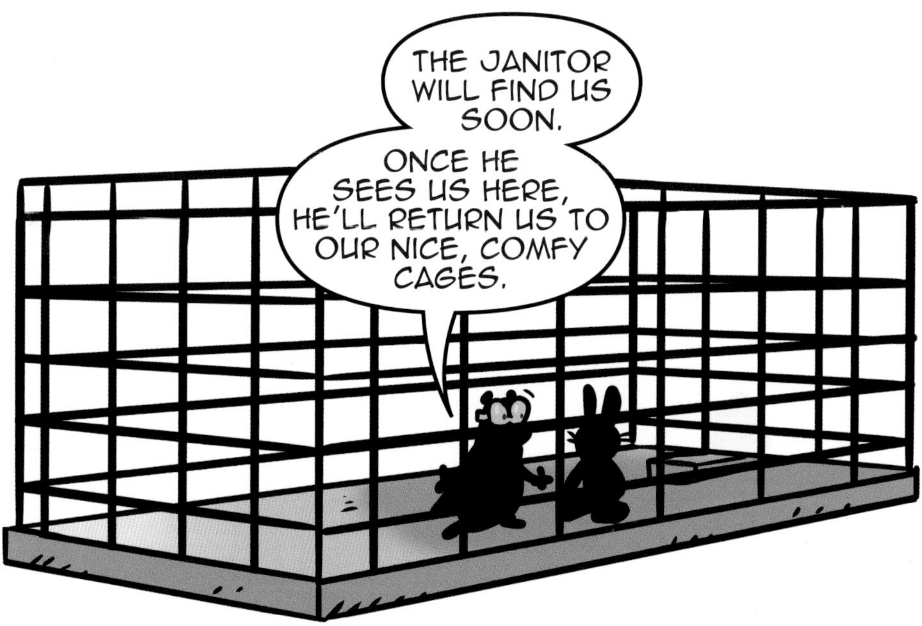
THE JANITOR WILL FIND US SOON.
ONCE HE SEES US HERE, HE'LL RETURN US TO OUR NICE, COMFY CAGES.

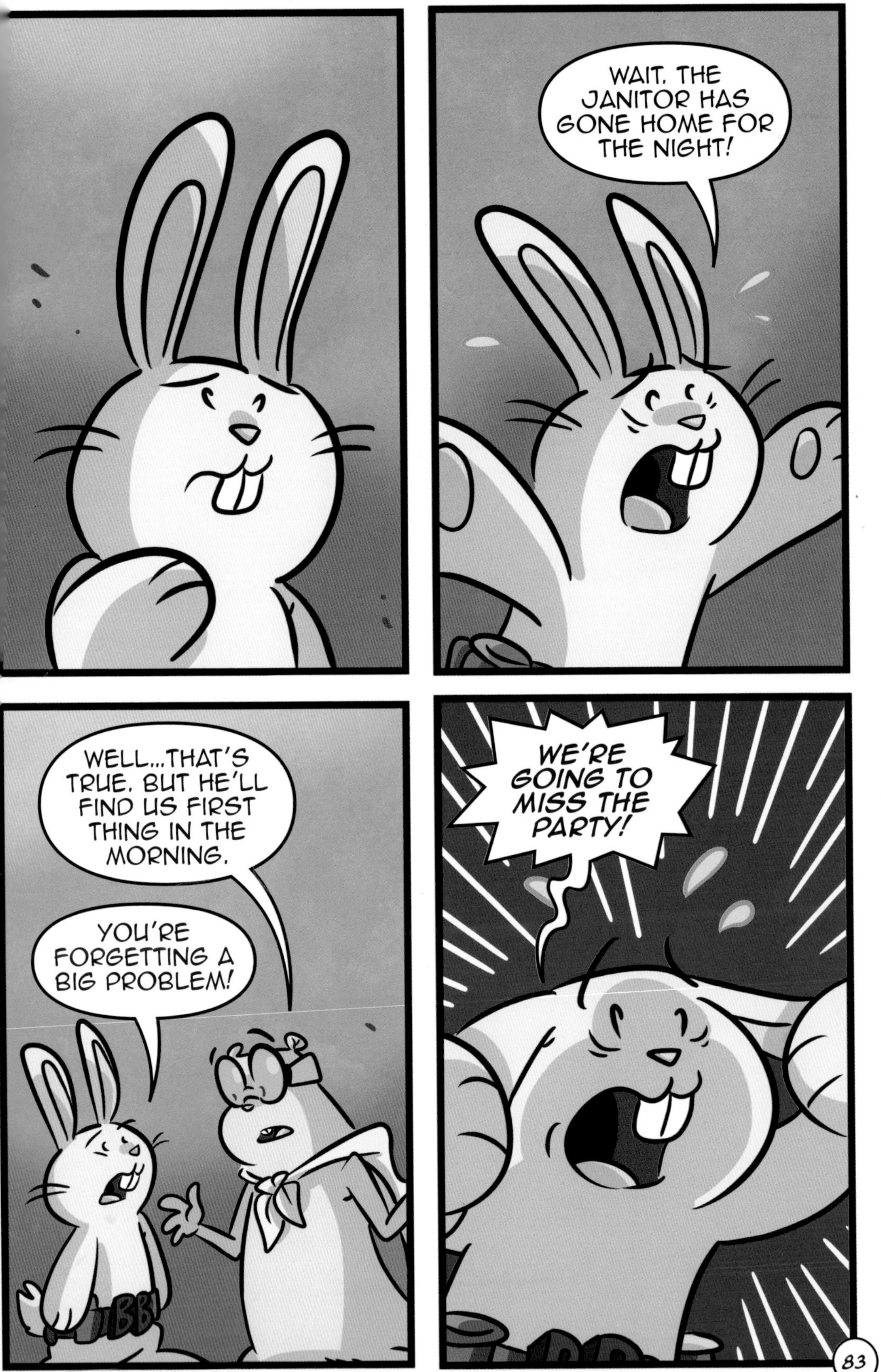
WAIT. THE JANITOR HAS GONE HOME FOR THE NIGHT!
WELL...THAT'S TRUE. BUT HE'LL FIND US FIRST THING IN THE MORNING.
YOU'RE FORGETTING A BIG PROBLEM!
WE'RE GOING TO MISS THE PARTY!

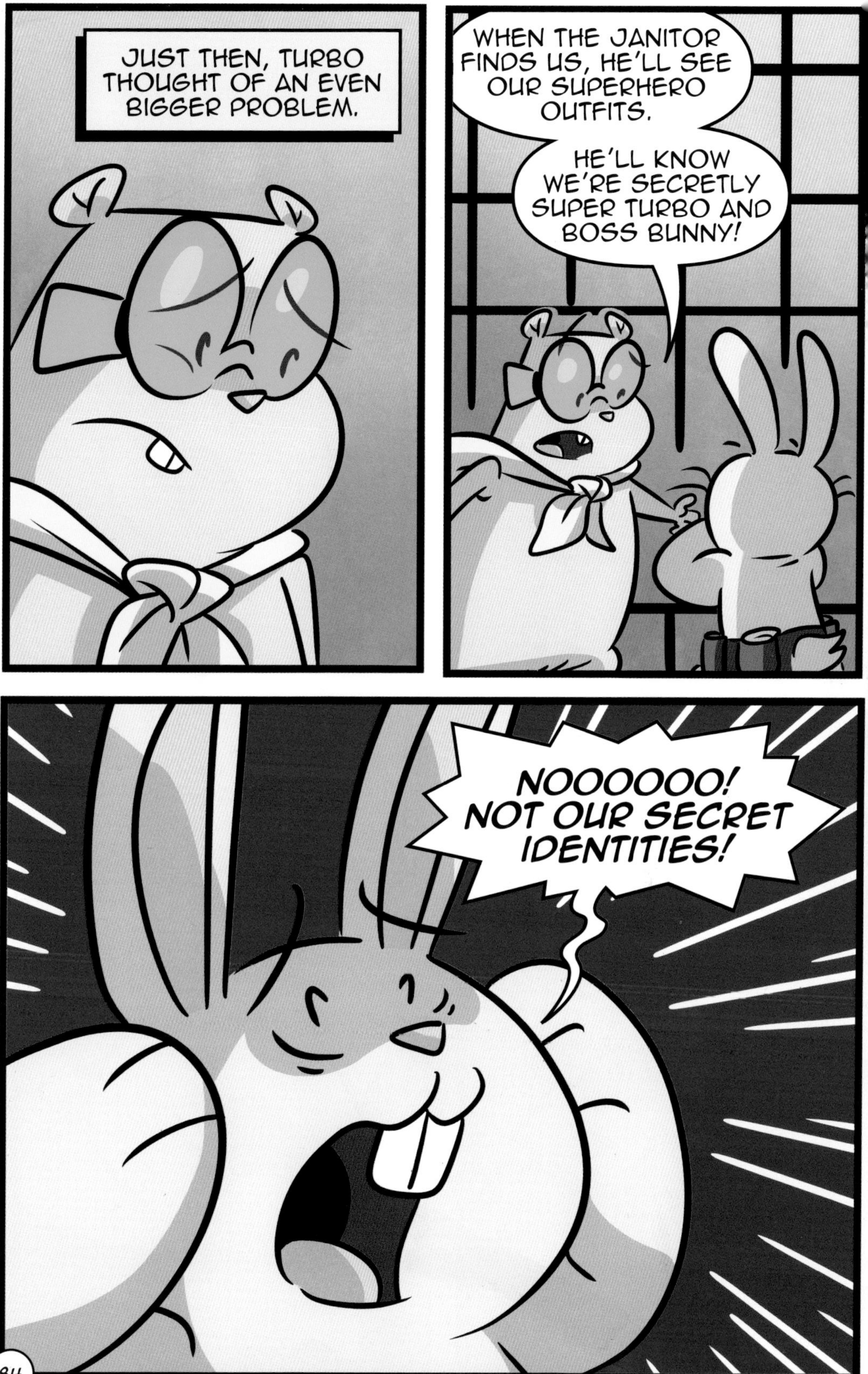
JUST THEN, TURBO THOUGHT OF AN EVEN BIGGER PROBLEM.
WHEN THE JANITOR FINDS US, HE'LL SEE OUR SUPERHERO OUTFITS.
HE'LL KNOW WE'RE SECRETLY SUPER TURBO AND BOSS BUNNY!
NOOOOOO! NOT OUR SECRET IDENTITIES!

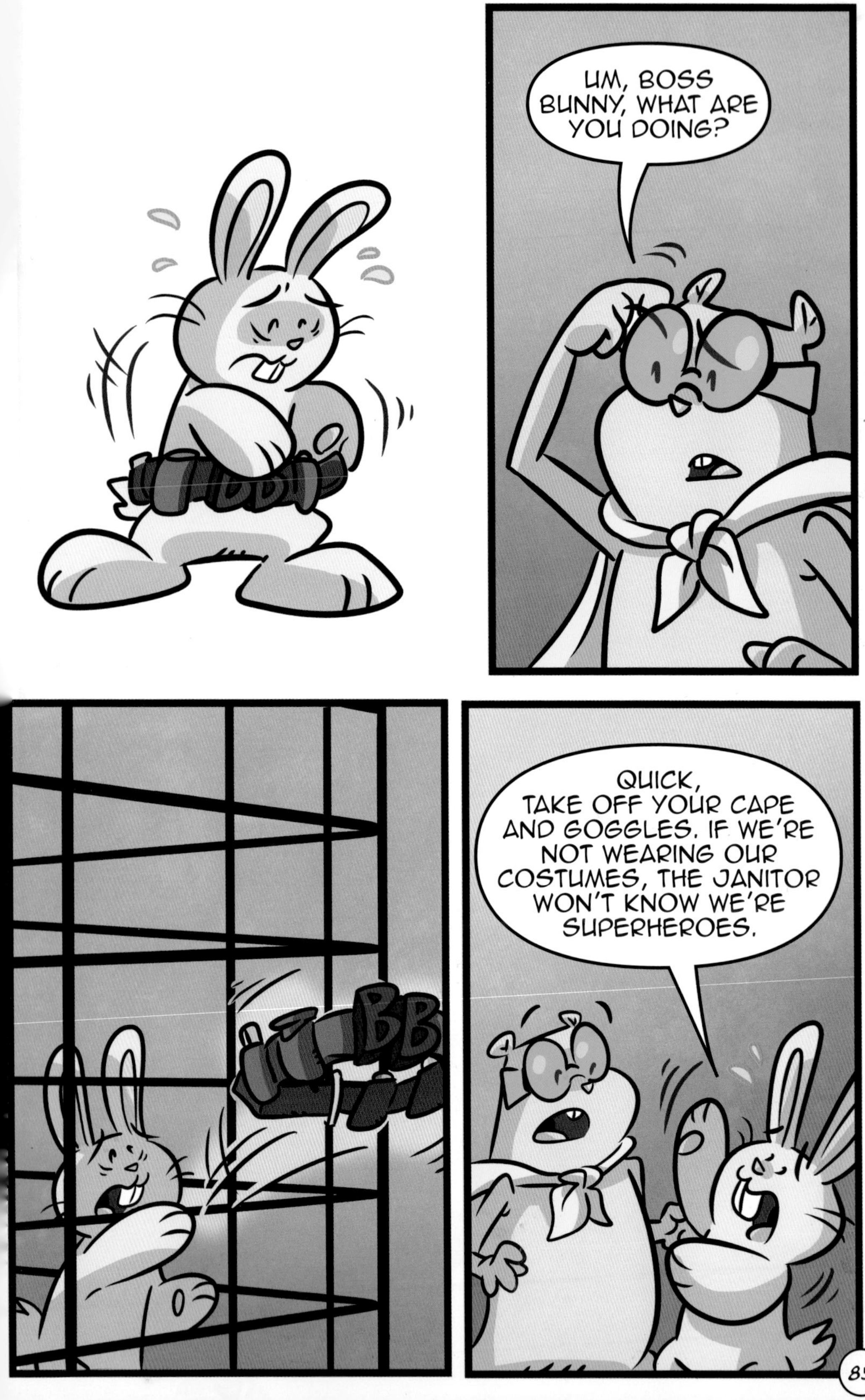
UM, BOSS BUNNY, WHAT ARE YOU DOING?
QUICK, TAKE OFF YOUR CAPE AND GOGGLES. IF WE'RE NOT WEARING OUR COSTUMES, THE JANITOR WON'T KNOW WE'RE SUPERHEROES.

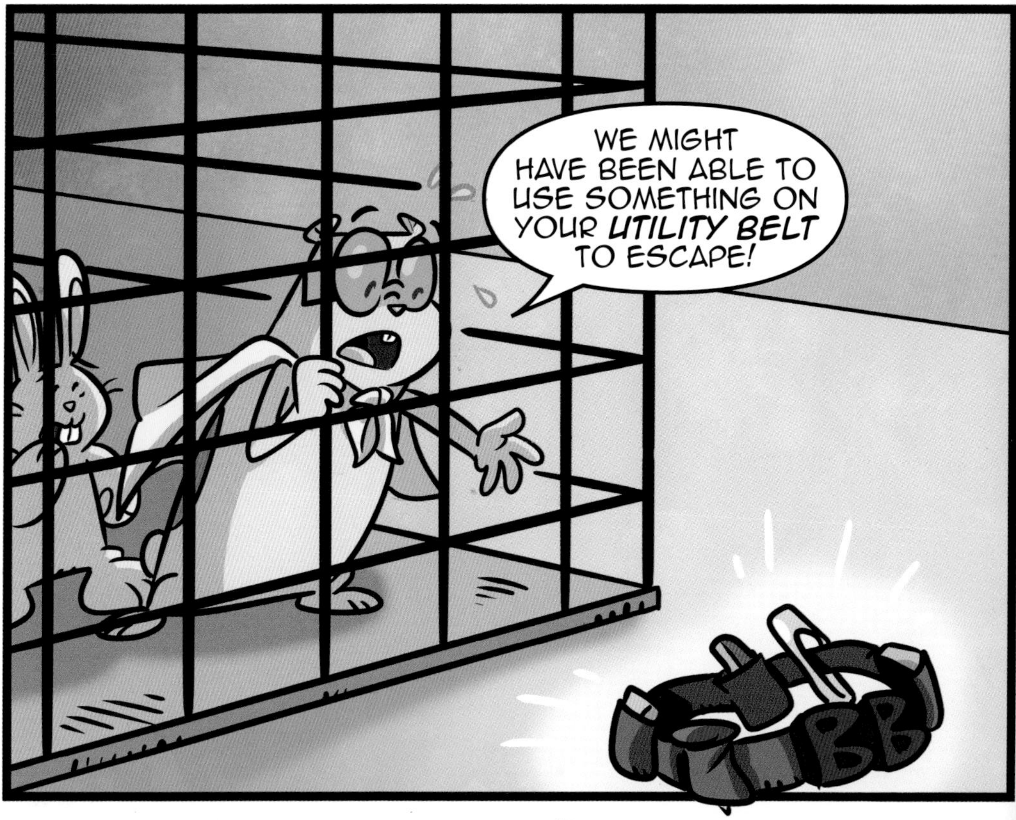
WE MIGHT HAVE BEEN ABLE TO USE SOMETHING ON YOUR *UTILITY BELT* TO ESCAPE!
BB

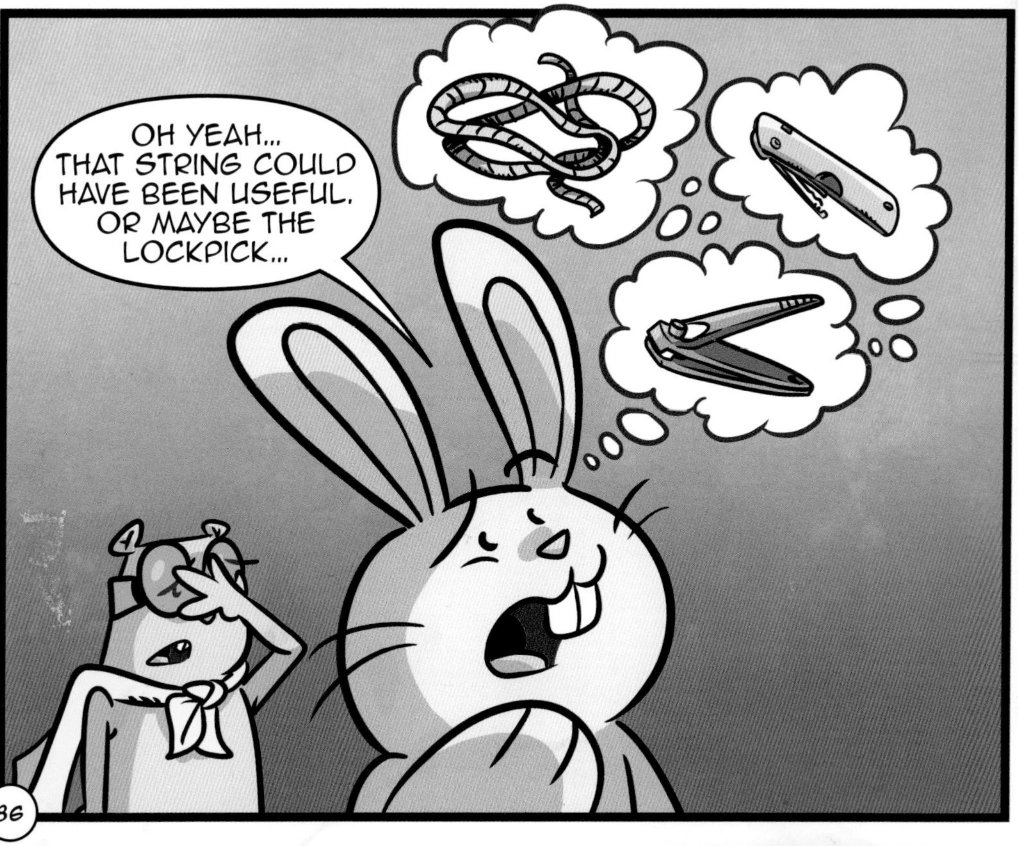
OH YEAH... THAT STRING COULD HAVE BEEN USEFUL. OR MAYBE THE LOCKPICK...

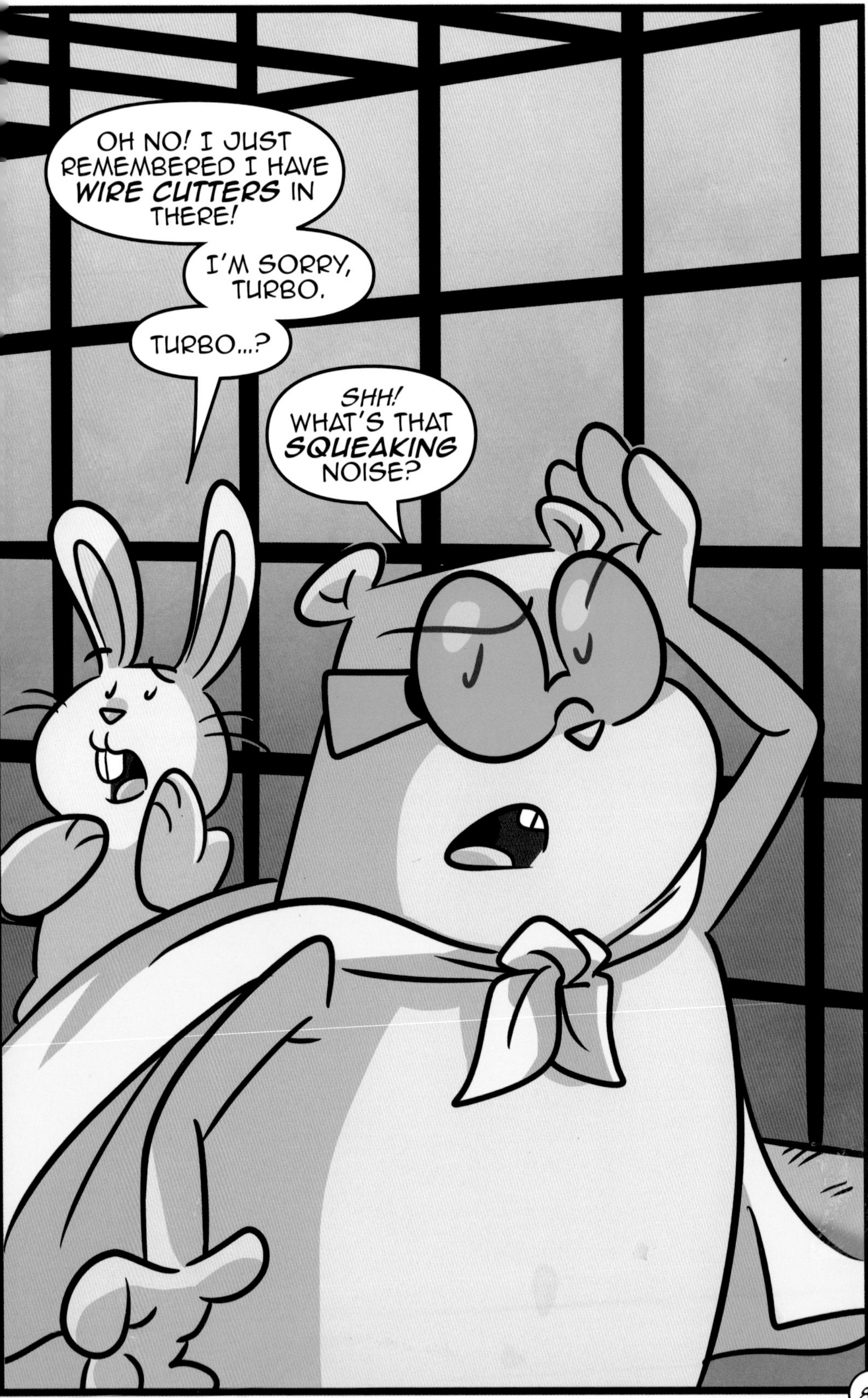
OH NO! I JUST REMEMBERED I HAVE *WIRE CUTTERS* IN THERE!
I'M SORRY, TURBO.
TURBO...?
SHH! WHAT'S THAT *SQUEAKING* NOISE?

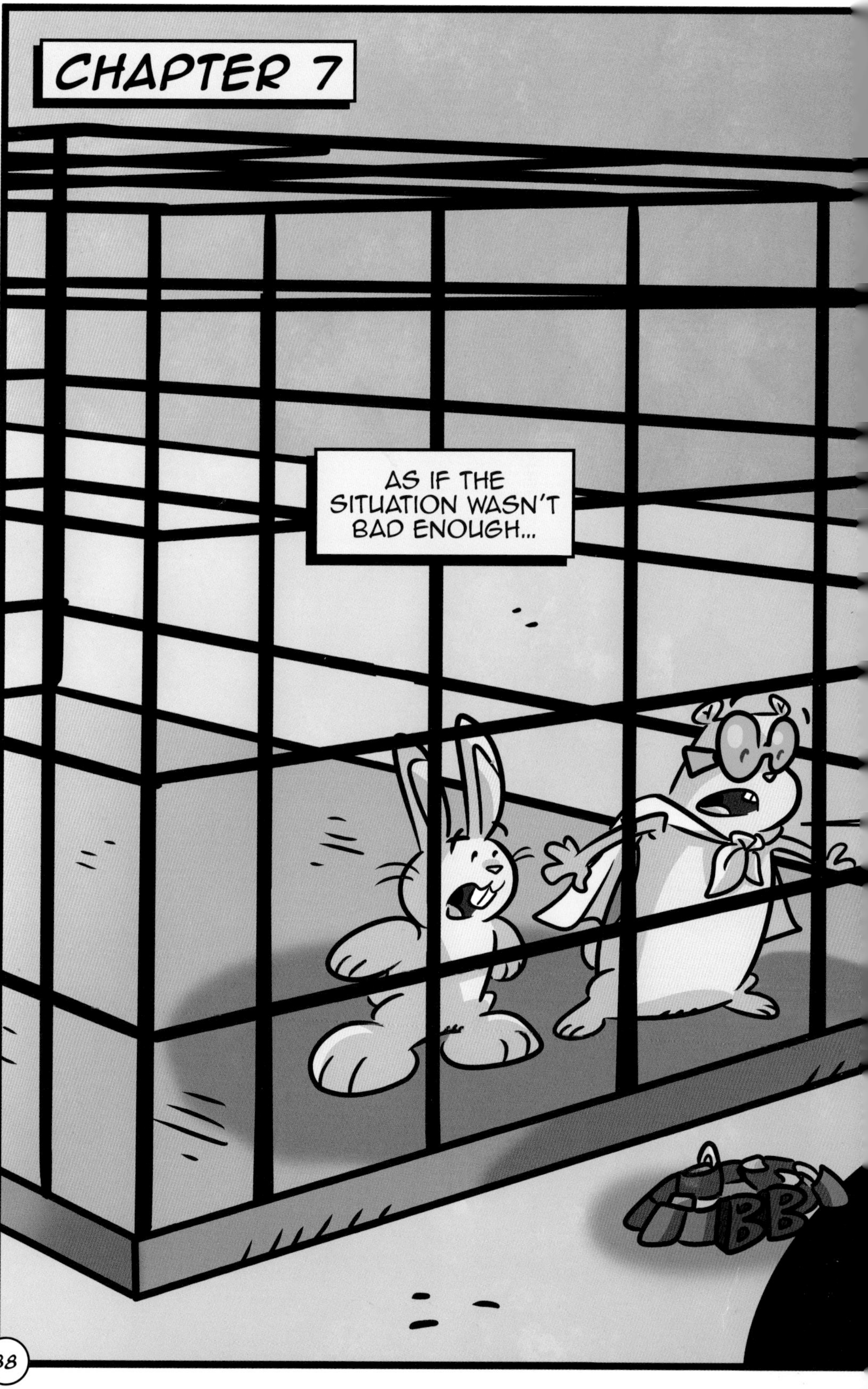
CHAPTER 7
AS IF THE SITUATION WASN'T BAD ENOUGH...
BB

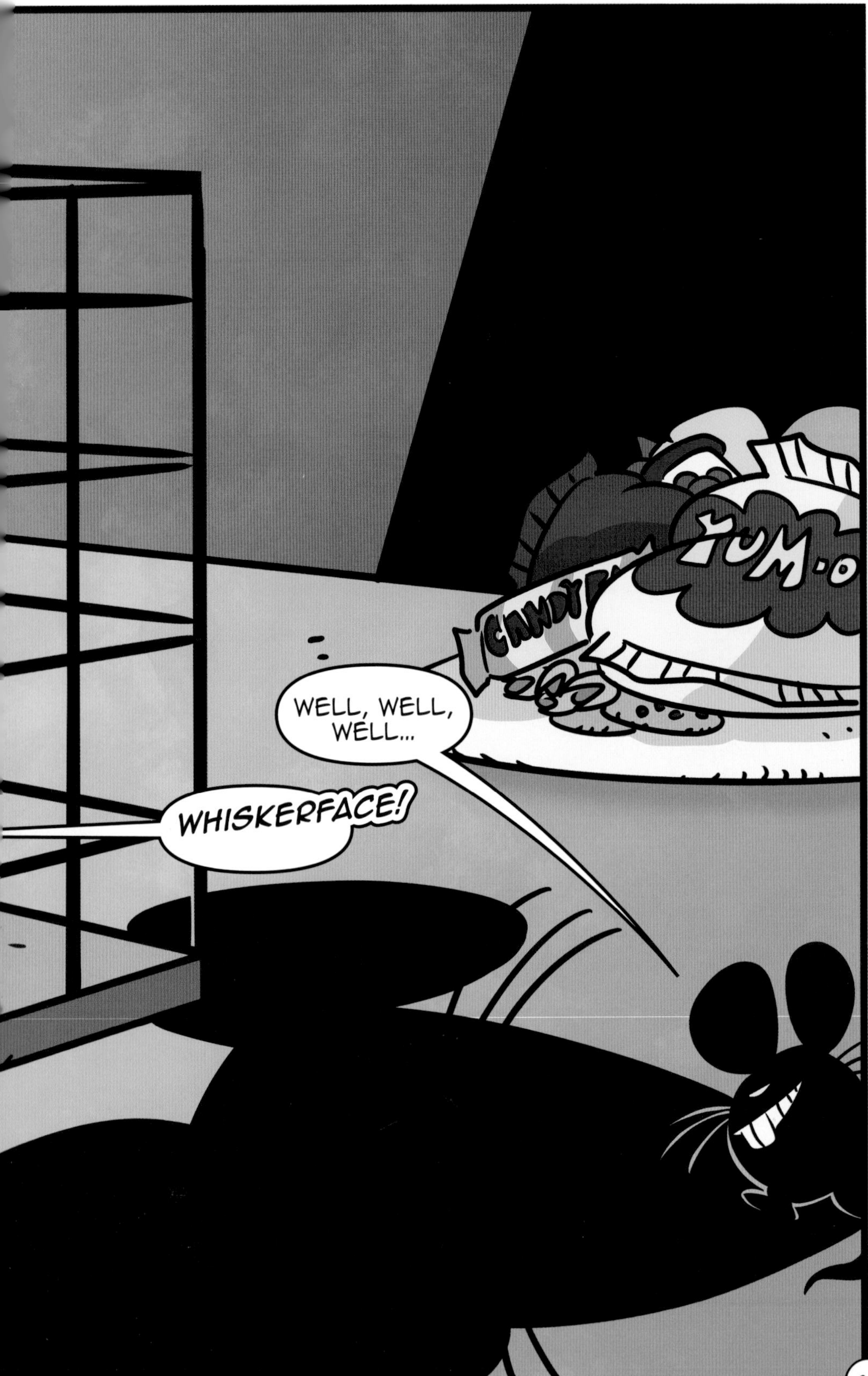
WELL, WELL, WELL...
WHISKERFACE!

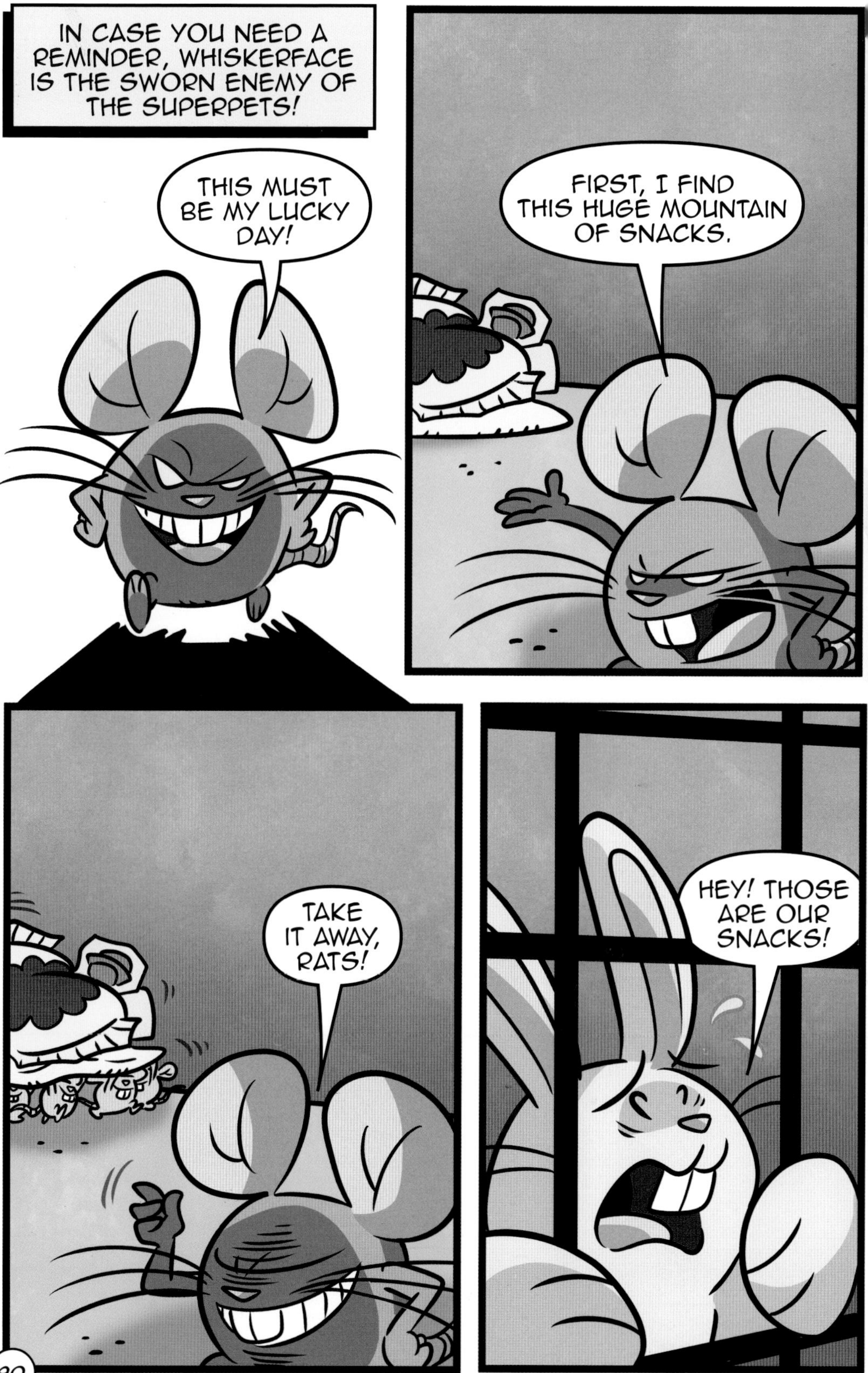
IN CASE YOU NEED A REMINDER, WHISKERFACE IS THE SWORN ENEMY OF THE SUPERPETS!
THIS MUST BE MY LUCKY DAY!
FIRST, I FIND THIS HUGE MOUNTAIN OF SNACKS.
TAKE IT AWAY, RATS!
HEY! THOSE ARE OUR SNACKS!

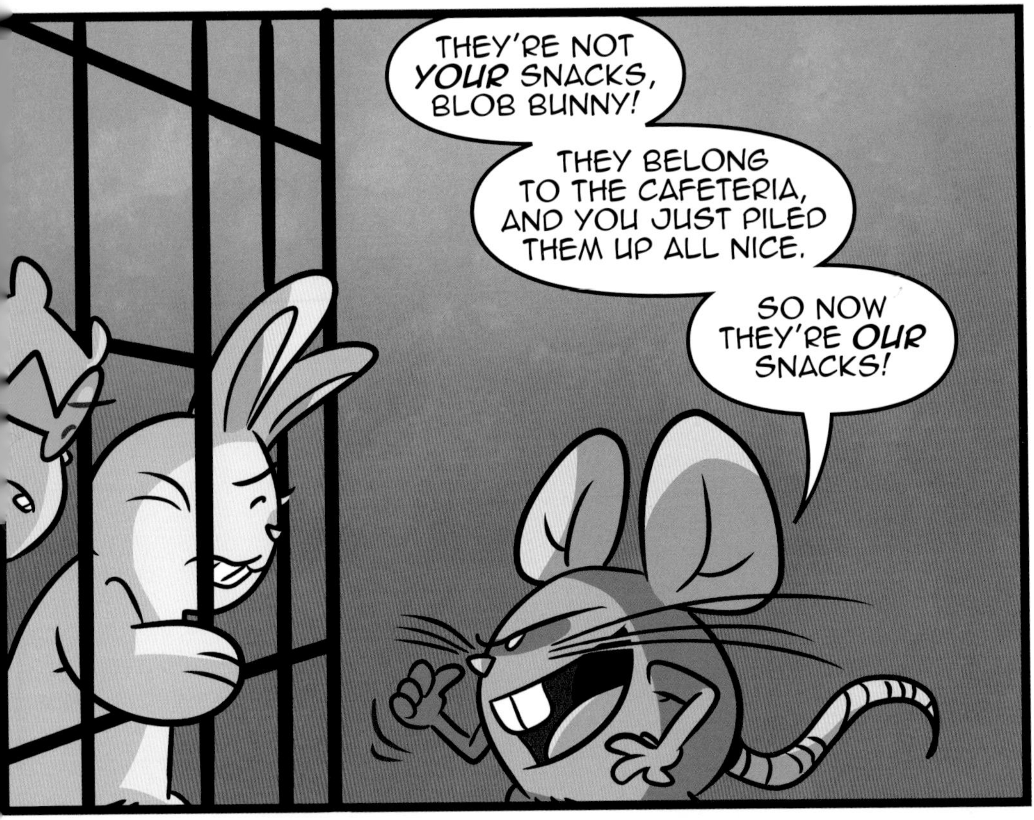
THEY'RE NOT YOUR SNACKS, BLOB BUNNY!
THEY BELONG TO THE CAFETERIA, AND YOU JUST PILED THEM UP ALL NICE.
SO NOW THEY'RE OUR SNACKS!

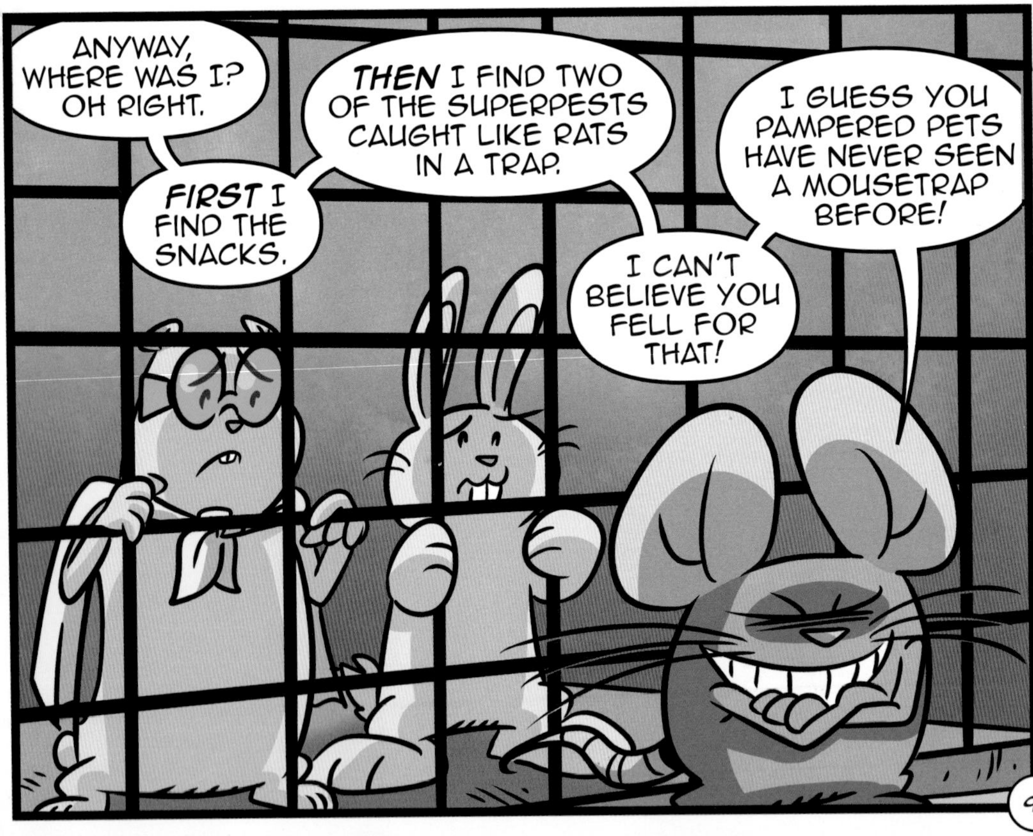
ANYWAY, WHERE WAS I? OH RIGHT.
FIRST I FIND THE SNACKS.
THEN I FIND TWO OF THE SUPERPESTS CAUGHT LIKE RATS IN A TRAP.
I CAN'T BELIEVE YOU FELL FOR THAT!
I GUESS YOU PAMPERED PETS HAVE NEVER SEEN A MOUSETRAP BEFORE!

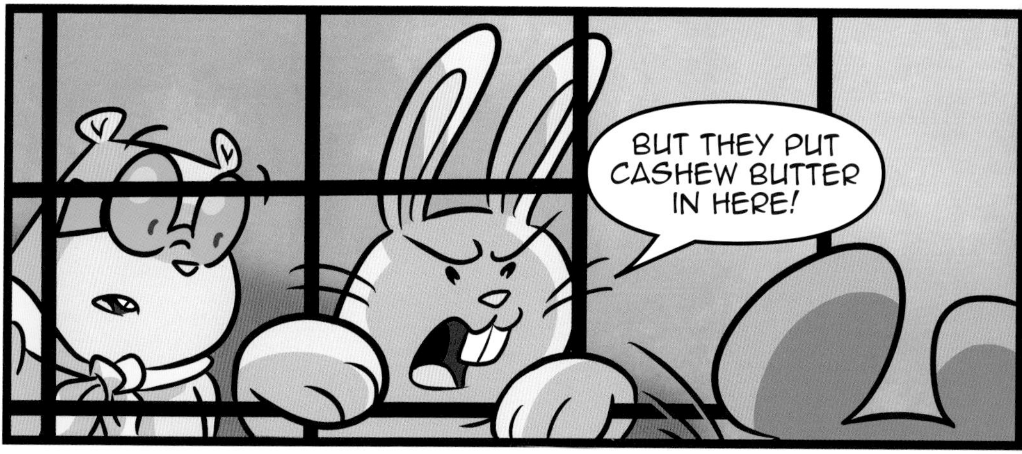
BUT THEY PUT CASHEW BUTTER IN HERE!

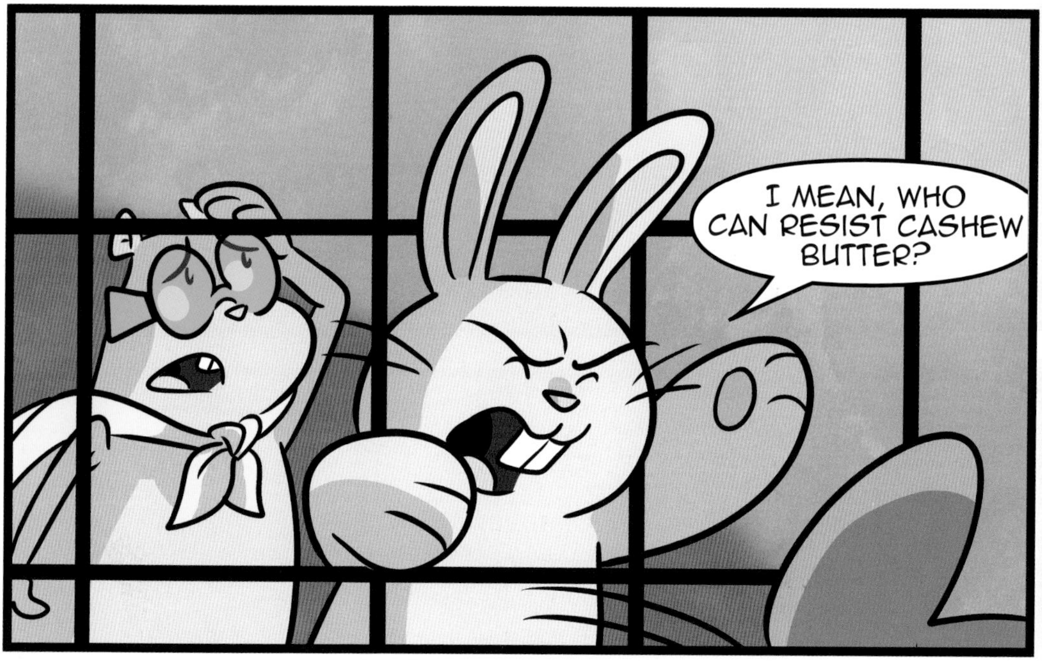
I MEAN, WHO CAN RESIST CASHEW BUTTER?

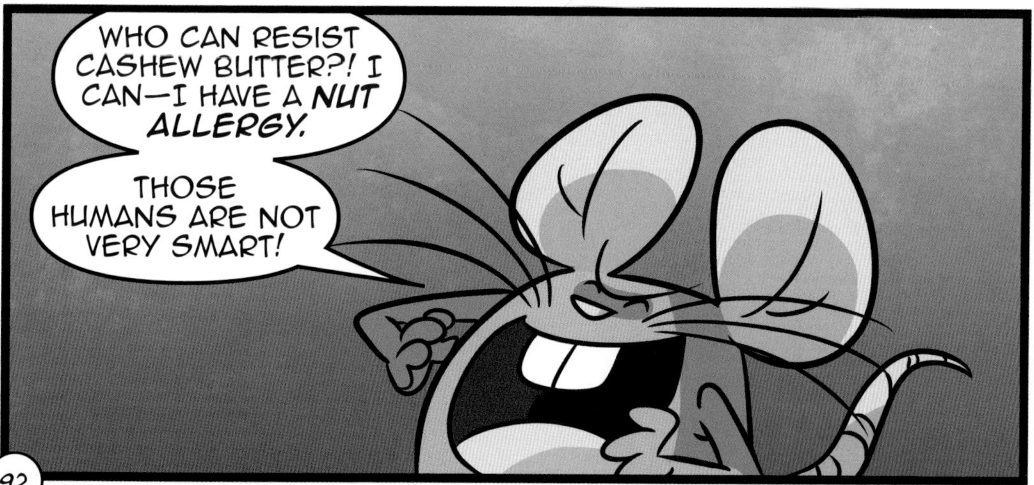
WHO CAN RESIST CASHEW BUTTER?! I CAN—I HAVE A NUT ALLERGY.
THOSE HUMANS ARE NOT VERY SMART!

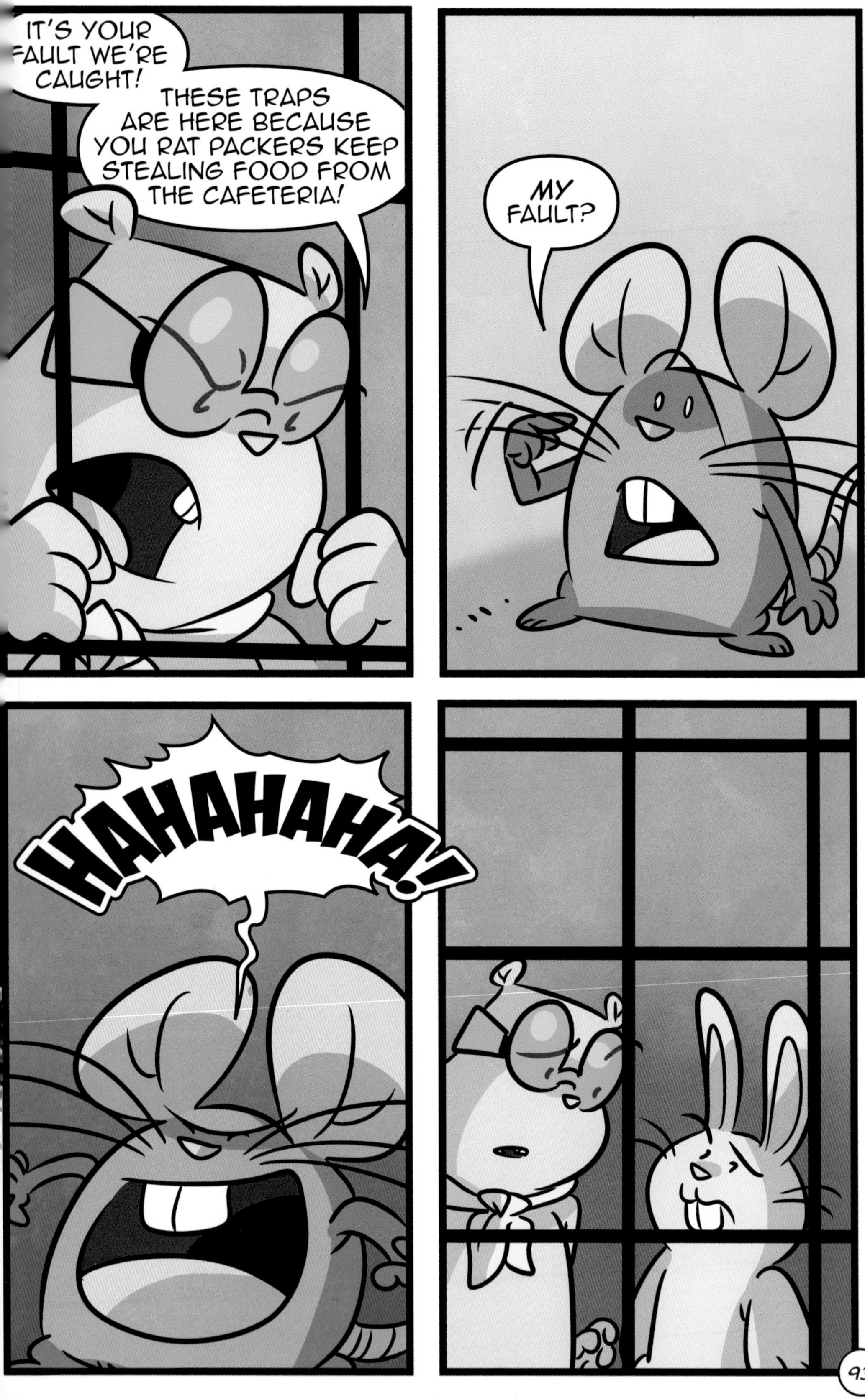
IT'S YOUR FAULT WE'RE CAUGHT!
THESE TRAPS ARE HERE BECAUSE YOU RAT PACKERS KEEP STEALING FOOD FROM THE CAFETERIA!
MY FAULT?
HAHAHAHA!

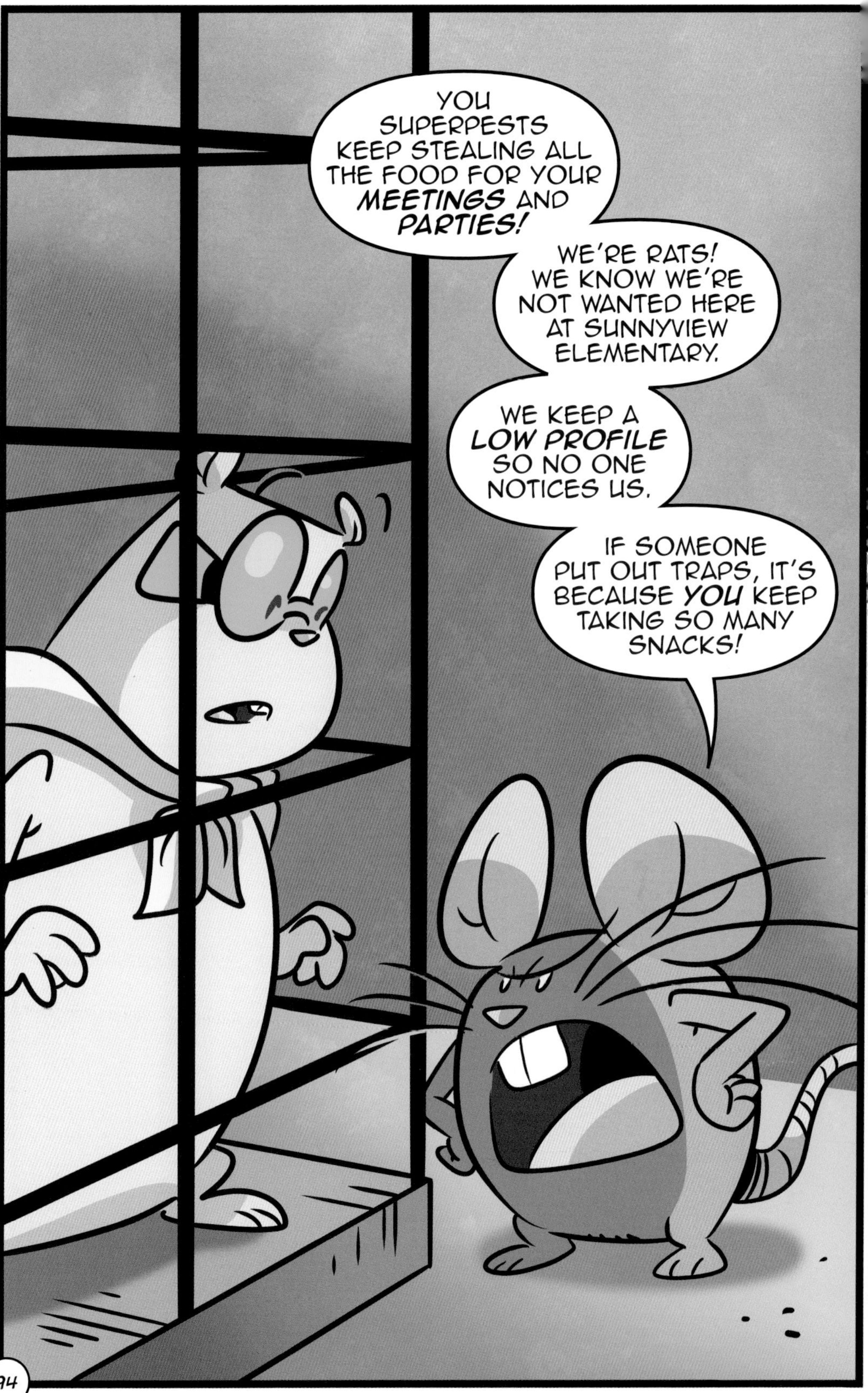
YOU SUPERPESTS KEEP STEALING ALL THE FOOD FOR YOUR MEETINGS AND PARTIES!
WE'RE RATS! WE KNOW WE'RE NOT WANTED HERE AT SUNNYVIEW ELEMENTARY.
WE KEEP A LOW PROFILE SO NO ONE NOTICES US.
IF SOMEONE PUT OUT TRAPS, IT'S BECAUSE YOU KEEP TAKING SO MANY SNACKS!

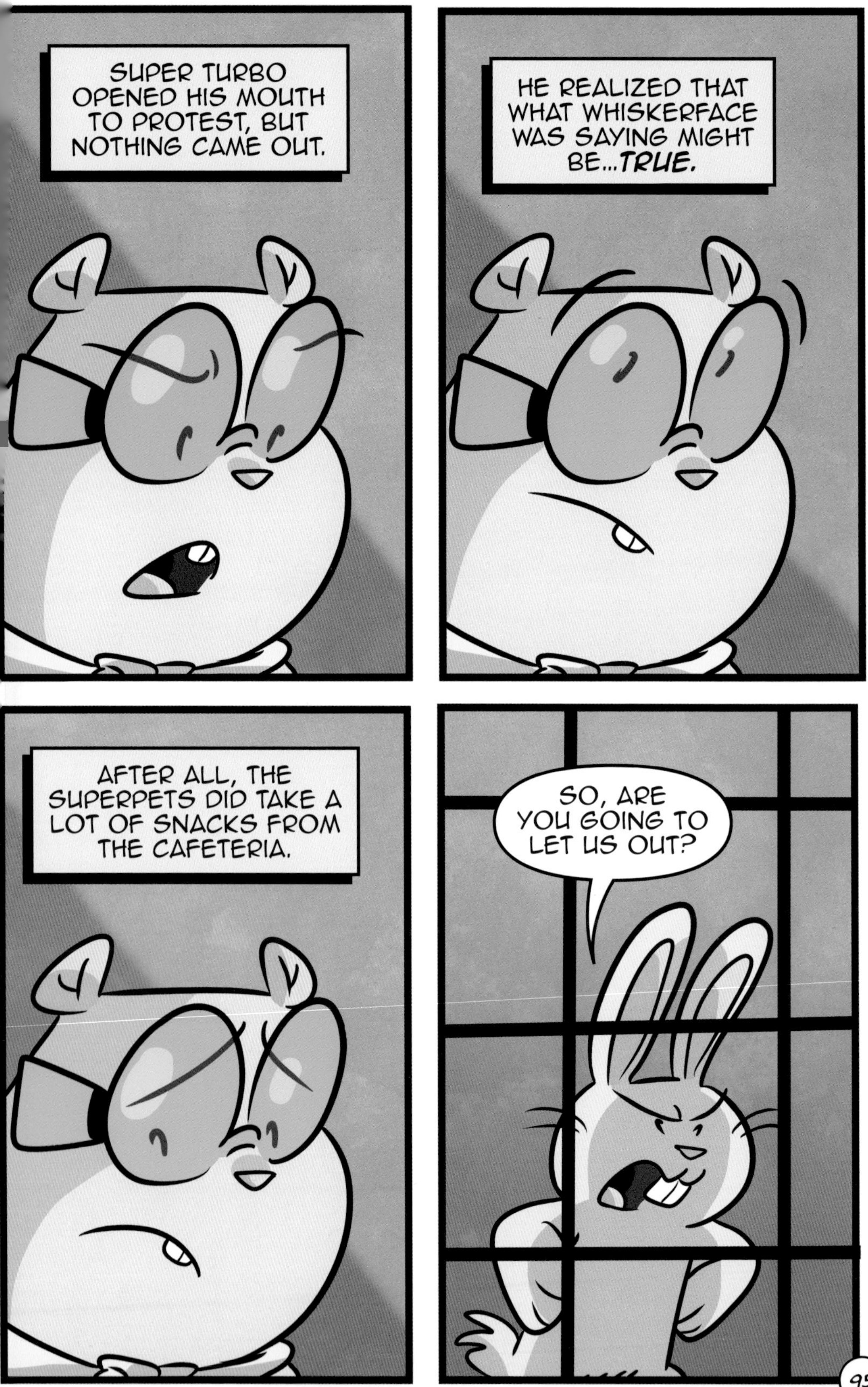
SUPER TURBO OPENED HIS MOUTH TO PROTEST, BUT NOTHING CAME OUT.
HE REALIZED THAT WHAT WHISKERFACE WAS SAYING MIGHT BE...TRUE.
AFTER ALL, THE SUPERPETS DID TAKE A LOT OF SNACKS FROM THE CAFETERIA.
SO, ARE YOU GOING TO LET US OUT?

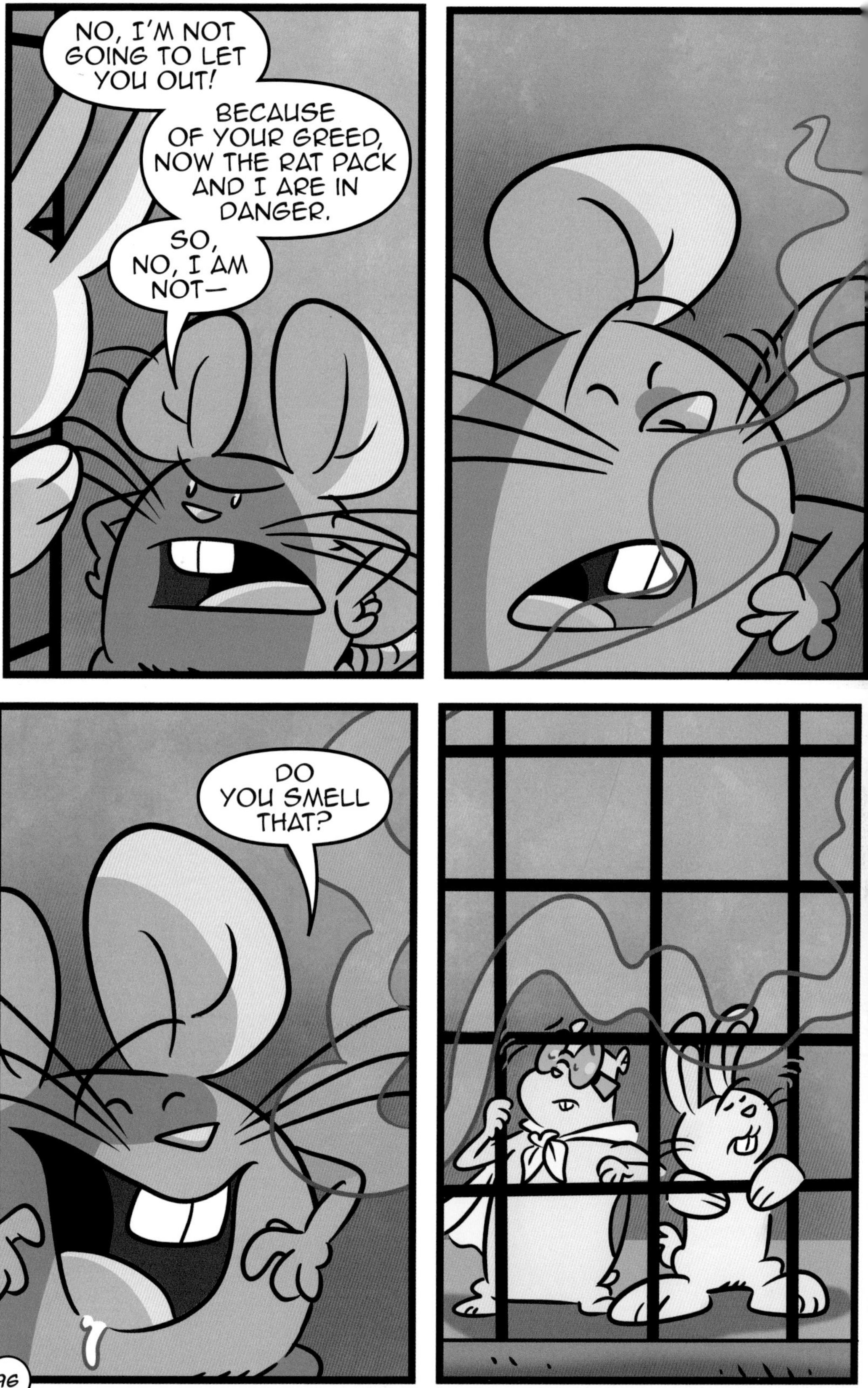
NO, I'M NOT GOING TO LET YOU OUT!
BECAUSE OF YOUR GREED, NOW THE RAT PACK AND I ARE IN DANGER.
SO, NO, I AM NOT—
DO YOU SMELL THAT?

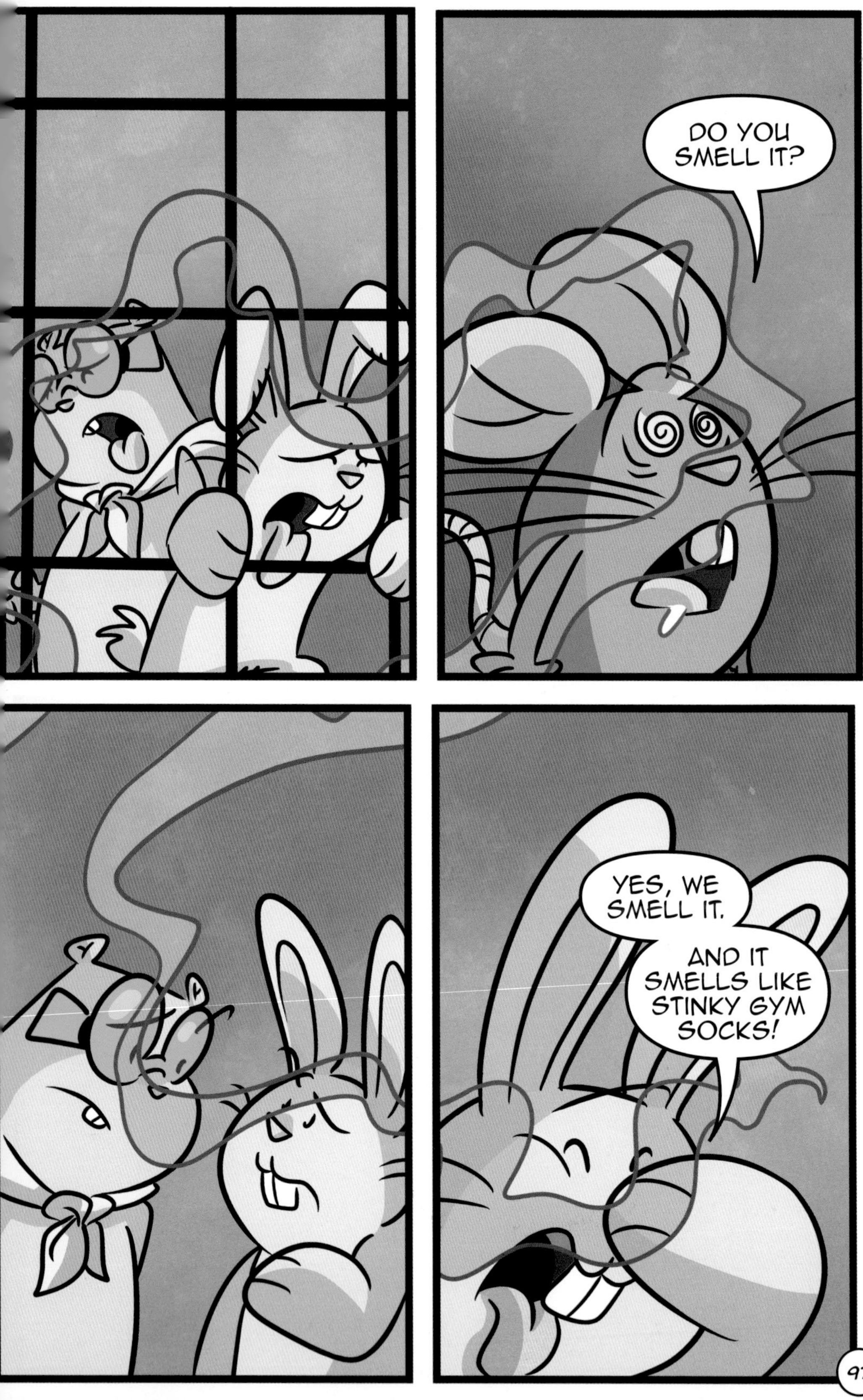
DO YOU SMELL IT?
YES, WE SMELL IT.
AND IT SMELLS LIKE STINKY GYM SOCKS!

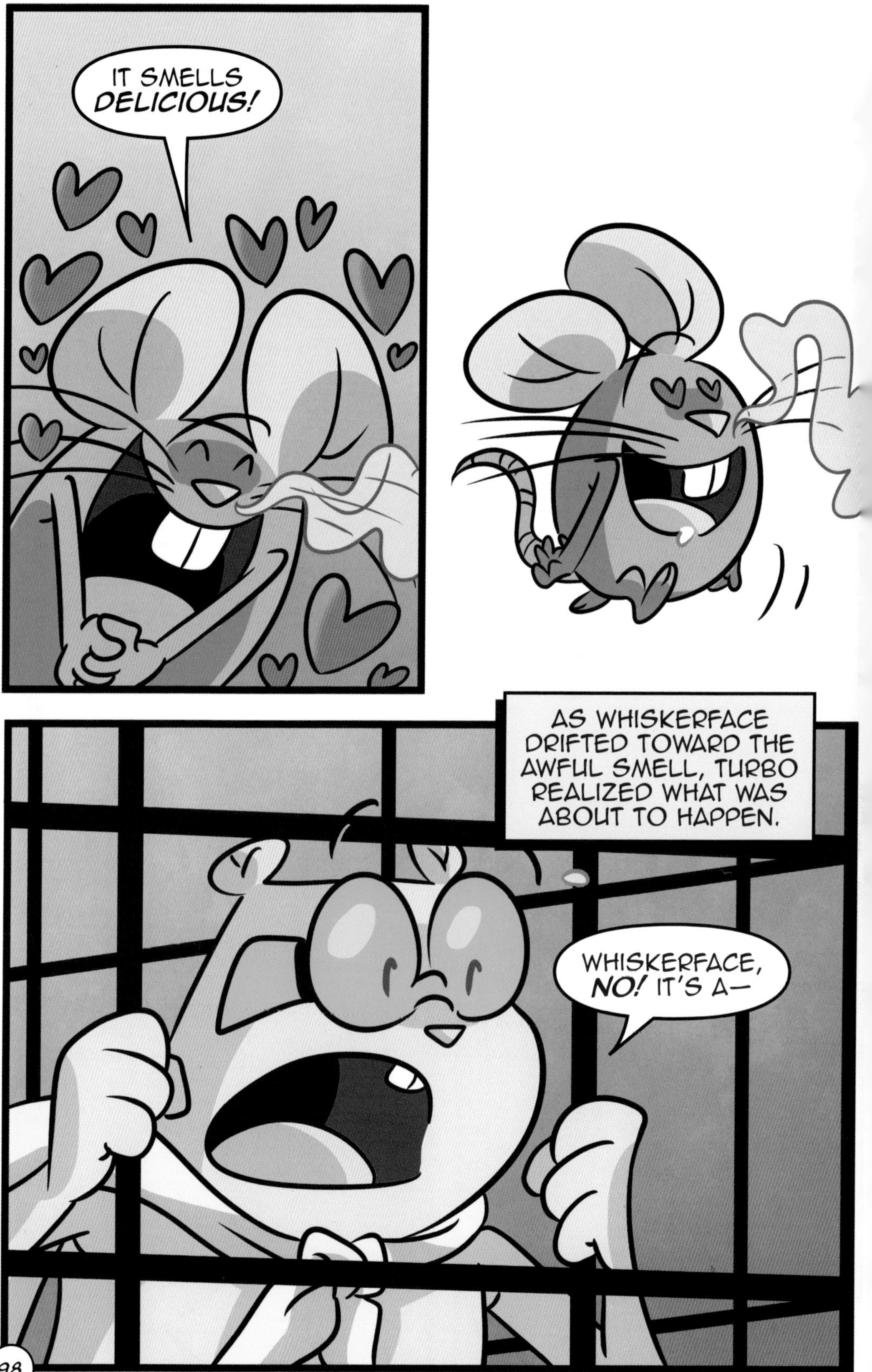
IT SMELLS DELICIOUS!
AS WHISKERFACE DRIFTED TOWARD THE AWFUL SMELL, TURBO REALIZED WHAT WAS ABOUT TO HAPPEN.
WHISKERFACE, NO! IT'S A—

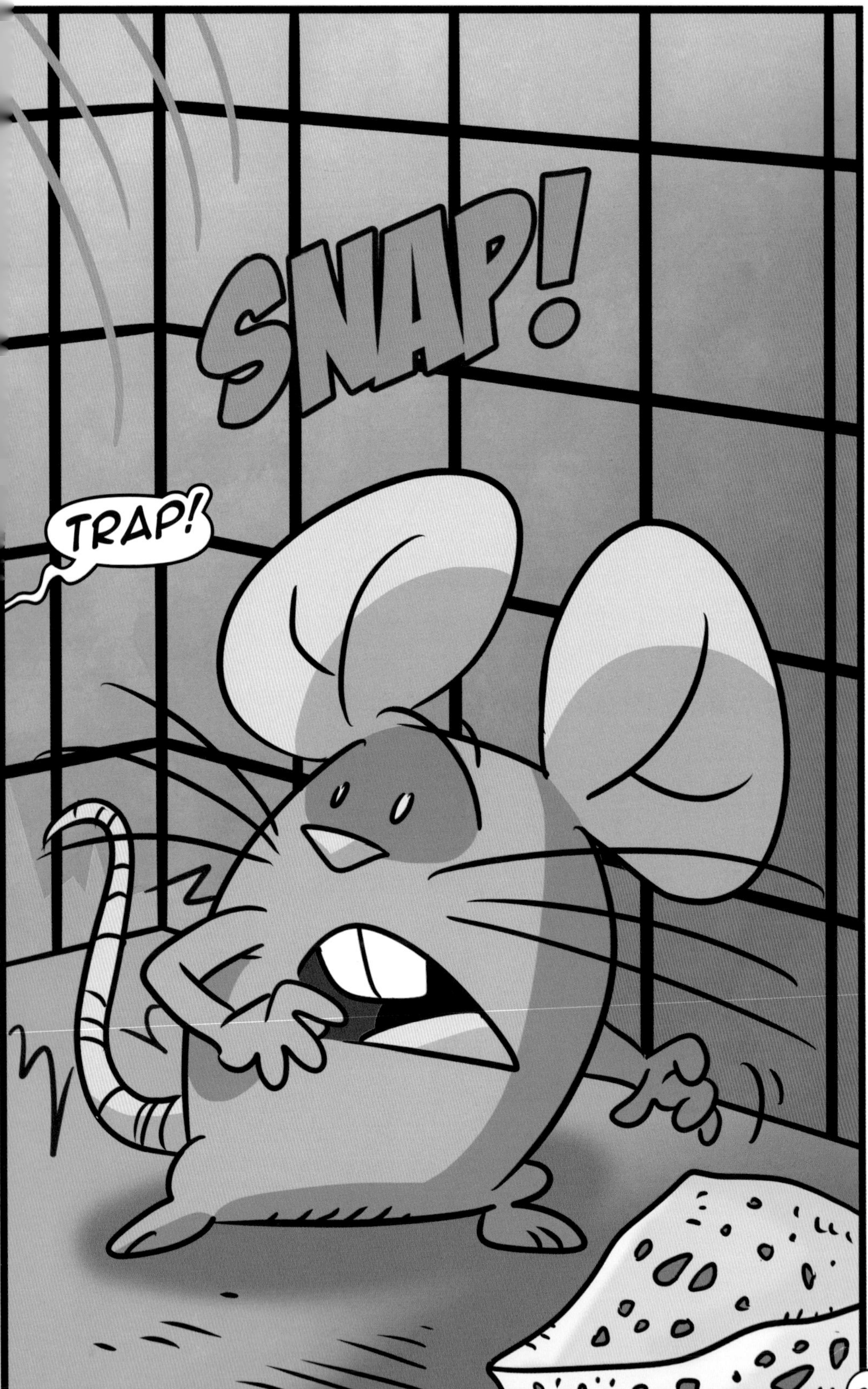
SNAP!
TRAP!

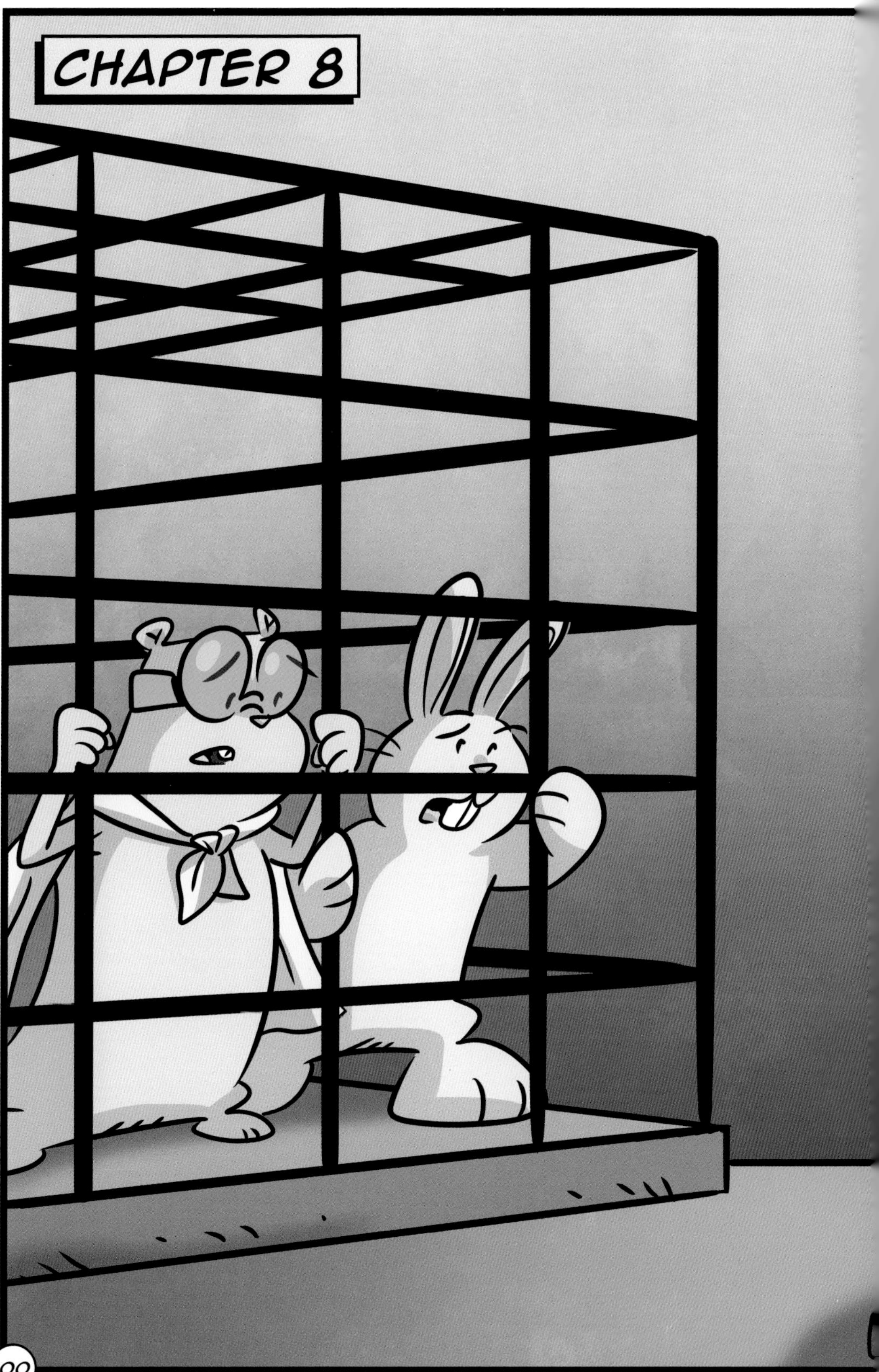
CHAPTER 8

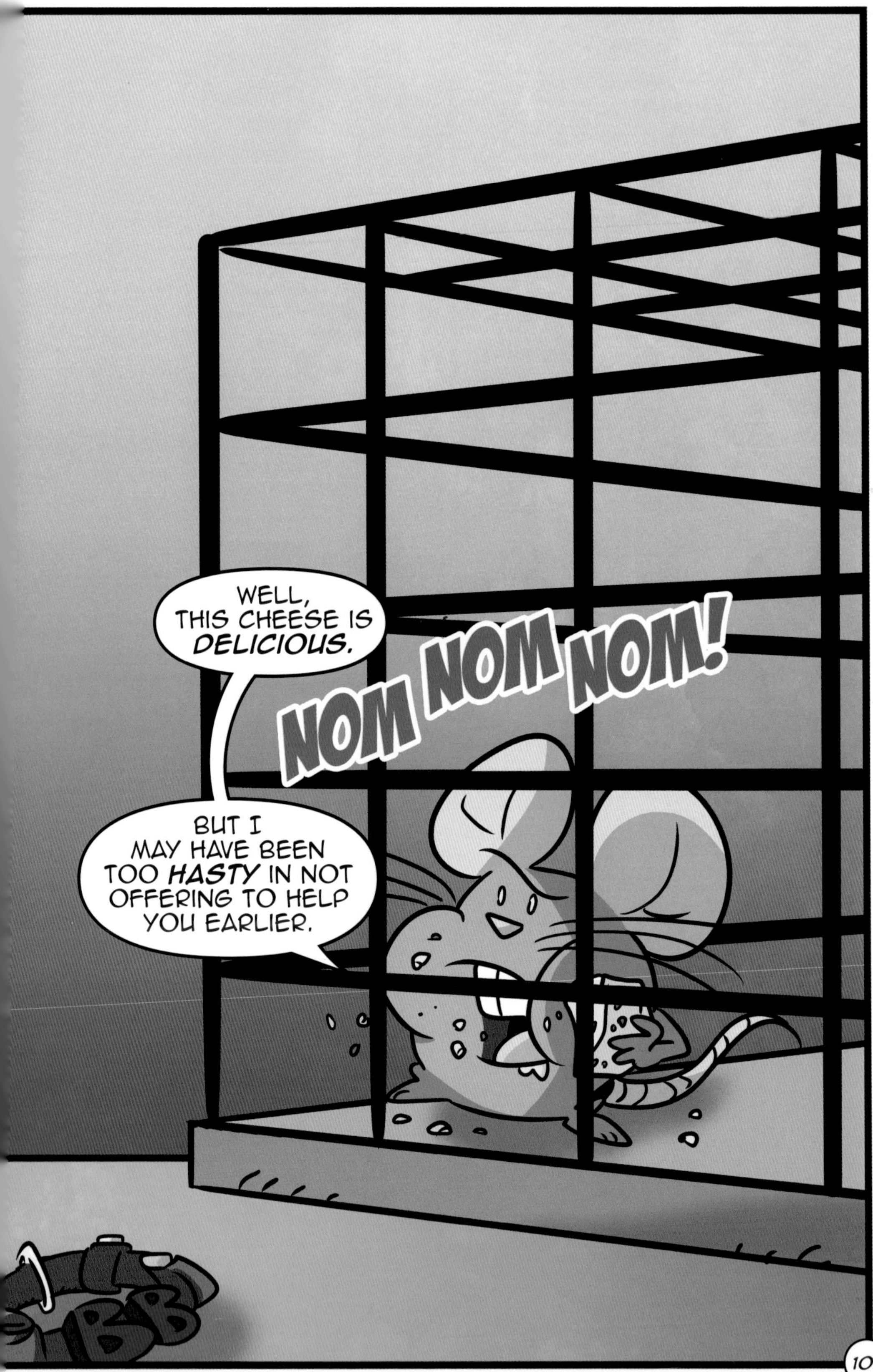
WELL, THIS CHEESE IS DELICIOUS.
NOM NOM NOM!
BUT I MAY HAVE BEEN TOO HASTY IN NOT OFFERING TO HELP YOU EARLIER.

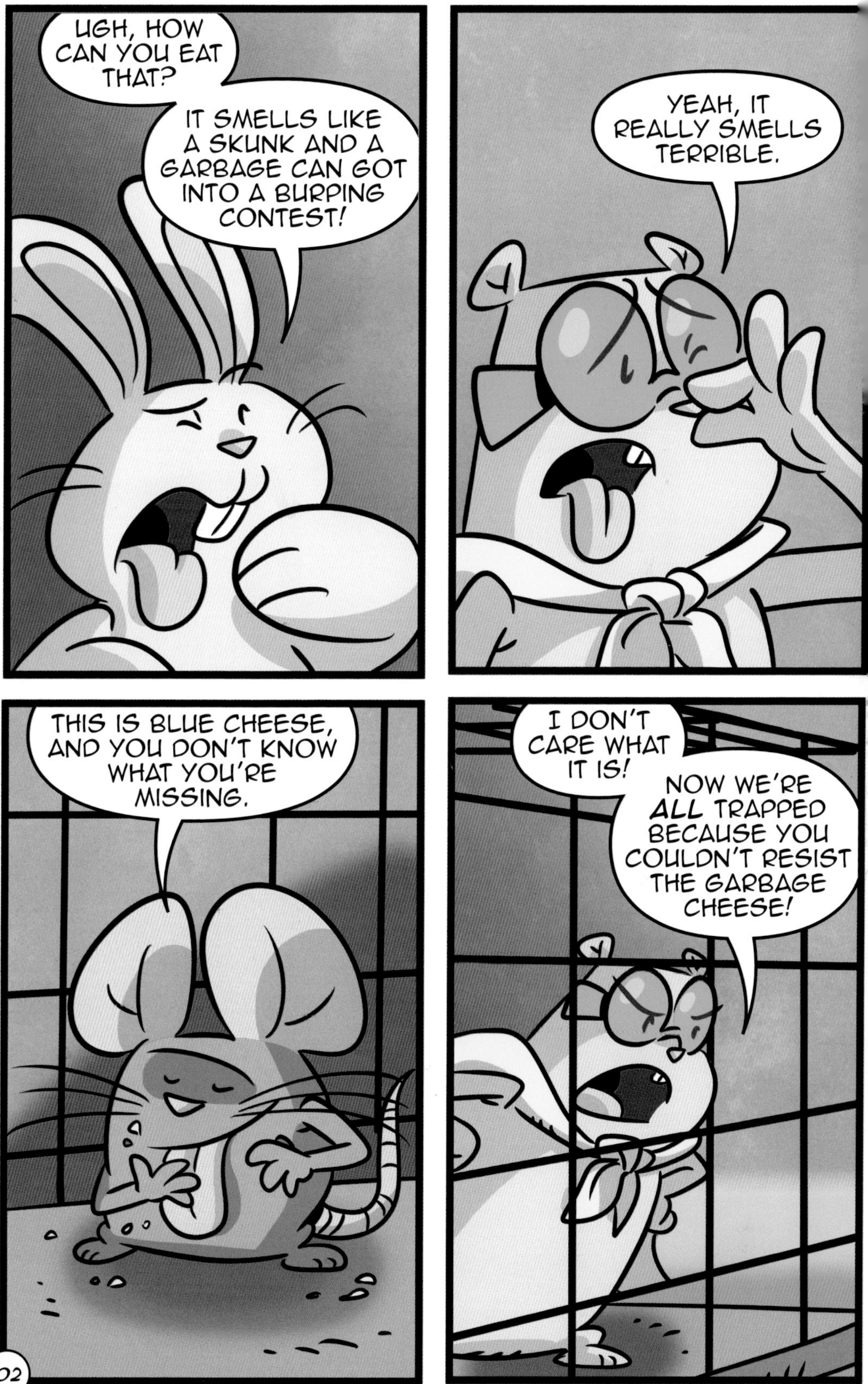
UGH, HOW CAN YOU EAT THAT?
IT SMELLS LIKE A SKUNK AND A GARBAGE CAN GOT INTO A BURPING CONTEST!
YEAH, IT REALLY SMELLS TERRIBLE.
THIS IS BLUE CHEESE, AND YOU DON'T KNOW WHAT YOU'RE MISSING.
I DON'T CARE WHAT IT IS!
NOW WE'RE ***ALL*** TRAPPED BECAUSE YOU COULDN'T RESIST THE GARBAGE CHEESE!

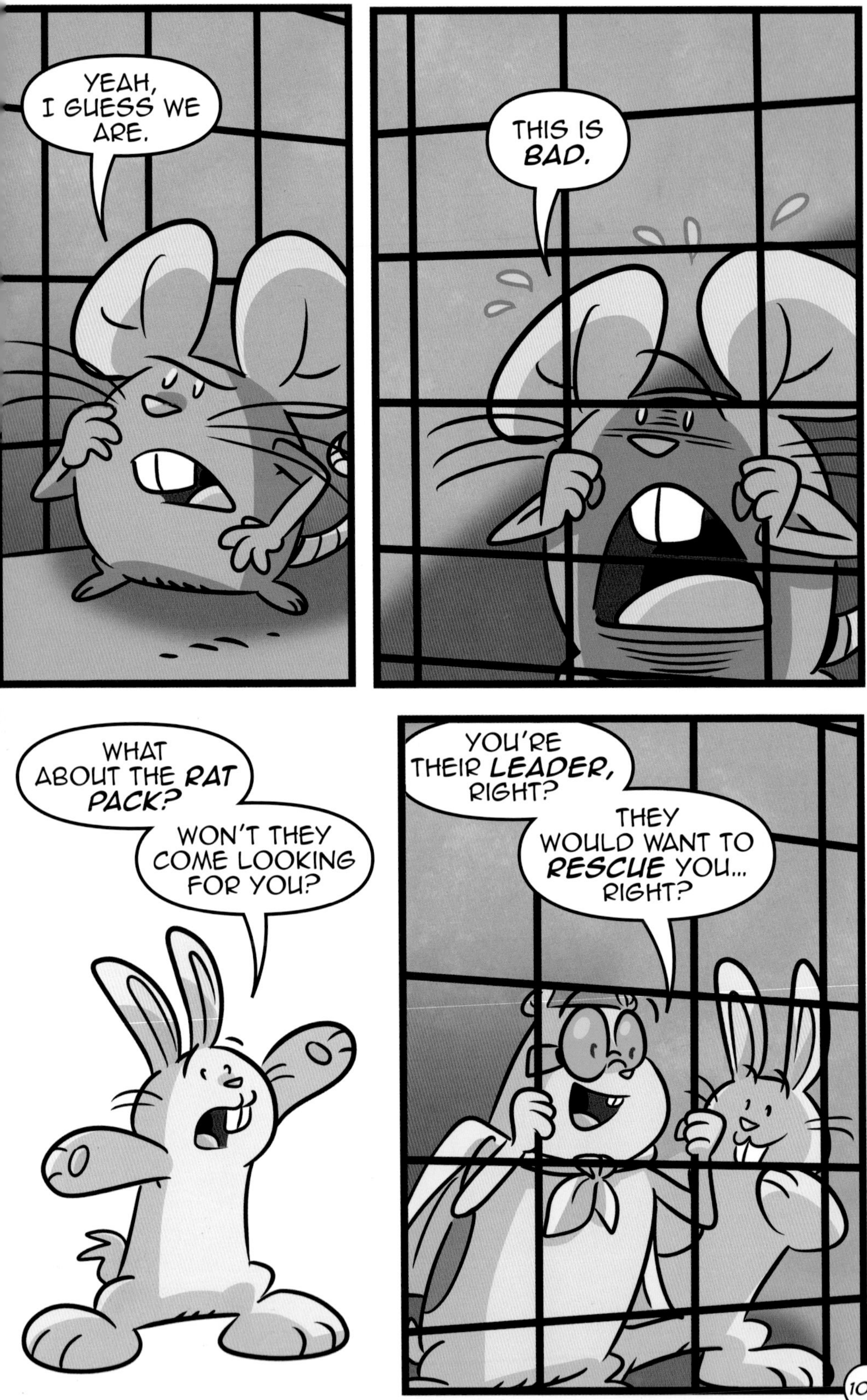
YEAH, I GUESS WE ARE.
THIS IS BAD.
WHAT ABOUT THE RAT PACK?
WON'T THEY COME LOOKING FOR YOU?
YOU'RE THEIR LEADER, RIGHT?
THEY WOULD WANT TO RESCUE YOU... RIGHT?

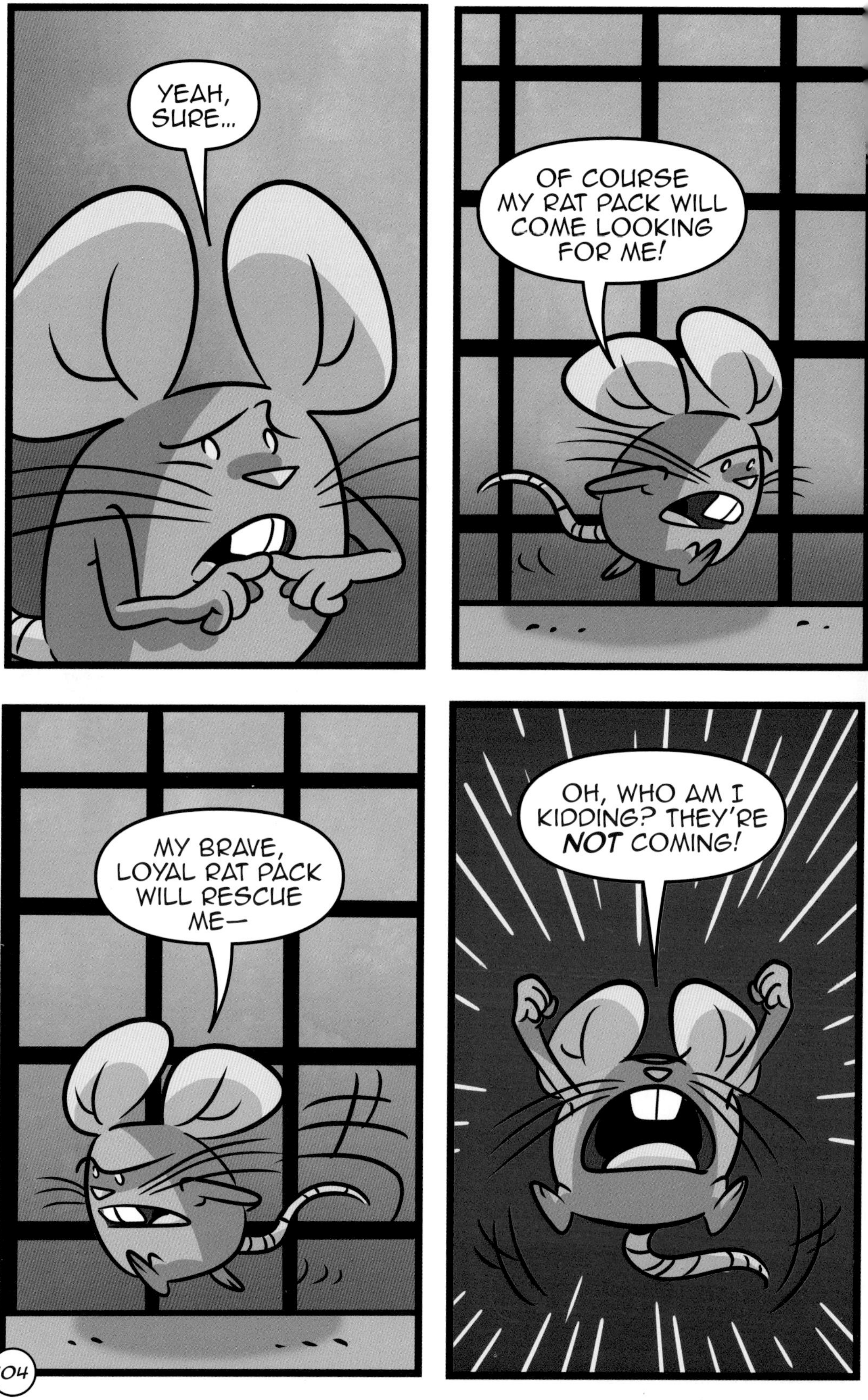
YEAH, SURE...
OF COURSE MY RAT PACK WILL COME LOOKING FOR ME!
MY BRAVE, LOYAL RAT PACK WILL RESCUE ME—
OH, WHO AM I KIDDING? THEY'RE **NOT** COMING!

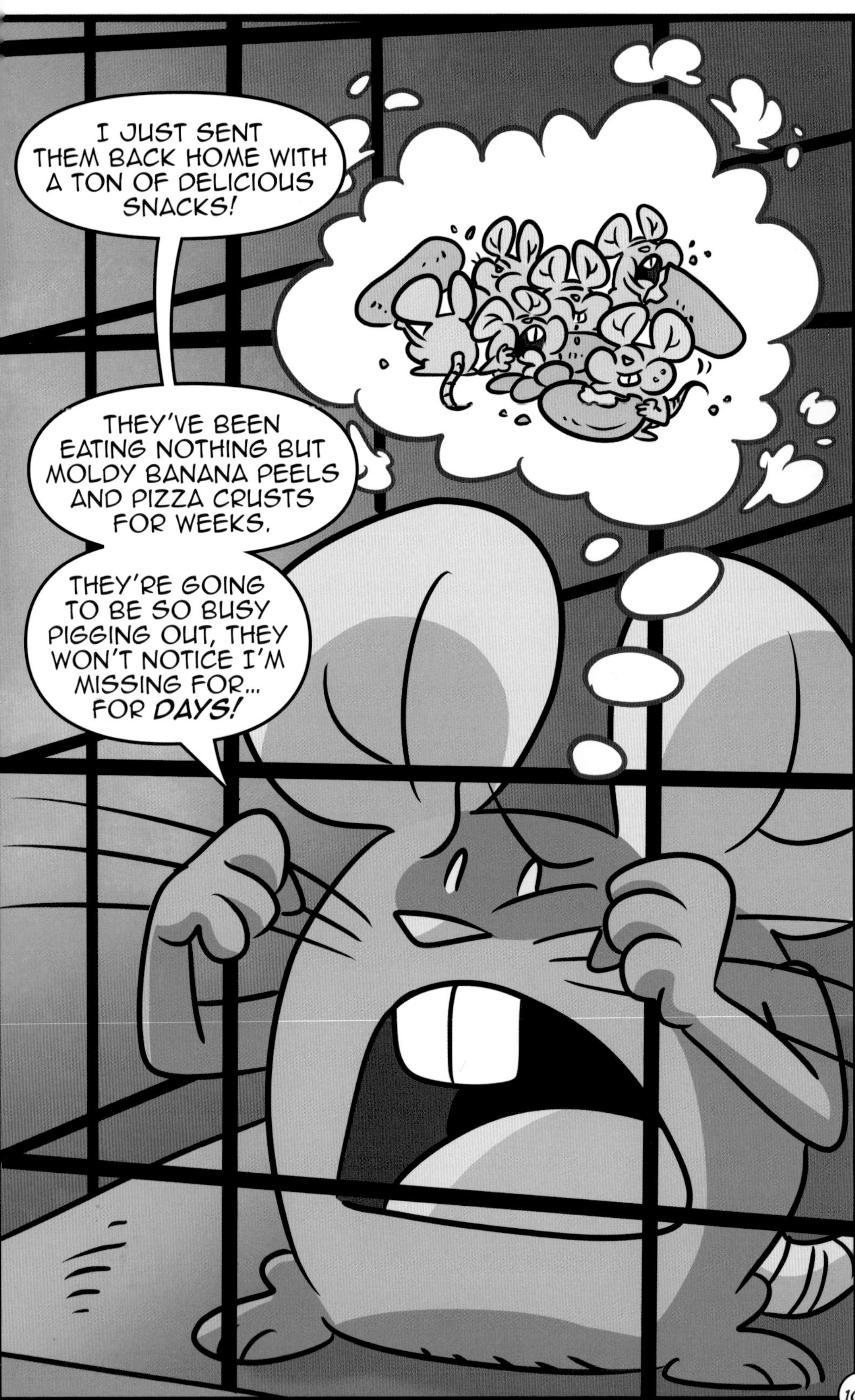
I JUST SENT THEM BACK HOME WITH A TON OF DELICIOUS SNACKS!
THEY'VE BEEN EATING NOTHING BUT MOLDY BANANA PEELS AND PIZZA CRUSTS FOR WEEKS.
THEY'RE GOING TO BE SO BUSY PIGGING OUT, THEY WON'T NOTICE I'M MISSING FOR... FOR *DAYS!*

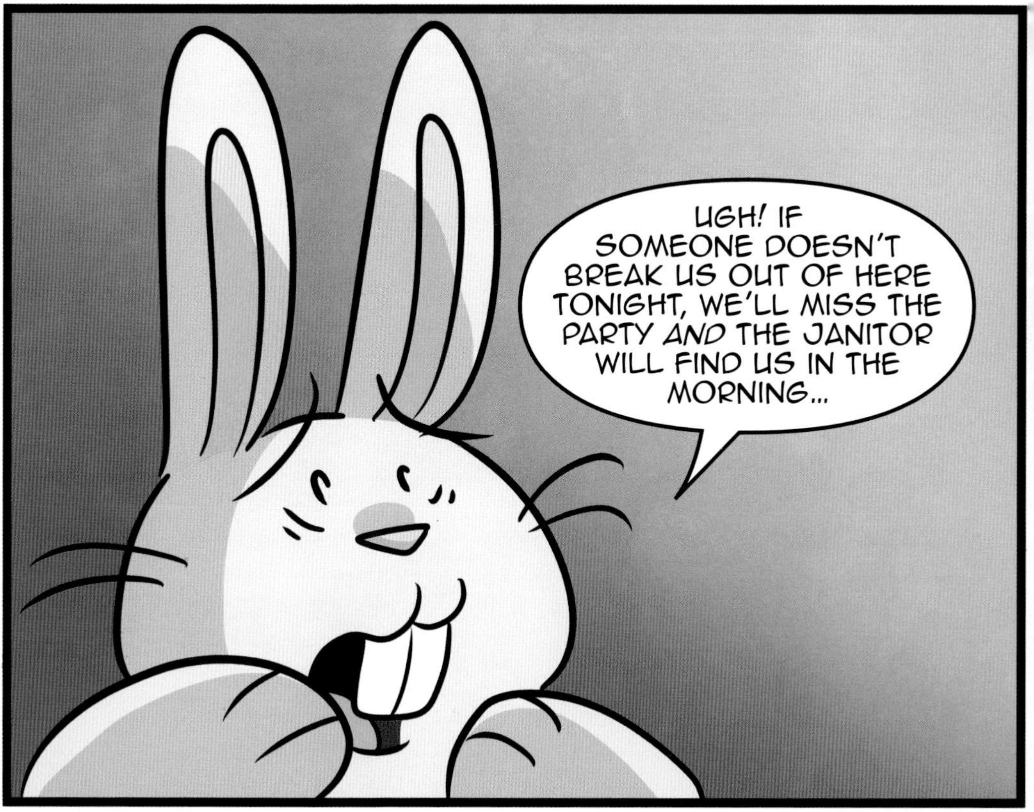
UGH! IF SOMEONE DOESN'T BREAK US OUT OF HERE TONIGHT, WE'LL MISS THE PARTY *AND* THE JANITOR WILL FIND US IN THE MORNING...

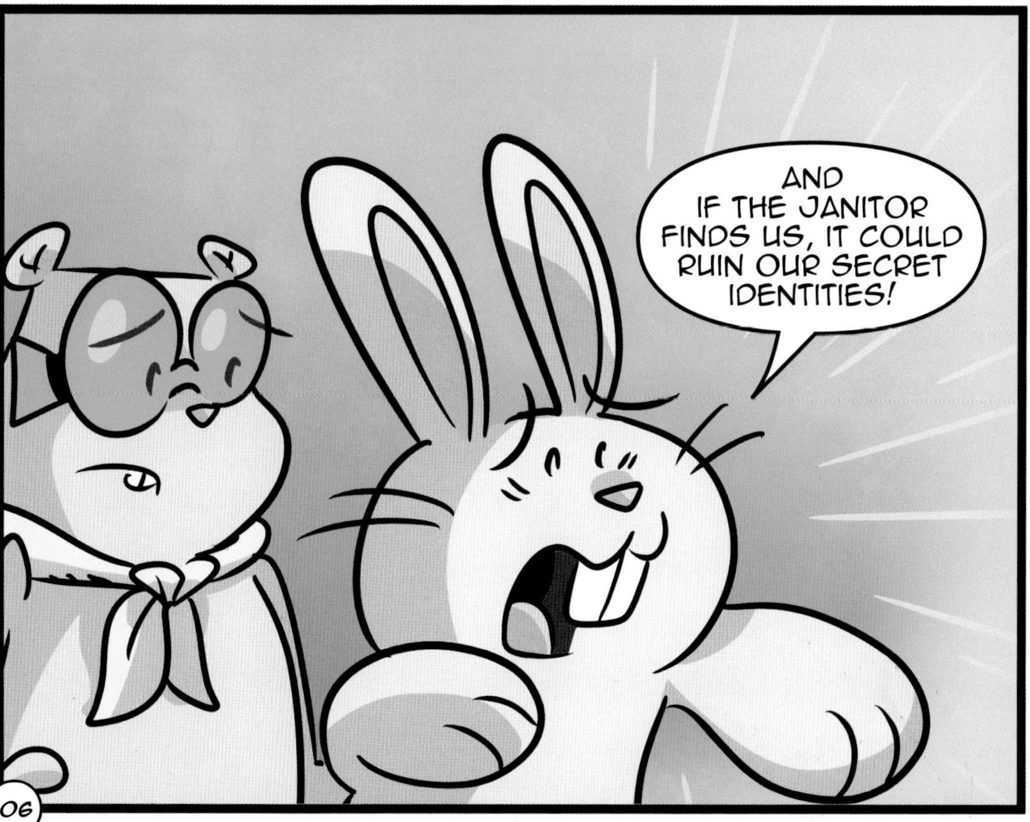
AND IF THE JANITOR FINDS US, IT COULD RUIN OUR SECRET IDENTITIES!

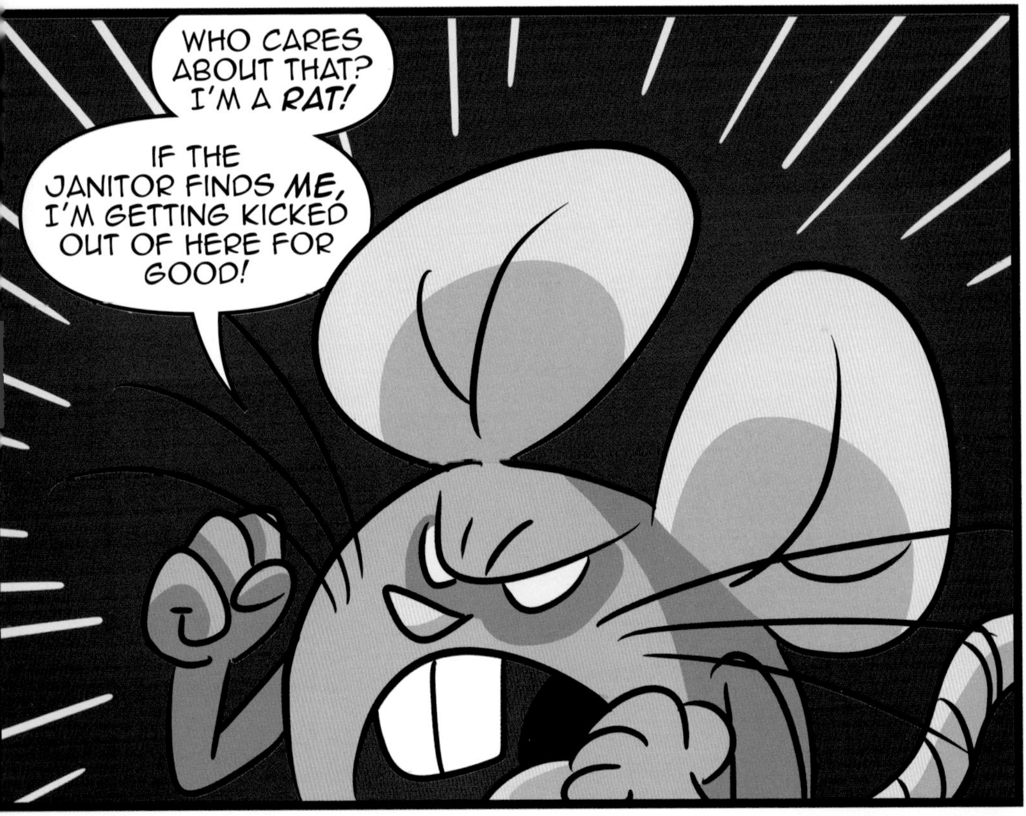
WHO CARES ABOUT THAT? I'M A *RAT!*
IF THE JANITOR FINDS *ME,* I'M GETTING KICKED OUT OF HERE FOR GOOD!

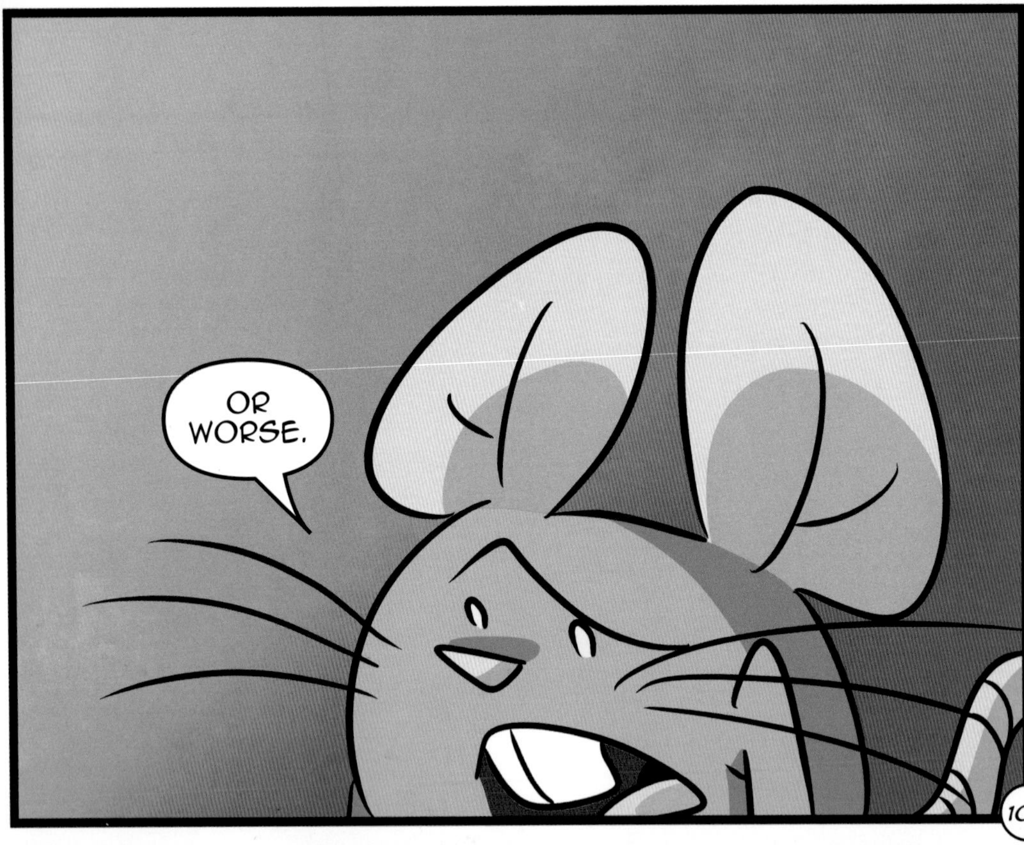
OR WORSE.

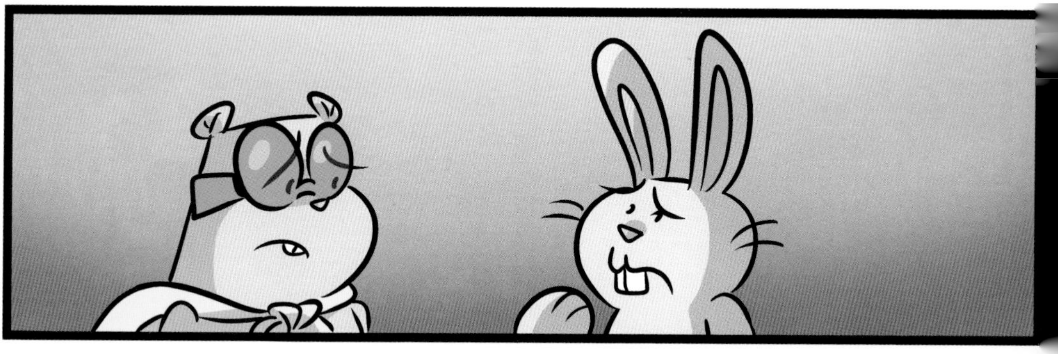

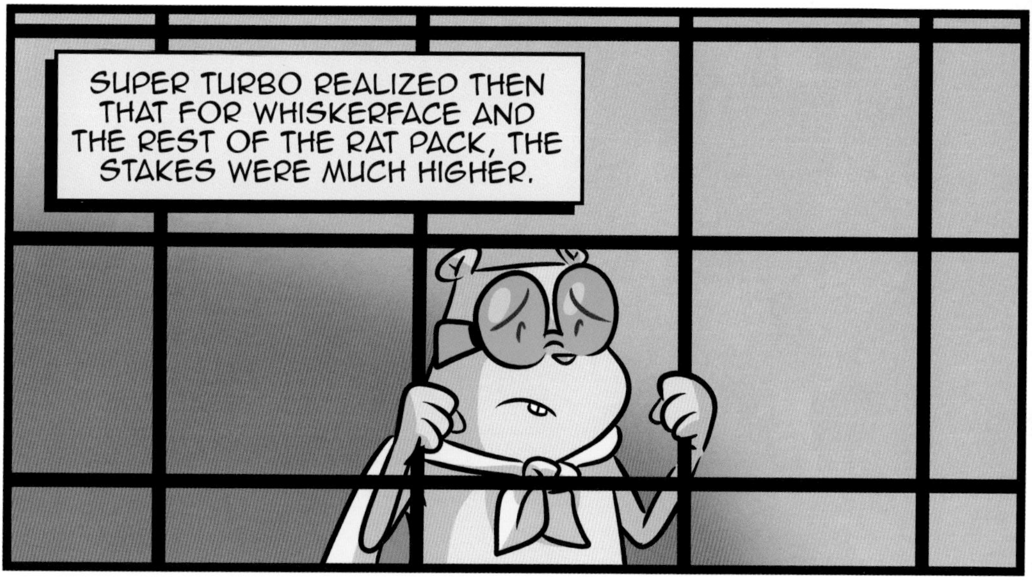
SUPER TURBO REALIZED THEN THAT FOR WHISKERFACE AND THE REST OF THE RAT PACK, THE STAKES WERE MUCH HIGHER.

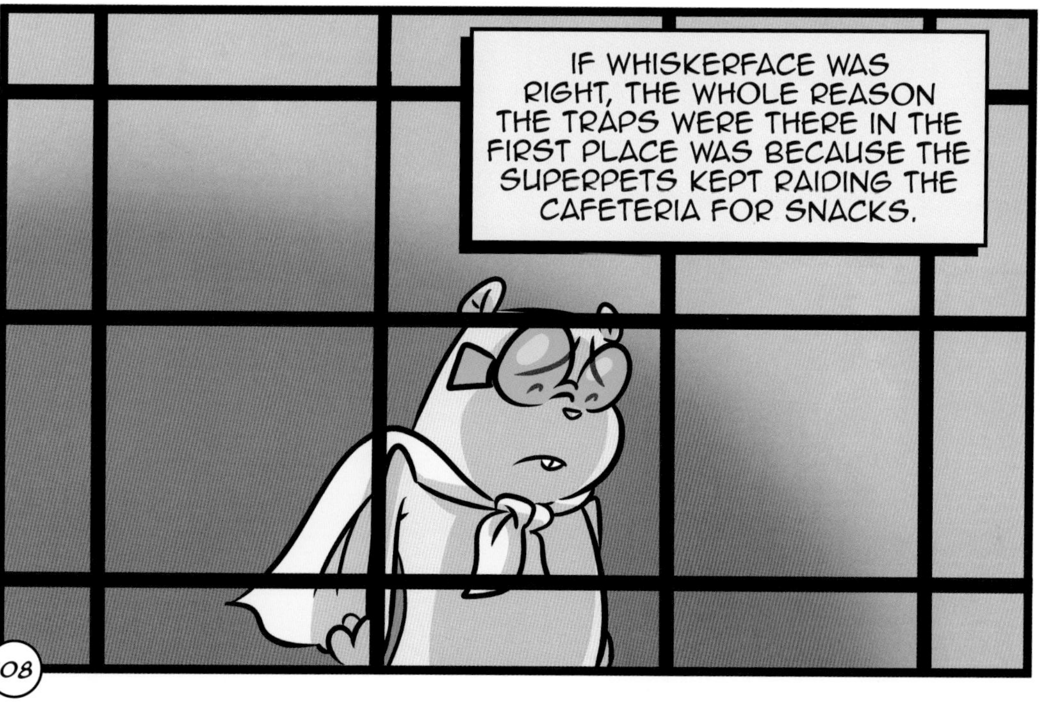
IF WHISKERFACE WAS RIGHT, THE WHOLE REASON THE TRAPS WERE THERE IN THE FIRST PLACE WAS BECAUSE THE SUPERPETS KEPT RAIDING THE CAFETERIA FOR SNACKS.

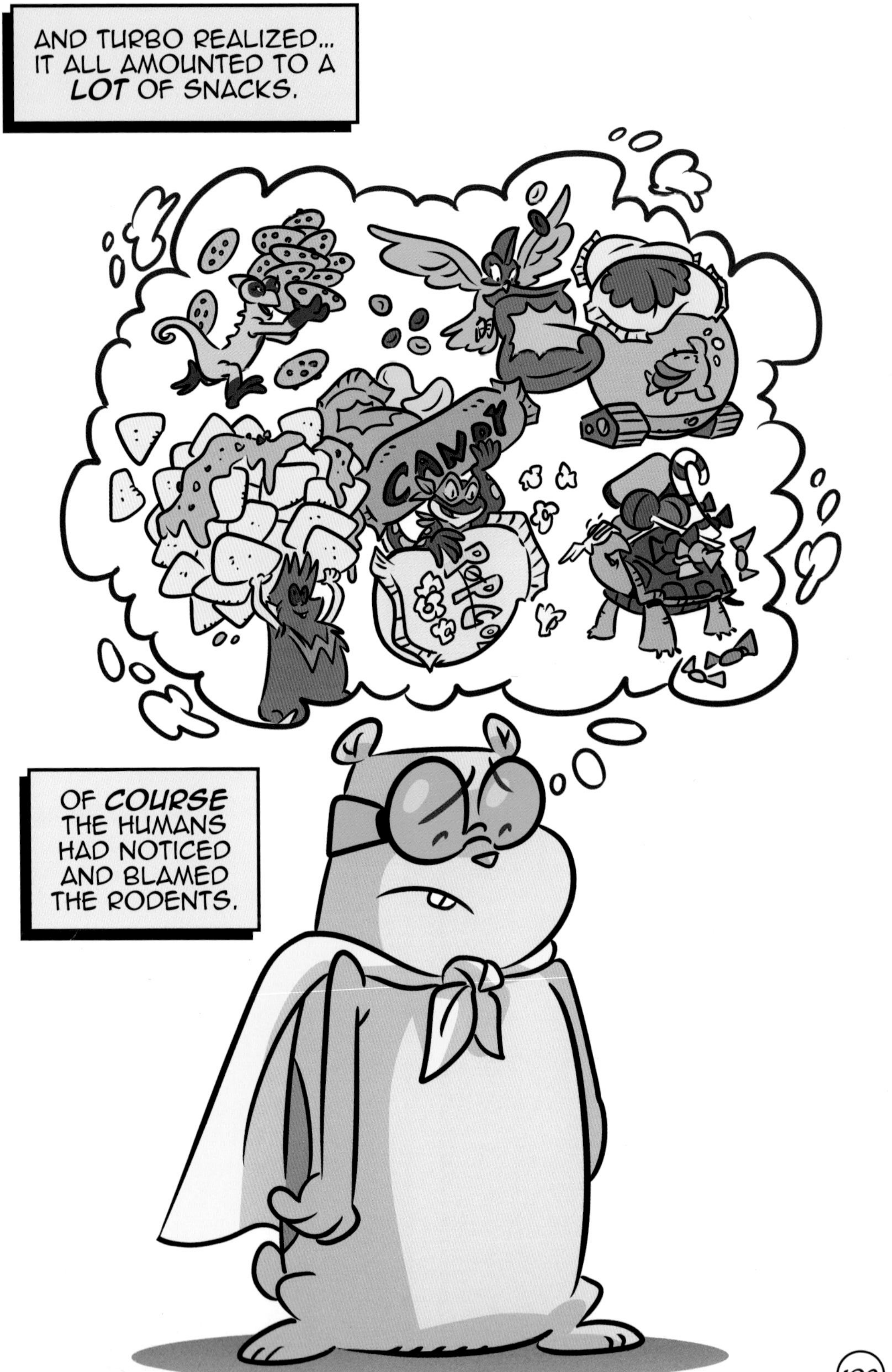
AND TURBO REALIZED... IT ALL AMOUNTED TO A *LOT* OF SNACKS.
CANDY
POP
OF *COURSE* THE HUMANS HAD NOTICED AND BLAMED THE RODENTS.

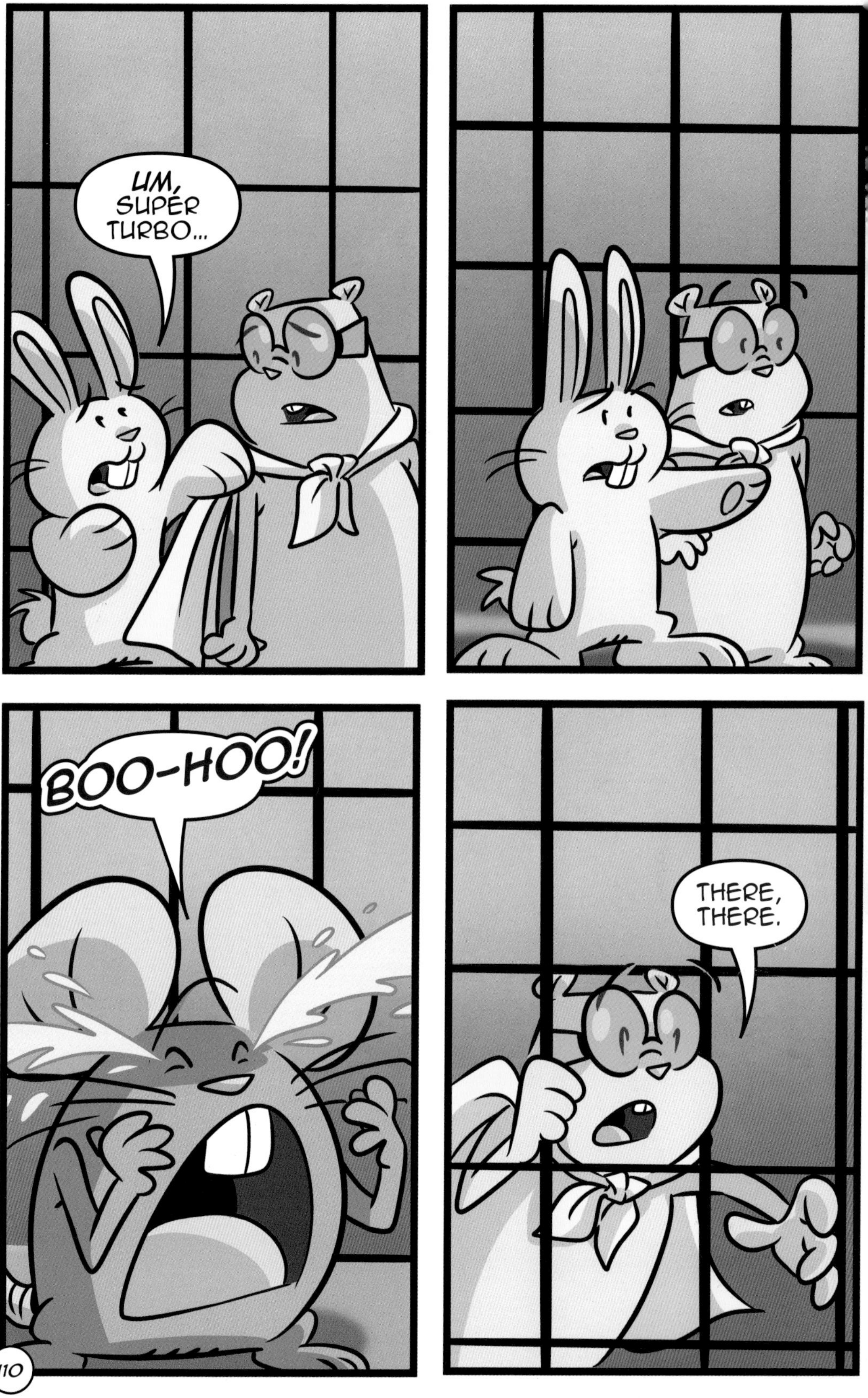
UM, SUPER TURBO...
BOO-HOO!
THERE, THERE.

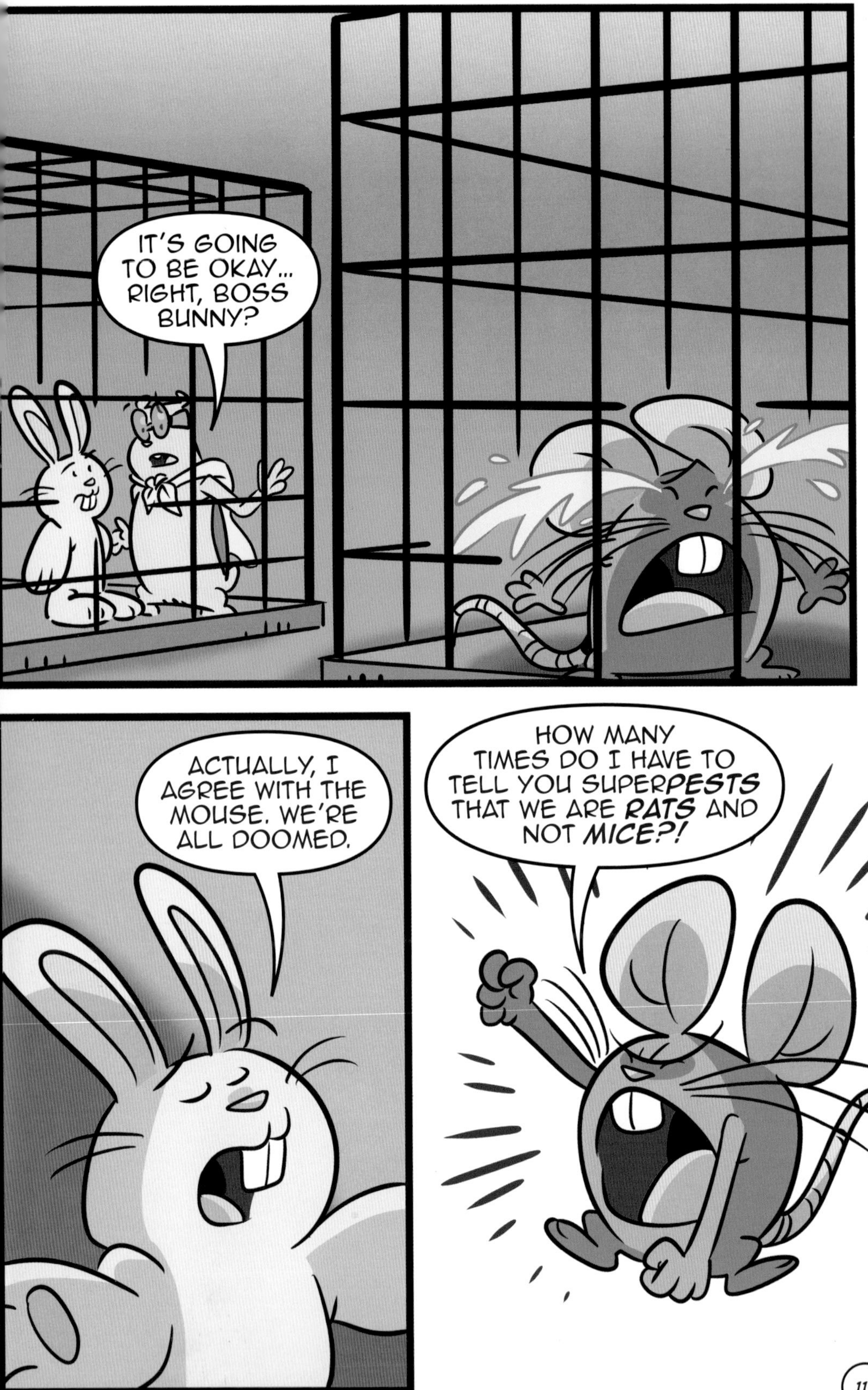
IT'S GOING TO BE OKAY... RIGHT, BOSS BUNNY?
ACTUALLY, I AGREE WITH THE MOUSE. WE'RE ALL DOOMED.
HOW MANY TIMES DO I HAVE TO TELL YOU SUPER*PESTS* THAT WE ARE *RATS* AND NOT *MICE?!*

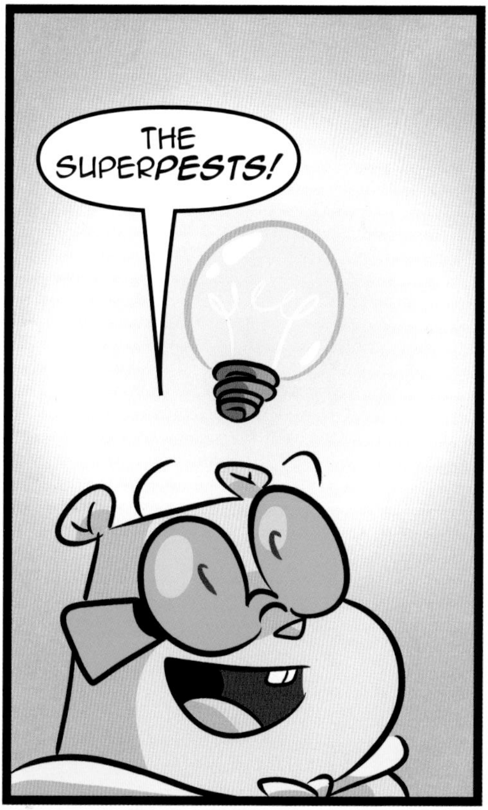
THE SUPERPESTS!

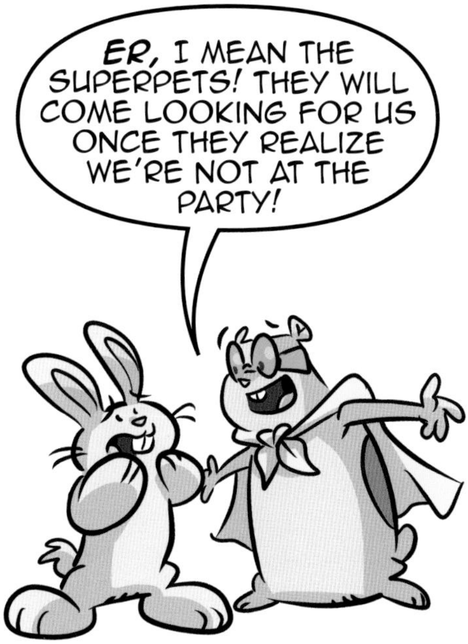
ER, I MEAN THE SUPERPETS! THEY WILL COME LOOKING FOR US ONCE THEY REALIZE WE'RE NOT AT THE PARTY!

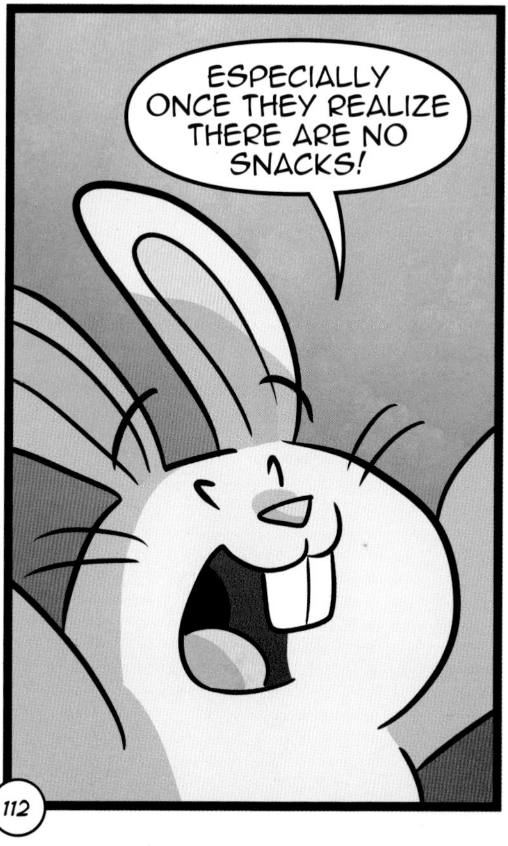
ESPECIALLY ONCE THEY REALIZE THERE ARE NO SNACKS!

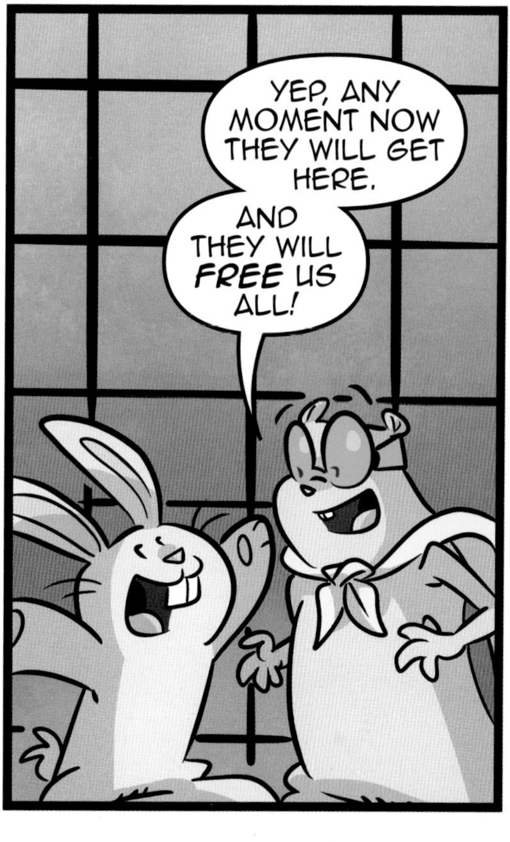
YEP, ANY MOMENT NOW THEY WILL GET HERE.
AND THEY WILL FREE US ALL!

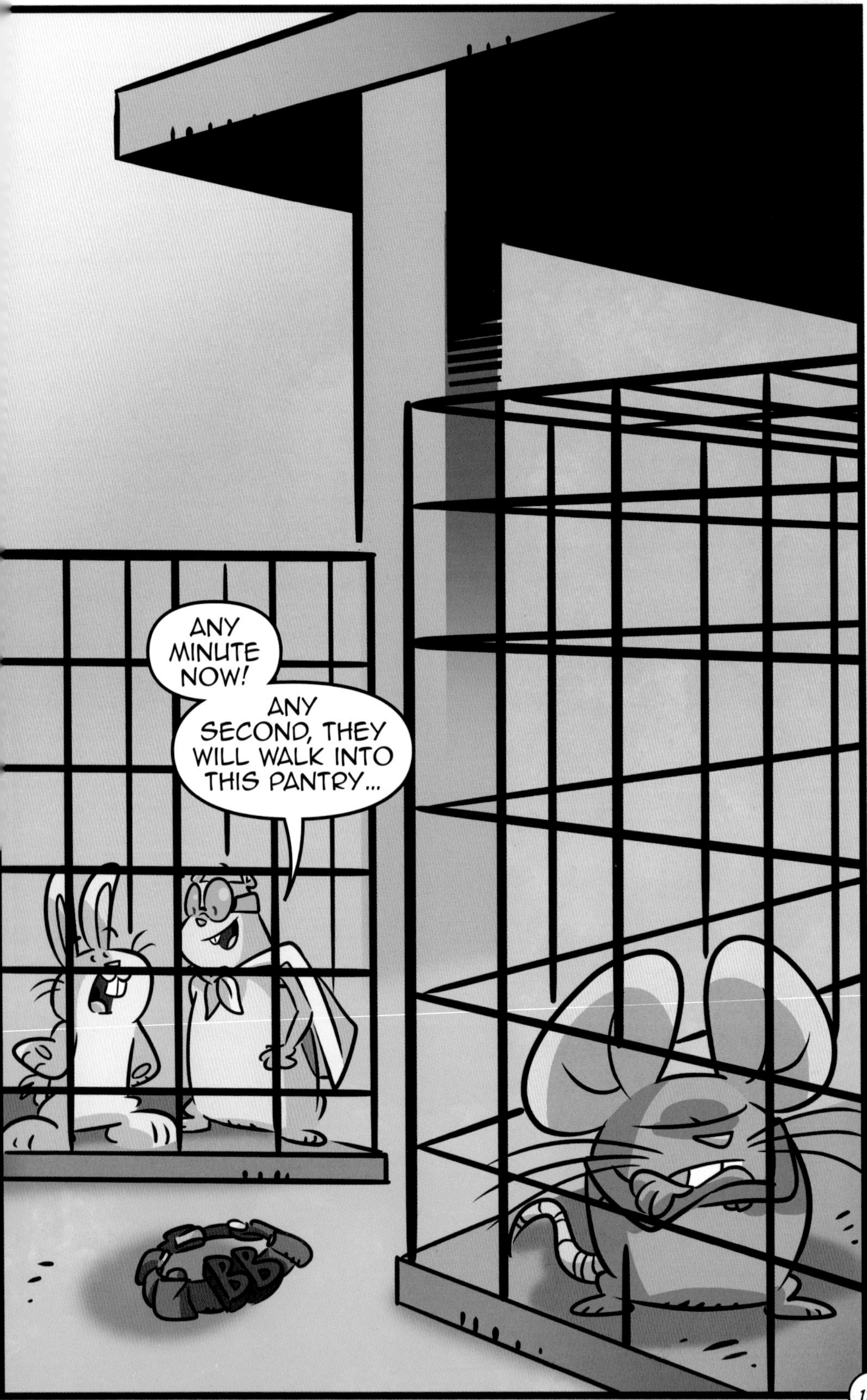
ANY MINUTE NOW!
ANY SECOND, THEY WILL WALK INTO THIS PANTRY...
BB

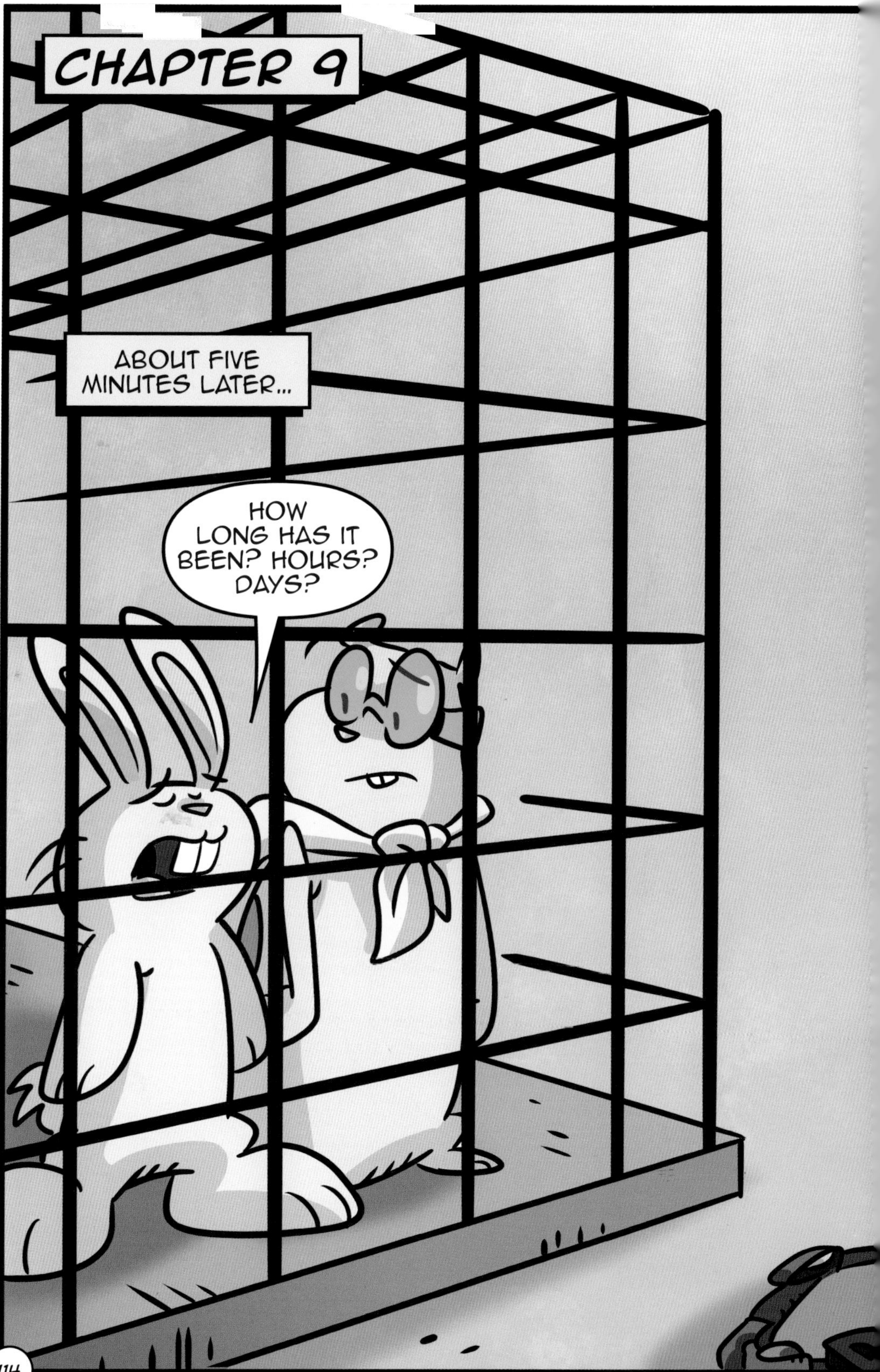
CHAPTER 9
ABOUT FIVE MINUTES LATER...
HOW LONG HAS IT BEEN? HOURS? DAYS?

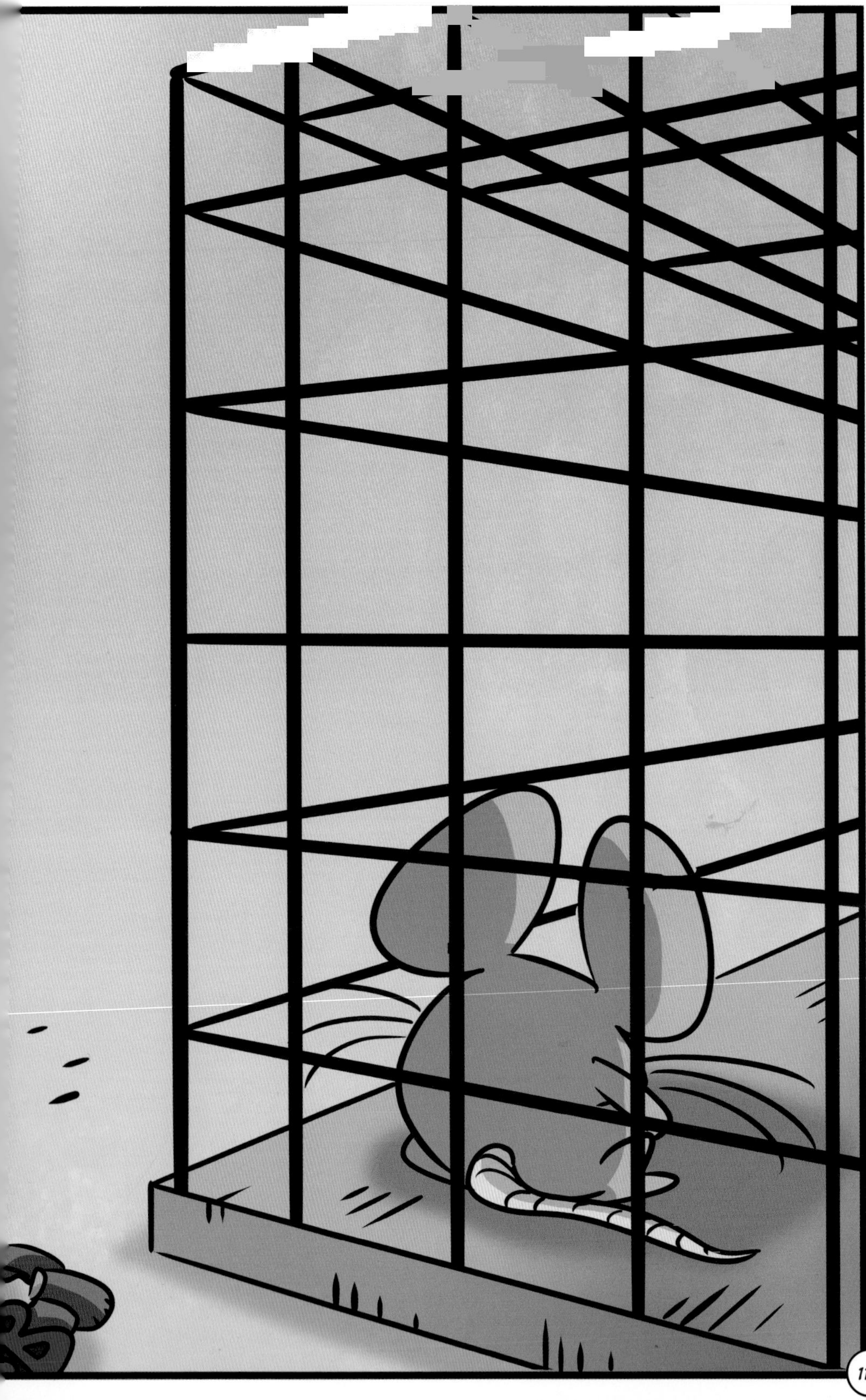

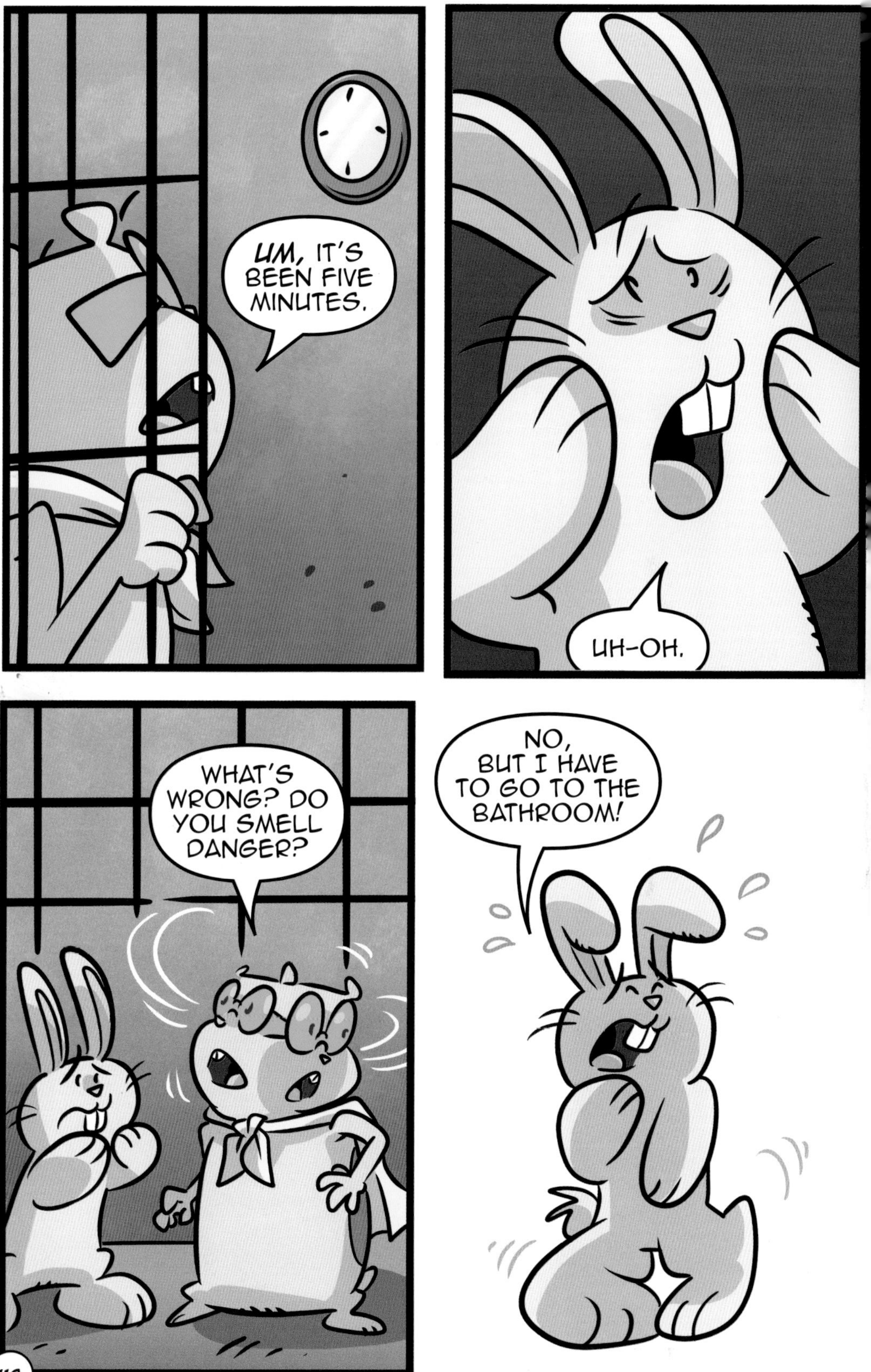
UM, IT'S BEEN FIVE MINUTES.
UH-OH.
WHAT'S WRONG? DO YOU SMELL DANGER?
NO, BUT I HAVE TO GO TO THE BATHROOM!

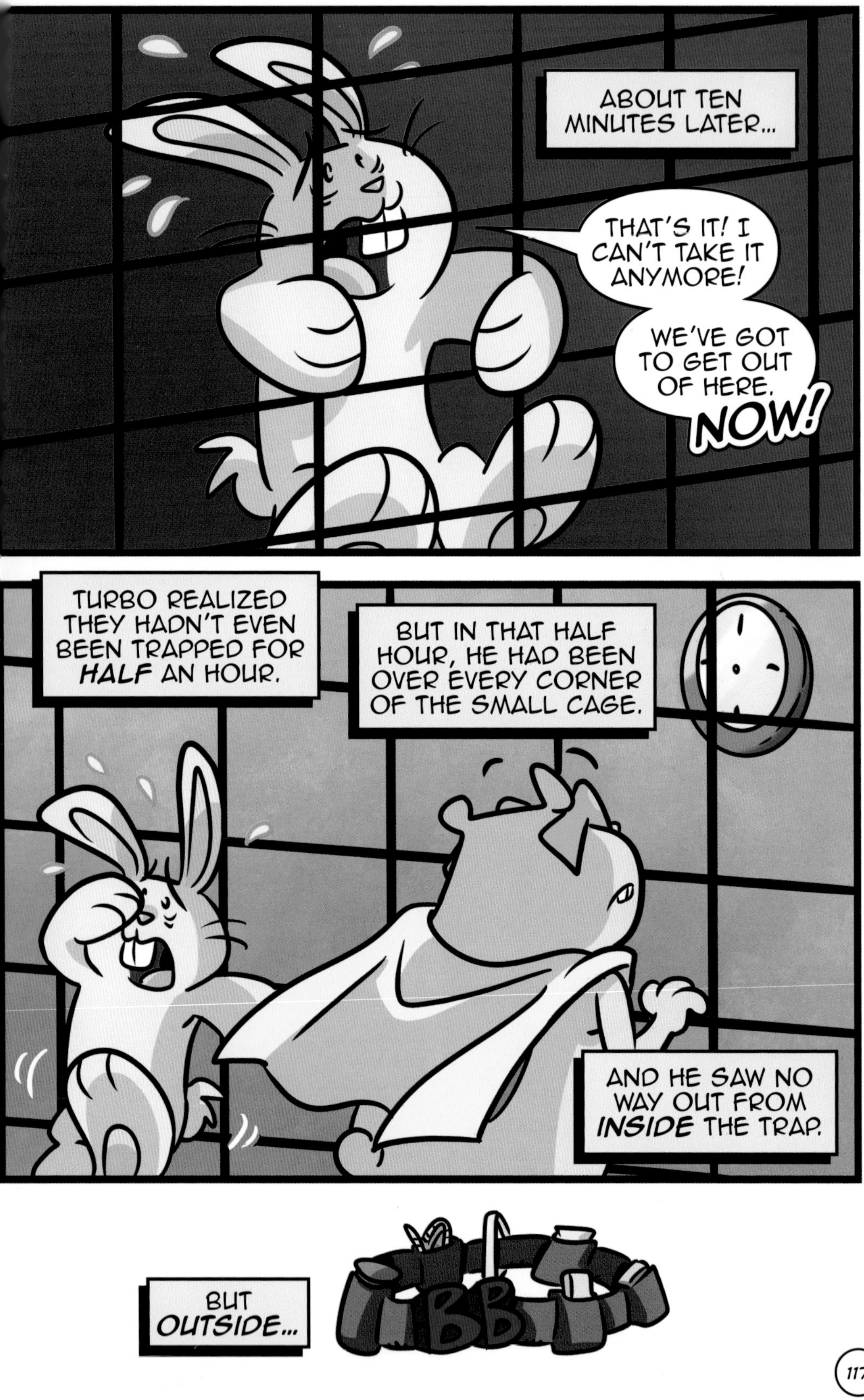
ABOUT TEN MINUTES LATER...
THAT'S IT! I CAN'T TAKE IT ANYMORE!
WE'VE GOT TO GET OUT OF HERE. NOW!
TURBO REALIZED THEY HADN'T EVEN BEEN TRAPPED FOR HALF AN HOUR.
BUT IN THAT HALF HOUR, HE HAD BEEN OVER EVERY CORNER OF THE SMALL CAGE.
AND HE SAW NO WAY OUT FROM INSIDE THE TRAP.
BUT OUTSIDE...
BB

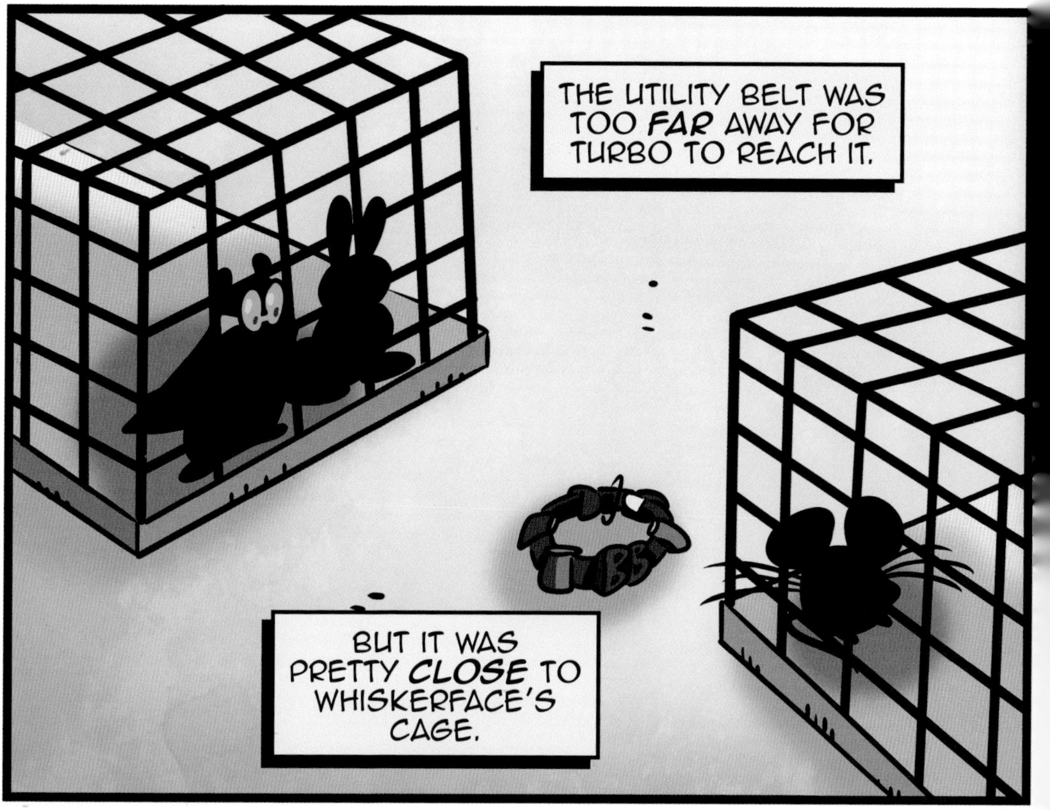
THE UTILITY BELT WAS TOO FAR AWAY FOR TURBO TO REACH IT.
BUT IT WAS PRETTY CLOSE TO WHISKERFACE'S CAGE.
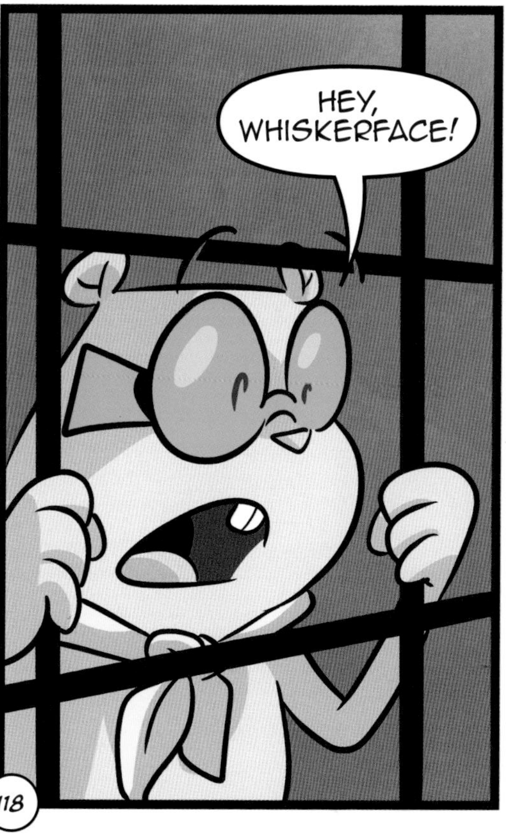
HEY, WHISKERFACE!
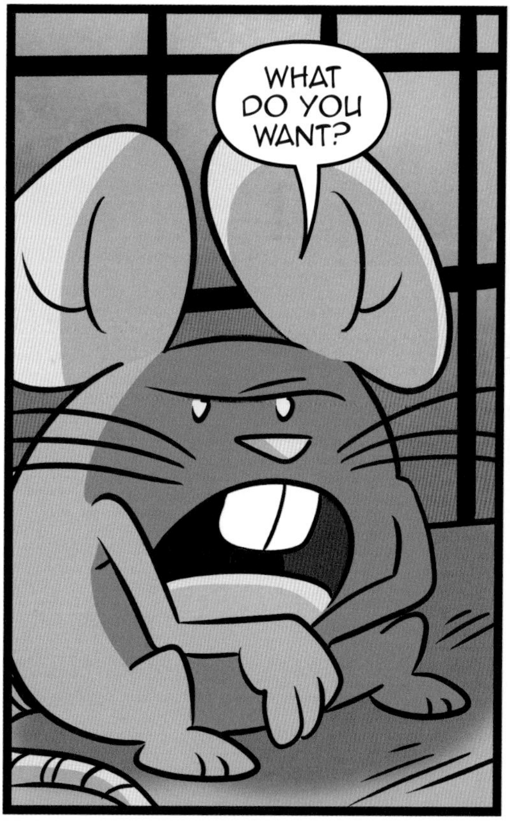
WHAT DO YOU WANT?

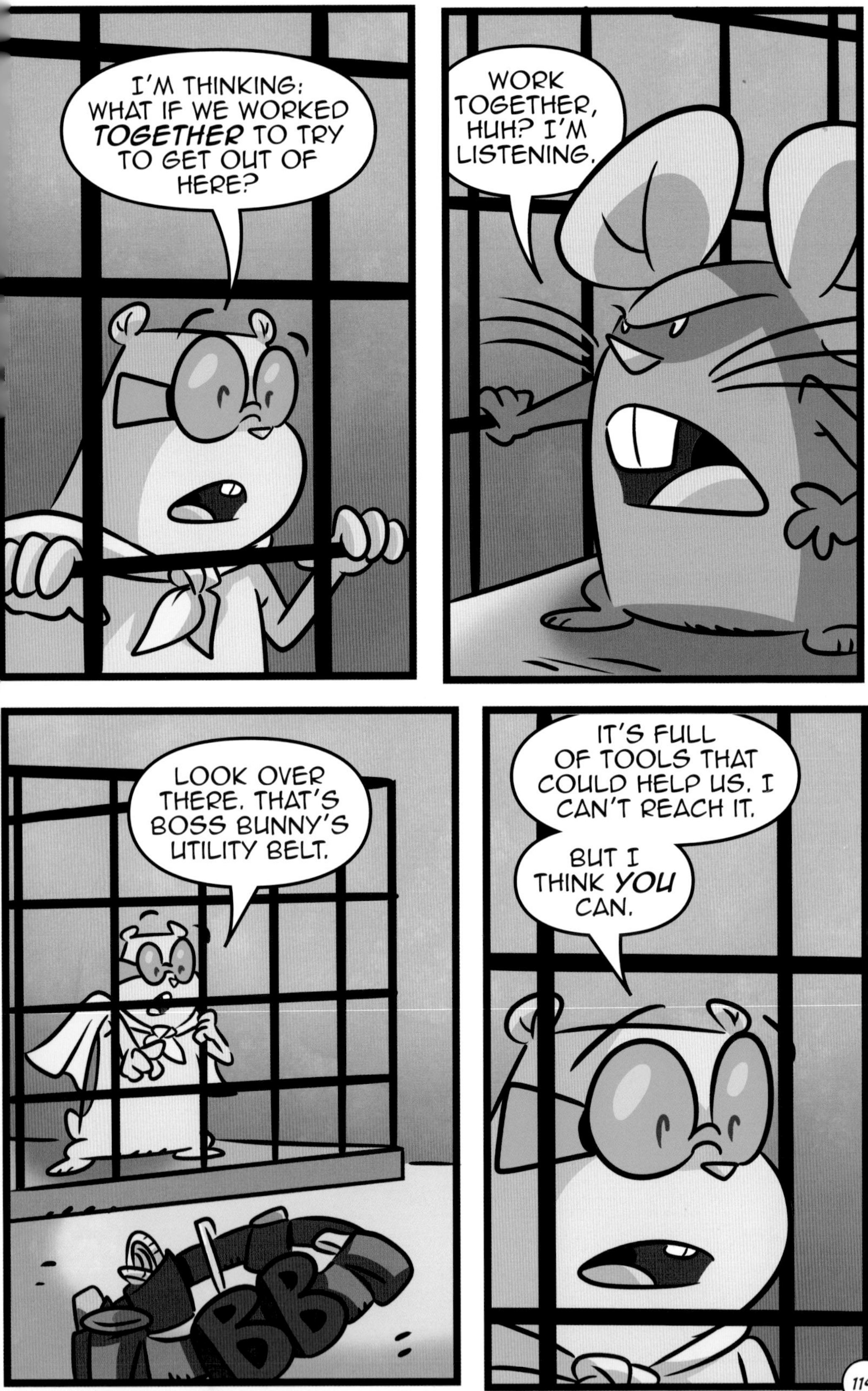
I'M THINKING: WHAT IF WE WORKED *TOGETHER* TO TRY TO GET OUT OF HERE?
WORK TOGETHER, HUH? I'M LISTENING.
LOOK OVER THERE. THAT'S BOSS BUNNY'S UTILITY BELT.
BB
IT'S FULL OF TOOLS THAT COULD HELP US. I CAN'T REACH IT.
BUT I THINK *YOU* CAN.

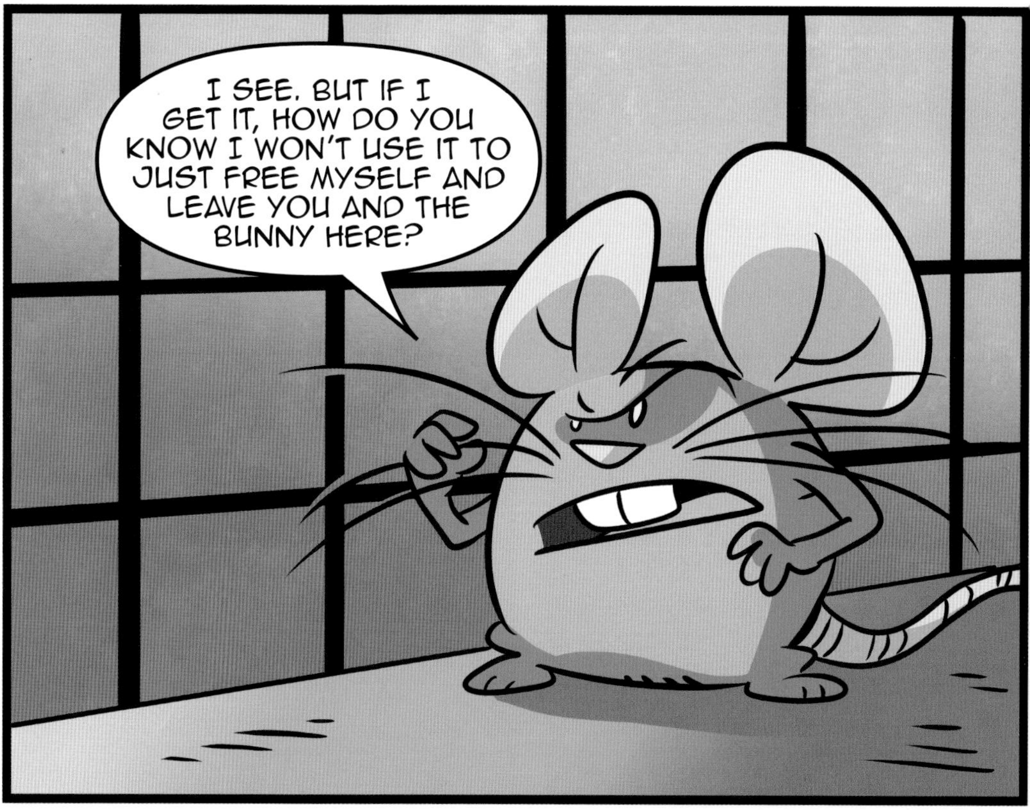
I SEE. BUT IF I GET IT, HOW DO YOU KNOW I WON'T USE IT TO JUST FREE MYSELF AND LEAVE YOU AND THE BUNNY HERE?

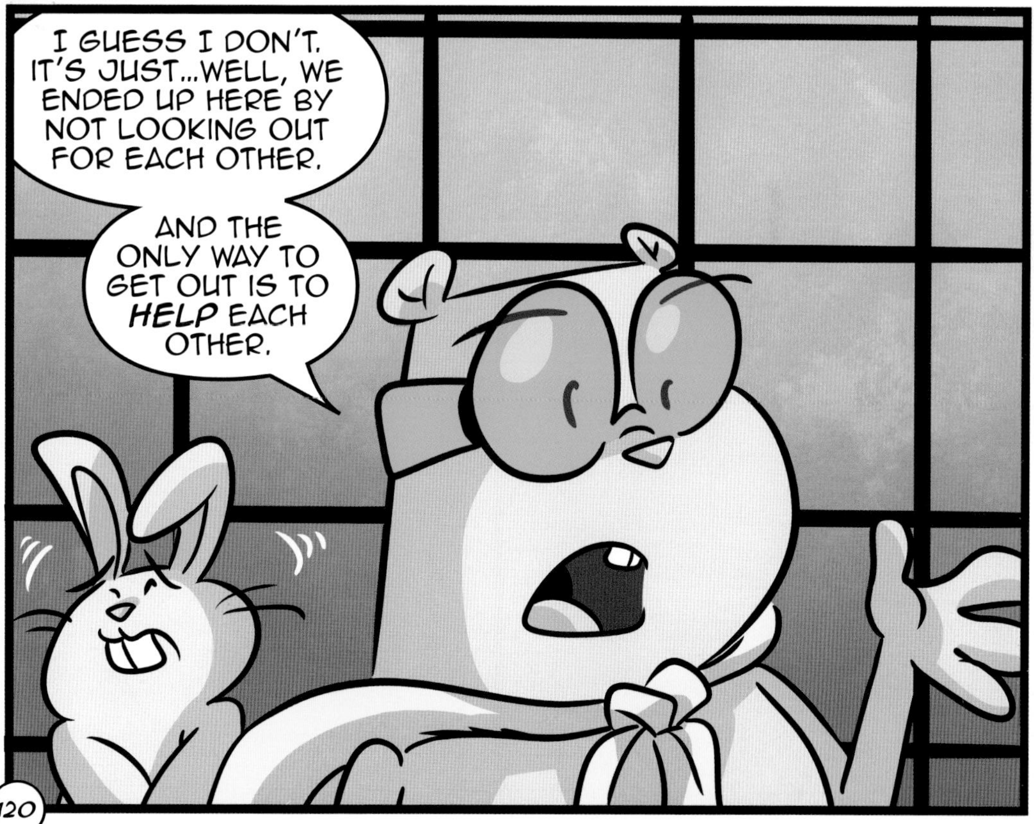
I GUESS I DON'T. IT'S JUST...WELL, WE ENDED UP HERE BY NOT LOOKING OUT FOR EACH OTHER.
AND THE ONLY WAY TO GET OUT IS TO *HELP* EACH OTHER.

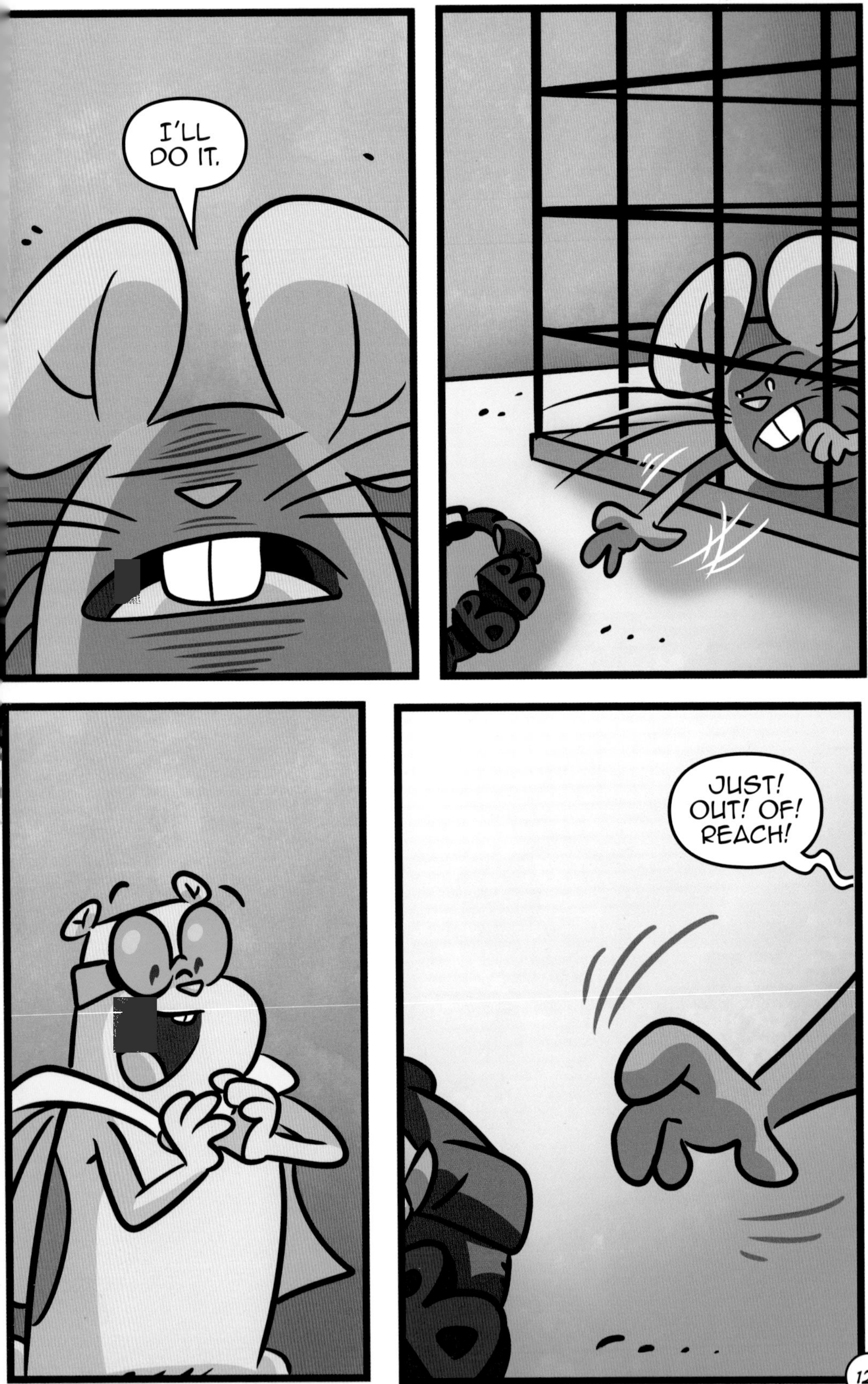
I'LL DO IT.
JUST! OUT! OF! REACH!

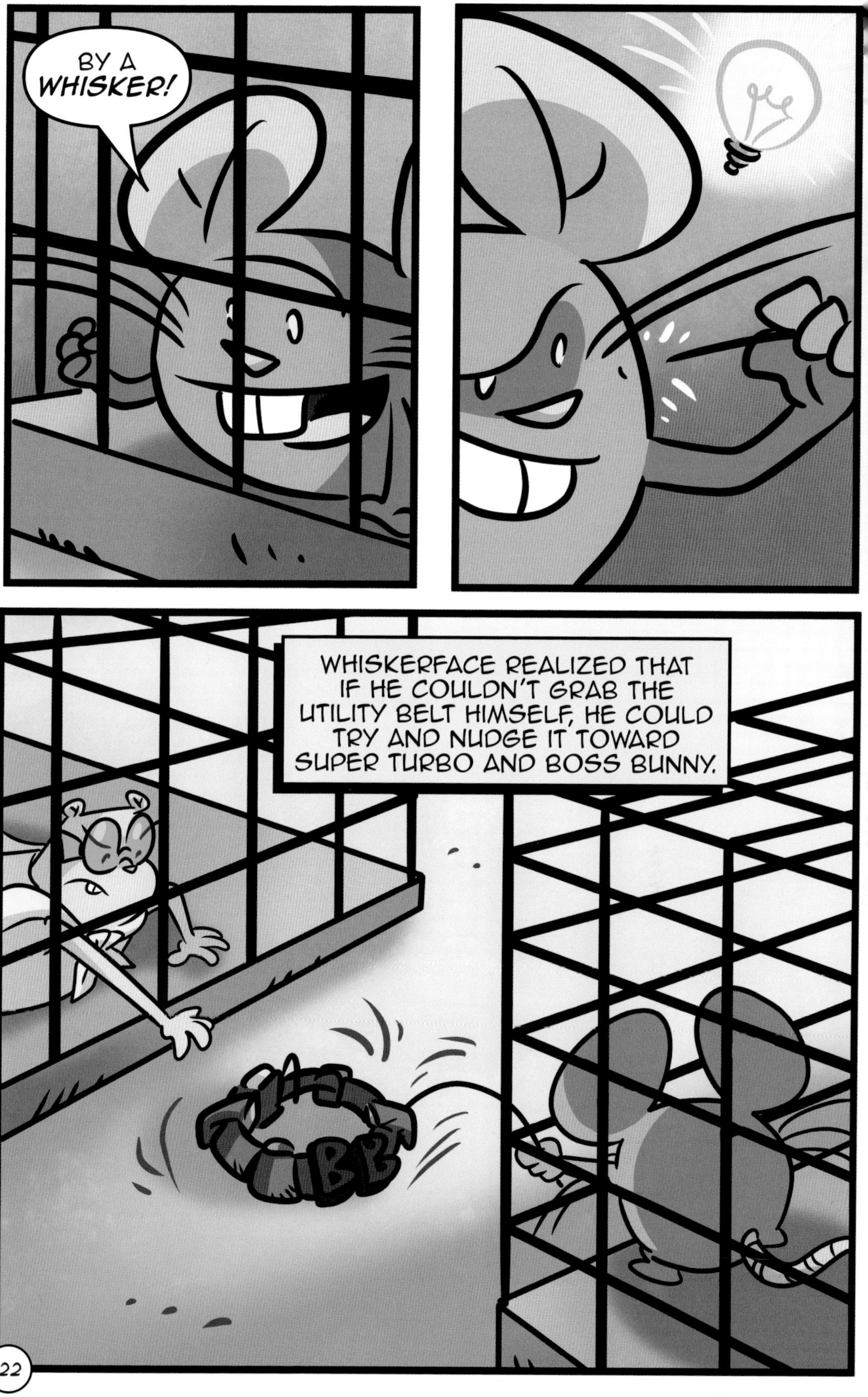
BY A WHISKER!
WHISKERFACE REALIZED THAT IF HE COULDN'T GRAB THE UTILITY BELT HIMSELF, HE COULD TRY AND NUDGE IT TOWARD SUPER TURBO AND BOSS BUNNY.

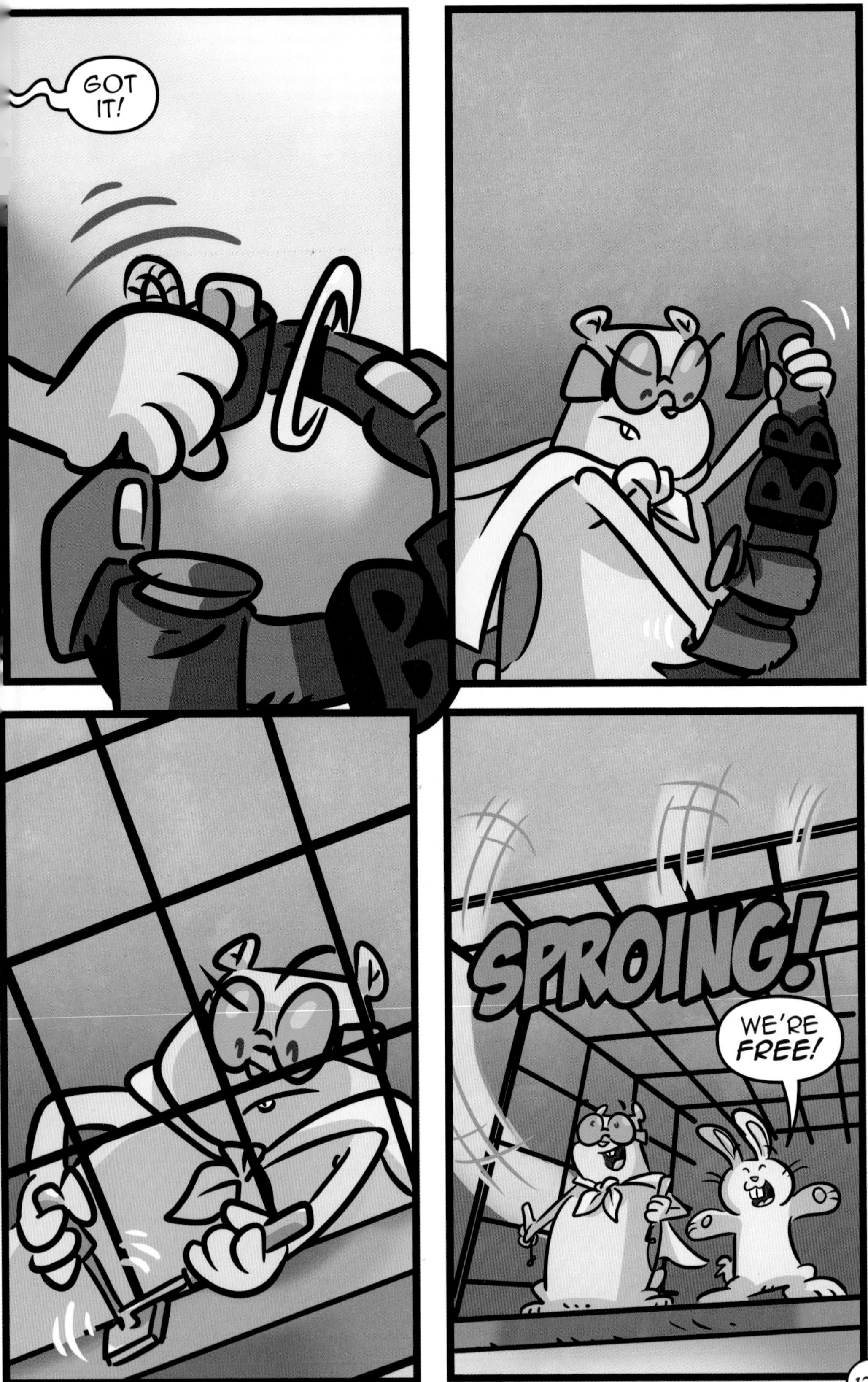
GOT IT!
SPROING!
WE'RE FREE!

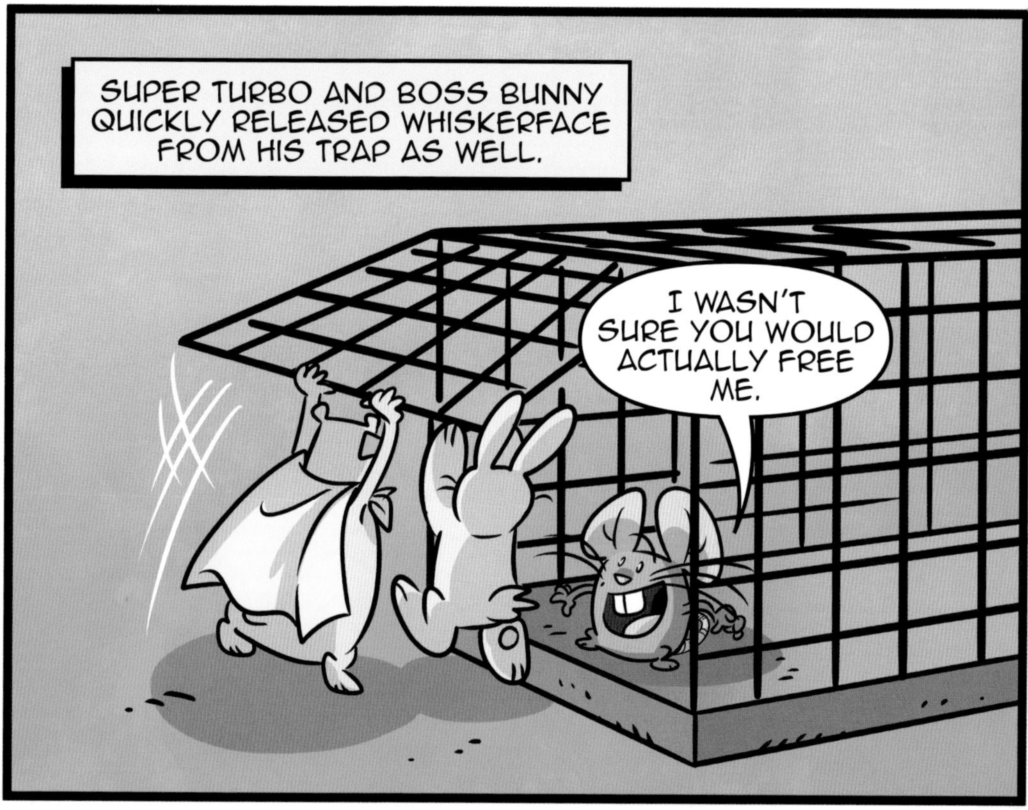
SUPER TURBO AND BOSS BUNNY QUICKLY RELEASED WHISKERFACE FROM HIS TRAP AS WELL.
I WASN'T SURE YOU WOULD ACTUALLY FREE ME.

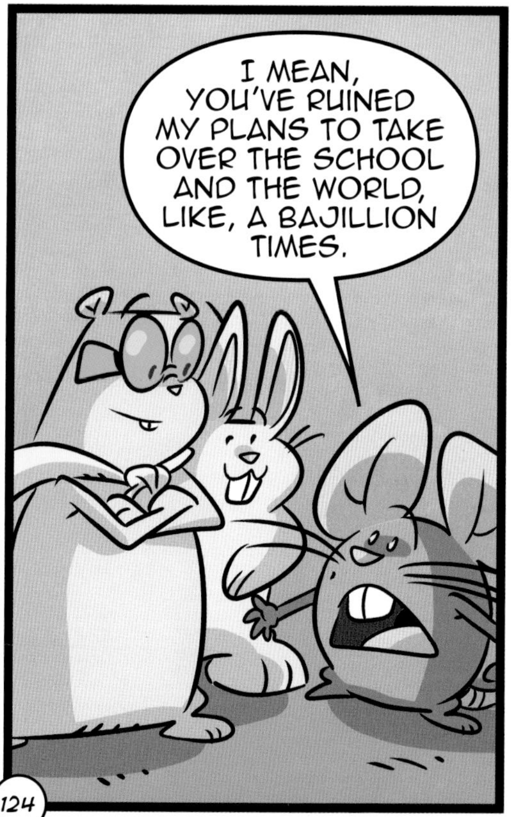
I MEAN, YOU'VE RUINED MY PLANS TO TAKE OVER THE SCHOOL AND THE WORLD, LIKE, A BAJILLION TIMES.

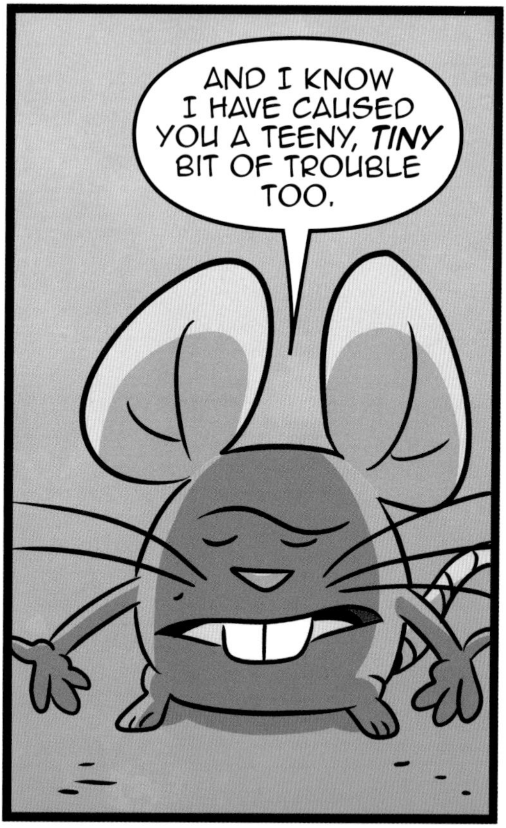
AND I KNOW I HAVE CAUSED YOU A TEENY, *TINY* BIT OF TROUBLE TOO.

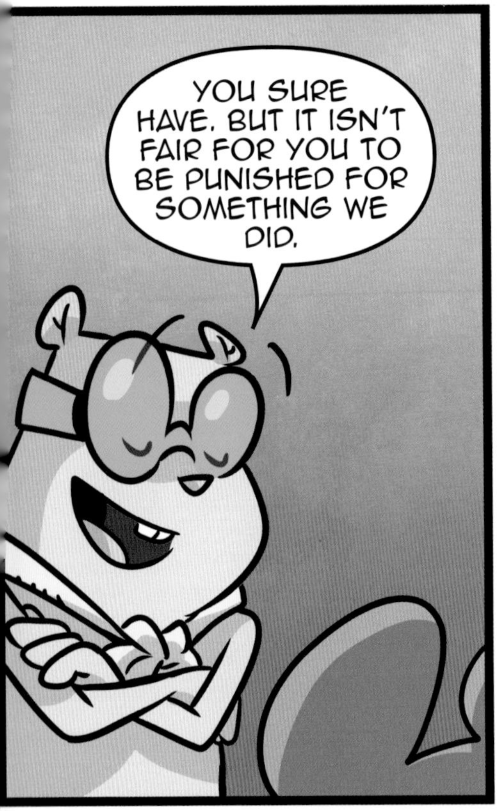
YOU SURE HAVE. BUT IT ISN'T FAIR FOR YOU TO BE PUNISHED FOR SOMETHING WE DID.

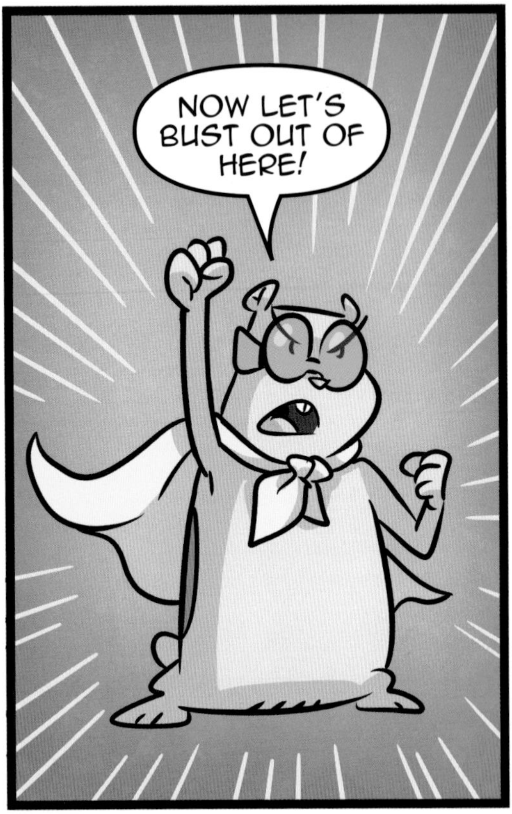
NOW LET'S BUST OUT OF HERE!

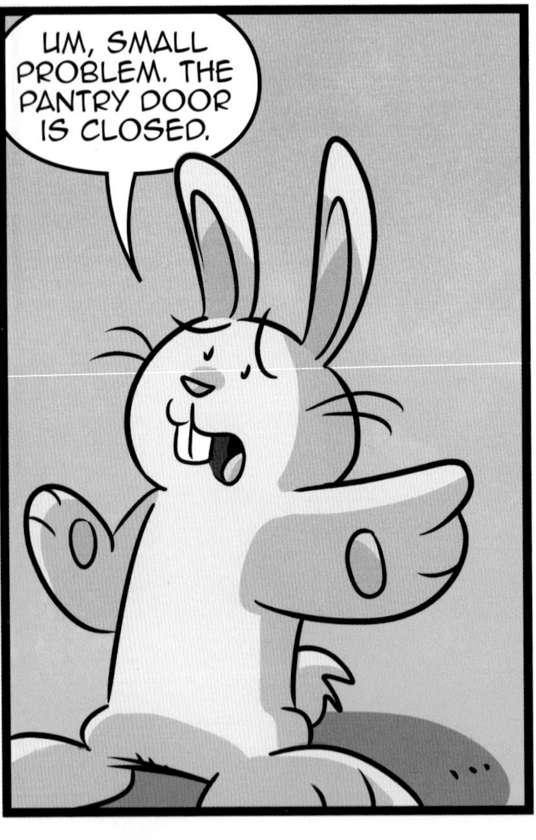
UM, SMALL PROBLEM. THE PANTRY DOOR IS CLOSED.
...

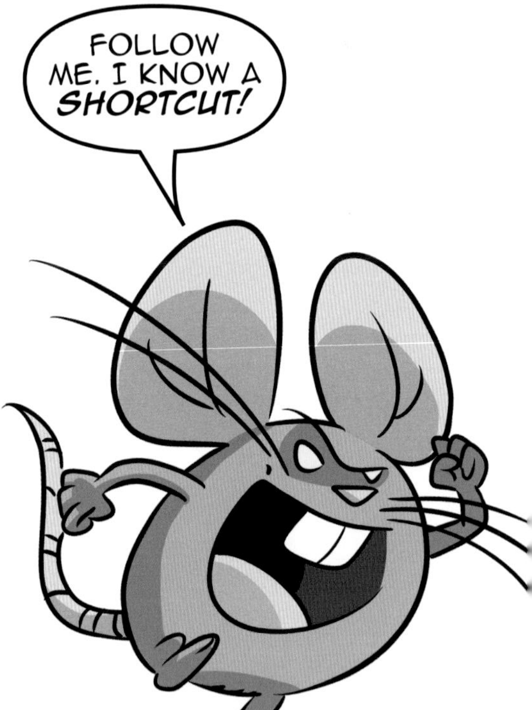
FOLLOW ME. I KNOW A ***SHORTCUT!***

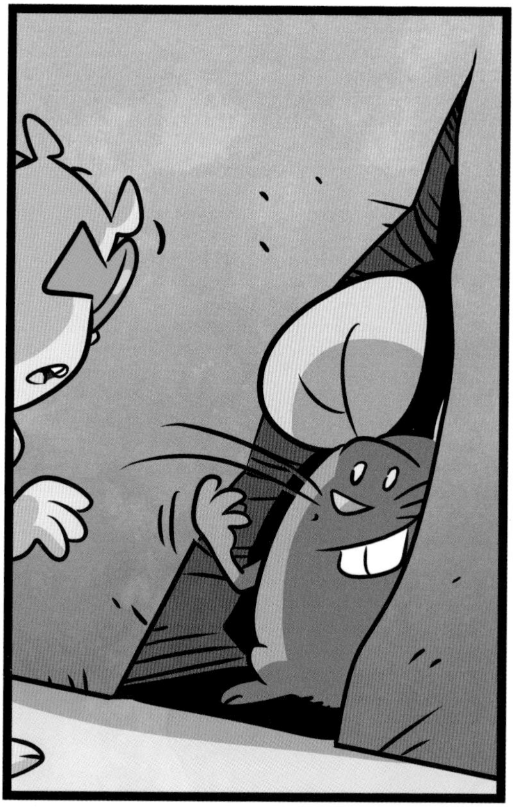

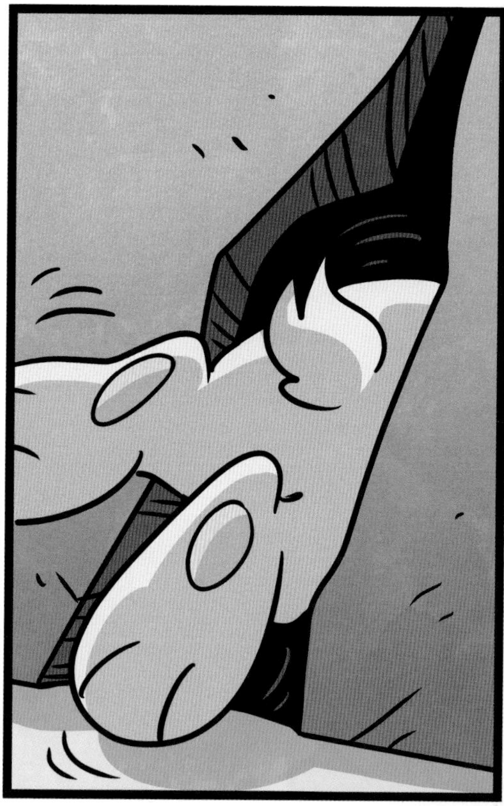

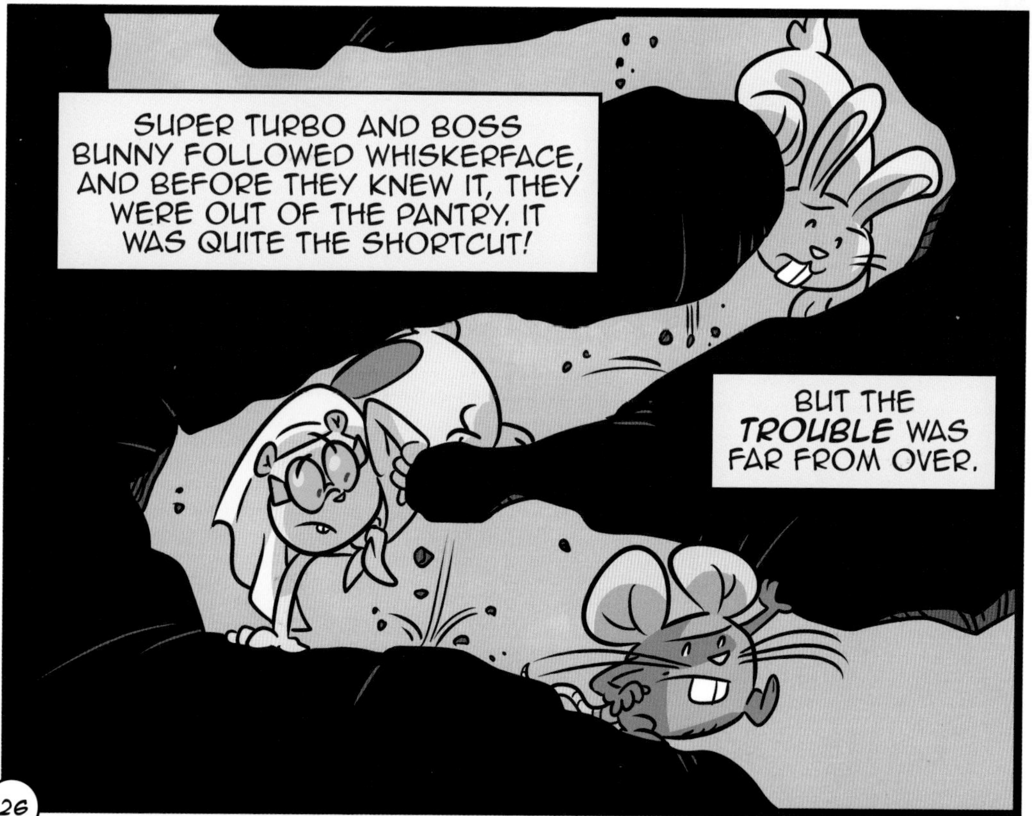
SUPER TURBO AND BOSS BUNNY FOLLOWED WHISKERFACE, AND BEFORE THEY KNEW IT, THEY WERE OUT OF THE PANTRY. IT WAS QUITE THE SHORTCUT!
BUT THE *TROUBLE* WAS FAR FROM OVER.

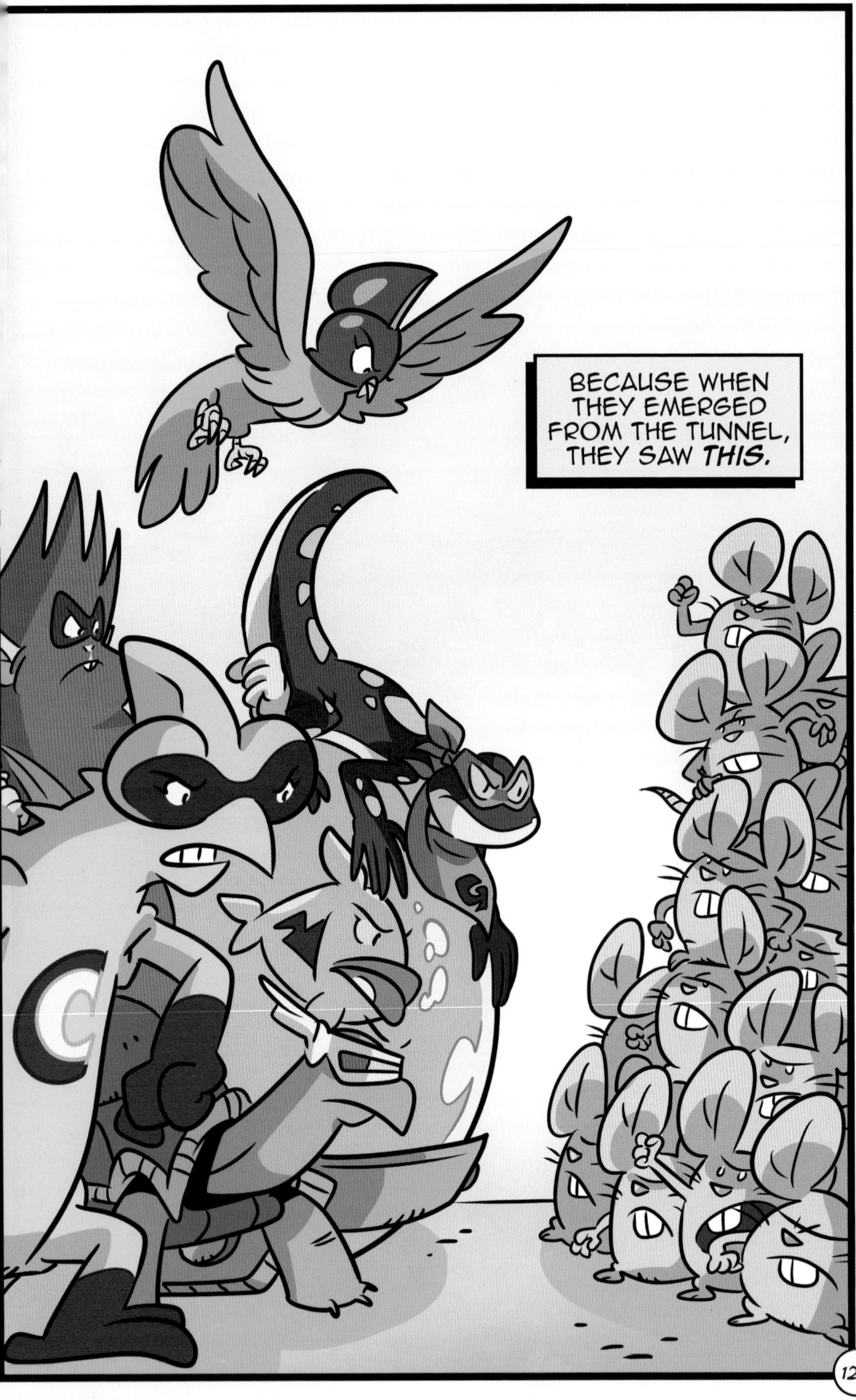
BECAUSE WHEN THEY EMERGED FROM THE TUNNEL, THEY SAW *THIS.*

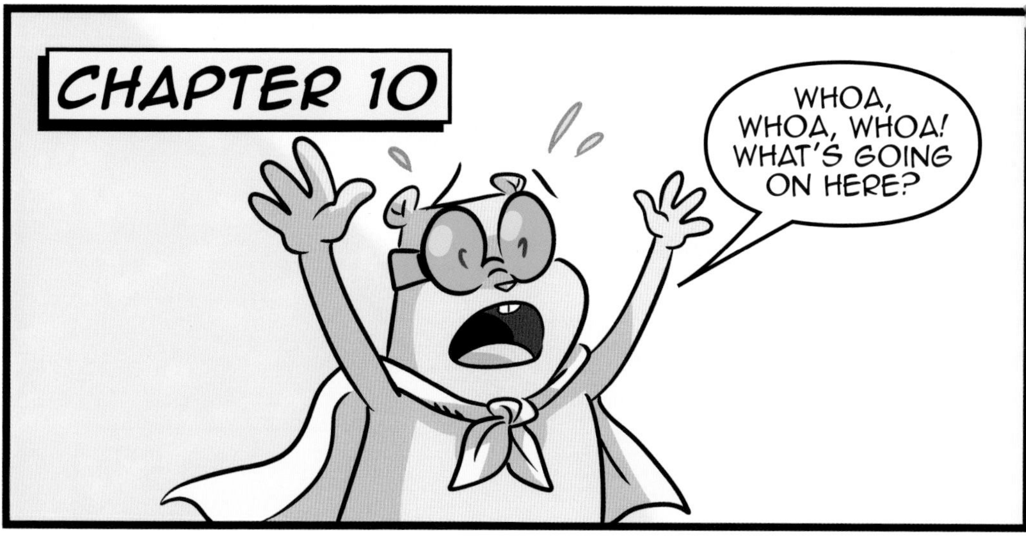
CHAPTER 10
WHOA, WHOA, WHOA! WHAT'S GOING ON HERE?

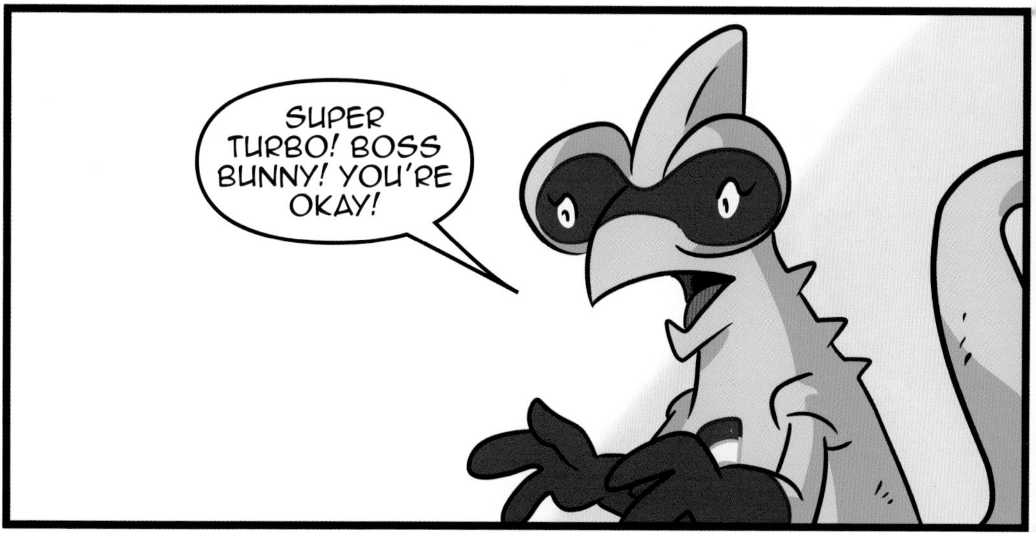
SUPER TURBO! BOSS BUNNY! YOU'RE OKAY!

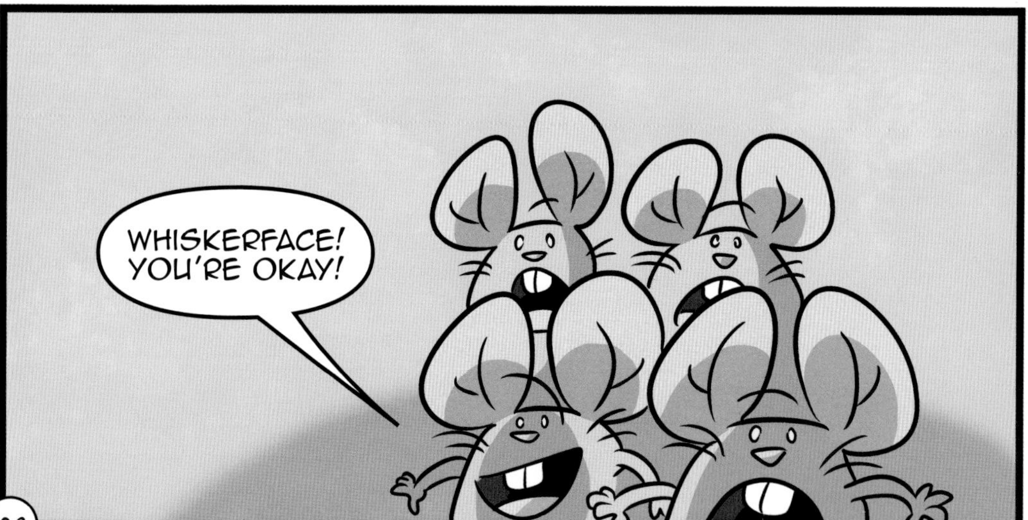
WHISKERFACE! YOU'RE OKAY!

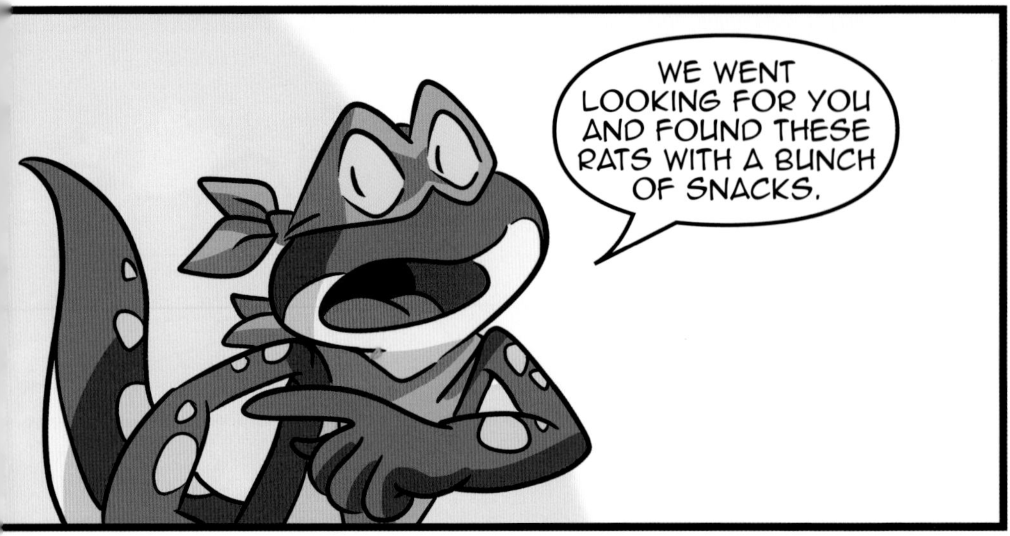
WE WENT LOOKING FOR YOU AND FOUND THESE RATS WITH A BUNCH OF SNACKS.

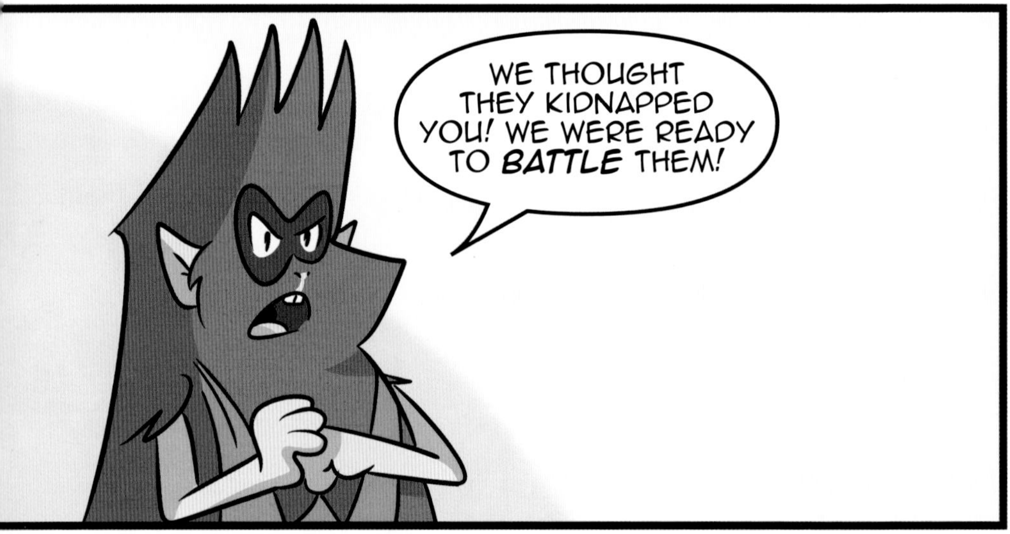
WE THOUGHT THEY KIDNAPPED YOU! WE WERE READY TO *BATTLE* THEM!

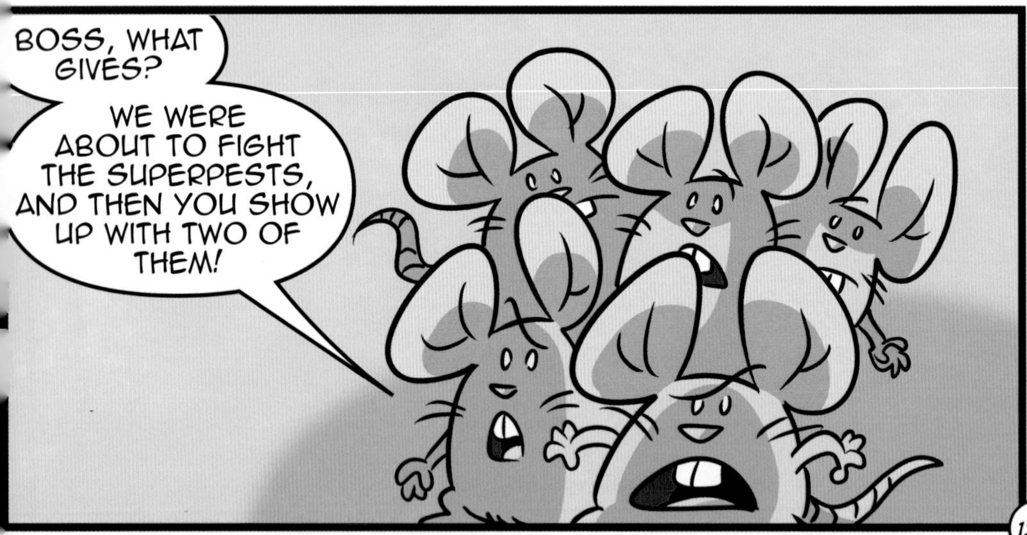
BOSS, WHAT GIVES?
WE WERE ABOUT TO FIGHT THE SUPERPESTS, AND THEN YOU SHOW UP WITH TWO OF THEM!

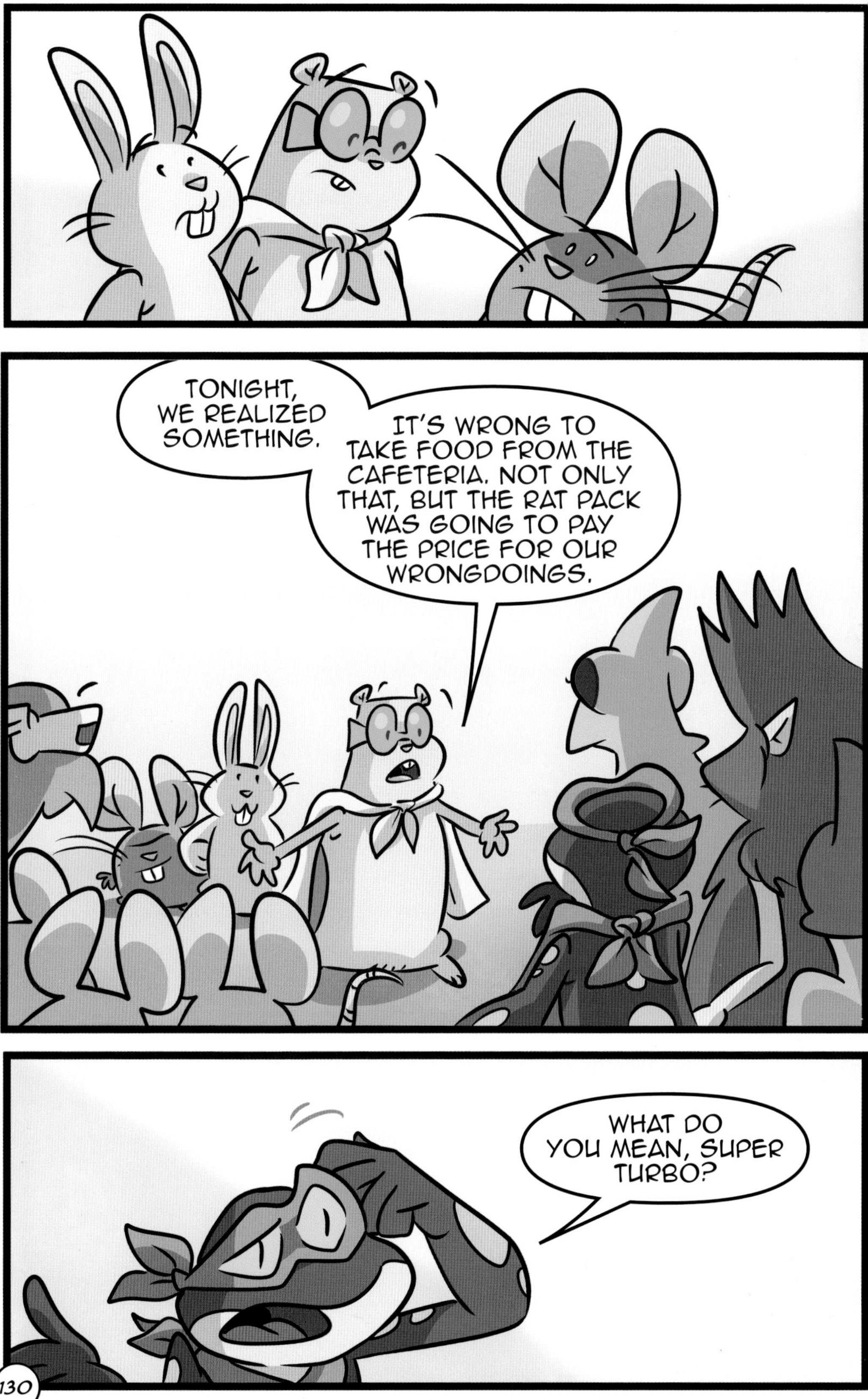
TONIGHT, WE REALIZED SOMETHING.
IT'S WRONG TO TAKE FOOD FROM THE CAFETERIA. NOT ONLY THAT, BUT THE RAT PACK WAS GOING TO PAY THE PRICE FOR OUR WRONGDOINGS.
WHAT DO YOU MEAN, SUPER TURBO?

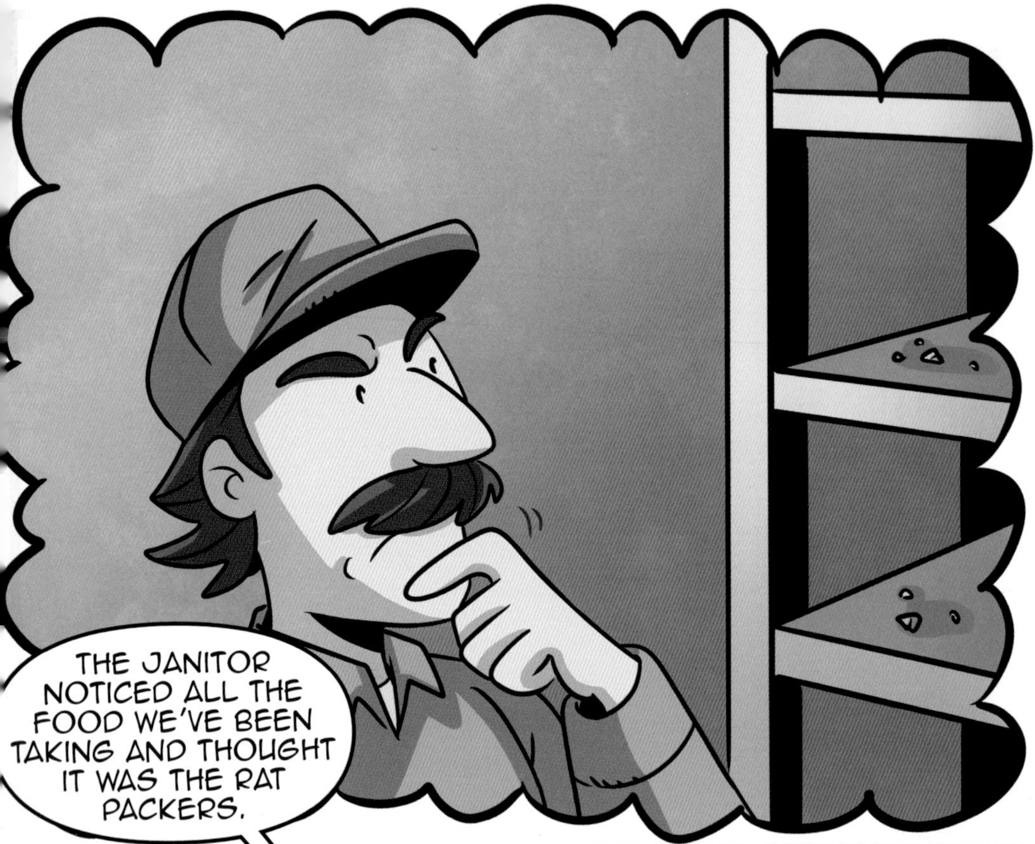
THE JANITOR NOTICED ALL THE FOOD WE'VE BEEN TAKING AND THOUGHT IT WAS THE RAT PACKERS.

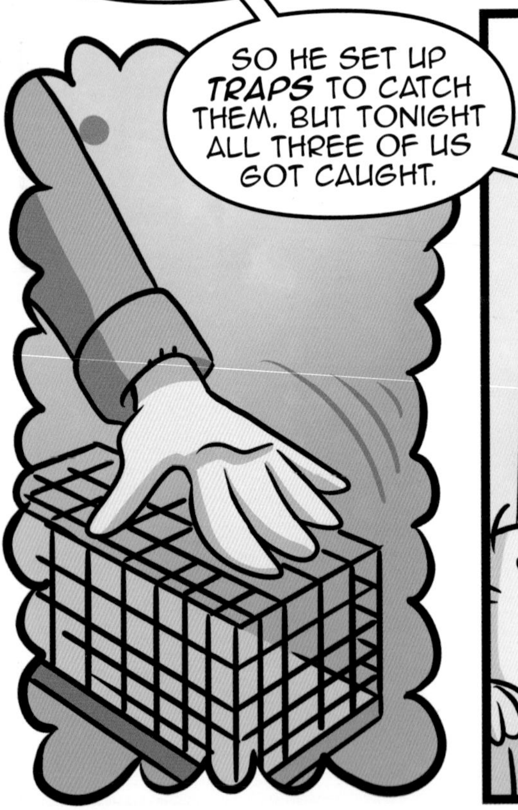
SO HE SET UP *TRAPS* TO CATCH THEM. BUT TONIGHT ALL THREE OF US GOT CAUGHT.

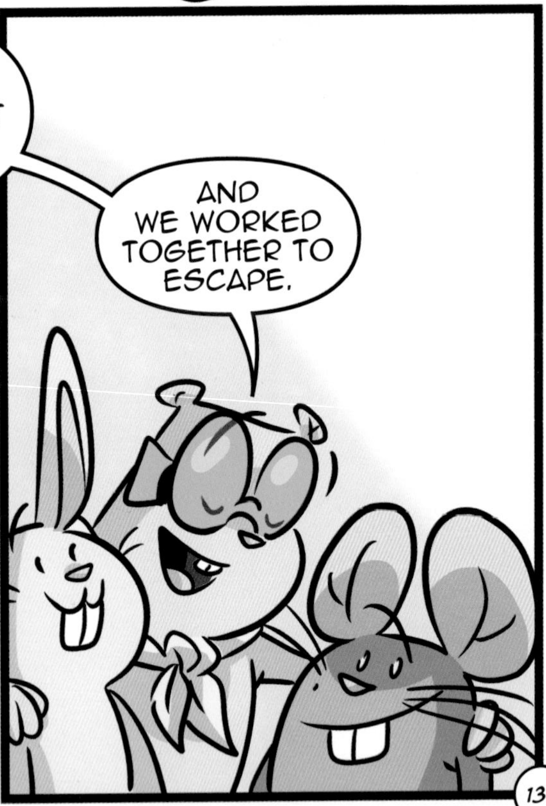
AND WE WORKED TOGETHER TO ESCAPE.

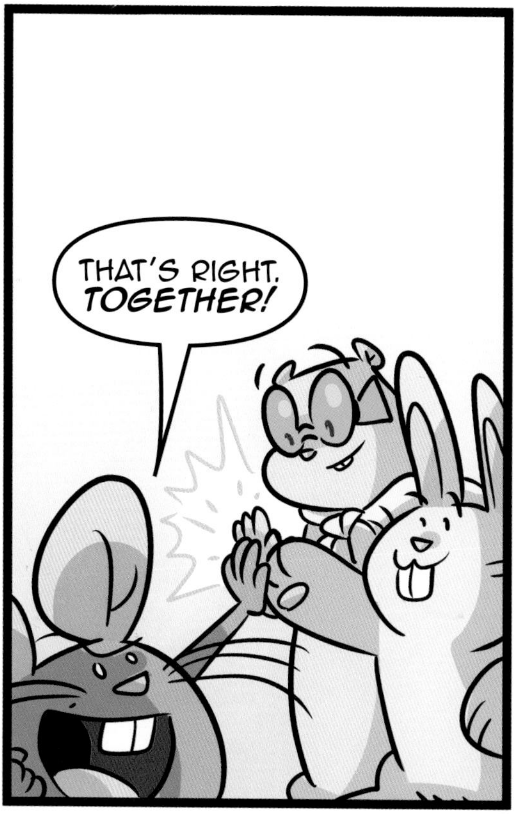
THAT'S RIGHT. *TOGETHER!*
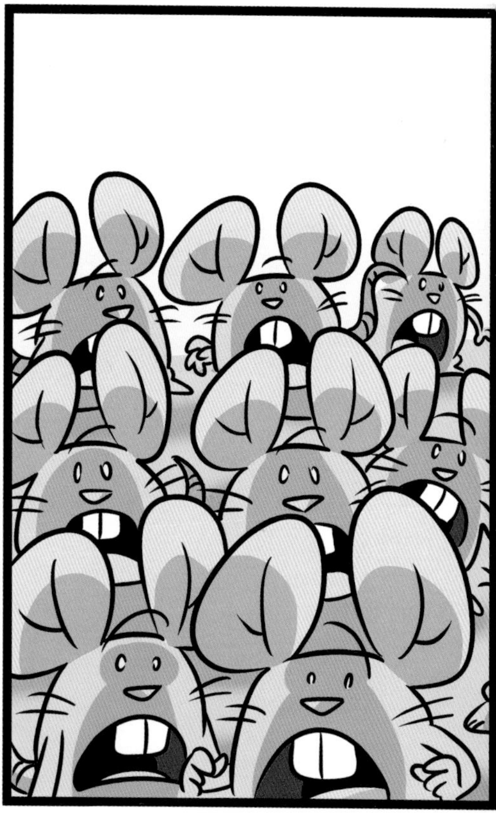
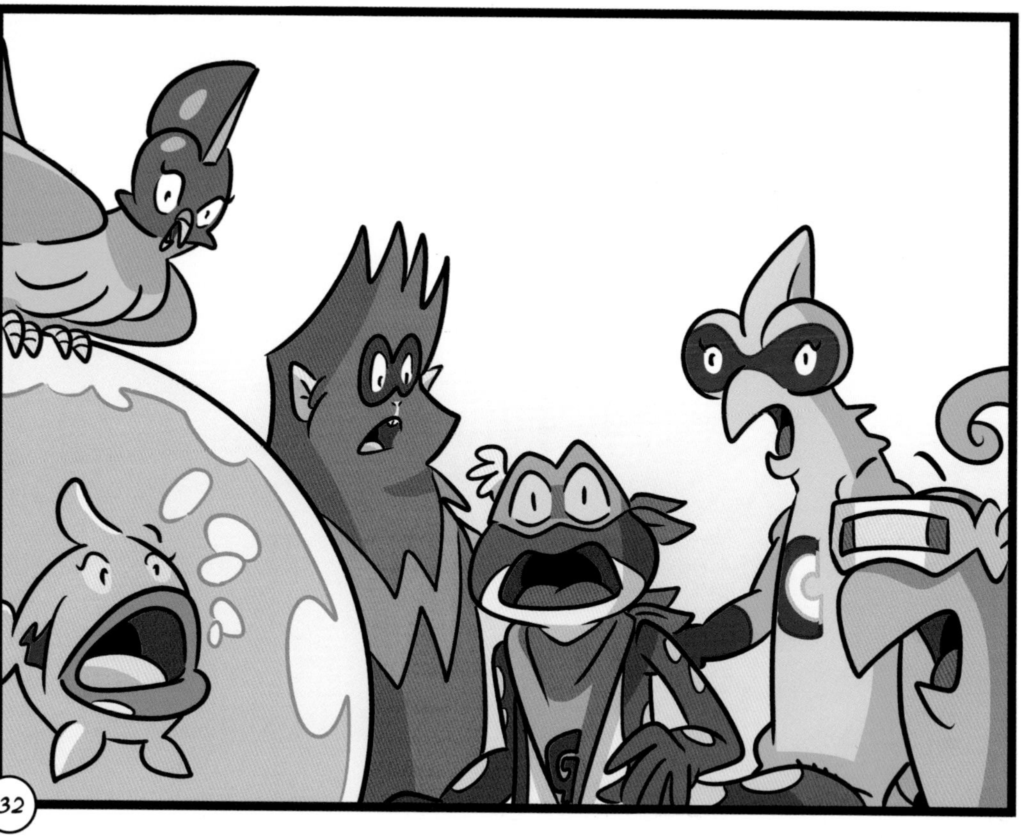

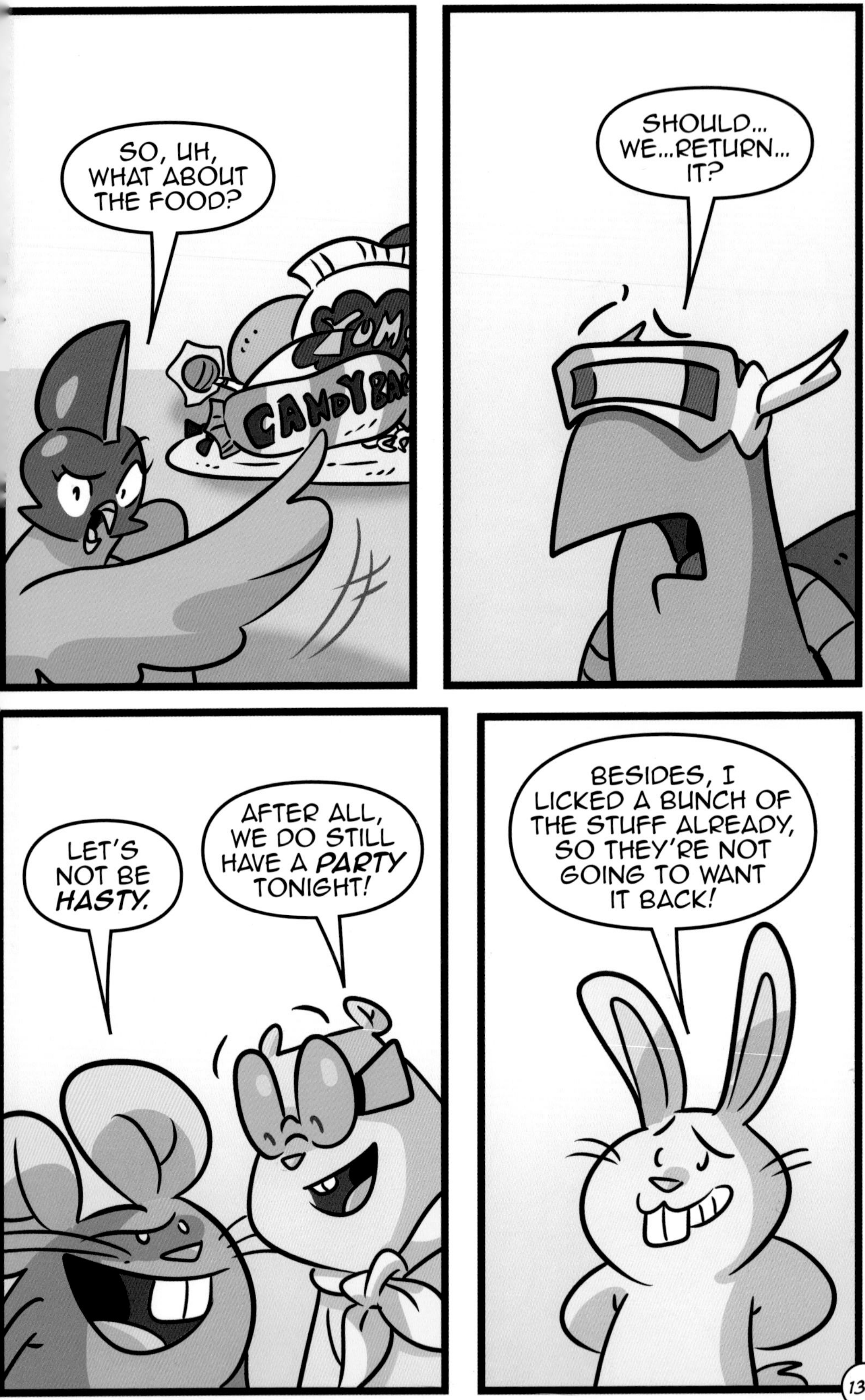
SO, UH, WHAT ABOUT THE FOOD?
SHOULD... WE...RETURN... IT?
LET'S NOT BE *HASTY.*
AFTER ALL, WE DO STILL HAVE A *PARTY* TONIGHT!
BESIDES, I LICKED A BUNCH OF THE STUFF ALREADY, SO THEY'RE NOT GOING TO WANT IT BACK!

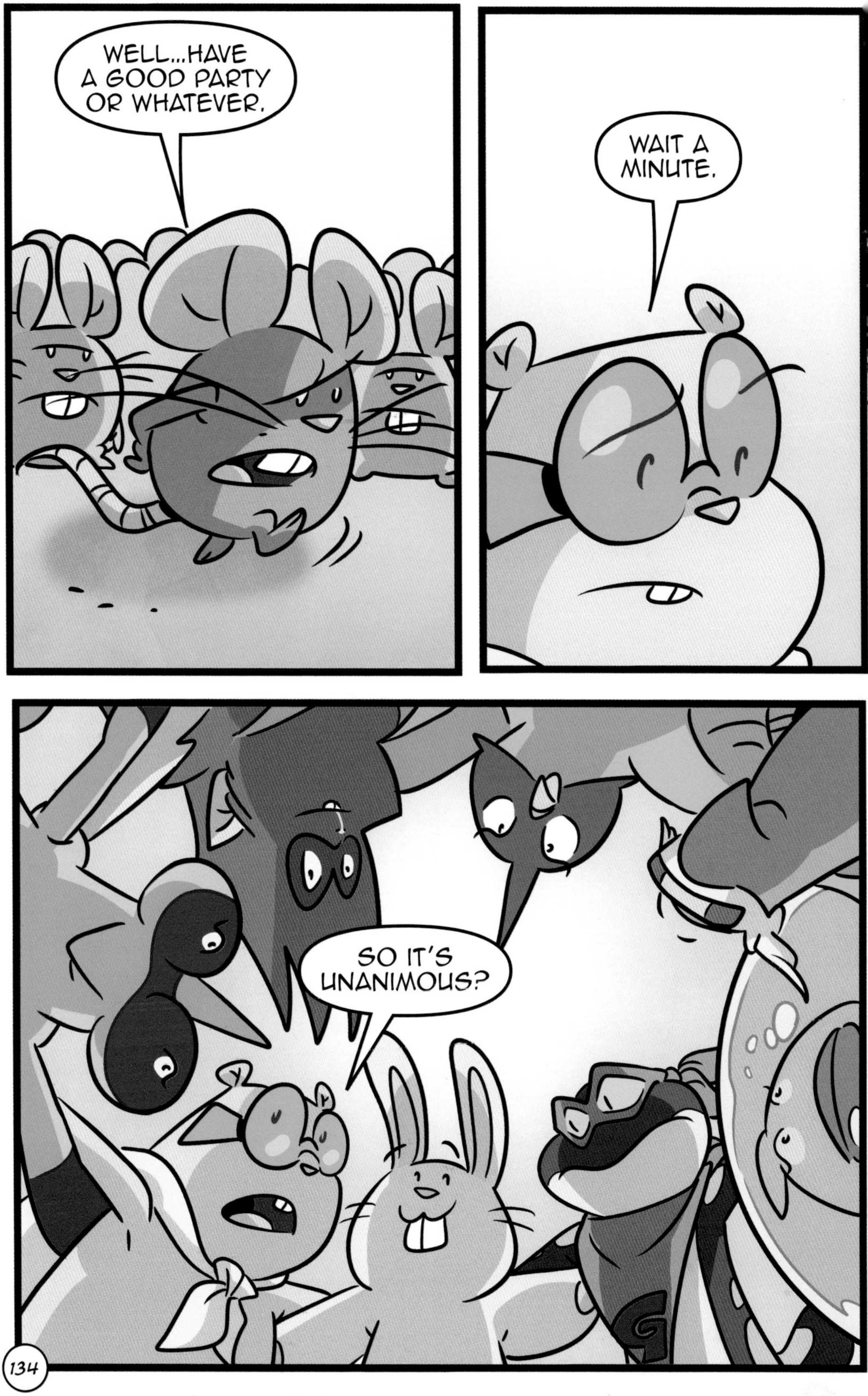
WELL...HAVE A GOOD PARTY OR WHATEVER.
WAIT A MINUTE.
SO IT'S UNANIMOUS?

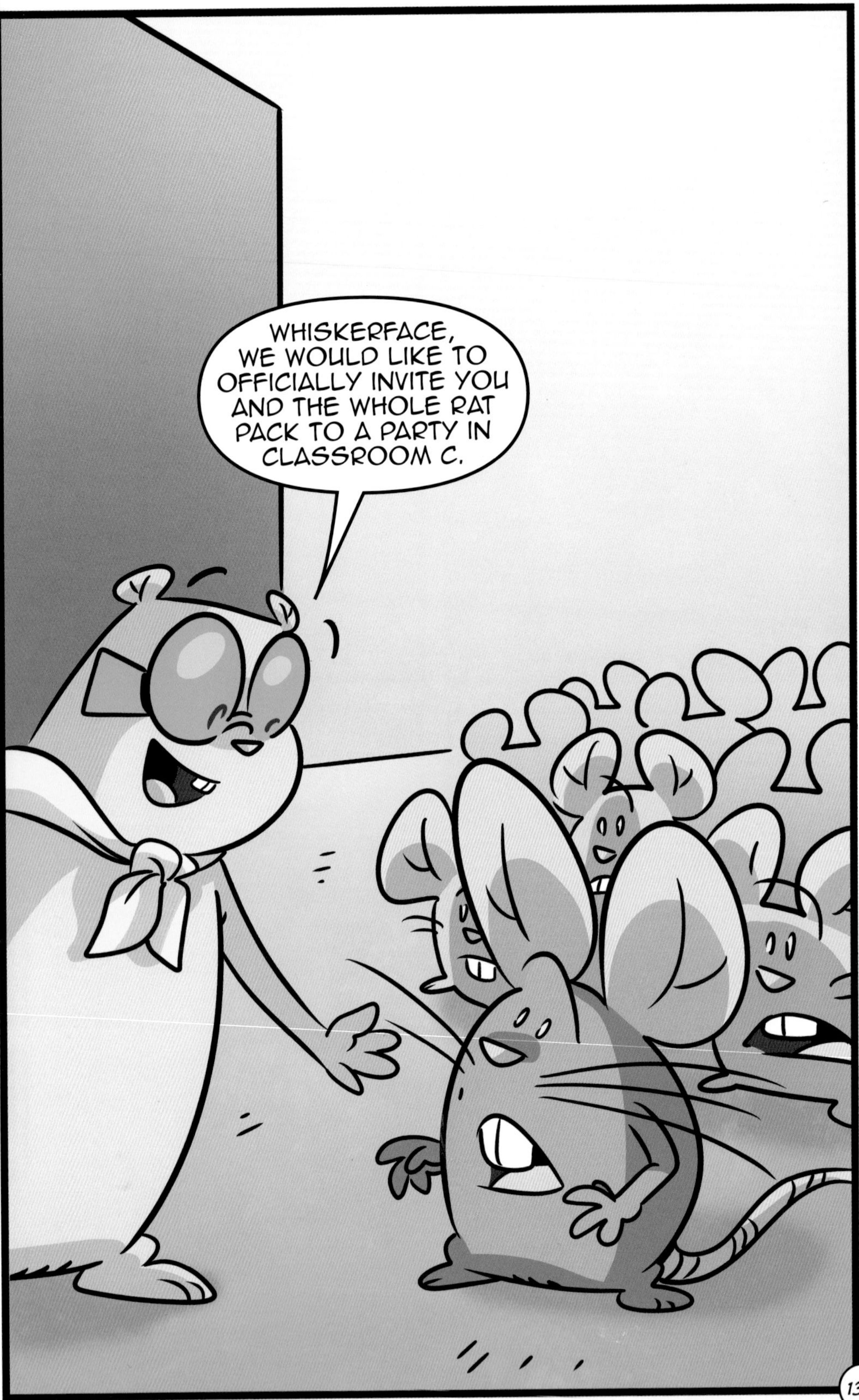
WHISKERFACE, WE WOULD LIKE TO OFFICIALLY INVITE YOU AND THE WHOLE RAT PACK TO A PARTY IN CLASSROOM C.

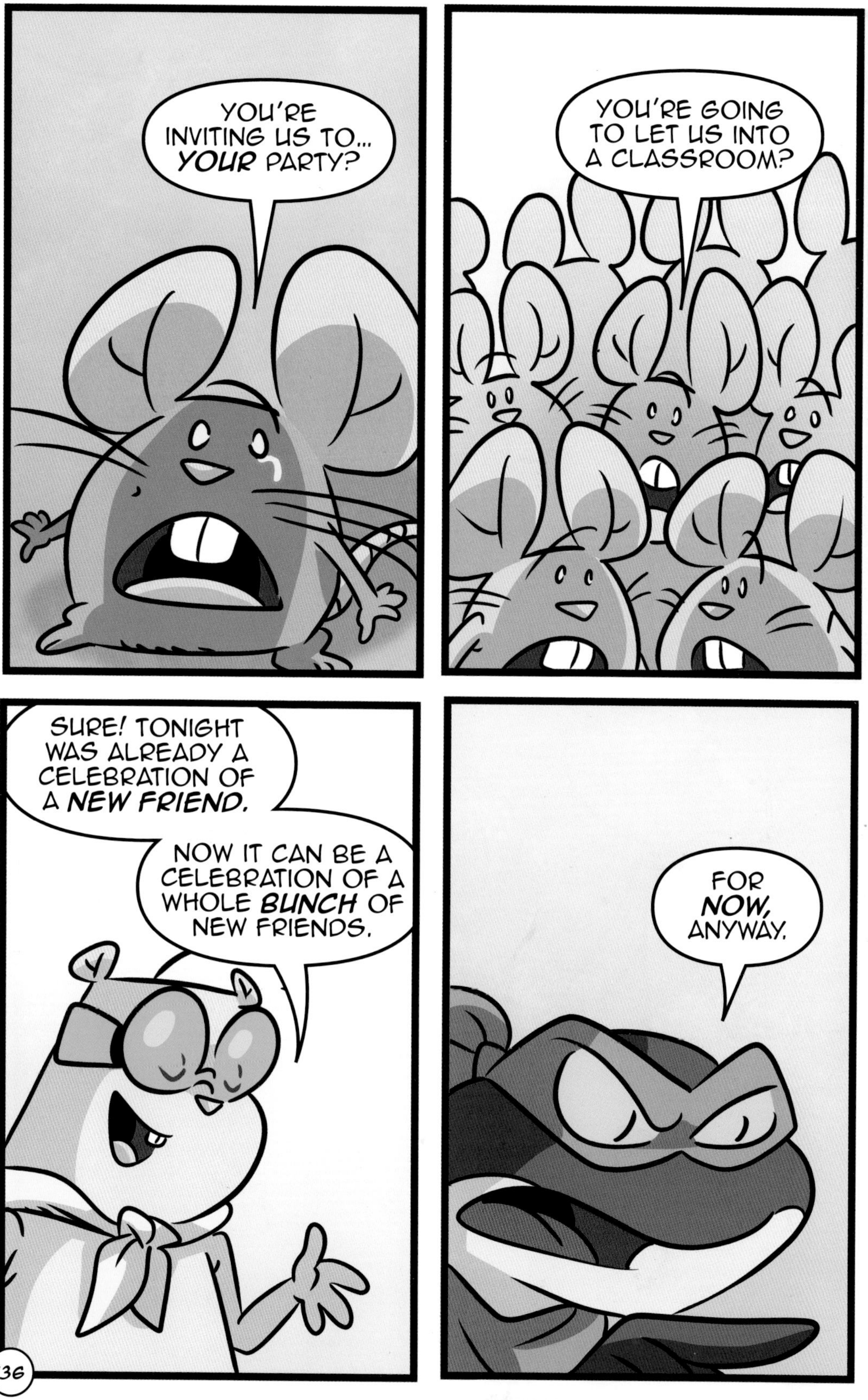
YOU'RE INVITING US TO... *YOUR* PARTY?
YOU'RE GOING TO LET US INTO A CLASSROOM?
SURE! TONIGHT WAS ALREADY A CELEBRATION OF A *NEW FRIEND.*
NOW IT CAN BE A CELEBRATION OF A WHOLE *BUNCH* OF NEW FRIENDS.
FOR *NOW,* ANYWAY.

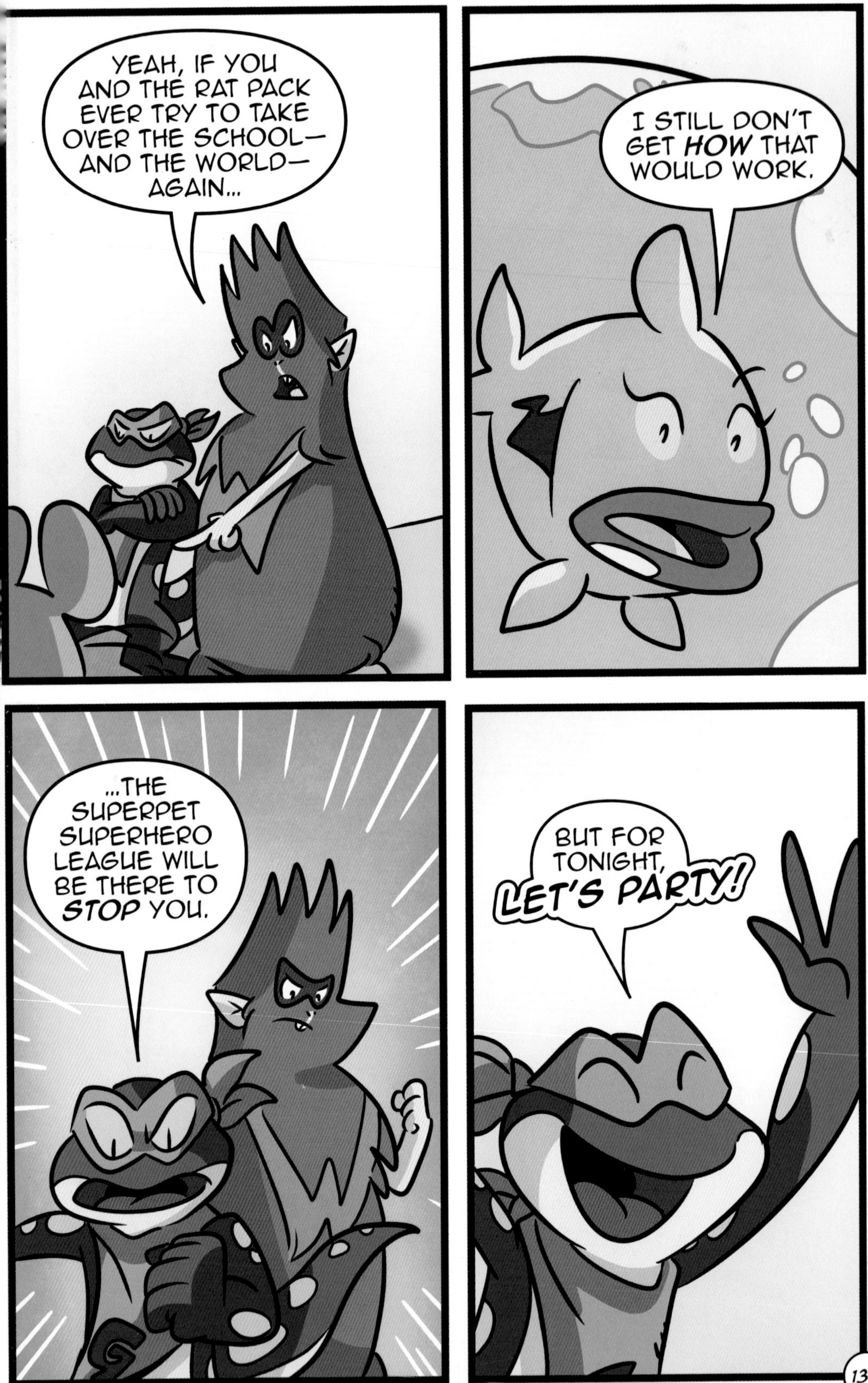
YEAH, IF YOU AND THE RAT PACK EVER TRY TO TAKE OVER THE SCHOOL— AND THE WORLD— AGAIN...
I STILL DON'T GET *HOW* THAT WOULD WORK.
...THE SUPERPET SUPERHERO LEAGUE WILL BE THERE TO *STOP* YOU.
BUT FOR TONIGHT, LET'S PARTY!

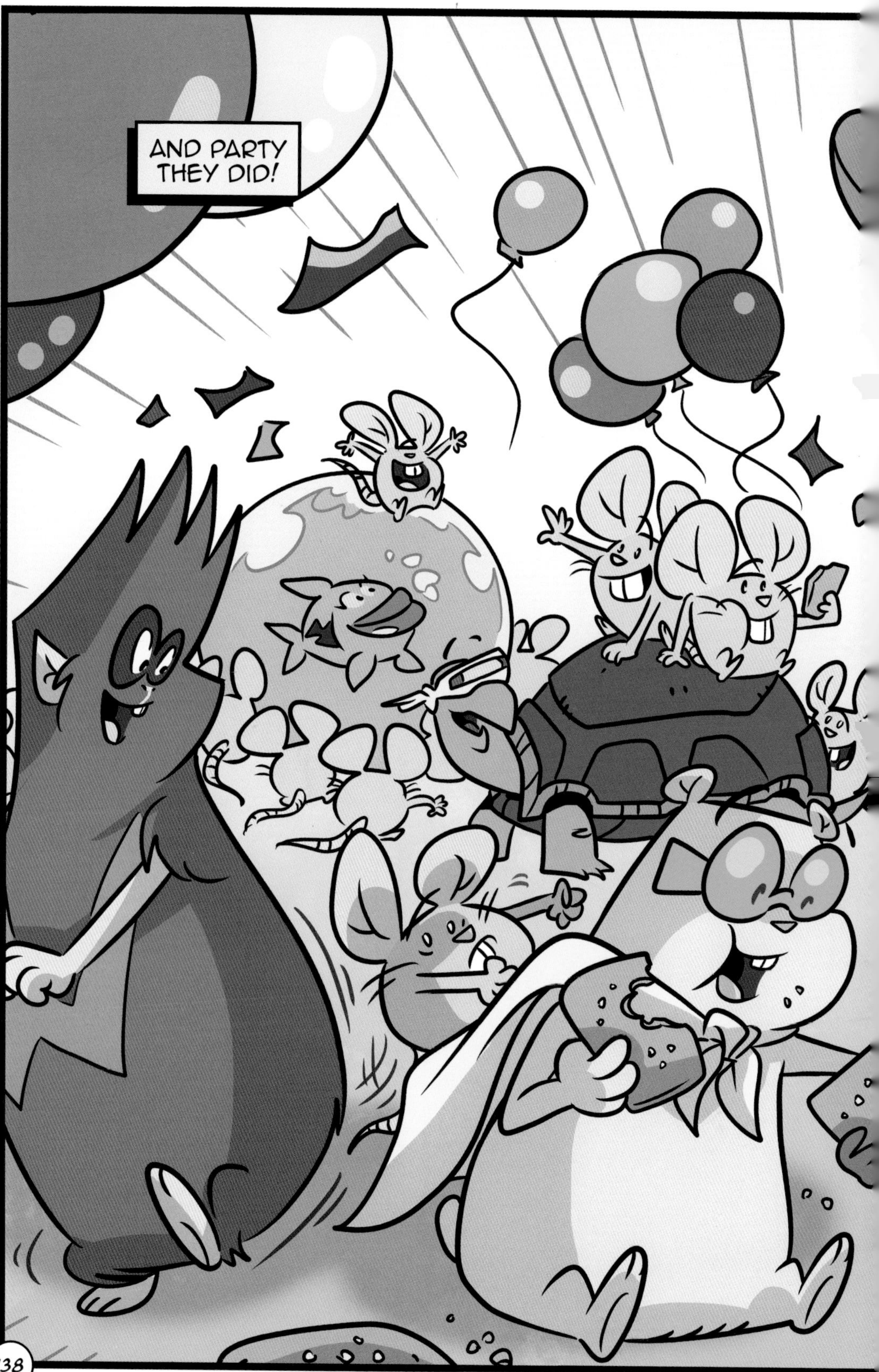
AND PARTY
THEY DID!

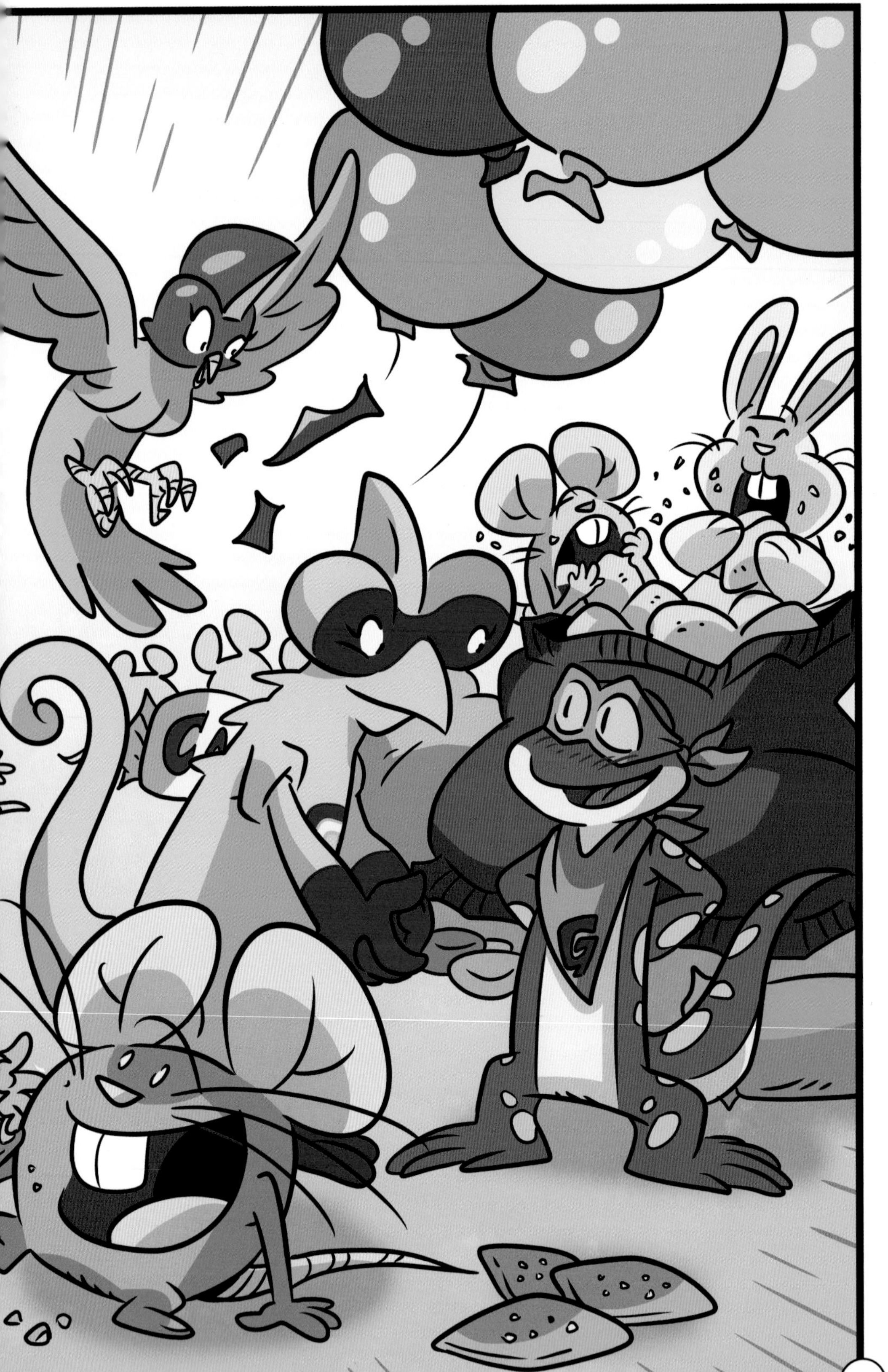

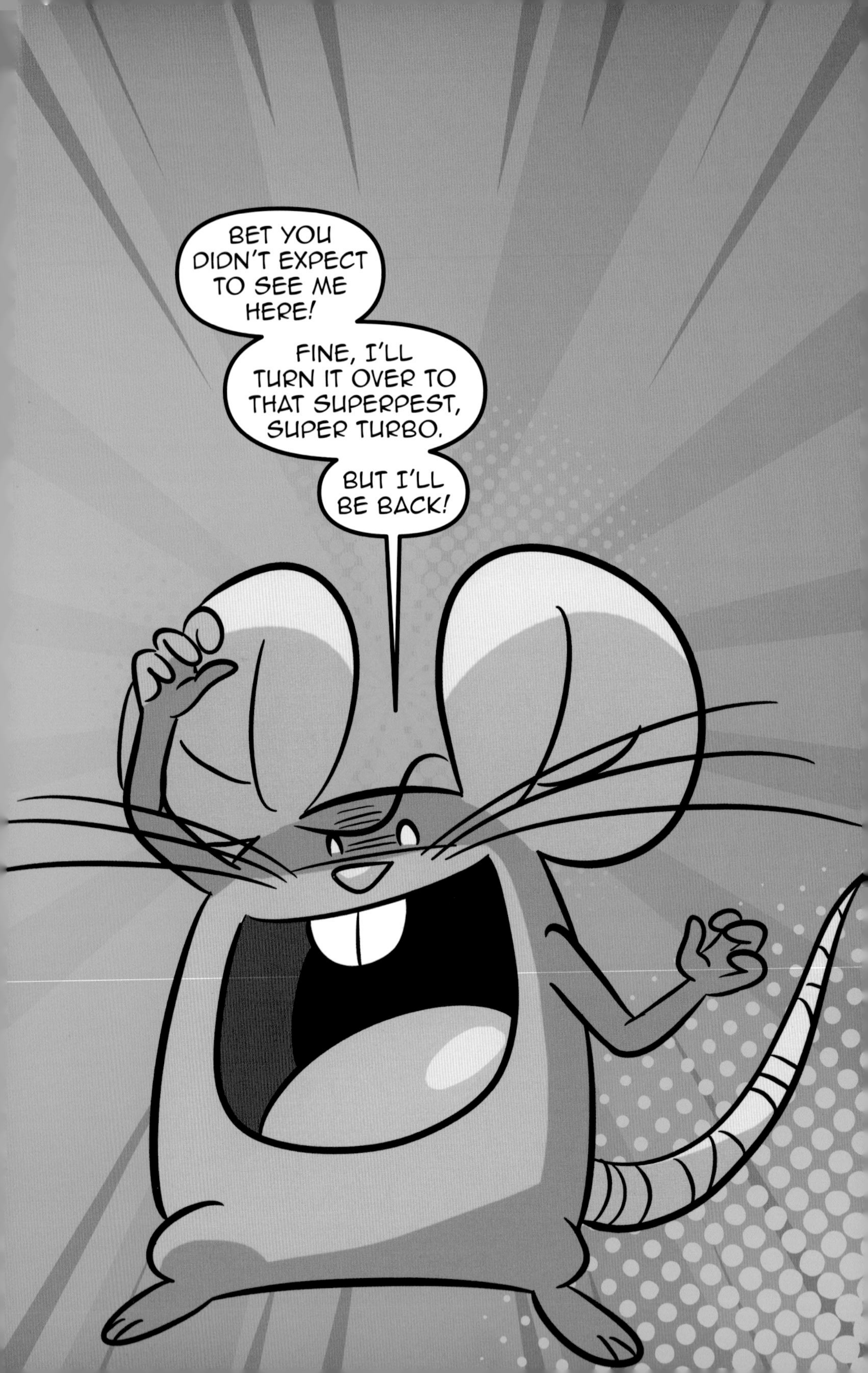
BET YOU DIDN'T EXPECT TO SEE ME HERE!
FINE, I'LL TURN IT OVER TO THAT SUPERPEST, SUPER TURBO.
BUT I'LL BE BACK!

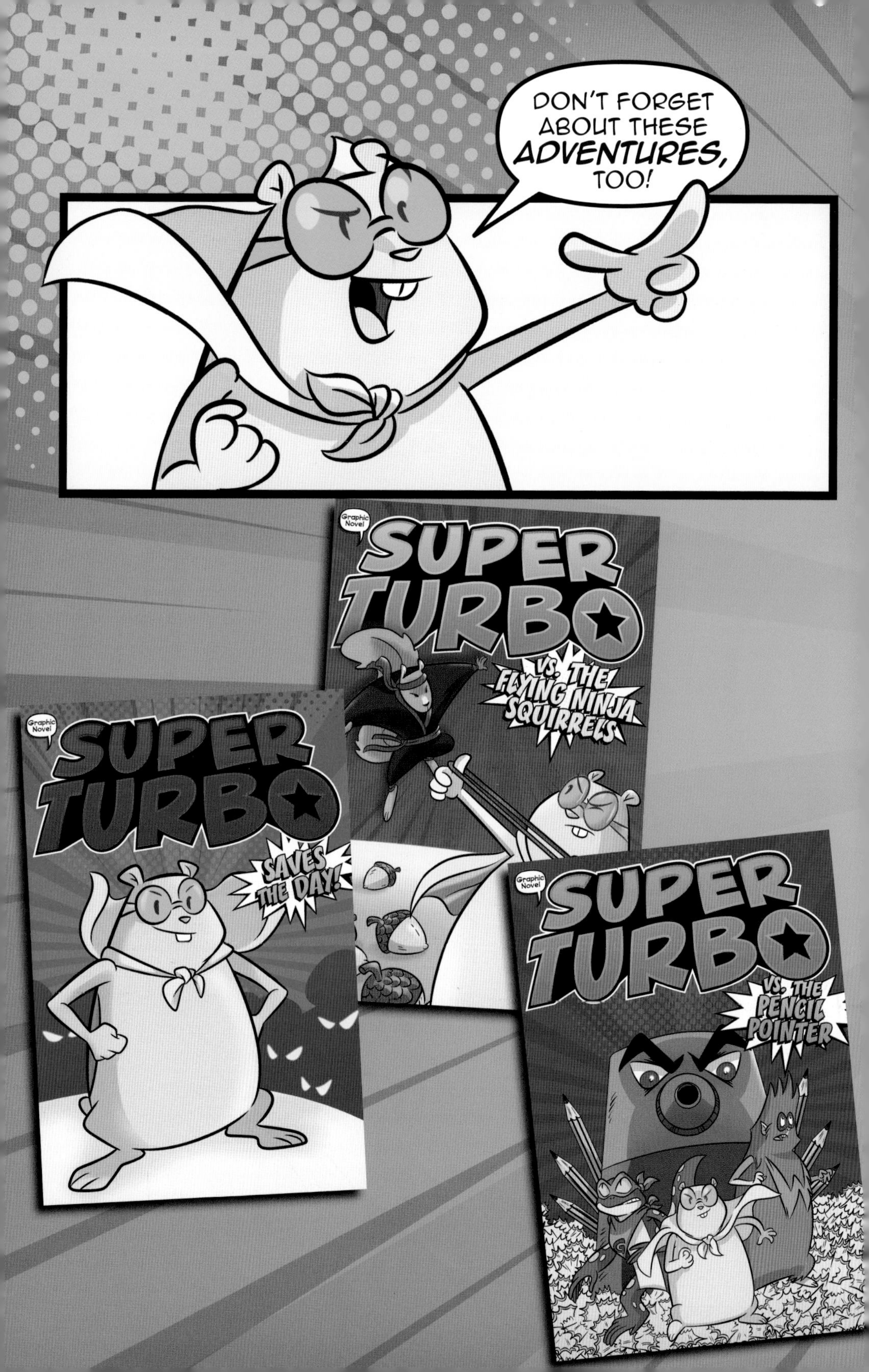
DON'T FORGET ABOUT THESE ADVENTURES, TOO!
Graphic Novel
SUPER TURBO VS. THE FLYING NINJA SQUIRRELS
Graphic Novel
SUPER TURBO SAVES THE DAY!
Graphic Novel
SUPER TURBO VS. THE PENCIL POINTER

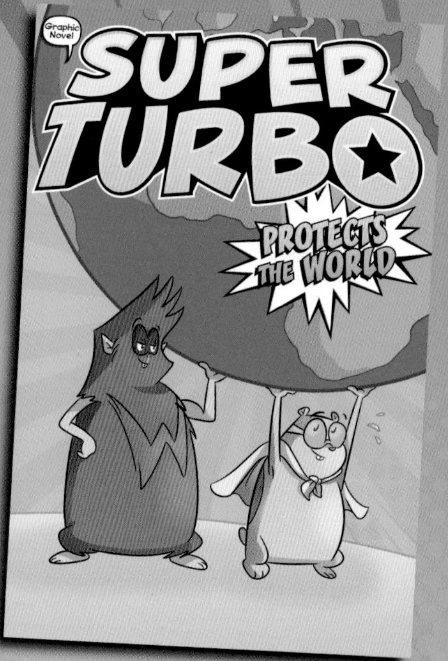
Graphic Novel
SUPER TURBO
PROTECTS THE WORLD
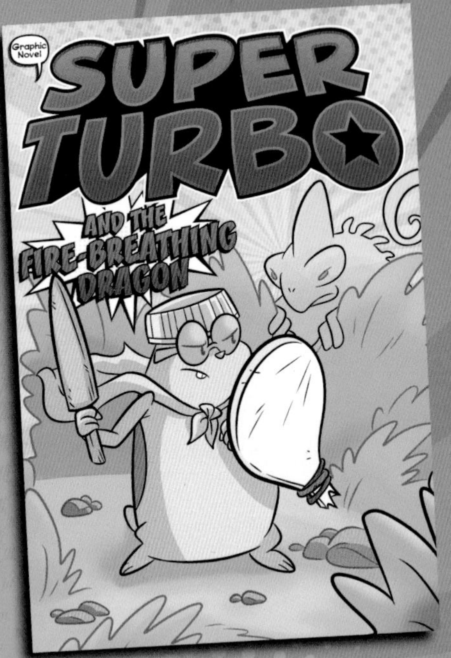
Graphic Novel
SUPER TURBO
AND THE FIRE-BREATHING DRAGON
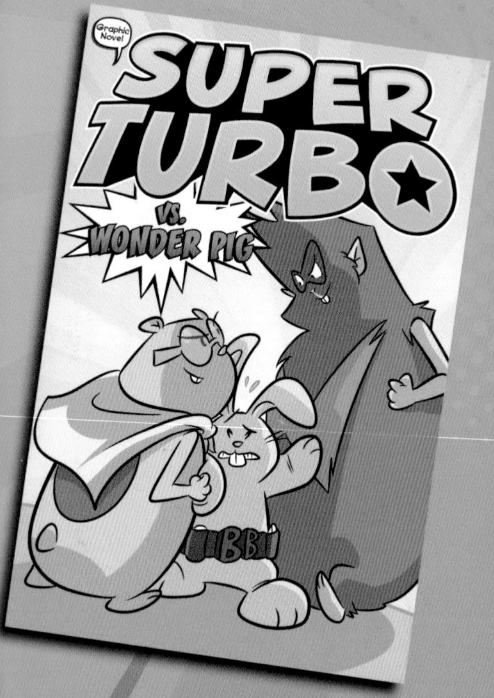
Graphic Novel
SUPER TURBO
VS. WONDER PIG
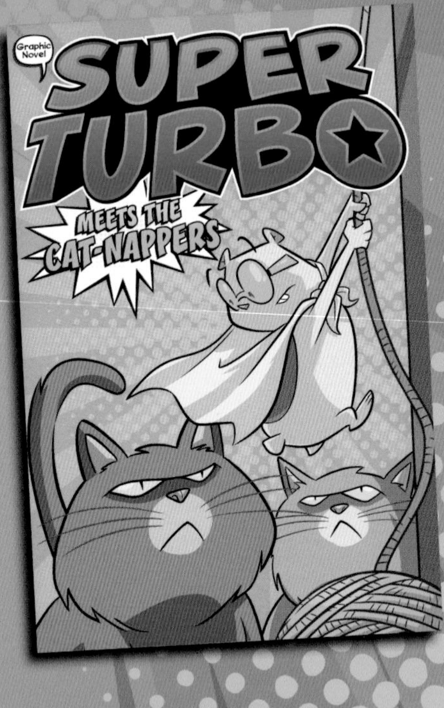
Graphic Novel
SUPER TURBO
MEETS THE CAT-NAPPERS

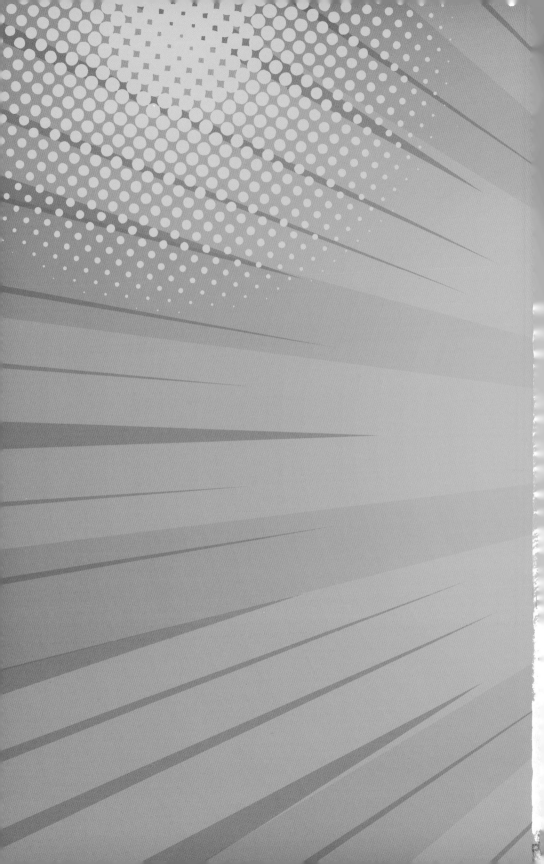